A
THOUSAND
DEVILS

ALSO BY FRANK GOLDAMMER

Max Heller, Dresden Detective Series

The Air Raid Killer

A THOUSAND DEVILS

A MAX HELLER NOVEL

FRANK GOLDAMMER

TRANSLATED BY STEVE ANDERSON

amazon crossing

Text copyright © 2017 dtv Verlagsgesellschaft GmbH & Co. KG, Munich/Germany
Translation copyright © 2018 by Steve Anderson
All rights reserved.

Previously published as *Tausend Teufel* by dtv Verlagsgesellschaft in Germany in 2016. Translated from German by Steve Anderson. First published in English by AmazonCrossing in 2018.

Published by AmazonCrossing, Seattle

www.apub.com

Amazon, the Amazon logo, and AmazonCrossing are trademarks of Amazon.com, Inc., or its affiliates.

ISBN-13: 9781503904323 (hardcover)
ISBN-10: 1503904326 (hardcover)
ISBN-13: 9781503904095 (paperback)
ISBN-10: 1503904091 (paperback)

Cover design by Shasti O'Leary Soudant

Printed in the United States of America

First edition

A
THOUSAND
DEVILS

February 6, 1947: Morning

Max Heller climbed out of the car and shoved his hands into the pockets of his long overcoat. His breath froze, his eyes watering from the cold. The days-old snow along the path was packed down and slick, and the cardboard cutouts serving as his shoe insoles couldn't stop the chill from creeping into his feet. His face was red. He had shaved using hard soap and water that was far too cold despite the pains he'd taken to thaw it. His stomach was rumbling. He had saved the slice of bread Karin had left him for breakfast so he could eat it at lunchtime with the thin soup served by the public kitchens. At least he'd have one real meal that way instead of two meager ones. This evening, Karin was making gruel yet again—as she did nearly every night. The stuff downright disgusted Heller by now, though he knew he should be thankful. Frau Marquart, who'd taken them in after they were bombed out of their home in '45, happened to know a milkman.

He leaned forward to look back inside the black Ford Eifel, then grunted with annoyance and slammed the door shut. He had been in such a hurry that he'd left his scarf on his desk. So he pushed up the collar of his overcoat and pulled his flat cap down tight. It really was bitterly cold. If their kitchen window thermometer was to be believed, it had been –13 degrees before sunrise. No wonder the pipes were frozen. The ice had spread across their bedroom windows overnight.

Heller took a few careful steps on the slick road. A throng of people blocked his view. A Russian military truck blocked Bautzner Strasse, which ran parallel to the Elbe River, so that even the streetcar had come to a standstill. Many of the riders had exited the overcrowded cars to gawk. Yet no one dared complain to the Russians.

Werner Oldenbusch climbed out of the Ford. He slammed the driver's door shut, rubbed his hands, and jumped from one foot to the other.

"Comrade Oberkommissar!" a cop called out to Heller. A member of the new People's Police, the cop wore a German Army overcoat dyed brown. He shoved through the crowd gathered on the steep slope above the Elbe, then saluted Heller.

Heller saluted by briefly raising his fingers to his flat cap. He'd steadfastly refused to wear a peaked cap. He was a police detective, not a military man. He'd gladly accepted his new overcoat, on the other hand. Karin could now wear his old one, something sorely needed even in their apartment.

Snow-covered meadows stretched below the slope. The snow wasn't very deep, and tips of grass blades poked up out of the white. Out on the Elbe, a little over two hundred yards away, little ice floes drifted by.

"How long have they been here?" Heller asked, glancing at the truck with the red star on the driver's door.

"Just arrived. Won't be much left for you, I'm afraid." The cop added an apologetic shrug.

Heller had figured as much. He still wanted to get a better look at the victim. "Clear a path for me. Werner, come on."

"Out of the way!" the cop shouted at the crowd. "Get a move on, pronto!"

The onlookers shoved each other out of the way.

"Wait!" Heller shouted at two Soviet Army soldiers about to remove a body with a stretcher. The deceased wore a Soviet Armed Forces uniform, his face covered by a uniform jacket.

Heller raised a hand and blocked the soldiers' path. "*Stoi!* Police detective."

The two Russians stood still and looked to their superior, a young man with Asian features who forcefully waved a hand and ordered the dead man onto the truck. He turned to Heller.

"Not your job, Comrade. Our job. *Do svidaniya!*"

Heller let it go. There was no point in arguing.

"Where was the corpse found?" he asked the cop instead.

"I'll show you," the cop said in a helpful tone, then walked toward the slope along the river. He pointed at a cluster of bushes about three yards below them.

"That's why no one found him sooner," Heller said, thinking aloud.

"A man went to relieve himself, found this instead. It was already good and light by then. Around eight or so. He was lying headfirst, and his legs—"

"One second," Heller said, barely stopping the cop from climbing down to the crime scene to describe it all. He needed Oldenbusch, his forensics man.

Heller used his official voice. "Kommissar Oldenbusch, come over here, please." He pointed at a few drops of blood in the snow. "Think you can get a photo in this cold?"

Oldenbusch nodded. "I think so."

Heller looked around, frowning at the crowd that refused to disperse. The Russian truck was still there. Restrained amusement was spreading among the onlookers. Heller turned his attention back to the bushes, warily eyeing the steep incline covered with the Soviet soldiers' footprints. They'd carelessly trampled all over the blood-soaked snow.

"A great deal of blood loss," Heller said. Dark tracks led down to the bush. Heller took a few steps back from the top of the slope to determine whether a person could only see the bushes from the street if they were standing right at the edge.

"The man who found the body—where is he?" Heller asked the cop.

"He's gone; he had to get to work. We got his personal details."

Heller looked at a dark patch in the snow. "Were you able to see the corpse? Could you tell the cause of death?"

The truck still hadn't started. Heller considered taking a look, but that young Soviet officer had expressly forbidden it.

The policeman nodded. "A stab to the carotid artery. Nothing could've saved him. I used to see that kind of thing a lot."

Heller knew what he meant. During the war.

"Russians having a dispute, I'm guessing," the cop said. "See it every day. Get drunk and start brawling. Sometimes it doesn't stop there."

Heller nodded impatiently—he wasn't asking for the man's opinion.

The truck's engine started, then died again. The soldiers were bickering while the officer stood next to the truck and smoked.

"Do their officers do it too?" Oldenbusch said. "Seeing how the dead man's an officer."

"Why not?" The cop shrugged. "Hey, get away from there!" he shouted at a couple of boys trying to climb down the slope to catch a glimpse of the large pool of blood that had frozen into the snow.

Heller pulled out his notebook and pencil and did a brief sketch, just in case. He didn't always trust Oldenbusch's old camera to work in these temperatures.

"I'm assuming someone attacked him here along the street. He stumbled, then fell down and bled to death in the bushes. Werner, you should try looking for clues regardless."

Oldenbusch sniffled, felt his way down the slope a few yards, snapped a few more photos. It took him some effort to climb back up. "If we at least had a footprint from the dead man, I could try to figure out what direction he was coming from."

Heller took another look at the army truck. "Couldn't you get a shot of his boot soles? They're still there."

"I'll go ask our Russian comrades," Oldenbusch muttered and marched off. Heller shoved his hands back into his overcoat pockets and

4

took a long look at the river valley. The early-morning sun was shining on the city ruins on the other side of the Elbe, making the snow-dusted remains of the walls and mountains of bricks glow pink.

"It's almost pretty," the cop said.

Heller looked at him, eyebrows raised. The cop pointed at the ruins to clarify. Heller wasn't sure if he should feel angry or amused, so he just shook his head. People said the strangest things.

"That was pointless," Oldenbusch told Heller when he returned. Right then the truck's engine started behind them with a roar, and a cloud of black fumes shot from the exhaust pipe. Some onlookers applauded, practically mocking their occupiers. The Soviets weren't exactly well liked and never bothered to try. They were perfectly entitled to that, Heller knew, but that didn't make it right. While waiting in line at the central exchange recently, a woman had whispered to him, "With Adolf, we always had butter." He didn't respond. Where would he even start? There was too much to say.

The truck was now driving away, and the streetcar driver rang his bell for the passengers to climb back on.

"The Russians never try to understand," Oldenbusch said, sounding resigned. "No point wasting another second here. There's that coal dealer who was held up. Maybe we go look into that instead?"

"I guess you're probably right, Werner."

"I said get away from there!" the cop shouted again. "Snotty little brats."

Heller looked down the slope. Farther below, where the bushes got thicker, a couple of curious boys were hiding out. Heller could see a few people gathering kindling among the bushes. Every twig and scrap of wood was needed for making fires. People were even stealing railings and display cases, garden chairs, fencing. Heller had seen others cutting down trees in Grosser Garten park. And winter still had a long way to go. Down at the bottom, along Körnerweg path and the broad meadow along the river, more people were scouring the snow, hoping to find clover or dandelions. The sight depressed him.

"Come on, Werner, let's get out of here. Once the streetcar's gone."

"Should I keep guarding the crime scene?" asked the cop.

Heller thought for a moment, then shook his head. The Soviets always played their cards close to their chests. They hadn't even let them take a photo of the dead man's boot soles.

"Either report back to your precinct or continue your beat," he told the cop. "Have a nice day. Dismissed!"

The man saluted and headed off. Heller went to the car and climbed in. Oldenbusch landed on the driver's seat with all his weight and started the engine.

Heller glared at a few onlookers who had rushed over to the spot where the body was found just as soon as the cop left.

"As if they haven't seen enough misery," he muttered, though lately he'd been trying to refrain from such comments.

"Well, at least the sun's shining," Oldenbusch said, hoping to brighten his boss's mood, and put the car into gear.

Heller placed a hand on his arm. "Let's wait till the streetcar's gone."

Oldenbusch leaned back, crossing his arms. They waited. The first streetcar had filled up again. Another one had arrived behind it, and a third coming the other direction had halted at the specified stop, according to schedule. Many riders got out, and most of them stopped to stare at the people gathered at the edge of the slope.

Suddenly Heller noticed a person who at first looked to be pushing aimlessly through the throngs but upon closer inspection was heading straight for the slope. The individual clearly wasn't interested in the crowd. The person wore an overcoat that must have been German Army issue, and he moved with surprising agility despite his corpulent appearance. But the coat was simply stuffed, it seemed. Heller tapped Oldenbusch's shoulder and pointed.

It turned out to be a young woman, practically a girl. She passed right by their unmarked car, and Heller had to turn all the way around to track her. She soon stopped and glanced down the slope. Then she descended the incline with careful steps.

Heller opened the car door and stepped out. The young woman had already climbed down ten yards, passing the bush where the dead man had lain, and stood near a hedge. She bent down and tried to drag something out. It was a backpack. One of the shoulder straps was caught on the thorny twigs.

"Halt!" Heller shouted. The woman looked up, startled.

"Drop it!" Heller ordered.

Oldenbusch had stepped next to him. "Think it belongs to the Russian?"

"Could be," Heller said as he rushed down the slope.

"Police! Leave that where it is." When Heller reached the woman, he grabbed at the backpack, but she wouldn't give it up. She pulled and tugged and eventually got the pack free; Heller's numb fingers couldn't hold on. She tried to hurry farther down the slope, but she slipped and fell. Oldenbusch caught up to Heller, sliding on the snow-crusted soil as he tried to keep balance. The woman had gotten back up, but Oldenbusch reached her and yanked the backpack.

With a furious snarl, the woman let go and stumbled down the steep terrain, half sliding, half running. Once she reached the bottom, she looked around, then ran down Körnerweg path toward the city center. Oldenbusch followed her for a good hundred yards, the backpack flailing in his hand, but it was clear that he wasn't going to catch her.

"Let her go, Werner," Heller shouted. It annoyed him that his junior partner hadn't been able to apprehend the girl. He would've liked to know who she was.

Oldenbusch returned and sighed after he made it back up the steep and slippery elevation. Still panting, he handed the backpack to the patiently waiting Heller.

Its weight surprised Heller. He set the pack down and pulled open the drawstring. He gasped.

Two dull eyes stared at him. He saw a blood-encrusted nose, thin hair, and ears leaking blood that had coagulated some time ago. It was the head of a man.

Heller let out a long, deep breath. Then he pulled the pack all the way open and took a closer look at the head without touching it.

Oldenbusch, watching over his shoulder, let out a low whistle. Heller glared at him.

"Sorry," Oldenbusch said.

"Is this backpack Soviet in origin?"

Oldenbusch shook his head, bent down, held up the underside of the top flap, and pointed to a patch showing a hand with a raised index finger and the word "Deuter."

"It's German."

"Doesn't necessarily mean anything." Heller stood, looking around.

"And look here, Max, it's got initials sewn on the tag. 'LK,' maybe 'SK.'"

Heller pulled out his notebook and wrote that down, though he knew that such a detail could mean little these days, when everyone either stole or took whatever they could find only to trade it soon after for something to eat.

"He could have lost it when he fell," Oldenbusch surmised. "And the backpack kept rolling."

"There any blood on it, from the Russian?" Heller asked.

Oldenbusch inspected the pack on all sides before shaking his head. "Maybe he dropped it when he was attacked."

"What about the girl?"

"She happens to be passing by, spots the pack, tries to take it," Oldenbusch offered.

Heller took a good look at the backpack, carefully lifting it. No fresh blood had seeped into the fabric even though the head wasn't wrapped. He put the pack back down. Why would a Soviet officer be out on the streets at night, carrying a severed head in a backpack? Why was he killed too? And why had the murderer left the backpack lying there? Could he have not known what was inside? Or could the two things simply have ended up in the same place by chance—one dead Soviet officer and a backpack with a severed head? Hard to accept that.

Heller pulled the drawstring tight, slapped the flap shut, and grabbed the pack by the handle. The cold had crept into his bones, and his fingers were frozen stiff. Oldenbusch, on the other hand, was still sweating from his brief chase, and Heller couldn't risk him getting chilled or sick.

"Drive me to the Justice Ministry, Werner."

"Soviet headquarters, you mean?"

"Yes. I want to see if the Soviet Military Administration will give me anything on the dead man. Meanwhile, find out if a corpse came in missing a head over the last few days. And give me your camera."

"Listen, you have to promise to take really good care of it; it's the first Retina model from Kodak, made in '34—"

"Werner, I used to have one just like it."

"Used to" meant before February 13, 1945. That was the day they lost everything except what they had on them—that, and they still had their lives. But Heller hadn't shed tears over it, not over the camera, nor his radio, nor their lovely display cabinet—not even the photos of his two sons. That night, simply staying alive was more than they could have hoped for.

"All I meant," said Oldenbusch, "was I was glad to get ahold of one."

Lieutenant General Medvedev, commandant of Dresden SMAD, looked up from his massive desk as his secretary led Heller into his office. It had been over a year since the Soviet Military Administration in Germany, or SMAD, had chosen the former Justice Ministry in

Hospitalstrasse as its local HQ. Heller had a little trouble finding his way inside the building; he hadn't been here since the Red Army started occupying Dresden, and his Russian-language skills hadn't substantially improved either.

The commandant stood, came around the desk, and held out a hand to Heller for a vigorous handshake.

"Comrade Heller. Always so unconventional." Medvedev laughed, returned to his chair, and gestured for Heller to sit. Medvedev had gained a little weight in the last year and a half, the collar of his uniform now tight around his stout neck. Heller glanced around, not knowing where to set down the backpack.

"Just put it on the floor." Medvedev shook his head in amusement. "You are unconventional and also stubborn, aren't you?"

Heller hadn't expected such a friendly reception. He relished how warm the office was, cracking his overcoat open a little, and he wondered how much coal they used to heat such a large building.

"In my profession, a person has to be stubborn if they want to get anything done."

"Well, it's not your profession I'm concerned about. It's your pig-headedness in political matters." Medvedev was still smiling when one of the many telephones on his desk rang. The general picked up, said no, and hung up.

So that explains his behavior, Heller realized. "I've been apolitical my whole life," he said, trying to be diplomatic.

"Which is why I was thinking of you for a completely different position. At police headquarters. Instead you're still an Oberkommissar, a detective, and I have to endure people like this Niesbach fellow, who studied Marxism and Leninism in Moscow."

Heller had no clue what his point was.

"Things are fine the way they are. I like my job."

Medvedev waved aside the notion—people always said that. "Heller, you don't have to be political. All that's required is one small signature, and the sky's the limit. A proper career. How am I supposed to get you into management otherwise? The old-school Communists would storm the barricades if I tried. The only reason you're back on duty is because of me."

Heller hadn't come to have this discussion. The Soviets thought highly of him for not joining the Nazi Party. Yet they couldn't accept that he wouldn't join the SED—the Socialist Unity Party of Germany.

"And I appreciate it very much, Comrade Commandant. But I'm here for another reason."

Medvedev raised his hands in submission. "Major Vadim Berinov."

"The officer who was found dead?" Heller asked.

Medvedev nodded.

"Your soldiers wouldn't even let me take a quick look at him."

"We wish to prevent rumors from spreading among the Germans that may suggest disputes exist within the Soviet Armed Forces."

"Truly?" Heller dared ask. All this supersecrecy only made people think the opposite. Medvedev didn't seem to realize this.

He ignored Heller. The phone rang again. The commandant picked up, listened, said *nyet* again, and ended the call. He turned back to Heller. "Now, this head—has the victim been identified?"

"No."

"Could it also have something to do with a member of the Soviet Army?"

"It's impossible to know so soon."

"He look German or Russian?"

"I'll let you decide for yourself." Heller pointed at the backpack.

Medvedev stood, grabbed the backpack, set it on his desk, and opened it.

"Please don't touch the head," Heller added.

Medvedev nodded and took a good look.

"Male, German, around fifty or even forty." He returned to his chair, unruffled.

Heller closed the backpack and set it back on the floor. It made him feel uneasy—the head had still not been registered with forensics but was instead proving vital for gaining access to the commandant.

"Four days ago, the body of an officer was found near the weapons depot on Carola-Allee. Colonel Vasili Cherin. He had several stab wounds and died from internal bleeding."

Heller took out his notebook. "On February 2?"

"They found him that morning."

"And the stab wounds? Knife-inflicted?"

The general shrugged.

"Is the body being kept somewhere? Has a coroner analyzed it? Is anyone looking into the matter?"

Medvedev laughed again. "Comrade Heller, you have many questions about a matter that does not concern you."

Heller sat back, annoyed. He didn't feel he was being taken seriously. Shouldn't it be in the Russians' best interest to at least try to resolve the matter?

Medvedev leaned forward, as if in confidence. "You remember Vitaly Ovtcharov?"

Ovtcharov. Heller thought a moment. "From the NKVD?"

Medvedev nodded. "We do not call it the People's Commissariat anymore but rather the Ministry of Internal Affairs. Ministerstvo Vnutrennikh Del. MVD. Ovtcharov, he looked into the death of Colonel Cherin. He came to the conclusion that it was an accident."

"An accident? So he thinks Cherin accidently and repeatedly ran into a sharp object?"

Medvedev started. Then he burst out laughing. "Heller, you should see your face. It's hilarious."

Heller stared back earnestly, without changing expression.

The commandant fell silent. He soon turned just as serious as Heller, forcefully tapping his index finger on the desk. "I'm interested in what happened. Heller, I'm telling you, there's plenty I'm being kept in the dark about. The MVD is not under my authority, so I can't learn anything new. Is it a feud between officers? Is it an attack on the Soviet military? I need someone with a good nose."

Heller stared at the lieutenant general, expecting more, but he stopped there. It was up to Heller to interpret Medvedev's words in the right way.

"For that, I'd need to have the corpse examined forensically."

Medvedev stood. "That you will have. I will arrange it. One more thing, Heller: Have you had breakfast yet?"

Heller shook his head.

February 6, 1947: Late Morning

Heller switched the backpack to his other shoulder, but the relief proved short-lived. He wasn't feeling great. And now the young Soviet doctor who found Heller waiting at his office door was eyeing him. Medvedev had arranged for Heller to have a car and driver, who had taken him up Königsbrücker Strasse and down Carola-Allee to the former German military barracks that the Soviet First Guards Tank Army had been using as a garrison ever since the war. Both victims, Berinov and Cherin, had belonged to this unit. According to Medvedev, the two were supposed to be lying somewhere inside the military hospital here. In charge of them was a doctor whose name Heller hadn't understood when he introduced himself.

The man wore a white doctor's coat over his uniform. He was about thirty years old and wore glasses with thin silver frames, which along with his slightly bored appearance made him look every bit the intellectual or aristocrat.

"Are you feeling sick?" the doctor asked, sounding concerned and keeping his distance.

Heller shook his head. He'd eaten too much breakfast in the Soviet officers' mess, the stomachache brought on by not being used to eating regularly. They'd had everything a person could imagine: warm white bread, butter, jam, honey, sausage, cold cuts, boiled eggs, pickled fish, pickles, cocoa, coffee. Heller was reluctant at first but overcame his shyness and ate until his stomach turned. Such abundance, he thought, while the people outside were stealing rotten onions, fighting each other for diluted bread, heading to the country to beg, and cooking fodder turnips and even leather. Adults and children alike risked their lives jumping onto moving train cars to steal coal. Many even killed for food. Not even a week ago, a nighttime intruder beat the butcher Richter to death inside his shop. Two days ago, the police had found a coal dealer who'd lost his life over just a few hundredweights of coal. How could any of this ever work out? How could the Russians ever be seen as their friends? All they were achieving with their repetitive slogans, constant self-praise as liberators, and posters of their glowing superman Stalin covering every building was feeding the population's anger.

"Would you like to sit down?" the doctor asked.

"No, thank you." Heller suddenly felt guilty about Karin. Should he have asked if he could take something home to his wife? Or simply slipped some food into his overcoat pockets?

"I'd like to see the body of Major Berinov," Heller said.

"I have it waiting for you. I received a call. If you'd please come with me . . ."

The doctor went first, and Heller followed, shouldering the backpack. It was cool here in this block of the barracks. It smelled strongly of ether. The high walls, the gleaming white tiles, and the compressed-wood flooring were all legacies of the old Imperial German military, and now their echoing footsteps awoke in Heller memories of the time he had had to endure a degrading examination by his grenadier regiment's doctors.

"Here." The doctor opened a door to a large, cool examination room. The two corpses, covered with white sheets, lay on normal treatment tables. The young doctor had that bored look again as he stepped up to one of the tables and pulled back the sheet.

"Berinov."

Heller set the backpack off to the side and got closer. "Can I turn on the light?" he asked. The smell of ether was so overpowering, it almost made him nauseous.

"Please do—right there next to you."

Heller turned on the ceiling light. It only gave off a dim glow. "Excuse me, but I didn't quite get your name before."

The young man sighed. "Kasrashvili, Lado Kasrashvili. Captain, or *Hauptmann*, as you call it."

The name Kasrashvili seemed familiar to Heller, but he couldn't place it. "Is that Georgian?"

"I am Georgian, yes. Now, are you going to take a look?"

Heller was certain he'd never known a Georgian. So he focused on the corpse.

The dead man was still in uniform. The shoulders of his jacket were covered in blood, but the uniform was practically clean below that. His head, on the other hand, was completely encrusted with blood, his hair caked with it and stiff from the coagulating. His face had been washed, though, presumably for identification. His nostrils were still clogged with blood, and his eyes were stuck closed.

"Had someone hung him by the feet?" Kasrashvili asked.

Heller glanced at him in amazement. Apparently, no one had told the doctor what had happened.

"They found him lying downward on a slope. Not far from here— about two hundred yards up from the Elbe."

Heller tried turning the dead man's head to the side, but the body was too stiff. Dried blood passed between his fingers after crumbling off the dead man's neck and ears. Heller grabbed the collar of the thick jacket and tugged to free it from the skin of the neck. Then Heller started stripping the upper body. He was already sweating, and Berinov's arms, stiff from rigor mortis, only made the work harder. The doctor, watching Heller labor away, didn't lift a finger or even offer him fabric shears.

And Heller wasn't about to ask for his help, because a person never knew if they were somehow wounding the Soviets' pride by doing so.

He was finally able to yank the dead man's arms out from his two jackets and sweater and then pull the sweater over the head. He stripped the undershirt off. The dead man's torso now lay bare, and Heller looked it over in detail. The officer looked well fed and didn't display symptoms of any particular deficiency. A scar on the chest indicated an old wound. A tiny red mark on the upper left arm caught Heller's attention.

He pointed at the spot. "Looks like the prick of a hypodermic needle."

"Members of the Soviet Army are regularly vaccinated against typhus," the doctor said.

This reminded Heller of those horrid typhus vaccinations every German was ordered to get back in 1945. The needle looked like it was meant for a horse, but the pain of the shot hadn't been the worst of it. It was the shrieks of the children getting vaccinated that caused downright panic among those waiting in line.

"Could you check? Maybe they receive some kind of vaccination certificate?"

Kasrashvili inhaled loudly through his nose and stared at Heller over the top of his glasses. It was clear he wouldn't check a thing.

"I'd really like to clean up the neck a bit—I'd need water and a cloth for that," he said and stared at the Georgian. He knew he was already exhausting the man's patience. There was no way around it, unfortunately.

The doctor hesitated, as if first having to consider whether this was an appropriate task for him.

"I could get it myself," Heller added.

"No, stay there." Kasrashvili left the room. Heller thought the cabinets might contain a cloth and a bowl, but he didn't dare look himself or touch anything. He didn't want to anger the doctor.

The doctor was soon back, and he had a metal bucket and wash-rag with him. Heller thanked him, rolled up his overcoat sleeves, and started washing off the dead man's neck. Doing so revealed two wounds, one on the right, one on the left. Kasrashvili watched him work without reaction.

"See here, a clean puncture." Heller stepped closer to examine the wounds. These weren't from a knife—they were more like small perforations in the shape of a four-pointed star. The left side of the neck showed the larger of the wounds, the right side the smaller ones, directly opposite. The weapon had likely severed the arteries on both sides and caused massive hemorrhaging. Berinov must have bled to death within seconds.

Heller took a few steps back and held out a hand, inviting Kasrashvili to look closer.

"It appears," concluded the doctor, "that the weapon entered the common carotid artery on the left side and exited through the same artery on the right, just above the collarbone. See that injury behind the ear? It's probable the perpetrator didn't find the neck on the first try, and the tip of the weapon knocked against the cranial bone."

Heller inspected the entry wounds again. "I know this type of wound," he said. He pointed at the other corpse. "That's Cherin?"

Kasrashvili nodded, went over to the other dead man, and pulled off the sheet. Vasili Cherin was completely naked and didn't look as if he'd been dead for four days. Once Heller touched him, he realized the corpse was frozen through.

He bent over and examined Cherin's stab wounds. There were four, spread over the upper body.

He let out an impatient sigh.

"Would you please help me turn the body?"

The doctor nodded but first went over to one of the cabinets, opened it, and pulled out two pairs of rubber gloves, then handed a pair to Heller. Heller's quick glance inside the open cabinet told him how meticulously clean and orderly everything was. He gave an anxious glance at the treatment table holding Berinov—his attempt at cleaning off the dead man's neck had left the table soiled, and a brownish puddle had formed on the floor. Heller looked up to find Kasrashvili staring at him.

"This here is my clean little realm among all the filth. But don't worry. I'll make sure it all gets cleaned up."

The two of them turned the dead man onto his stomach. Heller counted ten stabs on the back, with the same star shape as on Berinov.

"This was a bayonet," Heller said as he thought it over. "The killer attacked him from behind. But it doesn't look like the bayonet was fixed to a rifle. Otherwise the wounds would be somewhat lower, and the stab marks would run from bottom to top. The killer appears to have run the bayonet from top to bottom."

The Georgian looked as if he didn't know he was being spoken to. Heller glanced at him for comment, but Kasrashvili only stared at the dead man in silence.

"I used to see a lot more wounds like that," Heller continued. "In the First World War. I'm assuming this bayonet belongs to a Mosin-Nagant rifle."

"You were in the war? On the Russian Front?" The doctor suddenly took interest.

"No, in Belgium. I was wounded, and later in the hospital I saw some wounds and scars caused by bayonets like this."

Kasrashvili raised his head, as if to tell Heller something. He didn't. Instead, he went over to Berinov's corpse and yanked the sheet all the way back. Lying between the dead man's legs was just such a bayonet.

"He was holding it in his hand."

This only confused Heller. "Could be the murder weapon."

He carefully lifted the bayonet with his fingertips and checked the socket mount, which had been wrapped with hemp rope to provide a better grip. It looked like the weapon had been used in this manner for a long time. The cord was dark and greasy.

"From this, I think it's safe to assume that we're looking at a single perpetrator," Heller said. "The weapon being Russian-made doesn't necessarily point to ownership. I'm sure there are loads of bayonets like this floating around. Am I mistaken or is this an older version? I thought modern bayonets were shorter."

Kasrashvili barely shrugged.

"I wonder why Cherin was attacked from behind and repeatedly stabbed in the back while Berinov, by contrast, got it through the neck. The latter isn't very common. It's easy to miss the target. A frontal attack makes it much easier to stab the chest."

"That, or he was left-handed and standing behind Berinov," Kasrashvili remarked. It was hard to tell if he was just making light of it all.

"I'm assuming the killer got disturbed or surprised and had to flee. Otherwise he wouldn't have left the murder weapon behind, and certainly not this." Heller pointed at the backpack in the corner.

"Is the head in there?" Kasrashvili sounded surprised, apparently not expecting this.

Heller nodded at the backpack. These were bad times. Worse than ever. Everything seemed to be falling apart. When something did work, the Russians came and took it away. There was enough food out in the country, but people were hiding it. The people in the cities were starving. Black markets thrived on every corner. Those who didn't have anything to trade and tried to keep honest starved. Their liberators wanted to convert people, yet they ate everything up. And whenever the Soviets came marching down streets, people slammed their window shutters and barred their doors. It was all so absurd. So why shouldn't an Oberkommissar of the People's Police walk through the city with a backpack containing a severed head?

"We've been seeing an increase in robbery homicides over the past few months," Heller said. "Mostly cars ambushed on country roads and highways, but there's also theft and robbery on the outskirts of town, around the Dresden Heath. Anyone traveling alone in the dark is risking their life. So it's possible a single perpetrator attacked them both. A robbery, maybe?"

The Dresden Heath wasn't far. Anyone who knew their way around could vanish into the woods within minutes. Almost no one dared to leave home in the dark.

"Both officers still had their wallets on them, money, cigarettes," Kasrashvili said, leaving no doubt that he didn't think it was robbery.

"I'll arrange for the coroner, Dr. Kassner, to examine both corpses," Heller said. "Do you approve of my sending him over? And do you have anything against my taking photos?"

"No, go ahead." The doctor took off his glasses and polished the lenses on his coat. "Between us, Comrade Oberkommissar? I'm not certain what Lieutenant General Medvedev is after, but I do know that your work won't make you many friends. The Russians, they don't like it when people stick their noses in their business."

Kasrashvili's words preoccupied Heller as he exited the barracks. It was as if the doctor didn't feel he belonged and wasn't one of them. Heller passed through the guarded front gate, waving at the sentries. An engine revved, startling Heller. A Russian jeep with the top down drove up and stopped next to him, its long radio antenna whipping back and forth.

"There he is, my favorite fascist." The officer in the passenger seat smiled. He was bundled up in an overcoat, scarf, gloves, and fur shapka, his face barely visible between the thick earflaps. Yet Heller could immediately tell who it was.

"Colonel Ovtcharov."

"You recognized me." Ovtcharov clapped his gloves together. His nose was red from the cold, and his driver kept sniffling. "I just happened to spot you. What are you doing here?"

Heller knew the secret service colonel was lying. Ovtcharov had been waiting for him. He'd probably even been following Heller from the moment he left Medvedev's office.

"I'm investigating the Berinov case."

"That so? Me too. You must know that this matter concerns the Soviet Armed Forces?"

"I'm aware of that. But I was assigned to the case this morning. So I'll pursue it until German prosecutors drop the proceedings." Heller didn't know how else to respond. He couldn't exactly bring up Medvedev.

"There are no proceedings for this case," Ovtcharov said, then pointed to the backpack. "Is that it? The backpack with the head in it? Is there any proof it belonged to Berinov or that he had it with him?"

Heller shook his head.

"Well, that's what I thought. I am certain that it has nothing to do with this case. Has anyone found any other body parts? A coincidence, I tell you, nothing more. The men can't be prohibited from doing everything, you know. They're only human, after all."

Heller didn't understand what Ovtcharov was trying to say. Yet he didn't want to inquire further. The situation was awkward, and he just wanted to leave. Besides, he was freezing, he felt a sore throat coming on, and his stomach still ached. The sentries behind him must have heard every word. What would they think of him speaking in a conversational tone with an MVD officer? People like Ovtcharov had planted themselves in the regional court at Münchner Platz and in the former Hotel Heidehof after Soviet HQ had moved from there to the Justice Ministry, and their methods weren't much different from those of the Gestapo: confiscation, abduction, torture, imprisonment. People knew to avoid the cellar of the Heidehof at all costs. Many who were detained there were taken to the prison in Bautzen, guilty or not, without a trial.

"Is your son not back yet? I hear he's had the pleasure of enjoying over two years of our Russian hospitality."

"He's not back yet," Heller said, doing his best to keep his composure. Why would Ovtcharov mention Klaus? Klaus was supposed to have arrived the day before, but Karin had waited in vain at Neustadt train station for hours. Ovtcharov was tough to read. Did he know something about Klaus? Could he somehow be preventing Klaus's return home? No, Heller told himself, that was just paranoia. Until just a few hours ago, he'd had nothing to do with the secret service colonel.

Ovtcharov finally brought his little game to an end. "Well, it was a pleasure seeing you again. Here, take this, as a token of friendship." He reached behind his seat, pulled out a small bundle of rolled-up packing paper, and handed the package to Heller.

"What's this?" Heller asked.

"*Payek. Do svidaniya!*" Ovtcharov said, then ordered his driver to go.

Heller watched the jeep roll on, weighing the little package in his hands. It was surprisingly heavy, and he took a few more steps away from the gate before carefully unfolding the paper. He could hardly believe what he saw: a large piece of pork, a half stick of butter, two carrots, and a little pack of sugar.

He didn't receive these little packages often. Their Soviet occupiers used tactics like this to obtain the cooperation and favor of certain people. *Payek* was a magic word. Those who acted at the Soviets' discretion received *payek*, and it could be crucial to survival. Those who received lots of *payek* could in turn win the favor of other people. Heller closed the package, not exactly sure where to put it.

He heard someone calling for him. "Herr Oberkommissar!" It was Oldenbusch, waving at him from the Ford parked across the road.

Relieved, Heller crossed the street.

"Let's get going, Max," Oldenbusch said. "I don't like being around here for long."

"Why so worried?" Heller asked as he sank into the passenger seat.

"Some Russian just tried confiscating the car, that's why. Right in the middle of the street."

Heller snorted. That sort of thing happened a lot, unfortunately. In broad daylight.

"He tried to stop me, aiming his machine gun. I just held my ground and hoped he wouldn't shoot." Oldenbusch drove off, turned, and then headed down Radeberger Strasse toward the city center. "Was that one of those MVD men you were talking to?"

"Yes, and he was apparently waiting for me right there by the front gate. He hinted that we should stay clear of the matter."

"As expected. Fine by me. I don't want anything to do with their squabbles. No one's safe among them. Even the likes of Medvedev can vanish without a trace."

"True, Werner. But what are we supposed to do about this head?"

"That's for the public prosecutor's office to decide. We certainly don't have anyone on file complaining about missing a head."

"Werner, I wish you wouldn't always be so sarcastic. Soon it will turn into cynicism. And cynics don't believe the world can change. Hey, let's take a little detour by Neustadt train station."

Oldenbusch sighed. "We're nearly out of gas, and I'm not sure we'll be getting any in the next few days. We'd be in a real fix if we couldn't use the car."

Heller thought it over. Karin was sure to have gone to the station again, plus Klaus knew where they lived. His boy had survived both the war and a Russian camp, so he could certainly manage the last few miles on his own. "Fine. Drive to Dr. Kassner. Then to the police department. And these photos need to get developed soon." He held up the camera.

They drove on in silence before Heller finally lost the battle with his conscience and pointed at the little package on his lap. Oldenbusch had surely been wondering about it.

"Ovtcharov gave me an extra ration. Do you want to split it?"

"You take it, boss. You need it more than me. Besides, you have to provide for that older lady you and Karin are living with."

"Yes, true. And you're all provided for?"

"I get a package through the district committee."

Heller stared at Oldenbusch. "From the Russians? What for?"

Oldenbusch's look showed a certain degree of pity. "In a word: Socialist Unity Party of Germany."

So Oldenbusch received his *payek* for joining the SED. That was nothing more than favoritism, Heller thought, perturbed. He didn't even want to think where all this might lead. It hadn't even been two years, and already people had had more than enough of the Russians and their system of favors and privileges.

"That's actually five words," he muttered.

February 6, 1947: Late Afternoon

Heller's bad foot was making it hard for him to cover the last few yards of the Rissweg to get home. He was in pain, and the street was slippery with packed snow. Despite Ovtcharov's recommendation, Heller had arranged for the few remaining cadaver-tracking police dogs to start searching tomorrow for the body belonging to the severed head. They would start at Bautzner Strasse and Jägerstrasse, right above the slope where Major Berinov's body was found. Heller saw the matter of the severed head as an independent incident, separate from the Russian major's death, and thus Heller's responsibility. The MVD couldn't prevent him from doing the work, since the public prosecutor's office had initiated appropriate criminal investigation proceedings against persons unknown.

The ride home in the streetcar had taken an eternity. He'd left his dreary office in the cellar of the bombed-out police headquarters, where the detectives were currently housed due to space constraints, and had to take a detour over Augustus Bridge because Carola Bridge was still out of commission. The streetcars were crammed, the mood depressing. The train had even broken down for ten minutes.

"Power's out!" the conductor had shouted.

Many passengers were coughing; all looked ashen, haggard. They carried bags, packs, and suitcases in case they spotted anything edible or useful—though all too often they would return home with empty baggage. One person had a single coal briquette stuffed into their overcoat pocket; others bundled deadwood in their arms. Most looked around warily and avoided the gaze of others, scared of getting robbed.

Heller had to stand the entire way in the jolting train, anxiously pressing his briefcase to his chest. The smell of the meat was intoxicating, and those around him must have smelled it too.

The temperature had peaked at just 20 degrees that day and dropped severely once the sun went down. He felt chilled even with his scarf wrapped around his neck, mouth, and nose. Once he reached Frau Marquart's garden gate, he hesitated. Nothing indicated that Klaus was back. No one stood at the window or came to meet him. He passed through the little front yard, taking long strides, then knocked on the front door and opened it.

"Karin? Look what I have!"

Karin came rushing down the stairs, his old overcoat wrapped tightly around her. She balanced on her tiptoes to give him a quick kiss.

"Here, look." Heller opened his briefcase, but Karin only glanced inside.

"Max, Frau Marquart is sick."

"What's she have?"

"High fever. Severe chest pain. Hopefully it's not pneumonia. All she can handle is tea."

"But she was fine this morning."

"And now she's sick, Max."

"There's no one I could try right now," he said.

"What about that Dr. Ehlig at the hospital, the professor? You've worked with him before."

"I'll give it a try." Heller gave Karin his briefcase, which she took into the kitchen, and went to the hallway telephone they'd had installed when the new police force took him back about a year ago.

"Max, you even got meat!" Karin beamed when he entered the kitchen ten minutes later.

"A colonel in the secret service gave it to me."

Karin's expression dimmed.

"Don't worry, it was casual." Heller's voice lowered. "There's apparently a deadly feud going on among some Russian officers. He'd like me to keep clear of it."

"You mean that dead Russian they found over near Waldschlösschen?"

Heller was always amazed by how fast the news and rumors spread.

"A little farther down from there along that steep slope, but yes, him."

"And you're staying out of it, right?"

Heller nodded, but Karin's eyes kept searching his. "Don't lie to me!" she warned. "What about that Dr. Ehlig?"

"They wouldn't even put me through. Ehlig isn't on duty right now. All they told me was that we should take her to the hospital."

"Then let's do that."

"She's better off here, Karin. Trucks are leaving the hospitals every day with thirty, forty dead, heading for the crematories. I did speak to Dr. Kassner earlier." It was only a brief discussion, since Kassner had little time.

"So? Can he help?"

"What do you think? He's a coroner."

Karin bristled. "But we have to do something!"

"We'll make compresses and give her tea. Maybe she'll recover during the night."

"And if she dies?"

"Karin, there's nothing else we can do." Heller took Karin in his arms. She fought him at first, then gave in.

"I know, Max," she whispered into his chest. "When will all this end?"

Heller was reminded of the Soviet doctor—Kasrashvili. Maybe he could beg the man for help, at least to stop the fever.

"Does the name Kasrashvili mean anything to you?"

Karin thought a moment. "Sure. That piano concert."

"Right." Now Heller remembered. It must have been fifteen years ago.

"Tariel Kasrashvili, the Georgian piano virtuoso. It took some getting used to at first, remember?"

Heller nodded, lying a little. He couldn't even remember where the concert was. "I met a doctor today named Kasrashvili, a Georgian. Wonder if they're related." It was probably pointless thinking about it—the name could be as common as Müller in Germany. He let go of Karin. "Maybe he could help. Tomorrow. Let me try the neighbors and see if someone has some broth left over. I'm just afraid no one has any to spare."

"Take this with you." Karin pressed the little packet of sugar into his hand.

Heller reluctantly took it. He didn't like having to take it but didn't let on.

They heard an awful screech from upstairs. Heller whipped around.

"She's been doing that," Karin said and kept him from heading up the stairs. "She doesn't want to see anyone else. Just me."

Heller grabbed his cap and scarf. "Any news about Klaus?" he asked before opening the front door.

Karin bit her lip and shook her head.

February 7, 1947: Early Morning

Heller started awake and took a moment to get his bearings. The doorbell shrilled yet again, and someone knocked on the door. He tossed the covers aside, shuddering from the sudden cold, and thrust his feet into his worn-out slippers.

"Turn the light on," Karin muttered. "I'm half-awake anyway."

Heller switched on the night-table lamp and checked the clock. It was half past three in the morning. The doorbell rang again. He went into the hallway and turned the light on there too. He could hear Frau Marquart wheezing heavily in the neighboring bedroom. He had barely slept, worrying about her. He hadn't been able to find help. So Karin had made cold compresses to cool the sick woman's forehead.

Heller's heavy overcoat hung next to the door when he wasn't wearing it inside the cold house. He threw it around himself, shouted, "I'm coming already!" and went down the stairs. Another forceful knock. By the next ring he was sure it couldn't be Klaus—his boy would've never made such a racket.

Before Heller opened the front door, he reached into his overcoat pocket and grasped his duty pistol. He opened the door with his other hand. Freezing air rushed in.

The silhouettes of two uniformed cops showed in the dim glow of the gas streetlamps. From their distinctive stiff shako hats, Heller recognized them as People's Police.

"Comrade Oberkommissar?"

"Yes?"

"Corporal Neubert. You're needed immediately," one of them said. "There was an attack, with hand grenades and machine guns."

"There any dead or injured?"

"It's not exactly clear yet what's going on. They tried calling you but couldn't get a connection."

"Let me get dressed real quick." Before he went back upstairs, Heller checked the telephone. The line was dead. Sometimes the power was out, and other times it was as if someone were simply toying with them. He shook his head.

The two cops picked him up in an Opel Blitz truck with a wood-gas generator—captured by the Russians at some point, its original color had been painted over with the standard brownish green of the Soviet Army. They'd painted "POLIZEI" in stencil on the doors and tailgate. The truck bed was covered with a tarp.

The vehicle barely managed the climb to outer Bautzner Strasse. Right before turning back onto the road, the engine died. The driver spent several minutes trying to get it started again. The three of them were crammed into the little cab, yet Heller was still freezing.

They took Bautzner Strasse almost the whole way back in, close to Albertplatz, now renamed Platz der Einheit—Unity Square. The driver turned into Alaunstrasse and was stopped by a police barricade, then let through. A gaping void remained where the Palast-Theater movie house had stood before the air raids. The ground was leveled off, and temporary wooden shacks had been built on the open space for housing refugees.

The truck halted at Katharinenstrasse, about a hundred yards before the intersection at Louisenstrasse. Heller stepped out and looked around. Despite the cold, nearly all the surrounding windows were open, the residents watching with curiosity. Soviet Army soldiers with machine guns stood around smoking, and the German police waited next to the wall of an apartment building. Heller announced himself.

"Oberkommissar Heller, from detectives. I'd like a status report."

One of the cops stepped up and saluted him. "Corporal Berger. About an hour ago, someone attacked the Schwarzer Peter bar at the next intersection. One or more attackers fired rifles or machine guns, threw hand grenades and a Molotov cocktail. A patrol officer was the first on the scene but couldn't make out any attackers. Then soldiers from the Soviet barracks arrived and occupied the building. They encountered no resistance—the assailants obviously got away. It's looking like standard destruction. The bar was on fire, but it has been put out. The bar owner, a Josef Gutmann, was present and is slightly injured. The floors above aren't occupied, and the stairwell's walled up. Apparently, there were some eyewitnesses."

Witnesses or not, Heller knew that no one would willingly give a statement as long as Soviet Army soldiers were around.

"This Gutmann, where is he?"

"In his bar, in the back room. He's getting treated."

"Can I go inside?"

Corporal Berger glanced over his shoulder. The soldiers had set up spotlights that lit up the building, but Heller couldn't make out many details from a distance. "You can try. Our Soviet Army comrades sealed it off earlier. That bar was a popular meeting place for Soviet officers."

"I'll give it a try," Heller said.

None of the soldiers bothered him until he got close to the building. The windows of the bar, whose entrance was on the corner, were all destroyed, the shutters either broken off or hanging by their hinges. From the two windows facing Louisenstrasse, black smoke stains stretched all the way up to the fourth floor of the exterior. Luckily, the Neustadt neighborhood had a fire station just a hundred yards from the bar or the whole building would've burned down. The firemen were rolling up their hoses. Their water had frozen on the side of the building, lending the gray plaster an odd shine under the spotlights. A diesel generator chugged away.

"Are you the detective?" someone said to Heller.

"Oberkommissar Heller, yes."

"Fire Chief Steffens, head of this fire brigade. The fire was started on the ground floor with the help of an accelerant, probably a Molotov cocktail. We were able to keep the flames from spreading to the neighboring building even though the Russians wouldn't let us fight it at first."

"Why not?"

"Probably assumed the attackers were still inside. But they couldn't enter, because of the thick smoke. Maybe they thought it was a robbery," Chief Steffens said, then lowered his voice. "Or maybe it was one of them."

Heller looked up, craning his head way back. At first glance the building seemed habitable, but the well-preserved facade was probably deceptive. They wouldn't have walled off the stairwell for nothing, and the building likely didn't have a proper roof anymore—fire had probably gutted it the night of the big air raid, leaving only the fragile supporting walls. Many city neighborhoods had the same hollowed-out architecture.

"There weren't any other victims?"

"Only the ground floor's in use. All the staircases are walled off. We had some ladders up there, looked in the windows—it's all empty and open up to the roof. You can head inside if you like."

Heller entered the bar through the open door on the corner. There was a spotlight on the floor. It reeked of smoke. The wall paneling and much of the furnishings were scorched—the tables, chairs, and floor built of planks and sawdust had made sure of it. Water from the hoses dripped from the ceiling, gathering in gray puddles on the floor, thick with ash, or trickling through the floorboards. A slight crackling came from the cooling wood—the water was already freezing over. Heller faced right and went toward the bar top, which had been spared. A door stood open, and Heller entered another room with water trickling from the ceiling. He spotted a urinal—little more than a tiled wall with a ten-foot gutter mounted low. Two toilet bowls stood on the opposite wall, separated by a wood divider with no doors. Sheets of newspaper, spiked on long nails and fully drenched, had served as toilet paper. There was actually a sink, and when Heller turned the faucet, he was astonished to find running water. The main bar area was large, long, and drab. Heller tried counting the seating, but the mess soon forced him to stop. Still, he climbed over the upended chairs and tables to note the condition of the place. He also discovered a piano, but it was unsalvageable.

The ceiling had been temporarily bolstered against collapse with wooden supports and crossbeams, a stopgap solution that had held up for a good two years. The bar itself was built with crudely formed boards. The simple menu and prices were written on the back wall in chalk, most of the letters now washed out. "NO CREDIT GIVEN" read a warning in thick capital letters, and the Cyrillic letters below surely said the same. There had to be other forms of currency not listed on the chalkboard that could be taken on the sly and paid the owner even better. Not Reichsmarks, of course. There was better currency. Cigarettes, for example, but also eggs or bacon. Heller counted five bullet holes in the wall.

The bar had suffered severe damage, yet Heller guessed it would only take a few days for the place to reopen. This was no time for aesthetics—all it had to do was fulfill a need.

"Hello?" Heller shouted.

"Who's there?" someone shouted back. The voice seemed to come from a room behind the bar area.

"Police. Oberkommissar Heller."

"Here in back."

Heller pressed through a narrow passage and into a dark hallway. The only light came from the back room. There stood stacks of wooden crates, empty bottles, and cardboard boxes, some reaching the ceiling. A curtain hung down. Heller took a quick glance behind it but saw only wooden shelves holding laundry. Then he reached a small office lit by a kerosene lamp. On a makeshift desk—a board atop two sawhorses—lay piles of documents and slips of paper covered in a nearly illegible script. A small crucifix hung on the wall.

"Hello?" Heller tried again.

"Here."

Heller entered the small room. Behind the open door, a man sat in an armchair. He looked quite large even when sitting. He wore thread-bare corduroy pants, a thick turtleneck sweater, and slippers. He looked exhausted. His right arm was bandaged, and he had another bandage on his head.

"Are you the owner, Josef Gutmann?"

"That's me. Excuse my rudeness, but I'm dizzy and can't get up."

"Is your arm broken?"

"I'm not sure. It was bleeding a lot, and I was half-unconscious. Got hit on the head by something."

"Why are you here all alone?"

Gutmann shrugged and instantly winced in pain. He drew a sharp breath. "A Russian medic bandaged me up. At first there were a good dozen people in here, but they all beat it."

"You live here?" Heller asked, pointing at Gutmann's slippers. He put the man in his midforties.

"I have to. Someone needs to keep an eye on the joint." He glanced at a big club leaning against the wall.

"Things happen a lot? Break-ins?"

"Every week. You get actual gangs prowling around. Children, I'm telling you, gangs of children. They might look harmless, but they got a whole bag of tricks. They shadow a target, so they know when to make their move."

Heller remained wary. "You have other weapons? Firearms?"

"That's strictly forbidden," Gutmann said, not answering the question.

"Were you sleeping when the attack came?"

"Yes, here."

"In that chair?"

"I have a bed in the next room."

"You have a wife, children?"

Gutmann shook his head.

"So you were sleeping here, and the shots woke you? Or was it the explosion?"

"There was a bang, and I wasn't thinking explosion at first. Thought maybe something fell over. I go running into the joint, they fire at me, and the bullets pass over my head. I took cover, then there was this crash and a second grenade blew. That's when something hit me on the head and I went out like a light."

A sudden coughing fit overwhelmed Gutmann. Heller looked around to see if he could bring him a glass of water, but Gutmann waved him off, shaking his head.

"Probably took in too much smoke," he croaked. "If I'd lain there a couple minutes more, I would've been done for."

"So was it a robbery? Did they steal anything?"

"No. Everything's still here."

Heller raised his eyebrows. "You're able to confirm that already?"

Gutmann hesitated. "No, but I assume so."

"You have any valuables worth stealing? A storage room perhaps?"

"I have storage." Gutmann suddenly got up. "I'll show you."

Heller let Gutmann pass by, then followed him. Gutmann shuffled down the narrow hallway and passed three doors until reaching a fourth protected by an added-on metal gate. Its massive padlock was intact. Gutmann shook it as extra proof.

"Is this the only access to your storage?" Heller asked. "There's no window on the other side?"

"It's got bars on it. No one's getting in that way."

Heller looked the man in the eye.

Gutmann was starting to get indignant. "I thought you were here to investigate an attack."

"That's what I'm doing."

"Somebody looking to steal isn't throwing grenades and firing machine guns," Gutmann said and started coughing again. But eventually he pulled a key from his pants pocket and opened the gate. He used another key to open the storage room door. Once inside, he pulled a flashlight off a shelf and gave it to Heller, who shined it into the room.

Just like he'd figured. All the shelves were filled with precious items. Cans of food, packs of zwieback, bottles of schnapps and wine—sparkling wine and real champagne—plus jars of cucumbers, chocolate bars, sacks of sugar and flour. There were dried fruits, boxes of Maggi bouillon cubes, coffee, and noodles. Even hard sausages hanging from hooks. He also spotted a variety of cigarette packs and matchboxes.

Heller kept moving the flashlight beam around the room. The rear window was unscathed.

Gutmann said, "If you ever need anything . . ."

Heller shut off the flashlight and held it out to Gutmann but kept a grip on it for a second when Gutmann grabbed it. "Just what's that supposed to mean?"

"Well, I just meant, in hard times, people need to help each other." Gutmann said this with a crooked smile.

"I'd like to see the other rooms," Heller said.

Gutmann nodded and locked the storage room. Heller opened the neighboring door and discovered another little hallway leading to a well-secured back door. Behind the other doors were Gutmann's bedroom and a primitive kitchen that stank of stale grease. Two black pans sat on the stove, dishes stacked up beside it. There was a little table and two chairs. Heller sat and gestured for Gutmann to do the same.

"One second." Gutmann disappeared. Heller heard soft clanking. Gutmann returned with two glasses filled with schnapps, set one in the middle of the table, and sat down. He raised the other glass.

"Steadies the nerves," he said.

Heller ignored the invitation. He placed his notebook on the table and yanked out a short pencil.

"Ah, you're on duty, right." Gutmann tipped back the glass with panache. Then he took the second glass and tipped it back too. "It's all legal in there. Get it from the Russians. The schnapps I make myself. For money. Got all the receipts."

"You could do better with potatoes."

Gutmann's brow furrowed. "Potatoes?"

"The Soviets are requisitioning potatoes for vodka production, and in no small amount, I can assure you." Heller couldn't figure Gutmann out. Was he only acting like the attack didn't bother him, or was he truly this hardened? Either way, he'd dared two bribery attempts inside a few minutes, if one counted the schnapps—Heller couldn't take Gutmann's offer back in the storage room any other way. That he stressed everything was being done the proper way only made him seem more suspicious.

"Do you have any idea why this attack might have occurred?"

Gutmann laughed. "Of course. They're Nazis."

"Nazis?" Heller placed his pencil beside the notebook.

"Because I have all these Soviets coming and going. For people around here, it's just rubbing salt in the wound. They swear at me and scribble nasty things around my joint."

"And you believe that's enough for them to start throwing grenades?"

"It's Werewolves, I'm telling you."

"Werewolves?"

Gutmann leaned forward, and his schnapps-laden breath wafted into Heller's face. "Organized resistance. They're out there, all around! And I guarantee you they're responsible for those two officers as well."

"The two Soviet officers?" Heller wondered how much Gutmann knew.

"Look, I hear things, all right? I know Russian and was on the Russian Front, four years, rear echelon. I was able to make myself scarce right before it all went down the drain. They somewhat trust me. Heard one of them got knifed, and then another yesterday. They're shitting bricks, I'm telling you. That's why they're not letting anything get out." Gutmann crossed his arms, forgetting he was wounded.

"You smoke?" he asked.

Heller shook his head. "Aren't you bothered by all this? You could easily be dead."

Gutmann lit a cigarette, then shook out the match. He took a deep drag and expelled the smoke, shaking his head. "Could've been dead plenty of times. In Russia, then here in February of '45. All I know is, my time wasn't up."

"And you don't think the assailants will try again?"

Gutmann shook his head. "They'll try somewhere else. Be stupid of them to turn up here again anytime soon."

Heller picked up his pencil. "Let's go over everything anyway. The building, it belongs to you?"

"It was allocated to me. Year and a half ago. Belonged to a Party member who took off."

"What, so they just gave it to you?"

"What are you insinuating? I filled out the proper registration forms, got my business license, and applied for commercial premises, just like everyone else. They allocated me the joint."

"No competitors trying to buy it out from under you?"

Gutmann choked on his cigarette, coughed, and waved a hand in front of his face. "Look, I don't know. Wasn't like I was able to see the list."

"And the liquor license?"

"Got it the same way. I used to work in pubs, had all those permits too. It probably helped a little that I was in the KPD, sure."

"You were in the Communist Party? Before '33?"

"No, no, I joined right after the war. And I was able to show that I'd helped certain people. I gave them shelter when the Gestapo was after them. I also helped a few Jews escape. So they were glad to have me. And now I'm a member of the Socialist Unity Party. Granted, I've never been political. But when you're running with wolves, sometimes you got to howl along. Now, can I offer you some coffee?"

February 7, 1947: Midmorning

It took Heller almost three hours to get a reasonably sufficient record of the twenty witness statements down on paper—essentially the same story retold in nearly identical ways. During the night, around 3:00 a.m., people heard glass shatter and a grenade explode soon after. Subsequent bursts of machine-gun fire supposedly rattled on for several seconds. Then came a second explosion. People who dared look out their windows agreed that there was only one person involved. Probably a young man. He didn't try to enter the building. The whole thing had barely lasted a minute, though the fire had burned much longer. Flames shot through the front windows until the firemen could get close enough.

Heller then joined Oldenbusch, who'd been on the scene for two hours. The fire department had moved on after ruling out any possibility of the fire reigniting. Kids out on the street fought over the leftover cigarette butts and got shooed away by a man who then gathered up the butts himself.

"Were you able to find out anything, Werner?" Heller asked in a low voice on account of the large crowd that had formed across the street. Uniformed officers of the People's Police had their hands full sealing off the crime scene.

Oldenbusch tilted his head. "There's something I don't quite get. The gunman seemed really inexperienced in the way he went about it. I've found twenty-six bullet holes so far, which nearly match the twenty-eight shells. Two hand grenades were thrown, likely Russian make. I found the pins. Shells from the machine gun point to a nine-millimeter weapon of German origin, probably an MP 40. Magazine normally holds thirty-two rounds. Either there are four shells I haven't found, he didn't empty the magazine, or that was all he had. We found glass shards inside that likely belong to the Molotov cocktail. I'll try fitting the pieces back together in hopes of drawing some conclusion from that."

Heller was about to answer, then stopped and grabbed Oldenbusch's sleeve. "Werner, turn around slowly and look up Alaunstrasse. I think that's the young woman you chased down yesterday."

The young woman was strolling in a seemingly aimless way among passersby and onlookers. She still wore the long thick overcoat that made her look oddly plump; her hair was covered by a cloth, knotted at her forehead. She'd wrapped rope around her boots, which were coming apart at the seams. She looked like she was concealing something under her coat.

Oldenbusch tilted his head sideways, then frowned. "Not sure; lots like her running around. Should I trail her?" It was clear from his tone that he didn't think it was necessary.

The woman was farther away now, and passersby kept blocking their view of her. She was sure to notice anyone following her down the narrow street.

Heller conceded. Something else was on his mind. "Gutmann says it might have been some newly organized resistance group. Werewolves."

"Werewolves?" Oldenbusch frowned again. "That's a bunch of hogwash. You can see the shooter wasn't experienced from the bullet holes alone. Most of his shots hit the ceiling because he wasn't used to the recoil jerking him back every time he fired."

"Russian hand grenades but German machine guns?"

"There are plenty of both lying around. Hidden, or simply tossed out. They must have churned out millions of those guns."

"It's not inconceivable that Gutmann's competition was getting envious of his business. I got a look at his stocks—it's pure paradise, Werner."

"I know, he was serving coffee. The real stuff. I wasn't expecting that. Nearly keeled over."

"He also doesn't seem bothered about his place getting destroyed." Heller pondered that again.

"He doesn't do his main business inside his own joint. He's a rack-eteer, the king of the black market."

"Well, if he is, we haven't snared him on a raid. That face and build would have stuck in my mind. And that nice-sounding name. Gutmann."

Oldenbusch bent down and plucked another shell from between the cobblestones. "Number twenty-nine," he announced with pride. "No, a guy like that doesn't ever hit the black market himself. He's got people for that. Maybe you should talk to your young friend about it, you know, that one-legged fellow."

Heller immediately knew whom he meant. Heinz Seibling. He jotted the name down in his notebook. It was a good idea. A boyhood friend of Heller's son Klaus, Heinz lived in the neighborhood and was all eyes and ears.

"Which also raises the question of whether the assailant was intend-ing to kill Gutmann or if he hoped the place would be cleared out so late at night." Heller stared at Oldenbusch, waiting for his thoughts.

"If he'd intended to kill him, he would've broken in and emptied that magazine right into Gutmann. I'm thinking what you're thinking, Max. He only meant to scare the man."

"But apparently the prospect of killing someone was an acceptable consequence."

Oldenbusch blew air from his cheeks. "Well, that'd be a matter for the public prosecutor."

Heller knew what Oldenbusch was getting at. They both still had lots to do, and it was very cold. Heller turned up the collar of his overcoat.

"Keep me informed, Werner. I want to go ask Dr. Kassner if they have anything new on that severed head."

It took Heller nearly an hour to reach the municipal hospital in the Friedrichstadt district. There wasn't a vehicle available, so again he went by streetcar; he might as well have walked.

Inside the hospital he wasn't able to find Dr. Kassner in the pathology department and kept getting sent from one place to the next. After running around to three different buildings, he returned to pathology and simply waited inside the door for the doctor.

Dr. Kassner eventually came in.

"You been looking for me long?" he asked Heller as they started up the stairs.

"You could say that."

The coroner was around forty, with combed-back dark hair and a narrow mustache that, along with his thick-framed black glasses, gave him a stern look. He had returned safe and sound from the Russian Front after only arriving in the fall of '44, but he had lost his wife and child in the Dresden air raid. He never spoke about it and didn't let it show. He was one of those who endured their losses without lament, while others spent years mourning their living room credenza.

"I had a report sent to you at the police department," Kassner said.

"I haven't been there much," Heller said, "with so much going on around town." He was mad at himself for not making a quick stop at the office below the ruins of police HQ on Schiessgasse. There he could've used one of the permanent field telephones the city had allocated to the police and saved himself the long trip over.

"You're telling me. In the last three days my table has seen four fatalities from gunshot wounds and two from stab wounds. All robberies. People are bashing each other's skulls in. Since you're already here, should we take a look at that head?"

"Of course."

"Then come with me." Kassner took rapid strides down the long corridor. Heller followed.

"You working that incident involving the Russians?" the coroner asked, their footsteps echoing off the walls.

"I've been more or less forbidden," Heller said. Kassner didn't need to know what he'd discussed with Medvedev.

"What a disgrace! The Russians only have themselves to blame for no one liking them. There's hunger and distrust everywhere. In Cossebaude, people overturned a horse cart full of cabbage that was being delivered to a business. The poor driver had to sit and watch his cabbage being pilfered by moms, cripples, children, truly all kinds. Some started eating the cabbage raw, right there, standing in the middle of the road!" The doctor shook his head, looking dispirited. "The outrage is spreading. Here alone we see about ten deaths a day from typhus, and rising. The freezing cold is making everything worse. People are dropping like flies."

Heller couldn't help thinking about Frau Marquart being sick. "Tell me, doctor, how can you tell it's typhus? Is there a fever?"

"Yes, it jumps up quickly, but the pulse keeps steady. Congestion, stomach pains. Later, little spots. Typhus is caused by dirty water, and people get infected orally or from contact with feces. Spotted fever is transmitted by lice."

They had lice at home even though they used lice powder everywhere. And they were getting their water from the pump at the nearest intersection ever since a frozen pipe burst. Toilet paper was scarce. They had gotten shots for typhus, but there was probably nothing they could do for spotted fever and so many other illnesses.

"Heller, is someone sick at home?"

Heller nodded, which made Kassner raise both hands in defense.

"Typhus needs to be treated with penicillin. And before you ask, I don't have any. I couldn't even tell you where you could get some."

Heller was disappointed but tried not to show it. They'd finally reached the temporary rooms that Kassner used for forensics. The doctor pushed the door open and greeted a colleague, whom Heller acknowledged with a nod despite the man's face mask. Heller looked around. The doctors here had plenty to do. Corpses lay on several dissecting tables, and Heller raised his scarf to his face. But Kassner handed him a face mask and helped him tie it on.

"The head, please," Kassner said to a female assistant. "We're taking another look."

To Heller he said, "This dual burden is getting to be too much. I can't be working for both the hospital and the police. And I recently kicked a man out of my department because a colleague denounced him as a Nazi Party member. That's not the way this should work, Heller. Lots of people were forced to join the Nazi Party. People like me and surely you as well. They can't go locking everyone up, or there won't be anyone left."

"I've never belonged to a party. Never."

Kassner recoiled and gave Heller a surprised look.

"Well, be that as it may," he said, "we're very busy cataloging the various epidemics. We see many frostbite victims and lots of organ failure due to malnutrition. See, the body begins to break down muscle once it has no more fat reserves. The same happens with the heart muscles. Once that happens, the end comes fast."

Kassner's female assistant pushed in a rolling cart with the head under a cloth. Once she was gone, Kassner leaned close to Heller.

"Did you hear about the autobahn to Berlin? Last night two cars were held up, and the occupants killed and robbed. Supposedly seven dead. I'm telling you, there's going to be another war if the Russians keep letting people starve like this."

Heller took a deep breath. "We shouldn't forget whom we all have to thank for this."

Kassner nodded. "The Führer, that crook!"

But that wasn't what Heller meant. For many, Hitler had become the accepted excuse. Hitler was the guilty one, people simply said, and then didn't have to think about how guilty they themselves were. Hitler drove us into the abyss, they'd lament, as if a single person could be solely responsible for all misery everywhere.

Heller pointed at the cart. "Show me the head."

Kassner pulled off the cloth. "Male, age fifty, judging from the condition of the teeth. Appears to be in good health, no symptoms of deficiency. Cause of death unclear. No sign of poisoning, nor strangulation; hyoid bone is still intact. We know that the head was severed a considerable time after death. The body must have been lying on its back for a fairly long while as evidenced by the pressure marks here on the back of the head." The doctor turned the head around and separated the thinning hair, so Heller could see the dark spots where the blood had collected under the skin.

"Here, on the face, are two small scars that suggest he served in the war. They look like shrapnel wounds. The man could have been quite tall if you consider the size of the skull. The head was crudely separated from the torso, as if the perpetrator had been trying out different tools. There are signs here of a hatchet being used. These incisions here, clearly from a knife. The neck vertebra was first cut with a saw and eventually broken in two. Shows a certain brutality and steeliness."

"So between death and the head getting severed, how much time?"

"At least a day."

"Are there signs of a bayonet? Stabbing?"

"No, none. Have you made any progress identifying the victim?"

"Oldenbusch took photos. I'm hoping we'll be able to make them public. Possibly in the newspapers or with a public notice."

Kassner waved a finger. "Niesbach will never let you do that. He bows down to the Russians. Preemptive obedience."

"I think he's a little more capable of asserting himself than that," Heller said. "After all, he spent years in Moscow and surely learned how to handle the Soviets."

As head of the Criminal Investigation Division, Niesbach had mostly stayed in the background. Heller wasn't sure what to make of the man. Heller always had to think twice about how to state what he needed so he didn't make his boss look like some layman. They had selected Niesbach to become a police officer in a kind of crash course where his Communist Party membership and political training in Russia had proved the most critical factors.

"Bear in mind that Niesbach belongs to the Russians," Kassner added. "You shouldn't ever view him as one of our own."

One of our own, Heller repeated to himself. Kassner must feel quite safe in his job to go around trumpeting his opinions so loudly.

"In that case, I'll go see which prosecutor's heading the case. Have him take a shot at it. There must be some way of getting a dead man identified."

Heller left the hospital, heading for Friedrichstrasse, and as he turned toward the gutted Yenidze tobacco factory, he noticed a jeep with a long antenna idling across the street. Heller knew the vehicle. The man in the passenger seat stood and waved at him.

"Comrade! *Idi syuda!*" yelled Colonel Ovtcharov, far too loud and jovially.

Heller looked both ways and crossed the street in front of a horse and cart. The animal snorted out white puffs of steam, struggling with the weight of the overloaded cart.

"I'm starting to think you're shadowing me," Heller told the secret service colonel.

"I was told I could find you here. Where you heading?"

"Police headquarters."

"Splendid. Me too!" Ovtcharov chirped, whistling his *S*. "I like this word. Sssplendid. Come on, I will take you there." The colonel stepped out so Heller could squeeze by his seat and into the back, then sat down again.

Heller made room between the cardboard boxes and crates, and as a precaution turned up his collar, pulled his cap down, and wrapped his scarf tighter. The driver yanked the wheel and gave the engine gas.

Ovtcharov turned around to Heller. "After the attack on this bar so popular with the officers, we have to assume the attacks on Berinov and Cherin are assassinations directed against members of the Soviet Army. We're up against an organized band of insurgents. This is what you should investigate."

Heller squinted against the freezing wind, and the rough driving kept making him grab at the metal bodywork. He wanted to disagree, since he could think of a few more plausible motives. But all that cold air took his breath away. And Ovtcharov wasn't the right man for such a discussion anyway. Why would the colonel stalk him simply to tell him this? Perhaps the Russian was mistrustful and wanted to discover exactly what Heller had discussed with Medvedev at SMAD.

"The mood of the population is not good," Ovtcharov said.

Was it a question or a statement? Heller couldn't tell. He nodded.

"These are tough times, and tough times require tough measures. The people must see that we will not back down, and that the German police and judicial system are working closely with us. The Nazis must be exterminated; any resistance that flares up needs to be stamped out. Socialism in this land is a delicate little plant that must be tended with care. You have not yet joined the SED? You amaze me, Oberkommissar, truly. You are a very straight-ahead man. But everyone must overcome their pride at some point and conform to certain inevitabilities. This country needs men like you. You don't talk, you act. People look up to a man like you."

"It's called 'straightforward,'" Heller corrected. The driver kept hitting the brakes to traverse the many stopgap repairs made to the Marienbrücke, and they drove over the bridge's metal plates and plywood at a crawl. "And it has nothing to do with pride. I simply don't think it's essential for me to belong to a political party in order to serve the people."

The driver made it over the bridge, turned right, gave the jeep gas again, and raced by the destroyed Japanese Palace, heading toward the Justice Ministry. He stopped there. Ovtcharov jumped out so Heller could climb from the jeep. Just before he did, the colonel reached back into one of the boxes and pulled out a small package.

"It does have to do with pride, Oberkommissar Heller. False pride. You might think the war is over, but it is not. It has just begun, and you must soon decide what side you are on. Here, take it." He handed the package to Heller.

Heller took it. He touched the Russian's arm as he went to climb back into the jeep. "Tell me, would you maybe have some penicillin?"

Ovtcharov laughed and landed on his seat. "Dear Comrade Oberkommissar, do I look like a doctor to you? *Do svidaniya.*"

February 7, 1947: Afternoon

Niesbach, head of the Criminal Investigation Division, lifted a paper from his desk and placed it to the left, and then to the right. He was a slim man, balding, yet seemed younger than he was. He pushed his glasses back up on his nose, then picked up the paper again. Heller politely looked away until his superior was done sorting things out.

"You do know I'm not a policeman," Niesbach began.

At least he was able to recognize that, Heller thought, unlike Heller's previous boss.

"Before I went into exile in Russia, I'd learned to be a slaughterman, or 'butcher' as you call it here."

"A butcher?" This had to be a sick joke. Heller's superior in the Third Reich, SS-Mann Klepp, had also been a butcher.

"Yes. We say 'slaughterman.' I come from the Rhineland." Niesbach had placed the paper to the side. He nodded and took a wistful glance out the window, looking down at Carolaplatz.

"You see, I view myself as a functionary in this position, a link between party and police. And, Comrade Oberkommissar, I'm afraid I must deny your request. Or at least I cannot authorize us to seek the identity of the dead man in the newspapers. I would first have to get authorization from Police Chief Opitz, or better yet from the Soviet Military Administration. It's a political matter. You understand?"

"No, honestly, I don't." Heller didn't want to view things that way, and it was becoming a pain to keep explaining that he wasn't their comrade. It seemed pointless trying to explain to this Communist, who had such a confident view of his role, that the police should be independent of any political party.

"It's not an easy situation. Those Nazis still among us are spreading rumors, inciting the population, fomenting unrest. So we must carefully consider what to make public. Everything is political in principle, Comrade Oberkommissar. I know you don't take me for one of you."

Niesbach raised a hand to stop Heller, who'd straightened up in his chair, about to reply.

"Before you say anything . . . I was in Spain. Did you know that? I saw people die there, good people, freedom fighters from all nations, murdered by the fascists. And I saw what the German fascists did in Russia. I was in the concentration camps. Were you ever in one?"

Heller shook his head.

"Your job, Comrade Oberkommissar, is to solve crimes. And the rigor and determination you show in doing so is commendable. Even when you're conflicted. But I see a higher aim. Fascism must be exterminated, root and branch. There must never be fascism again. I see a better society, a socialist state with people who are equal and free."

Heller could hardly contain himself. As soon as Niesbach paused, he cut in. "But people need to eat, above all, otherwise they won't be able to think straight. You don't improve a society from on high, with orders and banners. You have to begin at the bottom and offer people a real future. Keeping things a secret creates the exact opposite of what you want. You think people don't know about the two dead Soviet officers? My wife already knew before I got home, just from going to the local water pump."

Niesbach nodded. "I understand, Heller. But the people you're talking about are the same ones who supported Hitler, or at least tolerated him."

The phone rang. He picked up.

"Yes, sitting right here . . . Absolutely . . . I'll send him down."

Niesbach hung up and gave Heller an almost-triumphant look, as if his view had been confirmed. "There was an attack on a meeting of the Victims of Fascism. Münchner Strasse, corner of Bienertstrasse. A vehicle's waiting for you downstairs."

The three-axle Russian truck hurtled Heller through rubble-laden streets. To Heller it seemed like the cleared roadways and pedestrian routes only emphasized the city's destruction, just as a doctor only recognizes the true extent of an injury after cleaning the wound. The tidy lanes cutting through the ruins gave the impression of pioneers carving trails through dangerous wilderness.

And yet life went on. The people made use of anything not entirely destroyed. Smoke rose from old downspouts, which had been converted to chimneys. Exposed facades were sealed with boards and blankets. Though it was strictly forbidden, children climbed through the ruins, searching for firewood. They ducked down when the truck neared, its retrofitted siren squealing. Streetcars traveled the ghostly roads. Women pulled carts. Bricks had been knocked apart and stacked up for reuse. Huge posters announced joyous socialist tidings and showed Marshal Stalin in uniform with his bushy mustache and puffed-out chest, so much like the Kaiser of old.

The truck droned by the ill-fated block of buildings around Münchner Platz, where first the Nazis' sham courts and now the MVD's secret offices resided, and continued on to Plauen, to the large hotel called the Münchner Krug.

Heller didn't know what awaited him. But he had his duty pistol, a Walther PP, in his leather briefcase. The uniformed police officers riding in the truck's canopied bed were armed with pistols as well, the Soviets forbidding them from having more powerful weapons.

Soviet soldiers who were blocking the street let the truck through. Heller sighed. The Soviets had appropriated official procedure yet again, apparently intending to deny the German police even the slightest authority. To make matters worse, Heller spotted Colonel Ovtcharov of the MVD exiting the hotel with a large entourage. A crowd of people had gathered at the junction of streetcar tracks across the street. They had all attended the event. The onlookers talked with one another, but most of the excitement seemed to have faded. In front of the building, Soviet soldiers and People's Police were picking leaflets off the ground.

Heller climbed out and went up to the intelligence colonel.

Ovtcharov gave out a few more orders before turning to Heller. "All right if I give you the latest?"

"If you would be so kind."

"The second meeting of the Victims of Fascism was supposed to begin at two p.m. The last of the attendees had just arrived when a young man asked to enter the building. He couldn't identify as VoF, so the guard turned him away. Shortly after, an explosion went off on the other side of the building, here along Münchner Strasse. A hand grenade had gone off in a guest room, then a second exploded on the street. The guards rushed around the corner and saw the young man throwing leaflets into the air before running away."

Ovtcharov gestured for one of the leaflets, handed it to Heller, and added, "I heard the explosions all the way at my office and headed over at once."

"'Defend Yourselves, Germans—Fight Bolshevissm,'" Heller read out loud. "They wrote 'Bolshevism' with two *s*'s."

"I noticed. We've gathered up hundreds of them already." Ovtcharov stepped closer. "Comrade, there are Nazis among us! Someone has a printing press, which is strictly forbidden. It's worse than murder. This must be your mission, Comrade Oberkommissar. *Our* mission! Our authorities must work hand in hand. And I want you to be my liaison officer. I will see to it. I am certain that both these attacks and the murders of the two Soviet officers were perpetrated by the same group."

Heller kept the leaflet, putting it in his pocket. "Any dead or injured here?"

"The attacker probably got the wrong window. One grenade landed in an empty room. The other missed altogether and bounced off the exterior."

"He got the wrong window? And then he had to take cover from his own grenade? Then he ended up tossing the leaflets around and running off?"

Ovtcharov raised an eyebrow in amusement. "Tell me, is this an interrogation? You don't believe me? The guards are right over there, you can ask them yourself. You do know Russian, don't you?"

Heller didn't respond. The Russian was just making fun of him. Ovtcharov and Medvedev were fighting a silent war. Each was envious of the other's authority and kept elevating his own claim to more power. And Heller was stuck between their front lines. He needed to navigate his way out of there as quickly as possible.

"Come on, Heller, no need to be glum. We will get you an interpreter. I know someone who speaks very good Russian."

Heller wasn't surprised to see Constanze Weisshaupt walk up to him at the scene. The young woman gave him a warm hug.

"Is your Klaus back yet?" she asked. "How's he doing?"

"He's two, no, three days late," he told her.

After the war ended, Constanze, who was half Jewish, had lived under their roof for nearly a year. She practically became a daughter to Karin during that time. They hadn't seen each other for some six months now. Constanze had gotten employment in the offices of the Victims of Fascism organization, as well as her own small apartment, which was practically a miracle these days.

"Are you all doing well? I've wanted to come visit for a long time, but there's always so much to do."

"Karin and I are well. But Frau Marquart is very sick. I'm worried it might be typhus."

"Have you taken her to the hospital?"

"It wouldn't help."

"But you could get infected!"

Heller was well aware of that. "Can you tell me what happened here?"

"There's not a lot to tell. The opening speech was about to start. We heard a bang, then another a few seconds later, down on the street. Someone screamed, 'Death to Bolshevism.' At first everyone hit the floor, but then things calmed down. Soviet soldiers came and secured the building. Then we were told to leave."

"Was it one person? Several? Did you see them?"

"No, I didn't see anyone. I dropped down right away after hearing the first bang. Still ingrained in us since the war, you know?"

Heller nodded, thinking it over. "Let's head over to those two guards."

Their conversation with the two Russians didn't produce much. They described the attacker as a young German, about eighteen, maybe younger, medium height, blond. He had tried to slip through with the other attendees, but one of the soldiers stopped him and asked for his invitation. Since he didn't have one, the soldier turned him away. The soldiers couldn't recall the man's clothing, his haircut, or if he wore glasses. They weren't even sure if he had been carrying a pack.

Heller wrote it all down, then looked up when he heard a familiar sound: Oldenbusch's unmarked police car. The Ford's engine had recently been pinging—the car would likely break down soon.

"Werner, you go in first," Heller said. "Secure the evidence in the room on the second floor. I have a sentry posted. I'm afraid any evidence outside the building has been trampled."

"Max, you sound so serious," Constanze said.

Heller showed her the leaflet. "From a printing press, even though they were all supposedly requisitioned. Private ownership of a machine like that is forbidden, under maximum punishment."

"Well, apparently they can't control *every* person."

"Just four hours ago, both Ovtcharov and Niesbach separately talked to me about Nazi resistance fighters. And now this happens. Mere coincidence? And take a look at this." Heller pointed to the last word on the leaflet. "'Bolshevissm' with two *s*'s."

Constanze looked over the leaflet and frowned. "Are you trying to say . . ." She started to whisper. "Say that this was faked? But doesn't it just confirm what Ovtcharov and Niesbach were telling you? Niesbach is a good man."

"I'm not trying to say anything, but something just doesn't fit. Why did the attacker get the wrong window? It's pretty obvious from outside where the main hall is located—all the lights were on. And yet he also missed the window with that second grenade? From how many yards away? Four, five?"

"He was definitely flustered, inexperienced. Max, I see assaults on Jews and Communists nearly every day, both veiled and open. I'm talking anonymous letters, graffiti, red paint on windows. Car tires slashed. Windshields smashed in. Plenty of the old phantom Nazi is still lurking inside people. So folks like me are happy that the Soviets are here. If they weren't, a brand-new fascism would rise up."

"Boss!" shouted Oldenbusch from above.

Heller pursed his lips in annoyance. How many times had he told Werner to call him by his proper title in public?

Oldenbusch loudly cleared his throat, then tried again. "Herr Oberkommissar!"

Heller looked up now.

"It was a German stick grenade. I'm coming down to see if I can detect signs of the second one down there on the street."

"Please do."

"Could that mean anything?" Constanze asked.

"Not on its own." Russian grenades were used in the attack on the Schwarzer Peter bar. Yet both attacks were carried out in a similarly clumsy manner.

"Max, listen. I can help you. Come to my office and enroll as a victim of fascism. I'll vouch for you. I know you were never a part of any Nazi organization, that you were passed over for promotion, and you helped a Jew. And you helped me. I can vouch for you."

Heller raised a hand. "I can't do that, Constanze. It would be hypocritical of me."

"Nonsense, Max. Don't be so narrow-minded. You'd get extra bread ration coupons and preferential treatment at the housing office. Once Klaus gets here, it's going to get cramped real quick. And you can get furniture too, seeing how you lost all you had."

"Constanze, stop, please. It feels false to me. And it *is* false." He'd be receiving an allocation of furniture seized from Nazis, who'd likely seized it from Jewish homes in the first place. The thought made him nauseous.

"You're too good a person, Max. And stubborn. That can be a good trait, but not always. The least you could do is join the Party."

"This is from Constanze?" Karin asked when Heller came home that evening and handed her the *payek* package.

"No, another one from Ovtcharov." Heller was about to take off his overcoat but decided to leave it on. It was too cold in the kitchen, even with a fire burning in the stove.

"What does he want from you, this secret service agent?"

Heller shrugged wearily.

"Look here—more meat, crackers, margarine, and a little tin can. What's this? Caviar?" Karin put the items down and shook her head. "This is just absurd! Where are they getting all this? Sometimes it seems like they want to see us starve."

"Karin!" Heller warned her, but she was already angry.

"Oh no, you don't—don't 'Karin' me. Can you explain it to me, Max? People have enough out in the country. Just ask the Schaffraths and the Meyers across the way; they're from the country. Just today they gave me two eggs for a whole package of sugar. I put them in some broth for Frau Marquart, and she spit it all right back up. And the Russians meanwhile? You've seen it yourself; they sure seem to have enough. We don't even get anything with ration cards. I stood outside Wippler's for two hours in the freezing cold, and once I finally got in, you know what I saw? 'All Out of Bread.' Two hours round-trip on foot, and for what?"

"But so? It's the Germans, after all. You just said it yourself. Anyone who can is getting rich. Anyone who's befriended a Russian is getting something and isn't about to give anything away. You get two eggs from the neighbors for a couple of cups of sugar? Karin, that's profiteering! The man I had to get out of bed for this morning? He's got so much stocked up, you wouldn't believe your eyes."

Heller sighed. He didn't want to argue, not now, not while Frau Marquart might be on her deathbed and Klaus still hadn't returned. Karin was clearly just as worked up.

He stepped closer to her, but she moved away. "And on the radio?" she shouted. "Always the same idiotic slogans. 'We Must Pull Through!' 'Socialism Will Prevail!' 'This Rail Line Is Open Again and Electric Power Restored.' It's all window dressing, just like with the Nazis. And these posters everywhere—'Progress,' 'Socialism,' 'Unity,' 'Stalin Is Our Hero,' 'Stalin Will Save Us,' 'Stalin Our Liberator'! Is that us Germans? No, it's the Russians. And why do they forbid us from getting newspapers from the western occupation zones? Why don't any packages arrive? Why is Erwin's last letter six months old? Where's Klaus? Why won't anyone tell us where he is?"

Karin had worked herself into a rage and now seemed to regret it. She leaned into him. He put his arms around her. There they stood a moment, in silence.

"I chopped up the chair by the telephone today—it's burning in the stove right now. Frau Marquart's going to be mad when she hears. She liked that old chair a lot." Karin's voice had lowered to a whisper. Heller said nothing. They stood in silence again, leaning into one another.

"How is Constanze doing?" Karin asked after a while.

"Good, apparently. She wanted . . ." Heller fell silent. His stomach suddenly growled and wouldn't stop.

Karin pulled away and started busying herself with pots and pans. "What did she want?"

Heller wanted to avoid putting Karin in the awkward position of contemplating posing as a Victim of Fascism. "Well, she thought it would be good for me to join the Party."

"But you're not going to," she said, and he could sense the reproach in her words.

The lights flickered. It was the warning from DREWAG: use less power, the municipal utility was telling them, or we'll shut you off. Karin quickly switched off the light.

"I'm cooking the meat from yesterday, making a stew out of it. We'll save it for Klaus."

Heller woke in the middle of the night because he was freezing. His down blanket had slipped off. He pulled it back over him and waited for his body to warm up. He wouldn't get to sleep otherwise. Now the alarm clock ticking on the nightstand bothered him. He made himself keep his eyes closed, but all the sleepiness had left him. Where was Klaus anyway? They hadn't worried as much after receiving that first postcard from him in the summer of '45. But this gap—for three days now, of not knowing what was happening and why Klaus hadn't returned home yet—sat on his chest like a huge weight, an invisible hand pressing him to the floor.

And then there were all the people pressuring him to join the Party. They had to know it was complete hypocrisy. Was that what they wanted, a giant following of hypocrites? Hadn't anyone learned from the Nazis' twelve-year reign? Many people only joined the Nazi Party because they hoped to benefit professionally and personally—or because they feared losing their jobs if they didn't. There had been so many joiners that the Party eventually stopped admitting people, because even the Nazis themselves weren't sure who the committed National Socialists were anymore. Nowadays, everyone claimed to have joined only because they felt they had to. So had they all been hypocrites? And what about now? Were there actually people who'd truly been swayed? Niesbach, possibly. He was an idealist, which was probably why Heller liked him—not simply because he was an idealist, but because he hoped for a better world for all people and not just for one Volk. He had put his life on the line for his ideals, had even left his homeland, and he really did seem to stand for what the Soviets and the Socialist Unity Party professed to be. But why? Because he did seem to believe in them wholeheartedly. And that made him blind to their faults.

Then there was Constanze. She had been a victim of fascism, yet she had never been a Communist. Was she interested in building a socialist state? Was she only seeking security? Or was this her own way of seeking amends for her suffering?

What was he supposed to make of Medvedev and Ovtcharov? Should he take their coaxing as simply good advice, because they liked him? Did they really value him enough to wish he'd become their confidant, someone they could speak openly to about needing to legitimize himself publicly by joining the Socialist Unity Party? Or were they only using him as a tool for their personal power struggles? If Medvedev had his way, Heller would've taken Niesbach's job. Such a position had once been his goal, many years ago. The Nazis had blocked Heller's career. So it would have been fair and correct for him to now take advantage. But maybe the cause of his refusal lay deeper? Maybe he didn't even want the position anymore. All the tedious office work and eternal meetings. Administration. Agitation. Playing politics. The cliques. Perhaps his refusal to comply had more to do with escaping that sort of obligation—that of playing the boring desk cop?

Heller heard a noise. Frau Marquart. She moaned and wheezed, and her lungs emitted what sounded like a squeaky pump. Then came a dull thump. Heller turned to Karin, but she was fast asleep. It was on him to get up. He tossed his blanket aside, put on his slippers, and left the bedroom.

He felt his way along the hallway to her room and opened the door. "Frau Marquart?"

She was having trouble breathing, letting out a disturbing whistle. Heller approached her bed with hesitation. A crack in the curtains let in weak gaslight from the streetlamps, making the ill woman's face loom like a death mask. Heller reached for the cloth lying next to the washbowl, moistened it, and wiped her sweat-soaked forehead.

Frau Marquart moaned and grabbed his hand. "Herbert?"

"No, it's Max."

"I'm going to die, aren't I?" she groaned.

"No, you're not dying," Heller said in a firm voice.

Frau Marquart wheezed, her wide eyes looking at the ceiling, and wouldn't let go of his hand. Heller didn't want to pull his hand away but was frantically trying not to think about the woman exhaling infectious germs. It would be a catastrophe if he or Karin got sick.

When he thought Frau Marquart was asleep again, he cautiously tried to break free. But she grabbed him again.

"I can't go on any longer," she wailed. "I don't deserve this. I don't want to go on like this; it's too pathetic." She clamped both of her hands around Heller's wrist and tried to sit up.

"You're not going to die. We'll get you through this. I'll see what else I can do." Heller gently pulled his hand away, lowered her back down onto the pillow, and touched her forehead. He recoiled when he felt how hot she was. Again he dabbed her forehead with water.

"We made it through so much," Frau Marquart said. Then she reared up and coughed into his face.

Heller shuddered and closed his eyes. "Don't talk so much. You need to rest," he said, irritated. He wanted to wipe his face but couldn't, because he had to keep Frau Marquart from falling out of bed. She was trying to get up at all costs. She was vehement about it and put up a fight.

"Ach, Herbert, help me, Herbert . . ." She sobbed and doubled over in a coughing fit.

Karin finally came into the room. She pressed Frau Marquart's shoulder back down to the bed. "You need to keep still! I'll make you tea. Drink it, and please try your best to keep it down." She looked at Heller. "Max, go wash yourself!"

Heller was relieved. As he left the room, his foot struck something hard, and he bent down to see what it was. It was his pistol, which was normally always inside his overcoat. A nasty shock shot through him—in her delirium, Frau Marquart must have taken his gun to finish herself off but dropped it. He quickly left the room before Karin noticed.

In the washroom, he turned a light on. When he saw his face in the mirror, he recoiled. It was speckled all over with blood.

February 8, 1947: Morning

Oldenbusch knocked and glanced in Heller's cellar office before entering. "Small miracles do happen from time to time, Max," he said, brandishing a folder. "These photos are already developed. Right as I was about to leave the lab yesterday, we got more developer fluid. I'd kicked up a little fuss and was sure to mention Medvedev's instructions."

Heller tried to blink away the weariness in his eyes but couldn't. He reached for the folder and pulled it a little closer to his desk lamp. The lamp was always on since the small high window reaching his cellar room brought in little daylight, and they had no lightbulb for the ceiling lamp. "Thanks, Werner. But please don't go around dropping his name too much."

Heller opened the folder. The photos Oldenbusch took at the crime scene looked sharp compared to the slightly blurry and underexposed images of the dead officers, Cherin and Berinov. He had photographed the head in a way that a person might think it was a normal photo of a man, which made it more suitable as an official search photo.

"He's staring right into the camera. If we cropped the picture right under the chin, no one would notice he's dead."

"Do that, Werner, and get some copies made if possible." Heller handed back the folder. A coffee would do him good about now. Instead he was drinking dull tea, likely reused. "Do you know if Kassner had a chance to look at the bodies of those two officers over at the Soviet barracks?"

"I believe he was planning to go up there today." Oldenbusch sat in the chair on the other side of Heller's desk. "You know, the way I understood it, we're not supposed to make that severed head photo public."

Heller picked up a typewritten page and handed it across the desk to Oldenbusch. It was an official order to investigate all manner of organized Werewolf activities as well as send a daily status report to Soviet MVD authorities. Upon reasonable request, he was being assigned staff and means of transportation. All manhunts, raids, or similar operations would have to be authorized by the MVD.

The document was signed by Police Chief Opitz and Lieutenant General Medvedev.

"I'm not even sure if the Russians would authorize it, or if Niesbach doesn't dare request it because he knows they wouldn't want to," Heller said. "As the victors, they're afraid it would look like their hold on the situation is slipping. Now, do you have a report for me regarding the incident at the Münchner Krug?"

Oldenbusch nodded, still reading the document.

He gave the page back to Heller. After a pause, he said, "Not being allowed to make the photo public doesn't necessarily mean we can't use it to question people."

"Let's hope so, Werner. I can't tell you what a rough night I had last night. And that idea you had yesterday of looking up my friend Heinz Seibling is a good one. I'd only need something to take him . . ." Heller didn't need to say any more, as Oldenbusch placed a pack of cigarettes on the table.

"From the evidence room. That's all you need to know, Herr Oberkommissar. The attack on the Münchner Krug, by the way, was carried out using two German stick grenades, the Schwarzer Peter bar with Russian ones. At the Münchner Krug no shots were fired, and there was no Molotov cocktail. That's how the attacks differ. Yet both were done in an amateur fashion, each one most likely carried out by a lone assailant."

"Which raises the question of why leaflets were thrown for one attack but not the other. And if both attacks were carried out by the same person, does that mean he was responsible for murdering the Soviet officers? The conclusion feels illogical."

"Maybe it's a group, rather than an individual? An amateur group, sure, but still."

"Our men with the dogs still out there?"

"Yesterday they searched the immediate vicinity of the crime scene, around Bautzner Strasse; today they'll expand the search area. There are only two police dogs right now, and they're only allowed to sniff for two hours since forensics demands high-level concentration."

"Did analyzing the leaflets reveal anything?"

"They seem to have been made using a simple rotary press or mimeograph. The paper can be found in any organization or office. Machines like that are common, but it's clear the user was highly skilled. Which fits the theory that it's someone from the trade. So I got an extract from the business register back in '39—listing all the printers in Dresden at that time. Canvassing them all is a tall order, but at least it would be a starting point." Oldenbusch drew a paper from his briefcase and, visibly proud, handed it to Heller.

Heller scanned the page. Then he drank his tea in one gulp and stood.

"Well done. Let's start here in the vicinity. It looks like a few print-ers are nearby, and maybe we'll run into Heinz Seibling while we're at it. Get the car."

Oldenbusch shook his head with frustration. "I couldn't get any gas and don't want to drive on fumes, in case we have to leave the car sitting somewhere."

Heller reached for the phone. "All right, I'll see if someone can take us across the Elbe. We can do the rest on foot."

February 8, 1947: Late Morning

The streets around the Neustadt area were full of people running errands or standing at the water pumps, which were warmed by open fires to safeguard against freezing. There were long lines at the housing and food offices. A constant stream of people advanced on the train station. After the center of Dresden was destroyed, the city infrastructure had relocated to outer-lying, less affected neighborhoods. Now buildings were slowly being repaired, bricks cleaned, power lines refitted. Soviet soldiers as well as German uniformed cops patrolled the streets. A master glazier advertised "Window Cardboard Now in Stock" on a chalkboard sign, and a long line formed immediately outside his shop. Schools had closed because of the persistent freezing temperatures. Children roamed the streets in mended and often-too-large shoes, and played in the ruins; if there was anything at all to grab, they snatched it up at once. Some went out begging, their small ragtag figures standing there mute with hands stretched out. Hardly anyone gave them anything.

Others made traps for pigeons, though there were few left and hardly any cats. People gathered around the notice boards and shook their heads at the latest directives. Pickpockets slinked through the crowds. People would pick anything off the ground, be it a cigarette, an old newspaper, or a small lump of coal. Those with a bicycle watched over their valuable possession like a hawk. Even more people crammed into the long lines outside the soup kitchens, at the water pumps. Whenever a Soviet Army vehicle approached, the people shrunk back. "72 Companies Already Returned to the People" proclaimed posters of the Socialist Unity Party in courting new members as well as the voters' favor.

Heller and Oldenbusch had already located two printers. One was now under state ownership, run by a former Communist who had spent six years in Dachau under the Nazis. He himself used to make leaflets and described to Heller the exact type of machine they needed to search for—a rather simple device that could fit on a table and was operated with a hand crank.

The other printer was privately owned, printing out applications, forms, ration coupons, and food stamps under strict supervision by order of the authorities. The manager gave Heller the names and addresses of all his employees.

Another printer was located on Tannenstrasse. The grounds were closed off and looked overgrown. The workshop stood wide open; all the equipment had been removed. Grass was now growing between the cobblestones of the main yard, clumps of it sticking out of the snow. The office building next door was deserted. "Schlüter Printing" it read in large, curving script on the exterior. "We Print It All."

Heller looked around. Across from the printer was a coal yard guarded by soldiers. He and Oldenbusch crossed the road, presented their police IDs, and were admitted onto the compound. Workers were shoveling large mounds of coal briquettes into jute storage sacks. A large Russian truck with another soldier in the passenger seat pulled in, and the driver honked at Heller and Oldenbusch for not getting out of his way fast enough. Once they reached the little office, the supervisor shot up from his chair in shock. He was around seventy, stocky, his short hair parted.

"You from the police?" he asked, so shaken by the surprise visit he could barely move.

Heller raised a hand to calm him. "We just have a question about the printer across the street."

"It's been closed since the war ended. The owners had it all dispossessed. The Russians took everything away."

"How long ago?"

"Last year. They took it all, even ripped the cords out of the walls and took the lighting."

"Dispossessed, you said?"

"The Schlüters, yes, real über-Nazis. Herr Schlüter and his sons never came back from the war. Frau Schlüter ran the business with a partner, but he's gone now too; Russians took him. Schlüters still have a residence, Nordstrasse 20, but I don't know if they're living there. Don't even know if any are still alive."

"All right." Heller jotted it all down. "Herr?"

"Dienhagen, Armin."

Heller wrote that down too, then took a look around. It smelled like coffee, real coffee. Herr Dienhagen didn't seem in need—it was clear he was earning a little extra under the table from all the coal. That was the Germans for you, Heller thought. You had to have it to do it.

"All right," Heller said. "Enjoy your day."

Nordstrasse was about twenty minutes away on foot, and the route took Heller and Oldenbusch right over Alaunplatz, the square where large military exercise halls once stood. They were later torn down, the grounds left idle. A crowd of people had gathered. They hurried every which way, whispering to one another, handing each other items, then nimbly making them disappear inside their pockets before pulling out other items.

It was a black market, one of many, yet this location proved especially good for it. From here a person could disappear in any direction if a raid happened. None of the streets could be quickly barricaded.

And here the people who possessed something essential got rich. The prices were always rising. A person had to give up a good pair of shoes for a loaf of bread. A half-dozen eggs cost a valuable watch; meat, all a family's jewelry if need be. The currency here wasn't money. The only solid currency was cigarettes—almost always American ones. That, too, was the Germans for you. Heller didn't blame them for it, but it seemed absurd how that once self-titled "master race" now robbed each other blind.

Heller and Oldenbusch kept out of sight as they moved along to avoid any unnecessary concern, since even without uniforms they were easily recognizable as police officers.

The Schlüters' residence on Nordstrasse was a large art nouveau villa with several stories, similar to homes Heller noticed in the Striesen and Plauen neighborhoods. It was clear at first glance that the Schlüters weren't the only ones living here. Frozen laundry hung from windows. Smoke rose from homemade vents. The surrounding area had seen air raid damage, and several homes were destroyed, as was the villa on the neighboring property. The four-story building had collapsed from the third floor down. Parts of the attic were still visible, as was a spiral staircase leading to nowhere. Yet while other nearby buildings were being rebuilt or cleared, this site was left fully overgrown. Blackberry bushes and rhododendrons formed an impenetrable thicket, and hedges ran wild, the ruins covered with dandelions and birch saplings.

Heller spotted smoke billowing up from the ruined building and soon heard a knocking sound. An old woman in an apron came out of a tiny door a few steps up from the ground floor. She carried a crate that she stood next to a chopping box, then grabbed a log and started splitting wood with a little ax.

"Who are you here to see?" asked an imperious woman from the second floor of the Schlüters' villa.

"Frau Schlüter," Oldenbusch shouted.

"And who are you?"

"Police detectives," Oldenbusch replied, whereupon the woman pulled the window shut.

Heller let out an indignant laugh and opened the garden gate. He wasn't going to tolerate that. Yet as soon as he reached the front door, the woman was there to open it.

"Can you show me your identification?" she asked. She was roughly Heller's age, not quite fifty, big, and blonde. She had her hair pinned up, and her clothes confirmed her former good standing.

"Frau Schlüter, I presume?" Heller said, showing his police ID.

Her unfriendly stance changed abruptly. "Oberkommissar Heller," she read. "Please excuse my impoliteness, but there's plenty of riffraff out there these days."

"We have a few questions regarding the printing business," Heller said.

"Would you mind coming up? Please. No one else in the building needs to know."

Heller and Oldenbusch followed her up a curved staircase. The large, open home had been partitioned into smaller spaces using plywood walls, and busy lives could be heard inside. Children screamed, mothers scolded, someone sang softly. On the upper floor, something clanked. Snippets of conversation in Silesian surged out of another room. A telephone set hung on the wall at the landing.

Frau Schlüter opened a door for Heller and Oldenbusch.

"This is what they left me." She sighed, sank into an armchair, and crossed her legs. The large room was full of valuable furniture. A sofa and two armchairs stood around a low table, and there was a makeshift kitchen on the window wall. Next to a glass cabinet was a black piano. "Emil Ascherberg," Heller read.

"A living room and a bedroom. You can see my kitchen there. Cobbled it together from what was left of my kitchen on the ground floor. I had to have a stove made; that cost me two hundred marks. Six families have been given quarters here in my own house. They're getting everything dirty, breaking everything. I lost it all! My husband, my sons. They took my business away, then the house. And we were good people. We had fifty employees—printers, drivers, apprentices, bookkeepers—and now it's come to this."

"The printshop was confiscated?"

Rage flared in her eyes. "I was dispossessed, unlawfully, and they carried it all off to Russia. Those barbarians. They wrecked all the presses with their hammers and tools, their big clumsy hands. They even made our foreman go with them to Russia."

"Tell me something: Did you keep anything from the printshop? Were you able to set some of it aside, or did you have any equipment at home?"

"They would've hanged me for that, Herr Oberkommissar. I have none of it left, nothing!"

Oldenbusch cut in. "What about a small manually operated press? Or basic mimeographs? A Greif Rekord model, maybe, or a Centrograph?"

Frau Schlüter reached over to an end table for a pack of cigarettes. Pall Mall, Heller noticed. Frau Schlüter took one out and lit it without offering them one. She took a deep drag, visibly upset at recalling all her losses.

"I already told you. It's gone. The pencils even, down to the last paper clip. I'm living off my savings. And I'm always scared of those Ivans roaming the streets at night, kicking down doors and doing whatever they please. This is exactly what Adolf tried to protect us from—from the Ivans and Bolshevism. But he was kept from doing so!"

"Could maybe one of your employees have set aside that kind of machine? Do you know anyone who could build such a thing?" Heller gestured for Oldenbusch to hand her one of the leaflets.

"Real fine work," she said after a few seconds, then gave the leaflet back to Oldenbusch. "It's possible that one of our people appropriated something."

"Anyone in particular?"

Frau Schlüter took another drag of her cigarette and shook her head.

"Could you provide us with a list of your employees' names?"

"From memory perhaps. I don't have any records anymore. But I can't guarantee I'll remember every single person."

"When do you think you could have the list finished? An hour? Two?"

"Ha!" Frau Schlüter laughed. "Tomorrow. Come back tomorrow, same time."

"I'll come back this afternoon," Heller said.

Frau Schlüter nodded, then gestured at the leaflet with two fingers clamped around the cigarette. "You looking for whoever started the fire in that bar? Let me tell you something. He should receive a medal. That filthy, whore-filled dive, the Russians coming and going. A disgrace. A disgusting bordello. Run by Germans. I'll be frank. This country of ours is sick. Traitors everywhere. Traitors to the Fatherland. Someone finally dared rise up against treason, against such a disgrace. And it must be such a disgrace for you personally, one of the old school, to have to capture such brave people for the Russians. Such tough times!"

Outside, Heller exhaled with relief. "How can someone be so self-righteous and unreasonable?" he asked Oldenbusch as they left the property.

Oldenbusch waved the leaflet. "She showed more than enough fanaticism to back something like this, don't you think, boss?"

"Yes, but it doesn't prove anything. We need to request a search warrant for that place."

"But our visit just warned her. She could make anything incriminating disappear." Oldenbusch thought about it. "I guess she wouldn't be dumb enough to keep anything at home anyway. She's a clever one."

Heller took him by the arm. "Let's go stand where she can't see us from the house. You go find a couple of uniformed cops to watch the building. Maybe there's a field telephone nearby? If you can't find the cops, there's a police station at Alaunplatz. I'll wait here. And please, don't call me boss. How many times do I have to tell you? Where did you pick up such a bad habit?"

Once Oldenbusch was gone, Heller strolled a little farther on but made sure to stay within eyeshot of the villa. There had to be another exit. He'd have to stay alert and hope she didn't make any sudden moves. Heller calculated how long it would take Oldenbusch to return, estimating a good half hour. He shifted from one foot to the other, looking around for something to fix his eyes on. Simply staring at the house the entire time would make it feel like an eternity in this terrible cold.

Over at the destroyed home, the old woman continued chopping wood. Heller took a couple of steps to the side, so he could watch her, standing on his tiptoes and craning his neck to see.

The woman placed a much-too-large chunk of wood on the chopping block. She could hardly lift it. Once she got it to stand, she took the little ax in both hands and swung. Her chop was so weak that Heller felt sorry her—the ax only sank an inch into the wood. The old woman got it loose, swung again, and missed the block. Undeterred, she pulled back and took another swing. This time the ax got stuck, and she couldn't free the head from the wood no matter how much she wrenched and pulled on it.

Heller couldn't take much more of this. He imagined how tough it would be for his old mother, if she were still alive, to have to struggle like this. He took a glance at the Schlüters' front gate. Then he looked back.

The woman was now attempting to drag the stuck-together ax and wood off the chopping block. The whole block toppled over. Heller couldn't stand it anymore. He marched the ten yards to her property, clearing a path through the bushes and weeds.

"Wait, I'll help!" he shouted to the old woman, as she couldn't see him from where she stood. When Heller came around the corner of the house, she was waiting for him, holding just the ax, the wood having dislodged when it fell.

"Let me help you," Heller offered again.

"Go away!" the old woman shouted, upset, and raised the ax to her apron smock, partly in defense, partly as a threat.

"My name's Heller. I'm a police detective. I saw you—"

"Go away! This is my property!"

"Listen, I couldn't help but see how hard it was for you to chop that wood. Just let me help. I don't want anything out of it."

"Go. I'll manage all right. I don't need any help. Not from anyone!" She was practically scolding him. Again she threatened him with the ax.

"All right, fine." Heller felt like a fool. What was he thinking? The woman didn't believe him, and why would she? He could've been anyone. He could've shown her his police ID, but that probably would have only confused her more.

"My apologies, enjoy your day," he added with a slight bow and turned back for the street.

An older man wearing a pom-pom beanie and pulling a handcart saw him coming from the property and spoke to him as he passed. "There's no point in trying with the likes of her. She's not letting anyone inside that house."

"We completely forgot about Herr Seibling," Oldenbusch reminded Heller. He had returned in twenty minutes with two uniformed cops. Heller instructed them to be inconspicuous and watch for anything stirring at Frau Schlüter's villa. They should only intervene if they spotted her taking something out of the building.

"I didn't forget," Heller said. "I was keeping an eye out for Seibling the whole way over."

"So what now? Back to headquarters? If we're back by noon, we might be able to get that search warrant. That or you get those MVD Russians on board, but then things might get a little hairy for Frau Schlüter and—"

Heller raised a hand. "We'll visit Captain Kasrashvili at the barracks up on Carola-Allee. It's ten minutes from here; we can use their telephone. Also, it might give you a chance to get some better photos of the two dead soldiers. I'll inform the MVD, but I can't have the house searched yet."

"Kasrashvili, that doctor? Doesn't sound Russian."

"He's Georgian. Very meticulous. Wipe off your shoes and don't touch anything."

Oldenbusch nodded. "Will do, boss!" Heller looked annoyed. "Sorry, Max—"

"It's one of those silly new buzzwords, Werner."

"But I don't mean it disrespectfully. It was a respectful title in the military, after all."

"Nevertheless. The way everyone speaks nowadays—hole up, go off the rails, use your noodle, have a screw loose." Heller could only shake his head.

They walked the last few yards to the barracks. At the gate they showed their identification, and Heller asked to see Kasrashvili. The duty officer made a call, and they were allowed inside.

The young Georgian barely seemed interested. He listened to Heller's request, then ordered one of his men to accompany Oldenbusch to the corpses. He stayed behind with Heller, who'd noticed that Kasrashvili's office also served as his sleeping quarters.

"I'll meet you back out at the gate," Heller shouted after Oldenbusch.

Kasrashvili furrowed his brow at Heller's shouting. Then he offered Heller a chair, went over to the window, and leaned on the sill. "Ovtcharov was here, making inquiries about your investigation. I told him I don't know what you're finding."

Heller nodded. He hesitated to get to the point.

"Didn't you want to make a call?" Kasrashvili gestured at the telephone on his desk. It was an old model, black, with a metal rotary dial.

"In a second. Um, I—"

"I can step outside if you'd prefer . . ." The doctor moved to leave the room.

"No, wait. Pardon my asking, but do you happen to know Tariel Kasrashvili, the piano virtuoso?"

The Georgian froze.

"My wife thought she remembered us seeing a concert of his some years ago."

Kasrashvili moved around the desk and took a seat in his reclining chair. "He is my father."

Heller laughed. "Your father! What a coincidence!"

The Georgian's expression remained blank.

"Is he still playing?"

"No, he's long since retired." Kasrashvili stared at the desktop. Then he looked up. "You know Rachmaninoff?"

Heller perked up. "Rachmaninoff! Exactly, that's what it was. Your father was playing Rachmaninoff."

"Did you know that Rachmaninoff lived in Dresden from the winter of 1906 until 1908? I think he still owns a home here. My father is an ardent admirer of Rachmaninoff. He defended him, where he could, against his critics."

"What about you? Do you play?"

Kasrashvili raised his hands in resignation, showing Heller emotion for the first time. A hint of regret flashed across the Georgian's face.

"The war hasn't given me much opportunity. And the piano I have here is missing pedals and completely out of tune. Now and again I give it a shot, but . . ." He frowned, resigned.

Heller wanted to know more. "Would you have become a pianist if not for the war?"

Kasrashvili hesitated, his face contorted as if in pain.

"I'm not a medical man. I only studied medicine to avoid getting called up. I couldn't see myself getting torn to shreds by a German shell just for the Russians. At home, we always considered ourselves more German than Russian. We spoke German and French. Russians were considered barbarians in our house. And then I became a doctor, went to the front, and had to see all these limbs blown off, the bodies riddled with bullets. Filth disgusts me. Dirt, blood, excrement. I can't bear it. All these illnesses, the sputum, the excretions. I find people disgusting, and sometimes I find myself disgusting."

Kasrashvili was working himself into a minor frenzy. "But when I play, everything is so clear. You understand? A lovely piece is like pure water, like a stream flowing through dense forest." His gaze wandered. "But would I have become a pianist?" He shook his head. "Three months ago, I was appointed the army's cultural advisor. Now I'm leading the choir."

Heller was intrigued. He wanted to give the doctor time to reflect, but he still had a request. Oldenbusch would be back soon. He considered the right words.

"Can I ask you something? We live in the home of an elderly woman. She's sick with a very high fever. I'm worried it's typhus. She'll die if I don't—"

Kasrashvili pushed back his chair and stood up.

"If it's medicine you need, I can't just give it to you!"

Heller kept at it. "But you do have some?"

"It's for members of the Soviet Army. I can't just give it to anyone who comes asking." Kasrashvili, upset, rubbed at his hands as if applying lotion.

"Please, sit down." Heller stretched out a hand, in appeal. "You shouldn't get so worked up. I was only asking. I didn't mean to be pushy."

Kasrashvili didn't sit, though he was calming down.

"I can't just give it to everyone. Not without . . ." He stopped.

Heller breathed a little easier. It wasn't the request that had gotten the doctor so worked up. Perhaps he regretted having revealed so much of himself. The Georgian was looking for something in return, it seemed. So there was hope for Frau Marquart after all. Yet what could Heller offer the man?

"Perhaps cigarettes would be—"

"I don't smoke. Just imagine all that tar in a person's lungs. Have you ever seen the lungs of a smoker?"

Heller had never given it much thought.

"I have everything. Food, heat, liquor. Everything a person could need." Kasrashvili went over to a cabinet, opened it, and pulled open a small drawer. He returned to his chair and placed two white pills on the desk.

"Here. Consider it gratitude for our pleasant conversation. I haven't thought about Father and music for a very long time. You can make that phone call of yours now. I'm going to lunch." Kasrashvili nodded and clicked his heels together, then rushed out of the room.

Heller picked up the pills but wasn't quite sure what to do with them. He wrapped them in a tissue and tucked them into the inside pocket of his overcoat. It wasn't much, but it was better than nothing. Then he picked up the phone and got connected to the public prosecutor's office.

"How did it go, Werner?" Heller asked Oldenbusch when they met outside at the gate.

"You're not going to like this, Max."

Heller stopped walking. "The bodies aren't there."

Oldenbusch sighed. "I almost thought someone was pulling my leg. The orderly was rushing around the basement, checking all over, but it was clear he was putting up an act."

Considering what Heller knew about the Soviets, he wasn't surprised. They were trying to wipe the slate clean. In this way, the Soviets were quite effective. Maybe Kasrashvili had known the corpses were gone, which would explain why he left so quickly. Maybe he'd even given the order. Who knew. But speculating was pointless. Heller checked it off the list for now.

"Did you know there's supposed to be another new head public prosecutor?" he said.

Oldenbusch shook his head. "That kind of thing happens every day. A person gets a position, then three months later? Gone again. Maybe it's a good thing you haven't been competing for a top spot, bos—Max."

Heller smiled.

"At least they were all out to lunch," he said. "But this pushes that house search to the top of the list. Werner, go to the nearby station. Find a way back to headquarters. I'm going to locate Heinz Seibling. I think I know where to find him. Once I've taken care of that, I'll find a phone and call you at the office. By then we should know more about the search warrant. Maybe you can help facilitate things. But be careful, Werner. No riot squads, you hear?"

"All right. And maybe next time we'll take the car after all."

February 8, 1947: Midday

Traffic was backed up at the intersection of Görlitzer and Louisenstrasse. A streetcar rang its bell at people to clear the street. There were two soup kitchens here where people could get a meal for ration coupons and a few Reichsmarks. They started serving meals around eleven, at which time long lines had already formed. By noon, all the tubs and pots were mostly empty. This intersection had also developed into a good spot for exchanging information and rumors. No one trusted the Soviet-controlled papers. Here, everyone knew the score.

Soviet headquarters didn't like people gathering like this. In their paranoia, they immediately assumed a conspiracy or uprising. So the German heads of the People's Police agreed to post a few policemen here to keep watch in the background.

For small-time crooks like Heinz Seibling, curious kids, day laborers, and poor rascals, it was the best place in the city. Something was always happening here. There was always something to eat, and say, and steal, and entertainment was assured.

Heller neared the intersection from Alaunplatz a few blocks north, where the morning black market had dispersed before blooming again in the evening. He knew he wasn't likely to spot Seibling among the teeming crowds, but he wanted to give it a shot.

Aromas of food rose up. Heller smelled turnip soup. It reminded him of that horrible turnip winter of 1917, when he had returned to Dresden, having just recovered from his wounds. For a few months, he, his mother and father, and millions of others had lived on nothing but turnips. Turnip bread, turnip casserole, turnip soup, and even turnip jam. It was nearly reaching that point again, and, just like then, when almost a million people died of starvation, there were always a certain number of people who hoarded food like it was treasure. And yet now, despite believing back then that he'd never be able to touch a turnip again, the smell was making him hungry.

Forcing his way to the front of the line was a hopeless endeavor; he'd get something to eat back at police headquarters, even though he didn't know when that might be.

Heller pushed his way through the throngs of people, looking for Seibling. A schoolboy passed by, and he nabbed him by the collar.

"You see a man on crutches, a one-legged man?" he asked.

The boy fought to get free.

"Listen, I'm a cop," Heller warned him.

The boy gave in. "That clown, ya mean? He was just over there!"

Heller let the kid go and headed in the direction he'd pointed, even though it was probably just a lie to get free.

Fortunately, Heller did find his one-legged young acquaintance. Sure enough, Seibling was performing minor stunts on his crutches for a small group of neglected-looking children. Balancing acts, pirouettes. He still wore the old overcoat he'd had back in '45, now completely worn out. A top hat rested on his head, and he'd drawn his clown face with ash, giving himself a big laughing mouth. A sad clown is what Heller saw. He stopped and watched awhile. Then Seibling recognized him.

"Shoo, shoo, scram!" Seibling raised one crutch as if to swing at the kids, which made them laugh hysterically before scattering. He then swung around to Heller.

"My dear Herr Heller," he said, sounding genuinely delighted.

"What's with the getup?" Heller asked and slapped Seibling on his shoulder.

"You do what you can." Seibling winked.

"This isn't what you live off, though. You do still pilfer!" Heller said it as a joke, though he knew it was true.

"What are you talking about? I'm a respectable citizen."

"Is there a place we could talk?" Heller directed his eyes downward, to the pack of cigarettes that gleamed from his overcoat pocket before tucking it away again.

"Quiet and warm, pure paradise! Let's walk a little. It's not far."

Heller nodded and followed Seibling down Louisenstrasse toward Martin Luther Strasse. Once they were halfway down, the young man looked around, gave a nod, and turned into a building driveway. The entrance led them into an inner courtyard and through a breached wall into a second courtyard. They squeezed between two walls running close together and went downstairs to a cellar. Seibling stopped at an unassuming hatch barricaded with a metal bar. He leaned his crutches against the wall and camouflaged them with a piece of old tar paper. Then he laboriously removed the bar and crawled through the square opening. Once he'd turned on an electric lamp, he waved Heller inside.

"Pull that hatch shut."

The space was warm and oddly cozy despite its cramped and unhygienic condition. A filthy mattress served as Seibling's nightly resting place, a mishmash of various blankets on top. Heller wasn't able to move around much inside. He took off his hat, ducking his head because of the low ceiling, undid his scarf and overcoat, and looked around. Seibling had collected a bunch of canned food, mostly the kinds of things that were worthless in better times but currently sufficed as barter for a meal. A busted little cabinet, some children's shoes, fabric scraps, severed cable, bent nails, picture frames, busted candlesticks, dented metal chests, bicycle pedals, saddles, a Wehrmacht helmet with a make-shift handle that he used as a pot.

Seibling hopped on his hands over to his mattress, dropped onto it, and offered Heller a seat on a low stool. Heller sat, and his fingers examined the little table Seibling had built for eating and fixing things. Various tools lay around, along with a dirty tin plate and aluminum cutlery. The cut-open end of a can served as an ashtray. Heller noticed the telltale pail next to the mattress. The heat came from a homemade electric heater that stood only a foot and a half from the mattress, its hand-wound coils glowing red inside the metal box.

Despite his wretched existence, Seibling seemed contented and cheerful. He smiled at Heller and appeared to take his glances around as appreciation.

"Nice digs, huh?" he asked with pride.

"You haven't registered your current residence, I take it."

"Herr Heller. People who need me know where to find me. I don't need to register. I was allocated an apartment a long time ago, but they just keep putting me off. I lived in the rubble for a year, Johannstadt district, gathered plenty of wood, yet I nearly froze to death last winter. After I got robbed for the second time, I thought to myself, Heinz, take care of you and you alone, do it all yourself."

"What about your family?"

Heinz snorted. "My brother died in Sicily. Dad in Aachen. Probably an accident, seeing how he was just a driver; drove over a German mine. Mom and my sister and aunt, along with her kids, got it on the big air raid. February 13." Seibling's gaze didn't waver, and his smile didn't fade.

Heller nodded, his lips pressed together. He felt bad for Seibling. His sons were still alive, and when they did come home, their parents would be there to greet them. But Heinz had no one left, neither parents nor siblings, and couldn't get work nor the apartment to go with it. And now he dwelled inside this hole and lived hand to mouth. Sometimes the unfairness was so unfathomable that Heller wondered how anyone could still believe in God. People like Heinz Seibling needed to be taken care of and given some kind of hope, even if only the chance to wash once a day.

Seibling seemed to read his thoughts. "I'm doing just fine here." He pointed behind him. "Beyond that wall is the public swimming pool, the Germania Bad, get my electricity from them too; it's all intact. Someone could get it back up and running. Just open it up for free for people to wash up and use the lavatory. That would be quite the socialist act, wouldn't it? Giving farmers newly cleared land doesn't do me much good." Seibling leaned forward, grabbed Heller by his arm. "You won't go telling anyone about the electricity, will you?"

Heller shook his head and, though he'd intended to use his cigarettes sparingly, placed the whole pack on the table.

"Heinz, can you tell me a little about the Schwarzer Peter?"

The way Seibling raised his eyebrows said plenty. He left the pack lying there. "Gutmann owns it. He's a real bastard, a degenerate!"

"Someone said it's a bordello."

"Yes, it's a brothel. Almost only Russians go there. I have a couple of friends in the Soviet Army, from the regular ranks, and they say only officers are allowed in. And a few of us the Russians like well enough."

"But for that they'd need rooms. That place doesn't have any. Just a back room and a storeroom."

"Well, I wouldn't know, never been there. But that proprietor, Gutmann, there's something fishy about him. He does business with the top tier. He's even providing Russian HQ with premium commissary items."

"Do you think the attack on the bar was because of the bordello business? There are certainly other bordellos around. You hear anything about that?"

Seibling thought a moment, shaking his head. "No, but there's more going on with that place. It's a heap of trouble. Maybe the pimps are having a dispute. Fighting over whores. But I'm not that close to things. Gutmann's also not one to mess with. Everyone keeps out of his way. He has this guy, I'm telling you, a real killer—One-Handed Franz. You can tell just by looking at him that he makes short work of people. He'd been in the war. People say he was SS, in Serbia most likely, but no one knows. Lost his hand. People say he hacked it off himself."

Heller nodded along. Facts were once again mixing with legend. Then Seibling remembered something. He reached behind his mattress and pulled out a small canning jar of strawberry preserves. "I got this from the pastor at Martin Luther Church. Every Sunday he hands out food and blankets for children and the invalids. He's a good man, more socialist than the Socialist Unity Party itself. I haven't ever gotten a thing from the likes of them. He could be rich if he sold it all. I was saving it for a special occasion. Would you like some?"

Heller hadn't eaten a strawberry in nearly three years. "Ah, Heinz, you keep it."

But Seibling wouldn't be deterred. He opened the clamp and pulled on the rubber gasket. The lid popped open. Seibling hovered over the jar, inhaling with glee. Then he dumped half the contents onto the tin plate and pushed it over to Heller. Heller hesitated. Seibling got the message, took the plate back, and handed Heller the jar instead.

"You'll have to fish it out with your fingers, though."

Heller snorted a laugh, reached into his overcoat pocket, and pulled out a spoon. Everyone had silverware on them these days. Heller and Seibling spooned up jam for a while. Heller was trying to hide it, but the incredible sweetness and beguiling aroma nearly sent him into ecstasy. So much good sugar, he thought, in just one jar of strawberries. For a moment he wondered whether it was possible to take some home to Karin, but Seibling would surely want to keep the glass. And Karin would surely want to share with Frau Marquart, and by then she would only have a few strawberries left. No, Karin would only chastise him for not eating them all, knowing that he was abstaining just for her.

Seibling slurped the juice off the plate and licked it clean. "I was thinking about that dead Russian. You need to find out if he was one of the ones visiting that brothel. And there was that other dead one too. So if he was in that brothel as well, then maybe he'd gotten in Gutmann's way somehow. Maybe they wanted to relieve him of his whores. The Russians do that sometimes—take one for themselves, keep them awhile. Which is maybe why Gutmann had those Russian fellows eliminated. By that thug of his, maybe. And since the Russians can't officially touch Gutmann, because he moves in high circles, they got at him this way."

It was a nice theory, but the attack was too amateurish for all that. And it didn't fit the attack on the Münchner Krug either. And what about Ovtcharov? Had he known about the bordello? Was he a guest there and knew about the dispute?

"Tell me something, Heinz. Would you be able to keep your ears open for me?"

"Oh no, my dear Herr Heller. You can't ask that of me. That's too tricky. I don't interfere with the likes of Gutmann. His One-Handed Franz could bump me off, and you'd find me in a ditch on the edge of town; then you'd really have a heavy conscience. You can't expect me to do that. And maybe one thing has nothing to do with the other. Maybe it's just a dispute among the Russians. I was only speculating."

"All right, Heinz, okay." Heller realized his information yield from the pack of cigarettes was looking pretty thin. But he didn't want to put the young man in a difficult situation.

Heller was about to get up when he remembered to show Seibling the photo of the severed head.

"One more thing, Heinz," he added, and handed Seibling the image, cropped just so.

Seibling took a look and handed it back. "Yep, that's him."

"Who?"

"Gutmann's thug. One-Handed Franz."

Heller had secured a patrol cop on the way to the Schwarzer Peter, and now the man pounded on the door. He listened for Gutmann but heard nothing. Heller nodded for him to knock again.

"Someone's inside," he whispered to Heller.

"Then knock again."

The cop hammered again. "Police, open up!"

Footsteps eventually sounded from inside.

"What's the problem?" barked a male voice. "I'm busy."

"Oberkommissar Heller here. Open up, please."

"Fine, wait there. I'm indisposed at the moment." The footsteps faded.

"Open up! Herr Gutmann?" Heller said.

"Should I open it?" the cop asked.

Heller shook his head. He was frustrated. Who knew what Gutmann was hiding in there.

It took a while for the bar owner to return. They heard bolts and locks clanking before the door finally opened.

"Hold your position," Heller told the cop. Then he turned to Gutmann, asking him bluntly and indignantly, "What took you so long?"

"I was in my underwear," Gutmann said. He didn't have a bandage on his head anymore, and his arm appeared to have healed rather quickly. He only had the scratch on his forehead. Gutmann had combed his hair back. It glistened with pomade, his hairline deeply receding at the temples. He wore a dark-blue suit, white shirt, and dark-blue vest with a gold chain hanging from the watch pocket. The bar still smelled from the fire, though other odors were starting to blend in. Coffee, schnapps, cooked fat. "To what do I owe the pleasure?" he said.

"If you'd please take a seat?" Heller pointed at the nearest table. Gutmann sat, and Heller took the chair across from him. All the surviving furniture had apparently been cleaned, and the bar looked ready to reopen.

"You know this man?" Heller placed the photo on the table and got out his notebook and pencil.

"That's Franz. I guess I don't have to keep looking for him. When did you nab him?"

"Who's Franz?"

"Franz Swoboda. My employee. Stopped showing up to work three days ago. Not like him at all. I figured something wasn't right. What'd he do?"

Heller ignored the question. "What sort of work does he do for you?"

"Oh, whatever you can think of. Receives goods, cleans up, shovels snow, gets the heat going, keeps an eye out, ushers certain people to the door. He gets two marks an hour."

"How do you know each other?"

Gutmann blew air out of his cheeks in spurts. "Can't recall. It's been a long time. I think he came asking for work. Fall of '45 or thereabouts."

"That's not so long ago. You didn't know each other before that?"

"No. Listen, did he do something wrong? Did the Russians pick him up—our Soviet Army comrades, I mean?"

"Would they have a reason to?"

"You know how it is. Do they even need a reason?"

Heller tapped his pencil on the table. Gutmann didn't seem to know Swoboda was dead. That, or he was especially clever. Heller wondered if he should tell Gutmann about the head in the backpack, if only to gauge his reaction. He decided against it. If Gutmann knew anything, Heller would need him to betray himself all on his own. If Gutmann didn't know what was going on, then he'd let things stay that way.

"Herr Swoboda is considered highly dangerous," Heller said.

Gutmann waved a hand, playing it down. "Come off it. He was just doing his job. You don't make many friends in this business. Sometimes certain customers try getting in, even when they aren't exactly wanted. He boots them out. It's not for the timid."

"Where does he live?"

"He's got a little place over on Pulsnitzer. But I've already been there looking for him. He's not around. His neighbors say they haven't seen him for days."

"Word is you're running a bordello here. For the Soviets."

"Look . . ." Gutmann stood, went over to the door, and checked to see that it was truly shut, then sat back down. "You're skating on thin ice here, Herr Oberkommissar."

Heller straightened. "Just what's that supposed to mean?"

"I'm only trying to help. For one, I thought you knew already. You actually believe the Russians just come here to drink? They can do that in their casinos. Second, I myself am doing nothing more than running a bar here. That's it. I'm not sure what goes on next door, and I don't want to know. And third, dear Comrade, the Soviets don't do such things, get me? That's why the ones up top, in the Party, not to mention any Soviets themselves, aren't taking interest—because it can't happen. You get my meaning? A story like this isn't exactly going to make you popular with the Soviets. Because such a thing doesn't exist, not at all."

Heller thought that over for a moment. Did Medvedev know about this? Should he be informed? After all, he said he wanted to know everything that was happening.

"Next door, you said?" he asked Gutmann. "Can I see the rooms?"

Gutmann stared at him, his face hardening. "There's nothing to see in there. Leave it be. I'm only trying to help you!"

Heller tapped his pencil on the table again. These were words to be taken seriously. Ovtcharov had already shadowed him twice. He'd even ordered a daily report. It would be easy enough for Ovtcharov to have him tailed permanently. Someone could even have been watching him as he entered the bar.

Heller stood. "Fine, let's leave it."

Gutmann exhaled, clearly relieved. "Tell me, when's Franz getting out? Or do I need to start thinking about getting someone else?"

"I can't tell you that because I don't know. Have a good day."

Heller left the bar, dismissed the waiting policeman, stood there a moment, and then turned to the right. He strolled up Louisenstrasse at a leisurely pace until he reached the building next door. He looked at the ground-floor windows with their closed shutters and eventually knocked on the front door. A small window let him see into the entryway, and he tried the door handle, but it was locked. He took a step back and looked up. Only the ground floor looked occupied in this building as well; the windows above were all boarded up.

Heller spoke to an elderly man who was passing by. "Excuse me, does anyone live here?"

"Just a few women been living there, but you already know that!" The man winked. "Three or four, changes sometimes. But it looks like they're all gone starting yesterday. Made themselves scarce."

Heller used the nearby police station on Katharinenstrasse to make a phone call. He got Oldenbusch on the line after some delay, losing the connection twice.

"Anything new with the search warrant?" Heller listened, frozen. "What kind of circumstance could they possibly still need to check on? . . . What's the prosecutor's name? . . . Speidel? You don't mean Detlev Speidel?" A sharp hiss escaped his lips. "Early tomorrow morning? Afternoon? Then the Schlüter villa needs to be watched around the clock, and we should intervene at the first sign of suspicious activity. We need at least *some* leeway! Try to make it happen. If Speidel doesn't agree, I'll step in. Listen, Werner, this means I'll be paying another visit to Frau Schlüter. She's expecting me anyhow, because of that list. I also get the feeling she'd open up to me if I came alone. And I need you to look into something. Franz Swoboda is the dead man's name, the head in the backpack. He was a bouncer at the Schwarzer Peter. Yes, Swoboda: Siegfried Wilhelm Otto Bruno Otto Dora Anton. Swoboda. Franz. Gutmann doesn't know he's dead, or at least he's acting like he doesn't. Find out anything you can about him. Delegate the task if you have to. We need to question registrar offices and locate relatives. I'm sure he's notorious around the area, considered dangerous. I'll be in the office early tomorrow to expedite the search warrant. Let's call it a day for once. Have a nice evening, Werner."

Heller hung up and needed a moment to reflect. Detlev Speidel! He couldn't believe it. He was still worked up as he left the station, heading toward Pulsnitzer Strasse.

Swoboda's apartment wasn't hard to find, Pulsnitzer being a narrow street along a cemetery. Everyone knew One-Handed Franz. Heller only had to ask once and was pointed to his building immediately. He climbed the stairs all the way up under the roof before coming to a door that opened to what looked like a storeroom—narrow, low, fitted with a handle knob. This wouldn't be a question of unlawful entry—there was imminent danger, for which he didn't need a search warrant. Heller cautiously pressed down on the handle. The door opened. Apparently, people feared One-Handed Franz so much that he could leave his door unlocked.

Heller slipped off his shoes and entered. Sparse light came in from two narrow windows. He spotted a steel oven in one corner, a bed under the sloping roof, a cabinet next to the door. In front of a small table, which had a neatly placed tablecloth, were two chairs at precise right angles to one another. A sideboard substituted for the kitchen. Everything seemed clinically clean, the wooden floor bare, nothing unessential. A pair of shiny shoes beside the stove. The bed was made in military fashion, with crisp folds, not a single crease. The whole room smelled of Ajax. A toothbrush and powder, soap, comb, and razor were arranged in rows on the shelf above the tiny sink. Heller opened the cabinet. Everything was in neat order, clothing perfectly folded and next to it a stack of papers on top of a photo album. Heller went through the stack and found nothing out of the ordinary. Then he pulled out the photo album, opened the first page, and looked at the images. He was so disgusted he felt nauseous, as if his stomach had filled with some black toxin. He went to sit down.

The album was filled with photos of people who had been hanged, shot to death, and beheaded. It wasn't clear where these executions had taken place, but he guessed Serbia, since Heinz Seibling had mentioned it. Swoboda himself wasn't visible in any of the photos, which could mean that he had been the photographer. Heller recognized the Waffen-SS uniforms the men wore. Some posed next to the dead, next to people hanged and possibly still struggling as they died; others stood nearby, some grinning, some looking into the camera with indifference. Heller looked into the faces of the dead men, women, elderly, and the young. He could make out large pits with people lined up at the edge, rifle barrels aimed at them. If these had only been a few shots among many photos of fellow soldiers, of countrysides, of destinations, Heller might have tried to dismiss them as shocking souvenir photos from an abnormal past. But this was different. This was sick. Swoboda's tidiness and orderly manner stood in stark contrast to his cruel and inhuman photo collection. It didn't take much for a person to lose all decency. It was true that Swoboda was dead now and hopefully had received his just punishment. He was only one of so many. And Heller's job now was to find the murderer of this sociopath.

Heller left the attic room and put his shoes back on, desperately trying to think of anything else. He had to reach Medvedev. He couldn't be sure if it would be as easy as it had been before. Though maybe Medvedev was just as interested in talking with him again too.

Medvedev either couldn't or wouldn't see Heller. According to the guards out front, the commandant wasn't in the building. Heller had come all this way for nothing. His right foot ached, the pain in his ankle now rising to his knee. This horrible cold weather! The persistent freezing cold in the teens and lower devoured his willpower and strength and life. Heller had been counting on being able to warm up a little in the SMAD building and was even hoping that Medvedev would invite him to eat again. And he wasn't planning on holding back this time, no matter what the Soviets thought of him.

Disappointed now, he turned away and walked over to Unity Square to take the 11 streetcar line to Nordstrasse. He was going to see Frau Schlüter.

Right before Heller reached the intersection of Hospitalstrasse and Unity Square, a black Mercedes braked hard and blared its horn. One of its rear doors opened. "Were you coming to see me?"

Medvedev. Heller nodded.

The Russian waved Heller over, then slid to the other side of the rear seat to let Heller climb in. He gave a terse order to the driver, who climbed out. "You must call! Are there developments?"

"The head belongs to a German named Franz Swoboda. He hasn't been one hundred percent identified, but it's looking certain. He worked in the bar that was attacked. Apparently, the only customers are officers of the Soviet Army and—"

"It's a bordello," Medvedev said. "So what? So that's your news?"

Heller didn't answer. Medvedev snorted and folded his arms across his chest. Heller searched for words to loosen the tension but couldn't find any.

Medvedev suddenly turned to him. "I will give you some advice, Herr Oberkommissar. I know that you are older than I and that we are not supposed to lecture our elders. But I advise you to let this matter rest. Men do what they need to do. You can forbid it, you can punish them for it, but they will do it anyway, and at some point you realize that you cannot punish them all. What else do you expect them to do, so far from their homeland, without their women? Concentrate on that other matter, so that Ovtcharov is satisfied."

Heller side-eyed the Russian with irritation. "But didn't you tell me there's a feud between certain officers? Maybe it has something to do with the bordello. I'd have to know if Berinov and Cherin had been there, and if they'd regularly visited the establishment. Isn't that a lead you'd want me to pursue?"

Medvedev laughed, his expression switching between amusement and anger. "Heller, you never know when enough is enough. Yes, I did say that. Do what you have to—but leave the bordello out of it."

February 8, 1947: Afternoon

Heller was frozen stiff by the time he reached the Schlüters' villa. There had been another power outage, and after the streetcar hadn't moved for ten minutes he decided to walk the last two stops. As a shortcut, he made his way uphill along Radeberger Strasse.

Outside the villa, he took one of his two patrolmen aside.

"You spot any suspicious movement?"

"Some people left the building, but they were only carrying empty bags with them. No boxes, no heavy objects," the policeman said. He appeared to be freezing despite his warm clothing. His nose was red, and he could barely speak.

"You see Frau Schlüter?"

"Someone who fit the description, yes. She's been gone about an hour."

Heller looked at his watch: 4:00 p.m. The days weren't quite as short now, yet they were still gloomy. The sky appeared as a uniform gray, growing dim in the east. He would be getting home in the dark again. He hadn't eaten today, apart from Heinz Seibling's strawberries. And those were just a faint dream to him now.

"You're not certain it was Frau Schlüter?"

"I only had the description. About fifty, blonde hair, an elitist look to her."

Heller knocked vigorously. He heard voices and footsteps inside. A man opened the door.

"Take me to Frau Schlüter, please," Heller said.

"She's not here. She's running errands." The man went to shut the door, but Heller stopped it from closing.

"Please, I have an appointment with her. She must be coming back any minute. I'm from the tax office. Klein's my name. Can you let me wait inside?"

The man hesitated, not sure how to handle the situation.

"I'll wait by her apartment door. If she's not back in ten minutes, I'll leave. Please? It's very cold outside."

"All right, fine," he said and let Heller inside.

"Thanks, I know the way." Heller nodded, rushed past the man, and went up the stairs. He waited at Frau Schlüter's door until the man returned to his apartment.

Then Heller knocked on the door.

"Frau Schlüter?" he said in a low voice, then listened. He bent down and looked through the keyhole. There didn't seem to be anyone home. For a moment, he entertained the idea of forcing his way inside. Instead, he quietly went down the stairs and found the cellar door.

It wasn't locked. Heller opened it and glanced down the dim, narrow stairs. The staircase had no light, and dusk was already falling outside. Heller could just make out the first four or five steps before everything got lost in the dark.

He hesitated. He wasn't scared of the dark, wasn't afraid of ghosts, didn't believe in evil spirits, but he knew that if he descended into that darkness something would happen to him. He would start hearing sounds that had long since faded, seeing things that no longer existed, start smelling fire, burned flesh, scorched hair. The darkness was already reaching out to grab him, wanting to creep up and drag him down. Heller straightened his shoulders and shuddered. He wanted to move, but he couldn't. He was frozen.

Noises from behind made him whip around. They were coming from the nearest apartment. "Be careful out there," someone said. "Don't walk through the ruins."

Heller couldn't let anyone spot him here. He quietly closed the cellar door behind him. The top of the stairs submerged him in utter darkness. He heard things out in the hallway. He pressed himself against the moldy-smelling wall, breathed shallowly, and searched for the door handle with his fingers. But it had disappeared, all transforming into stone. He was walled in.

Heller forced himself to breathe calmly, but it was as if the walls were pressing in, trying to crush him. Blindly, he groped around, touching the cool walls, the crumbly plaster, hearing the particles trickling to the floor. You'll get through this, he told himself. You've gotten through worse hells than this.

He felt the edge of the stair with his foot, then slowly glided onto the next step, his back pressed to the wall, as if fearing the next step would lead to a bottomless abyss.

He descended the ten steps this way, in slow motion, and only felt relief once he landed on solid ground. He spotted a weak beam of light. There was a small window, or even a door, possibly leading outside. Heller used the light to guide him. In the semidarkness he could make out furniture, baskets, and cardboard boxes. Everything dusty, coated with a thick layer of grit. The next room had a small window with light seeping in. He could see an old workbench, the wood warped and moldy. But in the next passageway Heller spotted clues in the dust, footprints that were damp, as if someone had recently been here. He drew his pistol from his overcoat and followed the prints until he came to a door. He touched the handle, feeling how cold it was. It led outside, likely into the backyard. Heller cracked the door open and looked out. The snow had been trampled down and was dirty—the door was frequently used. He shut the door again, then reconsidered and opened it wide. This gave him enough light to find his way around the cellar and follow the damp footprints. They led to another section of the cellar. He pulled off a sheet of cardboard tacked onto a metal gate and immediately realized that the little room beyond it had recently been emptied. There had clearly been crates or boxes in there, their contours still outlined in the dust, and the wooden shelving on the wall had been cleared. The floor still had a few boxes and crates, including an ammo crate, a metal toolbox, and some cardboard boxes. Heller discovered papers there. He took a few pages out, folded them, and stuffed them into an inside pocket of his overcoat. The other cardboard boxes held tools, pipe clamps, and door hardware. The ammo box was empty. Heller put his pistol away, bent down, and sniffed inside it. As expected, it smelled of metal and gun oil, but that didn't necessarily mean anything. Crates like this could be found in thousands of households these days, as stools, tables, firewood. The other boxes had old editions of *Der Stürmer* newspaper, a stack of booklets from the German Youth War Library, and other Nazi propaganda.

Heller was kicking himself now for not demanding an immediate search of the building. In the meantime, Frau Schlüter had apparently arranged for incriminating materials to be removed from her home despite two policemen keeping watch. Either the two cops didn't realize there was a path through the backyard or they weren't paying attention. The main thing now was to seize what was left before it could be removed. Heller squatted down to open the toolbox as well.

Before he could give much thought to the four hand grenades inside, something distracted him. The doorway had darkened for a second, it seemed. He quickly straightened up, pulled out his pistol again, and looked around. Nothing moved. He stepped silently to the side so he could peek down the passage. It looked empty and unchanged.

Heller darted toward the door and stood still, waiting. If someone was trailing him, the passageway was a decent place to be. He bounded out in two quick steps and checked left and right, but he was alone.

Aiming his pistol, he crept back over to the stairs. He'd obviously been deceiving himself. He lowered his pistol. He would have to send one of the two policemen to stand watch at the cellar door and the other back to the station for reinforcements. Oldenbusch had surely gone home by now. That meant he'd have to delay the forensics work until tomorrow. Heller didn't trust anyone else, as most of the staff working criminal investigations was new and inexperienced. This was why he'd insisted on keeping Oldenbusch as his assistant detective in addition to his role as Heller's lead forensics man.

As Heller exited the cellar door to the backyard, he found himself face-to-face with a young man who stared back at him in shock. He was right on the cusp of adulthood and already quite big. He wore a dark-blue jacket and a stocking cap with blond hair showing underneath. The boy spun around and ran off. Heller grabbed at him but missed. The boy scurried across the snow-covered lawn toward the bushes.

"Halt, police! I'll shoot!" Heller shouted and kept running after the boy. Then he raised his pistol and fired twice.

The boy dropped to the ground in fright. Heller had aimed high into the air.

"Over here! Police!" Heller shouted louder so the uniformed cops could follow his voice. The boy had jumped up again. He slipped and stumbled near the thicket at the edge of the property.

"Stay where you are!" Heller fired again. But the fleeing boy wasn't intimidated now. He busted through branches and brush and disappeared. One of the cops appeared on the path next to the house.

"There, down that street. He's getting away!" Heller ordered, running to the spot where the boy had vanished. He hesitated, not wanting to get surprised by the boy fighting back from the cover. Yet the boy was gone. Heller squeezed through the thick bushes, stumbled out the other side on the debris behind the elderly woman's house, and followed the boy's footprints in the snow. They disappeared in more thicket up ahead. The boy had gained even more distance on Heller and could have gone in any direction. Suddenly the old woman appeared in her apron.

"What are you doing here again?" she snapped at Heller. She held something, possibly an iron bar, though it could have been a gun. "You the one shooting?"

"I'm a police officer! A boy came through here, from the Schlüters' house."

"Didn't see him."

"He went through that underbrush. Where was he heading?"

"I don't know. I didn't see him."

Heller gritted his teeth. There was no point in chasing the boy now. He was sure to know his way around the area, and it would have taken ten policemen to catch him. He approached the woman and saw that the object in her hand was a bar.

"You know who that was?"

"You're police, you said? What did he do?"

That angered Heller. He didn't much like having his questions countered with questions. And he was mad at himself for letting the boy get away. Maybe he should have aimed lower. At a leg. Maybe he was just too kind?

"Oberkommissar Heller. I'm a detective. The boy was fairly tall, blond, maybe fourteen, sixteen at the most. Do you know him, ever seen him around? He was trying to enter the Schlüters' house." Heller looked back that way. A dozen pairs of eyes watched from windows.

"That'll have been young Friedel."

"Friedel?"

"Son of Frau Schlüter."

"I was told all the sons died."

"Two, yes, the older ones. Young Friedel was supposed to join the Volkssturm, but by then it was already over."

"He live here? With his mother?"

"Of course he does."

"So you know if he—"

"I know nothing! Right here is where I live, and all I worry about is myself—as you yourself have seen."

"Don't get smart with me!" Heller thundered. "Now let me get my questions out."

Defiance showed on the old woman's face, her eyelids twitching. She appeared to be thinking something over. She nodded as if talking to herself. Then she set the iron bar against her house.

"You'll have to excuse me, Herr Oberkommissar," she said, sounding far more obliging. "All kinds of people hang around here. The tiniest piece of bread isn't safe. I only know the Schlüters by sight. They were always looking down on everyone. Once they reported us for not properly displaying the flag on Hitler's special birthday. When our house was hit, they didn't do a thing to help us. They were dispossessed, I hear, which served them right. They used Jews as forced labor, and Russian prisoners. None of them fared too well with the Schlüters, I can tell you. Sometimes I saw them having to do yard work. One was supposedly shot for stealing an apple from a tree."

"You said 'us.' Someone else living here?"

"No, just me. My husband died in April of '45, from his wounds. People who'd been renting from me have all headed west."

"You've been living here alone ever since?"

"I'm doing all right, better than many others. I can still get around, and sometimes people give me a little something."

"Have you happened to notice when and how often Friedel leaves the house?"

The old woman shook her head.

Heller took out his notebook. "Your name, please?"

"Dähne, Sigrid."

"Comrade Oberkommissar!" someone shouted from the street.

Heller slapped his notebook shut. "Thank you very much, Frau Dähne, and please excuse the disturbance."

"Gone, without a trace!" the exhausted cop said to Heller out on the sidewalk in front of Frau Dähne's house.

"Your fellow officer?"

"Went around back, tried cutting him off at Jägerstrasse. Said he'd whistle once he spots him. But there's so many hiding places and ways out between houses that it won't do any good. The kid's gone."

February 8, 1947: Evening

It was already dark when the squad car pulled up with four more police-men. The gas streetlamps hadn't come on yet. They had already secured the cellar, so Heller assigned a cop to stand guard outside the Schlüters' apartment. He posted the other three at various locations outside and instructed them to detain Frau Schlüter, as there was a risk of her escap-ing or suppressing evidence. He had to assume she knew of Friedel's arms cache in the cellar. As required, Heller had informed Colonel Ovtcharov's office. Men from the MVD could show up any minute. He was hoping Frau Schlüter would come back before then, if she even intended to return.

As darkness fell, the temperature dropped further and the cold became nearly intolerable, especially since Heller had barely eaten that day. Already light-headed from hunger and the constant cold, he nev-ertheless positioned himself in a driveway along Priessnitzstrasse, so his uniformed colleagues could see him. He didn't necessarily have to do this. But the men should see that they were not alone in having to stand out in the cold. Respect, Heller knew, was never achieved with dictato-rial demeanor but rather through actions and commitment. Back in 1915, during the war, they had hated nothing more than those generals riding atop their horses as they passed the soldiers all standing at attention. Looking so well fed, their boots polished bright, with squeaky-clean uniforms, glistening spiked helmets, and shiny epaulettes. And every one of his fellow soldiers had considered toppling one of those prancing pheasants off their horses with his bayonet.

Frau Schlüter would probably come up either Priessnitzstrasse or Nordstrasse, depending on whether she came by foot or streetcar. Heller was just hoping she wouldn't resist.

Before he could consider that further, he heard her cautious footsteps on the trampled snow. He pulled back a little, letting her come nearer. He waited for her to pass without noticing him. She was groaning from the effort of carrying two bulging bags. Heller stepped out.

"Frau Schlüter?"

She let out a scream and spun around. "Herr Oberkommissar?"

"I have to ask you to come to the station with me."

"You're arresting me?" Frau Schlüter sounded spiteful, more disgusted than surprised.

Heller stepped closer. "I'm asking you to follow me over to the car without making any trouble. You'll be taken to the station and questioned there."

"What's the reason, if I may?"

"Soldiers from the Soviet Ministry of Internal Affairs could show up here any minute, Frau Schlüter. They won't bother asking nicely."

Frau Schlüter shook her head in contempt. "So there it is. You're a friend of the Russians."

Heller reached for the whistle he'd gotten from one of the cops. "Are you going to come with me or not?"

"How could you let yourself kiss the Russians' asses, even you, a solid patriot, a man of the Reich?"

Heller gestured at his whistle. "Frau Schlüter, I'm asking one more time! You can bring your bags."

"Just look around you. They're letting us starve while they go around whoring. Defiling our children. Defiling our Reich. Destroying, stealing."

Heller placed the whistle between his lips and alerted his uniformed colleagues.

"One day, people like you will be sentenced for treason against the Fatherland. To think that my husband and my sons died so suck-ups like you could live off the charity of Russians."

The policemen came running. Heller nodded to them to take the woman away. Two officers grabbed her elbows, a third took her bags. Heller glanced inside. They were full of potatoes.

"You'll see soon enough," Frau Schlüter snarled. "Another war will come, and I'll be sure to remember which side you took. Then you won't be able to change your stripes whichever way the wind blows." Windows opened all around as the officers dragged her to the car.

"You can't just go arresting everyone!" Frau Schlüter screamed over her shoulder, losing her hat in the process, her blonde hair unraveling. "There are still many of us left. Solid Germans. Real Germans!"

Colonel Ovtcharov of the MVD made a point of showing up personally at Frau Schlüter's home. Heller met him when he arrived.

"Splendid," Ovtcharov said, after Heller had explained the situation. "Let's initiate a manhunt for the boy. Friedel Schlüter."

"Colonel, I beg your pardon, but the boy's only a suspect. The fact that we found grenades in the cellar doesn't prove anything. Forensics first has to secure evidence, fingerprints, footprints. We need to find out where the rest of the evidence was taken. There's no connection to the murders of Berinov and Cherin. Different methods, different weapons. Even the fact that the boy ran away doesn't necessarily mean anything. Everyone runs away these days."

Ovtcharov smiled and patted him on the upper arm. "Do not worry, Comrade Oberkommissar. We're not going to shoot him on the spot."

Heller hoped no one had noticed Ovtcharov's almost comrade-like pat. "It's also crucial that I question his mother. Today. I've had Frau Schlüter taken to the nearest station."

"Dear Comrade, why so worried? I will not take the woman from you. But it is late, you know. Let the woman spend the night there. You can question her in the morning."

Heller knew he was supposed to be content with all this. But he wasn't. "I have to get some spotlights here. We need to follow the boy's trail, find out what he took from the cellar and where he left it. The apartment must be sealed so forensics—"

The MVD colonel raised a hand to silence him. "Halt, Herr Oberkommissar. You must leave a little work for me as well. I will arrange for a thorough house search. But I am amazed, I admit. At you. Good work, very good. You live up to the reputation that precedes you."

"Oh? Which is?"

Ovtcharov counted off fingers. "Determined, focused, fast, straight-ahead, always finds what he wants to find."

This wasn't what Heller wanted to hear, at least not the last part. "It's 'straightforward,'" he explained.

"Straight . . . forward," Ovtcharov repeated, taking the correction in stride. "Well, I must praise you most expressly for your work." He turned serious. "Comrade, do not become soft. Have no false sympathy. We must make an example of the boy. We must nip every reactionary in the bud."

"Provided he's guilty." Heller looked into the Russian's eyes. "I'm asking you. Don't be so hasty. Bring him in alive, which is in your best interest. If he's responsible, then maybe he wasn't acting alone." It was pointless to explain that the boy had grown up exposed to nothing but

Nazi propaganda. That all he had ever learned was to serve the German Reich and follow Hitler. That he was actually a victim, just like all the children. Far more of the guilt resided with his mother for not having taught him better.

Ovtcharov whistled loudly and waved over his driver, who brought a package that the colonel presented to Heller within full view of everyone. It was amazingly light.

"Here, take it. It's not edible, unfortunately, but I think you'll find a way to use it."

This was pure calculation on the colonel's part, and Heller knew exactly what it meant. It said: You are my man; no, better yet, you are my little dog. You sit up and beg when I tell you. And yet Heller felt forced to play along. He couldn't refuse without snubbing the Russian and embarrassing him in front of everyone. And Heller would end up feeling guilty about Karin and Frau Marquart missing out. So he took the package and tucked it under his arm. As he did, those venomous things Frau Schlüter had said to him still rang in his ears.

February 8, 1947: Night

It was nighttime when Heller got home. The streetcars had stopped running, and his walk up Bautzner Strasse had stretched on forever. All those dark arched passageways, heading uphill, past Albrechtsberg Castle, Lingner Gardens, and the bridge over Mordgrund Creek, keeping his pistol in his hand behind him as a precaution. On the other side of the road, the woods of the Dresden Heath loomed in the darkness. He had to consider the possibility of being attacked or robbed at any time, even killed. He kept turning around because he'd heard a noise. A soft crack, the squeak of a mouse, the call of an owl. A car passed him at one point with its lights off, and he had pressed himself against a wall. The relentless cold was all-pervasive, in his toes, his legs, his fingers, his ears. Sometimes it seemed as if the planet itself had renounced its sun and separated from its orbit and was now tumbling toward the deathly ice cold of the darkest parts of the universe. It was inconceivable to him that heat could exist somewhere on the other side of the globe. It seemed as if everything was gradually freezing over, as if there would never be another spring, warming rays of sunshine, budding trees. There was no life here anymore, only hunger and bitter cold. And until the end, the people would fight and wage war over all the remaining resources.

Heller shuddered, mad at himself for not being able to get Frau Schlüter's hate-filled words out of his head. People like her didn't want to understand who had driven this country to its downfall. They didn't see that they themselves had been among the ones who had done it. And they had not disappeared; on the contrary—they were all suddenly resurfacing and assuming high offices and important posts. Speidel was one of them. Nazi Party member since '34, now rehabilitated. He was allowed to become public prosecutor. These were the people Frau Schlüter should be blaming.

Heller was no friend of the Russians. He only wanted to do his job and ensure what was fair and just. The last thing he wanted to do was ask for charity. And yet here he was carrying this package under his arm. It had to be about ten packs of cigarettes. At the central exchange, these were good for several weeks of food. Absurd. And even more absurd was that others gave up their food for the cigarettes.

It was already quite late when Heller turned onto the Rissweg. Light came from the kitchen window—Karin was likely waiting up for him. His stomach growled. That feeling of hunger was permeating and unbearable. His thoughts had turned almost solely to food. He fantasized about bread with jam and fried eggs, fruit tarts, and roast pork. Hopefully there was some stew left. Or at least some gruel.

Heller opened the gate, crossed the front yard, and pulled out his keys with numb fingers. But he couldn't get the key in the lock—a key was already in it, from the inside.

Heller knocked softly at first, then more forcefully, until he heard hurried footsteps approaching.

"Who's there?" Karin asked.

"It's me!"

Karin rushed to turn the key twice and opened the door.

"Sorry it's so late, Karin . . ." Heller was startled by the sight of his wife. Her eyes were red, her eyelids swollen, a strand of hair dangling. She held a damp cloth in one hand.

"What happened? Is she dead?"

Karin shook her head. She grabbed him by the sleeve of his over-coat, giving him no chance to take his shoes off, and dragged him down the hallway into the kitchen.

"Max, look who's here," she said before pressing a hand to her mouth. Her other hand feebly let go of his sleeve.

Heller stared, frozen.

At their dining table sat a man who stared at him with wide eyes sunk deep in their sockets. He rose slowly, his limbs ponderous and stiff. His age was hard to estimate, maybe twenty or much older. He looked so down-and-out, with his tattered clothes and hollow cheeks, clearly starving, his hair shaved short. He eyed Heller indecisively, his mouth stretched into a hapless smile. A smile Heller knew all too well.

The package of cigarettes hit the floor with a thud.

"Klaus!" Heller pushed aside the table between him and this miserable figure, then wrapped his arms around his son. He clutched Klaus tight, pressing his face into the crook of his son's neck. "For God's sake, Klaus!"

He hadn't recognized Klaus at first. His own son. He had stared at him like a stranger. He might never forgive himself for it.

"Klaus!" He had to say it again. Yet it still wasn't enough, not even if he said the name a thousand more times.

And Heller suddenly saw himself thirty years ago, after he had returned home from two years of war and army hospitals and had to stand directly in his mother's path because otherwise she would have walked right by him. She had been heartbroken about that for the rest of her life and had kept asking him for forgiveness, even on her death-bed. Now he finally understood.

Klaus stank horribly, of delousing agent, mold, sweat, and grime. But Heller didn't care. He eagerly breathed in the odor. This man returning home was his son. Klaus leaned on his father as if he'd lost all strength, and his shoulders trembled. Heller ran his fingers through the stubbly hair on Klaus's head and patted him on the back like he used to when Klaus had been sad about losing a soccer game or had gotten a bad grade in school.

Karin stood next to them, staring at Heller, her eyes pleading. Heller gently let go of Klaus and handed him to Karin, who took him in her arms, sobbing, cradling his face, kissing him on the cheeks, the forehead, the nose, searching for any way to hold on to him.

Heller bent down for the package of cigarettes, picked it up, and placed it on the table. Which he then straightened, standing there indecisively, until he got an idea. He went into the living room to Frau Marquart's cabinet, where he kept a bottle of schnapps far down in back.

He carried it into the kitchen, got out three glasses, and poured. Klaus had sat his mother down on a chair, but she didn't want to let him go and kept holding his hand. So he pulled another chair over, and the three of them sat at the table, glasses in front of them.

Heller tried to keep it together as he again saw himself and his parents all those years ago, silent, groping for the words and the composure. There seemed to be no words worth breaking this moment, this calm. And yet something needed to be said, and back then it had been his father who had raised his glass.

"To your health!" Max said now, raising his glass.

Klaus looked like he could fall asleep at the table. He had reached the front door just ten minutes before his father. He had been delayed, the locomotive breaking down before they even left Russia. They had spent two nights in a barn before continuing their journey, and there hadn't been any way to inform anyone back home. Once back in Dresden, Klaus hadn't been able to get his bearings at first. Someone had shown him the way, but the streetcars weren't running by that point, and he had to go on foot.

In hindsight, it was a miracle that Klaus had been taken prisoner. He could just as easily be dead. A split-second impulse had proven decisive. The Red Army had their small infantry unit surrounded, giving them no choice but to surrender. Once they did, a dispute arose about what to do with the prisoners. A Russian officer eventually decided to let them live. That was June 24, 1944, and there had been moments since when Klaus had wished the Russian had decided otherwise.

All his possessions were in an old wooden suitcase and a large sack he'd knitted himself for carrying as a backpack. Klaus didn't want to talk about the camp. Perhaps one day. Not one bad word about the Russians passed his lips. He had even brought liverwurst, fatty Russian liverwurst. He had saved it for home.

Later that night, Heller lay in bed and listened to the darkness. Klaus was sleeping downstairs on the sofa in the cold living room. Frau Marquart had tried refusing the pills at first but then started burning with fever and eventually gave in. She now slept soundly for the first time in three nights. Karin had fallen asleep the second her head hit the pillow. The only thing that would not rest was Heller's mind.

The only one missing now was Erwin, he thought. They knew he'd been released long ago and was living somewhere in Cologne. He had even found a job and wanted to begin his studies at some point. He'd prefer to be in Dresden, of course. But his fear of the Russians prevented him from returning home.

Heller's limbs were slowly warming under their thick down blanket. Finally, after so many years, he had been relieved of a great burden. He wanted to show gratitude, but he didn't know whom to show it to. He knew so many people whose sons were never coming home from the front. He had known so many who had lost their lives in February of '45. Gratitude itself felt misplaced somehow. It was thanks to mere happenstance that he and his family were still alive. And yet he knew as well as anyone that everything came at a price. He could see in his son's eyes that the boy had already paid some.

Heller turned on his side and stared at the luminous hands of his alarm clock, ticking and counting off the seconds, as if his life were trickling out of a faucet. He turned back over.

Klaus had always been a pensive boy. He never handled defeat well. When something didn't work out, he blamed himself first and wanted to make things good and right again. He couldn't understand why others would threaten to beat him up simply because he'd wanted to explain things to them. Heller often used to find the boy staring into space, deep in thought.

That was what wouldn't let Heller sleep. He needed to know how high a price Klaus had paid.

Heller got out of bed quietly, careful not to wake Karin, and went down to the living room. Klaus was not there. Then he saw that he was lying on the floor in front of the sofa. Klaus had apparently been awake too, because he raised his head right away. "Dad?"

"I can't sleep. Like you, I'm guessing."

Klaus got to his feet. He pulled on his jacket and moved close to Heller. Father and son stood like this for a while in the dark, saying nothing. Klaus was the first to speak.

"What happened to the city?"

Heller wanted to answer, but he couldn't speak. The return of his son had opened a door inside him, one that he had locked for a good two years. But suddenly those fountains of flame were shooting into the sky once more, melting metal and glass, the rolling barrage of fire advancing down the streets, bursting all the walls, while permeating everything with an ear-deafening roar like that of some giant wounded beast.

He grew dizzy and had to brace himself on Frau Marquart's round table that they never used. Then he sat on one of the good upholstered chairs.

Klaus was about to sit with him, but then he went into the kitchen and came back with the bottle of schnapps and two glasses. He poured in silence. They emptied their glasses.

Heller tried to start over, but his throat tightened again.

Klaus sat with his head lowered and whispered in a barely audible voice, "I'd heard about Dresden. When I was a prisoner. I tried, but I couldn't believe it. I didn't believe it." He ran a hand over his stubbly head. "I prayed you two survived. I prayed like never before. I sound like such a hypocrite."

Heller shook his head and kept running his hands over the table. Klaus leaned forward and placed his hands on his father's. His boy's hands were rough and calloused.

"The Leutholdts?" Klaus asked.

Heller shook his head.

"Frau Porschke? Frau Zinsendorfer?"

Heller tried to pull his hands away, but Klaus held on tight.

"They're dead," Heller whispered.

"Frau Zinsendorfer was always so nice to us. Odd, but nice. She gave us chocolate."

"I know, Klaus."

"The Müllers, the Kaluweits? Henkels? What about their girls?"

Heller rocked back and forth.

"Old Frau Müller, the Eschweinlers? And the twins? The Reichs? Your friend Armin?"

"Dead. All of them."

"The Missbachs? And Trude? Daughter of Herr Schreiner?"

"Klaus, please!" An intense pain had overtaken Heller and made his chest cramp. Like it had all happened yesterday. And that was just how it was. There had been so much to do. No time to reflect. There was no one to talk to about it. Only the ones who'd made it out, the survivors, who too had suffered more than enough loss and yet believed they could heal their wounds through silence. Nobody wanted to look back, nobody wanted to think back. Only now, here with his son, did the memories of that night roll right over Heller with full force.

Klaus pulled his hands back. He poured another schnapps.

He spoke deliberately, as if having to force every word out. "How did you two survive?"

"I wasn't home. I had to . . ." Heller's voice broke. It didn't matter what he had gone through; it was bad enough that he wasn't able to be with Karin that night. "Your mother, she had to make it on her own . . ." He saw her standing there before him again, like a phantom, in her partly scorched cardigan, in slippers, surrounded by a world destroyed. The way she said his name, once, twice, as if she didn't believe her own eyes.

Klaus placed a hand on Heller's arm. "It's okay. You're both alive, and that's what counts."

The two of them fell into silence again.

"Heinz Seibling—he's still alive!" Heller blurted out as the silence threatened to stretch on too long. "He's missing a leg. You remember him, right?"

Klaus nodded, but Heller couldn't read his face. It was too dark for that. They stared at the strange shadow patterns on the curtains.

"Well, I guess a person should try not to think about it too much," Heller said. Then he shut up. What was he talking about? There was no way not to think about it, of course there wasn't.

Klaus didn't respond.

Heller wondered how it must feel for him. Everyone he'd known was dead or missing; his home didn't exist, nor did anything that had ever belonged to him, not one piece of clothing, no schoolbook, no drawing, no photo, no toy, no book.

But that wasn't all. Heller knew Klaus well enough. Klaus wasn't attached to material things. There was another reason why he'd needed to ask. All that had happened here must have seemed so horrendous and surreal to him that he'd wanted to confirm it all—that the man opposite him truly was his father, and the place where they were truly was his city, that this home he'd come back to was not just some fever dream.

Heller scooted a little closer, so his son could touch him.

Klaus had apparently been waiting for that. He grabbed Heller's hand and stared at him. "Father," he whispered almost inaudibly, "I've seen things that, that . . ."

Heller waited.

"I saw people, who . . ." Klaus stopped talking for a moment, but he kept looking at Heller without lowering his eyes, their foreheads nearly touching. "People who did things . . ."

Heller nodded. He knew the things that people did. And the way they could force others to do things.

"I had to . . ."

Heller gently patted his shoulder. "You had to do it, Klaus. You had promised your mother something. You promised you would make it back home. And you kept that promise." When he tried taking his hand away, Klaus grabbed it again.

"But shouldn't there be rules in war too? You shouldn't be allowed to simply kill indiscriminately. I mean, isn't that right?"

"It is."

Klaus nodded and released his father's hand now. Heller looked his son in the eyes. Searching them. Searching for that pensive little boy.

"Klaus, what is it?" he finally asked. "What was it you had to do?"

He didn't want to know, but it was his duty to ask.

Klaus nodded again. "In the POW camp. January '45. I ratted them out," he whispered. "They were dressed like ordinary privates, but I knew them. They were from the SS."

Heller was patient, silent. Klaus was searching for the words.

"I reported them to the heads of the camp. They pulled those two out the very same day and shot them dead."

Heller took a deep breath. Klaus must have known that would happen if he betrayed them. But he wouldn't have done so without good reason.

Heller sensed that they needed to discuss this somehow. His son was struggling with it. "Were you forced to blow the whistle on them, or were you maybe hoping to gain favor?"

Klaus didn't answer for a long time. He eventually shook his head. "No. No one made me do it. When we first got to the camp, we were all interrogated. Those two came later. But I knew them. I had seen them, in Vitebsk, them and many others. Father, I had seen what they did there, and I went to report it. I wasn't looking for anything! You have to believe me." He stared at Heller in near despair.

"But two days later the Russians gave me a job in the camp kitchen, and I was recommended for training. You can imagine what happened then. To the others, I was a traitor. And I was one too. I could've just let it go, couldn't I, Father? It couldn't have helped anyone at that point. And the two of them are dead now. They needed to be punished, but they had worried mothers too!" Klaus's voice nearly gave out.

Heller shook his head. "One day you will know why you acted," he said.

He'd always seen that Klaus never tolerated injustice. Erwin wouldn't have betrayed those two. The fact that Klaus was calling himself a traitor revealed how irreconcilable the conflict was.

"They were criminals, Father!" Klaus cried out and feebly let his head drop onto Heller's shoulder. "They were murderers. Not soldiers, real murderers!"

It had long been clear to Heller that people like that rarely received just punishment. And Klaus knew it too. He could not bear the thought of those murderers living on. "You did the right thing, Klaus," Heller said, stroking his son's hand. "You did the right thing, considering the circumstances."

Klaus gently sobbed. "They pulled them out of the barracks and beat them half to death, then shot them dead. Not even an hour after I reported their names."

Here was another price Klaus had to pay. And he was likely paying a far higher price than those two dead men. "It's never easy. It's never simple," Heller said.

Klaus straightened up and wiped his face on his sleeve. "Please don't tell Mother."

Heller nodded. "It stays between us."

Klaus straightened up again. He had something else on his mind, it seemed. He cleared his throat. "I applied for the police," he said. "That's why they let me come home."

February 9, 1947: Morning

Public Prosecutor Speidel was angry. He directed Heller to sit with a gruff swipe of his hand. Heller reluctantly complied. He wasn't feeling well. He had slept for barely three hours, and the schnapps hadn't helped. His head was aching, and his temples pulsed. The cold was especially unbearable today. Klaus was accustomed to even worse. This morning he'd walked to the water pump to get water for Karin, wearing only a light jacket.

Heller's bag held two slices of bread spread with Russian liverwurst. He couldn't think about anything else.

Speidel took his time. He wrote something down, calmly stamped some papers. Heller played along with his childish game. He knew Speidel hadn't called him here for fun, and he wouldn't have wanted it any other way.

Speidel finally looked up, glowering at Heller through his wire-framed glasses. He was clean-shaven, the little Hitler mustache that had adorned his upper lip for a decade long gone, and he wore his hair somewhat longer than he used to, though with a clean part.

"Comrade Oberkommissar, were you trying to insult me by entering the Schlüter family's home without an authorized search warrant?"

"There was imminent danger. I arrived in the afternoon, as arranged with Frau Schlüter, to pick up a list of her former employees. I noticed suspicious activity in the yard and investigated. Something had obviously been removed from the cellar, and I made the decision to act. I obtained access to the cellar and seized evidence. In doing so I surprised a young man, likely Friedel Schlüter. When he fled, I took chase."

"You shot at him!"

"I fired warning shots into the air."

"The patrol officers at the scene described the situation differently. You entered through the front door after inquiring about Frau Schlüter's whereabouts."

Heller forced himself to remain calm. He didn't want to show that he was tense. He crossed his legs and folded his arms. "I knocked, and a resident of the house opened the door. It was cold. I asked to wait inside for Frau Schlüter."

"Thereupon you entered Frau Schlüter's apartment?" Speidel eyed him over his glasses.

"No, because I had no search warrant."

"So you secured evidence in the cellar and informed Colonel Ovtcharov of the MVD. Why? Don't you think the public prosecutor should be informed first?"

"I was given explicit instructions. The order was signed by the SMAD and Police Chief Opitz."

Speidel clearly didn't want to hear this. "And then you let our Soviet friends go and plunder Frau Schlüter's apartment?"

"I had nothing to do with that."

"Be that as it may, Comrade Oberkommissar, it seems you're making that family pay as part of your personal vendetta against the Nazis. You surely know what a manhunt for Friedel Schlüter means for the boy. He'll either be shot or end up in a camp."

Heller gritted his teeth. He kept control of himself. "Herr Prosecutor, first off—"

"It seems to me that your sense of fairness and justice needs a little refreshing—"

"Don't you dare cut me off," Heller thundered. "And don't you dare allege that I have no sense of justice. If anyone needs their sense of right and wrong examined, it's you!"

Speidel made a point of leaning back in his chair and acting calm, yet a nerve twitched below his left eye. "Control yourself, Heller. I possess a clean record; I have nothing to apologize for. My case has been reviewed. I've been rehabilitated. I was only in the Nazi Party so I could earn a living."

Heller burst forward, propped his fists on the prosecutor's desk, and pointed at Speidel. The man had already recoiled so far back in his chair he had no more room to move. He squinted at Heller as if looking down a gun barrel. Heller no longer saw any reason to keep it together. What Speidel needed was a dose of reality.

"It was only luck that you ended up passing their review. You were a Nazi of the first degree. And you headed countless criminal investigations against anyone who resisted, anyone found 'hostile to military power.' They were all executed!"

"That was my job, and those were the laws. I didn't create them; I merely carried them out. And stop acting so high and mighty! You also had to have your record cleared at some point." Speidel's face had turned bright red.

Heller pounded his fist on the desk. "Goddamn it, how many times do I have to tell people? I've never been in any party, either as a fellow traveler or real National Socialist!"

Right then he noticed Speidel glancing past him. Heller turned around and saw the prosecutor's secretary standing in the doorway. Only now did he realize how much of a rage he had worked himself into, and that it must have sounded as if he were about to really let loose. He thought better of it now, stood up straight, and pulled his overcoat down tight. Then he looked the secretary in the eye until Speidel waved at her to withdraw.

"I could make a formal complaint against you," Speidel told him in a low voice.

"You do that." What a poor attempt at saving face, Heller thought.

"And I could take the case away from you. Both cases."

"You'd be doing me a favor, Herr Prosecutor." Heller knew this was all ridiculous, both Speidel's threat and Heller's reply, but it was apparently the only way to reach Speidel. "Feel free to discuss it with Lieutenant General Igor Medvedev."

He detested throwing the commandant's name around. After all, he was the one who had never wanted to be dancing to the Russians' tune. People lost their posts so easily these days, even people like Medvedev. Then he'd be left without connections, with no one to have his back, and at the mercy of Medvedev's enemies. At best he'd lose only his job.

"For your information, Herr Prosecutor, once I've questioned Frau Schlüter, I'll move on to questioning witnesses about events surrounding the Schwarzer Peter bar. By the way, the severed head belongs to one Franz Swoboda, a disabled vet working for Josef Gutmann. But I assume Officer Oldenbusch has already informed you of that. Have a nice day."

As if Medvedev knew his every move, the general called the police headquarters on Schiessgasse right as Heller arrived. Niesbach's secretary found Heller in the hallway and informed him that the general wanted to see him in his office at Soviet HQ. Heller nodded, then went into his office. Oldenbusch was waiting for him. Crossing back over the Elbe again would take a half hour or more, so a few minutes wouldn't matter.

Oldenbusch rose from his chair.

"Mornin', boss. Been plenty going on with you, huh? You send me home on purpose just so you could have all the fun?"

Heller ignored being called boss again. He had to sit down. His altercation with Speidel worried him. He needed a moment to compose himself, and he tried to stop thinking about it, drumming his fingers on his desk. His dark office, not much bigger than a prison cell and no more comfortable, wasn't helping. But then a smile flashed across his face. He looked at Oldenbusch.

"Guess what, Werner? Klaus is back!"

Oldenbusch bounded over to Heller and shook his hand heartily. "Congrats! He safe and sound?"

Heller nodded. "Yes, but he's got plenty on his mind."

Oldenbusch waved it aside. "That'll pass, I can assure you."

How would he know? Heller wondered. Typical Oldenbusch, always speaking off the cuff.

"The way I heard it," Oldenbusch said, "you went and waylaid Frau Schlüter."

Heller didn't mind Oldenbusch changing the subject. He always felt more comfortable keeping things on a professional level.

"Speaking of, take a few men and head over to her place. The cellar needs to be combed for evidence, her apartment too, even if the Soviets have already gone through it. I want fingerprints of everyone living there. Anything new about Swoboda?"

"Investigations are under way. I should know more today."

Heller nodded. "I actually wanted to go see Frau Schlüter myself, but Medvedev needs to speak to me. I'll come find you later at her place."

Lieutenant General Medvedev had coffee and cake waiting for Heller. It was only a simple pound cake, but it was covered with a chocolate glaze, something akin to a miracle these days. The commandant had it all set out on his desk and waved Heller over.

"Now don't hold back, Heller. Help yourself."

"Thank you very much." Heller wasn't sure how to proceed. He waited for Medvedev to take a piece.

"Sugar, cream?" Medvedev pointed to a sugar bowl and a little pot. Medvedev apparently thought nothing of offering up what people had been missing most, and in excess, though Heller also got the sense that he was being played with.

"What can you tell me about this case concerning that woman and her son?" the commandant asked.

"It's still unresolved. We've barely secured evidence. The hand grenades are the same type used in the attack on the Münchner Krug—German model 43 stick grenade. Solid wood stick, not hollow like the 39."

Medvedev stuck half a piece of cake in his mouth and chewed but couldn't keep the crumbs from covering his mouth, then took a loud slurp of coffee.

"I'm looking for your opinion, Heller," he said once he'd swallowed it all down.

Heller pried his eyes away from the enticing plate of cake and sighed. "This Friedel is just a misguided boy who thinks he's standing up for a good cause. Kids like him will be plaguing us for years to come. His mother's a committed Nazi. But if he was the attacker, I don't believe she knowingly supported him."

"He can't be connected to those two dead officers?"

Heller didn't like Medvedev's probing tone. "When you put it like that, most likely not."

Medvedev took another piece of cake and carefully nibbled away at the chocolate glaze. "How, then, do you explain those items that were found?"

Heller, having no idea what the general was talking about, didn't hesitate to make his point. "I can crack these cases, but I need to be allowed to do my job properly."

"What do you mean?"

"I just had an altercation with our rehabilitated new public prosecutor."

Medvedev set the partially eaten piece of cake on his plate. He looked Heller in the eye. "Speidel." The Russian wiped the crumbs off his hands, then planted his elbows on his armrests. "I wish to be candid, Herr Oberkommissar. There are some of us who feel that denazification needs to proceed more radically. In which case you wouldn't be seeing anyone in office with a Nazi past. But circumstances demand a few compromises that you must live with as well. We need capable people, or else it will be decades before the Germans are able to run their own affairs again."

Heller started to reply, but the general raised a hand.

"And before you get too worked up, think twice. Because there are radicals among us who would not stop even at a person like you. Speidel is a good man, good at his job. He joined the Social Democratic Party as early as '45 and then the Socialist Unity Party. He's already showing himself to be a good comrade. Heller, I can see you're angry, but you're going to have to live with people like him."

Medvedev paused. "I will ask him to show restraint." He picked up his piece of cake and dunked it in his coffee. The sodden piece fell apart in his fingers, most of it landing inside the cup. Medvedev frowned and started fishing for the crumbs with a little spoon.

Heller shook his head in distress. "No, please. Please let me handle this on my own."

Medvedev nodded with satisfaction. "You see? This is exactly what I expect of you. Now will you finally take some of this cake? You can wrap it up in newspaper." He pushed over pages of newspaper to him, the *Sächsische Zeitung.*

Heller read: "Unity and Progress . . . Two Factories Back in the People's Hands . . . Looking to the Future Together." He loathed how these socialist slogans were always the same. But then he helped himself to some cake, wrapped up four pieces, stood, and gave the commandant a military salute as he left.

February 9, 1947: Late Morning

Heller knocked at the Schlüters' front door. "Werner?"

"Coming!" Oldenbusch shouted from inside before opening up. "Come on in, boss, but stay over there."

Oldenbusch went over to a window. "I just want to finish this real quick, then I have to show you something."

Heller looked around. What he saw unfortunately matched every cliché about the Russians. They had ransacked the place, ignoring the typical house search code of conduct. Cabinets stood open, drawers pulled out, doors torn off. Papers lay strewn all over the floor, laundry and broken dishes too. The sofa had been sliced open.

"I have enough fingerprints to keep an expert busy for a year," Oldenbusch said. "And it's not just one set." He came back over, holding a little piece of transparent film that he carefully tacked to an index card.

"I can't tell you if any of these are usable, though. You can see the job the Russians did. I'm hoping I can at least match a few prints with those in the cellar, mainly on the ammo crate where the grenades were. From around the house itself, we mostly have fingerprints of the women and children, since the men are usually only home in the evening." Oldenbusch put away his brush and container of black carbon powder.

None of this was Heller's main concern. "Werner, Frau Schlüter isn't at the police station I took her to yesterday. They say the Soviets took her away right before I came. No one knows where, and no one at the MVD will tell me. In any case, what else have you found here?"

"You really haven't heard? Come on, Max. You're not going to like it."

Heller followed Oldenbusch down to the cellar. He said hello to other colleagues whose names he couldn't remember. Most of them had recently joined up and received a quick course in criminology. Oldenbusch passed through the cellar so they could exit through the cellar door into the yard. A tarp was spread out, with cardboard cartons and crates on it.

"These officers have been here since we started working. They relieved the MVD's people. They started following the boy's tracks at daybreak. Those led to a neighboring property over on Löbauer, where we found all this hidden in a hollow space under a pile of rubble. The print roller's here, the self-made template, some leaflets, some failed attempts too. Our initial check tells us the leaflets came from this equipment and match the ones from the Münchner Krug crime scene. In this bag was a hunting knife, some Hitler Youth badges, a pennant, photos. And this here." Oldenbusch knelt down, grabbed an old doctor's bag, folded open its dual-handled metal closure, and gave Heller a look inside.

Heller saw an ax with a blade splattered red, a jigsaw, a butcher's knife, and a sharpening steel. He crouched down. "That's not rust, I take it."

Oldenbusch reached his gloved hands into the bag, pulled out the ax, and pointed at the crusty splotches. "This makes more sense considering what comes next." He placed the tool aside and reached back into the bag. He took out something wrapped in newspaper. He laid it down and unfolded the paper. Heller winced. Two hands lay before him, a right and a left, severed at the wrists. He let out a fatalistic sigh.

"Why so glum? After all, we just might have found the hands that go with that head," Oldenbusch said.

"No, Werner. This is a new victim. They didn't call Swoboda 'One-Handed Franz' for nothing."

"I guess that's true," Oldenbusch muttered, his mood souring.

Heller took a closer look at the hands. They were masculine, strong, with short fingers, the nails clean and well groomed. On the right ring finger was a small gold wedding band.

"Can you remove it?"

"Already tried, but the hand's frozen stiff. Needs thawing first."

Heller bent down again, this time to take a closer look at the news-paper the hands had been wrapped in. He turned up a corner of the paper. It was a page from *Der Stürmer*, already yellowed.

"There's a stack of them in that cellar room," Oldenbusch said.

"So did we find this?" Heller asked. "Us, not the MVD."

"We did. Wolpert, to be exact. About an hour ago."

"Was anyone from the MVD still here?"

"Yes. They took some photos and cleared out after."

"And none of them thought to follow those tracks across the property? Even though I'd clearly described the situation yesterday to Ovtcharov?"

"What are you getting at, Max? No, they were only inside the apartment turning everything upside down. They posted a sentry overnight and questioned people in the building. They all still look intimidated."

"Werner, this bag needs to get to the lab at once and these clues secured. The wedding ring might be engraved, which could help us identify the victim. That's the highest priority. I want you to do it personally."

Keeping his eyes on the ground, Heller slowly crossed the lawn and followed the beaten path all the way to the thicket at the edge of the property. He ducked under the low-hanging branches of a fir tree and took bounding strides over tangles of roots. That brought him to the old wooden fence separating the property from the one behind it. Some slats had been broken off, and Heller bent down to clamber through the opening. The boy's hard work amazed him, considering all those boxes and crates he'd hauled to his temporary hiding spot. And all of it more or less under the eyes of two cops who were there to prevent it.

The neighboring property was even more overgrown, the house uninhabitable. Heller only crossed the yard. The tracks ran left down a slope and to the next property over. The whole stretch of fence had been pushed down. Heller climbed over it and found himself in a small copse of beeches, the old leaves like soft carpet under the snow. He tried walking alongside the path, figuring he wouldn't spot any useful prints. It seemed clear either way that Friedel was the one who had hidden the evidence. Heller had seen him. Yet he still needed proof. To make matters worse, his inexperienced colleagues had ended up using the same path while seizing the material—highly unprofessional.

Heller scratched his chin, deep in thought. Time for a shave, he thought, which sparked no joy at all, with no shaving cream and his worn blades. He stared into the snow. What reason would Friedel have to cut off a man's hands and possibly the head of another? Did he even have the nerve for such a thing? Heller didn't know the boy, but there was a big difference between tossing a few grenades before running off and mutilating a man, dead or alive. And where were the bodies? Could the other victim also have some connection to the Schwarzer Peter?

It was up to Heller to find the answers. He also needed to know why the Russians hadn't set up spotlights. The crates had been sitting out unguarded all night, and anyone could've set down that doctor's bag with its horrific contents.

Heller kept following the tracks. He passed through the copse, then spotted a completely unscathed building to the left with black smoke billowing out its chimney and a villa with boarded-up windows to the right.

He stopped at a collapsed garage. The side walls had toppled inward, and only the back wall still stood. Here the tracks ended. Heller reached for a piece of tar paper and bent it upward. Underneath was a hollow space. Friedel had stashed the crates here, though it didn't seem like a very secure hiding place. The houses within view were inhabited—someone would've found this garage sooner or later. It looked more like a temporary hiding spot. Yet where had the boy wanted to take the crates? Did he have a handcart for hauling them away in one go?

Heller scrambled into the hollow space. It smelled strongly of martens. Feathers and little bones lay on the ground. He pulled a flashlight from his overcoat pocket. It didn't provide much light, the batteries having suffered from the cold. He shined it over the ground and hesitated when something caught the light. Heller knelt in the rubble and spotted a syringe lying between two chunks of brick. He carefully lifted it out with his fingertips, touching only the metal nozzle so as not to smear any clues on the needle, cylinder, or piston. He crawled back out into the daylight with his find.

It was a medical syringe, the injection needle clearly used. The glass cylinder still held a little bit of frozen liquid. Berinov had a fresh injection mark on his upper arm, Heller recalled, and Kasrashvili hadn't been able to tell whether it was from a typhus immunization. Heller wondered if the syringe was German or Russian.

A strange feeling hit him. He looked up and pivoted, eyeing the buildings, trying to see if someone might be watching him through the trees.

His ears pricked up. He thought he heard the blare of a police siren coming closer. He turned back for the Schlüters' villa, holding the syringe between his thumb and forefinger.

"Comrade Wolpert!" he yelled since it was the only name he could remember.

A tall, gaunt man came out of the cellar, ducking his head so as not to bump the doorframe. "Yes?" he asked without any greeting or salute.

"Oldenbusch is already gone, I take it?"

Wolpert shook his head. "I think he's still upstairs."

Heller frowned. That wasn't what he'd meant by leaving immediately, though he had to admit it wasn't bad timing.

"Werner, I found this in that collapsed garage." Heller handed Oldenbusch the syringe. The police siren had now faded.

"I'd really like to know who used this and if it's a standard model. The content needs to be analyzed. At once!"

Oldenbusch didn't seem to pick up on the urgency. He took his time looking over the syringe and even held it up to the light. "No clues on it at all." Then he unscrewed the needle and smelled the nozzle. He eventually tried pulling out the piston but couldn't, since the contents were still frozen. He cupped a hand and breathed into the opening of the syringe.

"Either this was cleaned or someone was wearing gloves, likely the latter."

Heller struggled with how Oldenbusch was treating such crucial evidence. Heller had to trust that there really were no clues on the syringe and swallowed his objections. "Our men trampled all over the path," he said.

Oldenbusch nodded, then offered a sad smile and a conciliatory tone. "We evidently have to choose between laymen or die-hard former Nazis. I don't even want to know where they find these people. In construction, administrative posts, power plants, waterworks—who knows?"

Oldenbusch took another sniff of the syringe's opening and moved the glass cylinder back and forth. An oily drop ran down the glass.

"I'll analyze it to make sure, but I'd bet it's Evipan."

"An anesthetic."

"Right, commonly called a knockout drug, with a short-lasting effect. Used in surgery. Also at the front. Saw it used often in '45, when I was lying in a field hospital. The patient quickly loses consciousness. Side effects range from impaired senses to dizziness to nausea. Frequent use can lead to dependence."

Heller pulled off a glove and massaged the bridge of his nose with his thumb and forefinger. He needed to sort out his thoughts. It didn't help that another police siren was blaring.

"I have to speak to Gutmann and Frau Schlüter. I don't know whom to try first. And we have to find Friedel, no matter what, before the Russians do! Where were the men killed? Apparently not here in this house. At least that's how it looks. Why were those hands in that bag? And why the head in a backpack?"

Oldenbusch looked at the window. The siren was coming closer. "Maybe he was some kind of trophy?"

"Berinov was probably just an accessory who got eliminated. Maybe Gutmann did have something to do with it."

The siren stopped. A uniformed cop jumped out of the passenger seat of a small truck and hurried up to the front door. He obviously wanted Heller for something, and he went over to the apartment door.

"Comrade Oberkommissar? Herr Heller?" someone called from downstairs.

"Up here," Heller yelled back.

"But what does all this have to do with the Schlüter boy?" Oldenbusch asked. "He needs to be questioned, either him or whoever foisted that doctor's bag on him."

The cop ran up the stairs. He stopped at the door and gave a military salute. "A body's been found! You're needed at once."

"Is nobody else available?" Heller asked, indignant.

"It's quite possibly a young woman. Comrade Niesbach said that falls under your responsibility. She was found in the courtyard behind the Schwarzer Peter."

That got Heller's attention. "Very well. Werner, take us there before heading to the lab. Make sure someone takes care of this *right away!*"

A loud drone from the street made Heller glance out the window. Two large Soviet Army trucks were coming up the street. They stopped in front of the house. The driver of the small police truck was forced to give up his parking spot.

Oldenbusch groaned. "The Russians are here to clear out the apartment."

Heller could only shake his head.

February 9, 1947: Midday

Another large crowd had gathered. Oldenbusch hit the horn along Alaunstrasse, just fifty yards from Gutmann's bar, passing all the people who begrudgingly cleared a path. Once the uniformed cops recognized the car, they forced people out of the way to let the Ford through.

"Comrade Oberkommissar," one of the officers said to Heller as he climbed out. "We'll have to go up the street a little to a passageway. The body was found in the back courtyard."

Heller nodded and gestured to Oldenbusch to drive on and take care of his tasks. "Let's go," he told the cop.

Heller followed the cop up the street to the passageway. Through that was an open area about a hundred yards long. Several buildings facing the inside courtyard had been fully destroyed by the air raids, creating a rubble landscape that had evidently served as an adventure-filled playground for some time now. The children had built shacks here. Flags and pennants made of fabric remnants gently fluttered. The retaining walls of two buildings still stood, and the remains of stairs rose into the sky like skeletons.

The wasteland amazed Heller; he'd never have guessed it existed judging from the intact buildings facing the street. He followed the cop into the rubble. They walked the well-trodden paths to reach a large crater that descended steeply and held frozen-over water at the bottom. Yet someone had cleared a path all the way down. Heller and the cop managed to descend several yards using steps dug by hand. There they saw an opening, which led into what apparently used to be a cellar.

Heller hesitated but then spotted light shining a few yards ahead, and he pulled himself together. He didn't want to show weakness. They went a short way, and Heller was amazed to find a staircase leading up to the ground floor, then reaching up two stories more. The final portion of stairs was in acute danger of collapsing, the steps suspended by a few rusty reinforcing bars. The top landing was riddled with cracks. The cop pointed at a loose pile of debris on the highest floor.

"The victim's lying up there, under that debris. Just visible. Someone had wrapped her in fabric. Curtains or something. Then they laid stones and wood over it. Some children found her."

"Who hides a body in a spot where children obviously play? She'd be found sooner or later."

"But up there?" The policeman pointed to the nearly free-floating portion of the third floor. "That'd get you killed. Not even a kid's going up there!"

For Heller there was no question. "Exactly the kind of place a kid would find interesting. Danger isn't a deterrent. Same reason they play with dud shells and discarded ammo. Has anyone been up there yet?"

"I have," the cop told him. "But I'd rather not climb up there again. The thing moves under your feet."

Heller climbed a level higher. The man was right—it was dangerous to walk around on such a shaky surface. "Well, the body made it up there somehow."

"The fire department will have to get a ladder up there."

"Go. Get them out here," Heller ordered. He waited until the man had disappeared before looking around. There were people in all the windows and courtyard entrances, and all the children were sure to have come running up for a look at the body before the find had been reported. He'd already sent Oldenbusch away. So to secure evidence he'd have to use the policemen on the scene—men who, much like Klaus, had been recruited after serving in the military and were completely inexperienced in police matters. Heller thought it over for a moment and then bounded up the final rickety steps onto the upper landing. He now stood fully out in the open with no more walls to support himself. He could feel the floor swaying under his feet. He tiptoed onward. A freezing wind whistled up here, making his eyes water. He squinted and eyed the portion of the floor before him with skepticism. It was already sinking. He would need to step around it, even though that would put him perilously close to the ledge. If he fell, he was sure to plummet ten to fifteen yards before landing on the rubble. Yet he moved onward, and Karin could never know about this. She'd think he was crazy.

He finally reached the spot where the body lay. It was so gray and dusty that at first he couldn't make out a thing. Only one bare foot fully stuck out of the loose debris and fabric. Heller pulled away pieces of wood and placed them to the side, removed stones, and rolled some larger brick sections off the pile. One slipped out of his hands and fell.

"Look out!" Heller shouted, then heard the bricks crash and tumble. Finally, he could unwrap the fabric with the foot sticking out. It was a very small foot. Heller feared the worst. Since he didn't know how else to manage it, he grabbed the fabric with both hands and tugged. That made the rest of the piled-up stones start to slide, and they too plummeted off the other side. A cloud of dust rose up and was driven away by the wind.

Heller now faced his next problem. He had no knife or scissors to open the bundle and couldn't just roll the corpse out.

"Herr Oberkommissar?" shouted the policeman from below. "It might take a while for the fire department to get a telescopic ladder here."

"Come up here," Heller shouted.

It took a while for the policeman to make it. He stared at Heller in amazement.

"You can stay there, but take an end from me once I'm on the stairs so we can carry it down together." Heller bent down, grabbed the head end of the large bundle, and dragged it toward the stairs. He needed to make sure he didn't step in a hole or onto some especially unsteady spot. The policeman decided to come all the way up. He grabbed onto the foot end, and without wasting any words the two men hauled the bundle down the stairs, through the cellar, and back up the crater.

Panting heavily, they finally laid their load on solid ground.

Heller, looking for an end of the fabric, found it and unrolled, pulling fabric away from the dead body with each turn.

"Such a goddamn disgrace," the cop muttered once the frozen body lay exposed.

Heller, kneeling, only nodded. It was a girl of fourteen, maybe fifteen. Her eyes and mouth were still open, her hands and arms bound with a long rope that had been repeatedly wound around the body. All she had on was a short dress and underwear. The foot sticking out of the debris was bare, but the other had a sock and a shoe.

Heller took several deep breaths, then leaned over the dead girl. He looked her over and couldn't determine a cause of death. There were no wounds or strangulation marks. Yet her expression indicated that she must have suffered, her rolled-back eyeballs showing only the whites, her tongue swelling out of her mouth. Agony.

"Let's turn her on her side," Heller ordered. The cop helped him, and Heller inspected her back. He didn't spot anything unusual here either. The girl's long hair was hard and stiff and stuck to her skull. It had frozen oddly flat at the back of her head.

"It must have been wet there, then froze. She was wrapped in the fabric later."

"Did she drown?"

Heller considered that, then pulled a handkerchief from his over-coat. He rolled it into a point and used it to wipe at the inside of one of her nostrils. The tip of his hanky turned black. He stood and patted the dust off his coat.

"Have the body brought to the hospital in Friedrichstadt, to a Dr. Kassner in pathology. Use a stretcher. You do have a truck out-side?" The policeman nodded and left. Heller figured Kassner must have examined the two dead Russians by now. He hadn't received a report yet, but he was certain it would be on his desk today. Kassner was very reliable.

Heller waited with his shoulders hunched up and hands in his pockets until the policeman came back with a colleague. They lifted the dead girl onto a long board since they lacked a stretcher. They scrambled along the path out of the rubble, through the building passageway, onto the street. It wasn't a simple undertaking and required the help of four men at various spots. Heller followed at some distance and looked at Gutmann's bar as he did so, at those small barred windows to his store-room and the larger, also barred windows to his back rooms.

A crowd of onlookers had already gathered, jostling for a look, by the time the policemen exited the courtyard and reached Alaunstrasse. The children's eyes bulged as much as anyone's.

"Anyone know the girl?" Heller asked in a loud voice. "Anyone know her name, where she lived?"

"She's not from around here," replied a man.

"Not true, I'd seen her," countered a boy of about ten.

"Where was that?"

"Just around, in the neighborhood. Running errands. Getting water."

"You don't know where she lived? Maybe in the rubble here?"

The boy shook his head. "Nah, no one lives in there."

"But where was she taking the water?"

"Dunno, maybe it wasn't her?"

"She's one of Gutmann's, see? That's who she is," someone else said.

"Who said that?" demanded Heller. A man separated from the crowd. He looked old and gray, wore a tattered overcoat, and had a thick scarf wrapped around his head and neck.

"You live here?"

"Yes, in Louisenstrasse, in the metal shop. Little room under the roof, even got a little oven."

"What did the deceased have to do with Gutmann?"

"She belonged to him."

Heller tried to simplify his questions. "She live there? She have a room in the building next door?"

"Nah, guessing she lived with him."

"With Gutmann? In the bar?"

"I think so, yeah. Never saw her come out of the building next door."

"But it's not his daughter, right?"

The man gave Heller a quizzical look. The other people had stepped to the side.

"You don't know?" Heller added.

"No, how could I? He's got other girls there sometimes. That's what people say."

People. It's always just people, Heller thought, as if you're not one of us. "So what are people saying? That it's a bordello?"

"That the girls work there. Young things. You know, to get by."

Heller guessed what the man was getting at. He took him by the arm. "I'll need your name and age."

"Koch, Fritz. Born 1902."

Heller looked up, astonished—the man was younger than he. "Were you in the army?"

"Nah, was doing time in prison."

"Political prisoner?"

"Nah, nah, nothing political."

Heller gave up; he had more important matters. "So you think the girls were working as prostitutes?"

"Hookers, that's right. But not no more."

"Not anymore? Why not?"

"Not since Franz disappeared."

"*The* Franz? Franz Swoboda? The one-handed man?"

"He was probably keeping 'em in line. But they aren't there no more, all cleared out."

"You can see all that, from your window?"

"Sure can."

Heller was certain this man wouldn't be found on the official witness list. "But you never saw the attack, did you?"

"Gutmann probably did it himself. Him or Franz, because they were having this fight, see?"

"Fight?"

"That's what people say. But that Franz, he don't take no half measures, and he makes short work of it. Maybe he torched the place because of that."

"Do you know Swoboda?"

Fritz Koch stared at Heller, puzzled.

"*That* Franz," Heller emphasized. He glanced at the policemen. They had reached the truck and were setting the board with the dead girl on the pavement.

"'Course I know him. He was in Serbia, lost his hand there too. Crushed somehow. So it was back to the home front for him. They didn't mess around there."

"Well, a one-handed soldier isn't a whole lot of good to the military."

"Nah, where he was, I mean. They didn't mess around. Made real short work of things there. Bumped 'em off, hanged 'em. Told me one time when he had a drop too much. And sometimes he got . . ." Koch tapped his forehead.

"What?" Heller said.

"Y'know, crazy, raving, twitching, could hardly speak. The man was real bonkers, I'm telling you. That's why people kept out of his way."

"All right," Heller said. "Wait here."

Heller ran over to the truck and yelled, "Hey!" because a man in a black suit was bending over the dead girl and about to touch her face.

"Stop that!" Heller grabbed the man's hand, then shouted at the uniformed cop standing there, "You're not supposed to let anyone near the body!"

"That's the pastor," the policeman said. "From Martin Luther Church."

"Doesn't matter. No one touches the corpse."

When Heller looked at the pastor's face, he was surprised to see how young he was. He was indeed wearing a collar. "You're not allowed to touch the body," Heller explained. "We have to examine it first."

The pastor looked at him with glassy eyes, not giving the impression he'd understood. He had to be freezing in his simple cassock. He didn't even have a cap on.

"Did you know the girl?" Heller asked him.

The pastor tightened his lips and shook his head.

"Did you happen to be passing by?"

The pastor wiped at his mouth and chin. "I was told someone had died. I wanted to see if I could do something."

"There's nothing you can do."

"I could pray for the salvation of her soul," the pastor said softly.

Heller waited a few moments. "You don't know her? Do you know if she had family nearby or where she lived?" he added.

The pastor gave Heller a look of despair and helplessness. "I already told you: I don't know anything. Except that these aren't good times. Not at all." He suddenly turned around and walked away. The crowd parted for him.

Heller gave a signal, then watched the cops load the body onto the truck and drive off. Only two policemen stayed behind to disperse the onlookers. Heller looked around for Fritz Koch, but he couldn't find him. He started walking toward the little metal shop on the opposite corner and still didn't see the witness. At least Heller had noted his residence. He took another look at the Schwarzer Peter. The bar was barricaded. He studied the sooty wall and the blackened icicles on the windowsills. He definitely had to question Gutmann. But considering both the good relationship the bar owner cultivated with the occupiers and the poor relationship Heller had with the public prosecutor, it was questionable whether Gutmann could even be summoned, let alone made to appear before a judge. The odds of a search warrant were grim. If what Fritz Koch said was true, then Gutmann's place wasn't just a prostitution ring—minors were being abused as well. Breaking that news to the Soviets would prove tricky. It surely meant that Soviet officers were playing a decisive role. Niesbach wouldn't help, that was clear. He'd probably just file the matter away and ride it out. So if Heller wanted to get Gutmann, he would need to take a different approach. The murder of Franz Swoboda provided his best chance.

Heller looked at his watch, which confirmed what his stomach had been telling him for a long time: it was far past lunchtime, and he was incredibly hungry. The next soup kitchen wasn't far, and he had a few coupons in his pocket. Nevertheless, he went to Gutmann's bar and pounded on the door.

"Herr Gutmann?" he shouted. "Police detective!" He heard nothing from inside. He gave up and headed down Görlitzer Strasse to where the public kitchens had been set up.

After making the short march up the slight incline on Louisenstrasse, he realized he was too late—again. There wasn't anything left.

He looked around for Heinz Seibling but didn't spot him. So he continued on, following the secret route through building entranceways and inner courtyards until he stood at the one-legged man's hiding place. The wall hatch was open. Heller stayed a few yards back.

"Heinz?" he called in a muted voice. Heller wanted to at least give him a chance to hide whatever needed hiding.

"Herr Heller!" Seibling stared out the opening, looking pleased. "Come on in."

Heller stepped closer but only squatted at the entrance—today wasn't a day for crawling inside. "Listen, what else can you tell me about Gutmann's bar? Do you know anything about the girls?"

Seibling's smiling face transformed into a woeful one. "Why must you always burden me with such things, Herr Heller? Can't there ever be something good?"

"Actually, yes. Klaus came back."

Seibling's face brightened again. "That's splendid! He's all in one piece, then?"

Heller nodded.

"Give him my best regards."

"Gladly. Now, Heinz, this is important. What about the girls? What are people saying?"

"Please, my dear Herr Oberkommissar, I don't want to get dragged into this."

"Franz Swoboda—what else do you know about him?"

"Nothing, nothing, I know nothing about him."

Seibling pulled back inside and looked busy, as if searching for something.

"Heinz, you don't have to be scared of him anymore. He's dead."

Seibling popped up, crawled back to the opening. "Dead? Actually dead?"

"Dead in a way only a man without a head can be. Heinz, you must have heard about the dead girl. Found only a few blocks from here just this morning. Someone said she belonged to Gutmann. She wasn't even fifteen."

Seibling hesitated. Heller could see the inner conflict. He frowned with agony. "All right, yes, people were saying he had something going on there. He gathered them up and pampered them, and they worked for him. But Herr Oberkommissar, there's nothing you can do. They'll settle that with each other. You've seen it yourself. They're killing each other."

Heller didn't relent. "There was a dispute between Gutmann and Swoboda."

Seibling finally stuck his head out of the opening, looked up at the walls surrounding the back courtyard, then waved Heller a little closer.

"Actually, they were more like buddies, real close. But that Swoboda was crazy. Sometimes it was like he was boozed up but even worse somehow. They say he sometimes beat the girls real bad and supposedly one got bumped off that way."

"Rubbed out?"

Seibling nodded. "The two of them were probably fighting about it. But that's only what I heard."

"So Gutmann wasn't scared of Swoboda?"

Seibling shrugged. "Apparently not. He did give him food and lodging."

"So when did Swoboda supposedly kill a girl?"

"Just recently," Seibling said.

"Recently?" The dead girl didn't look like she'd been beaten to death. But sometimes it only took one shot. An unlucky fall. Maybe her neck was broken. Kassner would find out. And why had Seibling kept this from him yesterday?

Seibling held up his hands with regret. "I don't know any more than that. Promise. Head cut off, huh? I'm sure he deserved it, the pig."

Heller wasn't any wiser by the time he was standing back out on Louisenstrasse, and his stomach was no fuller. He had to go see Niesbach, or better yet Speidel, whether he wanted to or not. Gutmann had to see the dead girl, as Heller hoped to learn something from his reaction. The public prosecutor was certainly obligated to act accordingly—hopefully today. Heller decided to pay another visit to the police station on Katharinenstrasse.

At the Görlitzer Strasse intersection, he pushed through the crowds. Acting on impulse, he went to one of the public soup kitchens and yanked a coupon from his wallet.

"Anything left?" he asked a lady manning her serving station, just to see. She wore an apron over a thick jacket.

"Barley broth an' a hunka crust. Bread coupon an' five marks fifty."

Heller pushed the money and coupon over to her, but the woman held up her hands for him to wait. "You got no bowl? No pot?"

Heller raised his hands in regret.

"Wait a sec." The woman went in back and returned with a well-filled porcelain soup plate and a piece of bread.

"Thank you. I have my own spoon."

"You need to eat it here, though, so you don't go walkin' away with that plate."

The soup tasted bland, the barleycorns bloated, turning the broth into porridge. There was no salt or pepper, pretty much the only things that could make the meal tasty. But it did fill his stomach in a pleasantly bloated way, which gave him some hope that the feeling might last awhile.

Heller wasn't quite finished eating when he noticed something moving out of the corner of his eye. It was a child, about four years old, all bundled up in a much-too-large jacket, the seams of the sleeves stitched with wire. Its head was covered with what looked like a homemade cap cut out of a sofa cushion cover, filled with cotton, and sewn back together. The little face looked out, all grimy and smeared with soot. Heller couldn't tell if it was a girl or a boy. Its big eyes looked up at him.

Heller looked around, hoping to find who the child belonged to. But he couldn't spot anyone.

"Where did your mother go?" Heller asked.

The child stared at him. Its mouth moved, the tip of its tongue appearing, then vanishing.

"Is she not here?" Heller tried again.

"Don't talk to 'em, they'll steal that hat right off your head!" warned the kitchen lady.

Heller ignored her.

"What is it, are you hungry?" he asked the child.

The child nodded almost imperceptibly. Heller glanced at the rest of his soup and fought with his conscience. Then he held the soup plate tight, bent down, and extended the plate to the child. The child didn't hesitate. It picked up the spoon and quickly ate the rest of the soup. It didn't seem to chew at all, just swallowed all it could get in its mouth.

"You want this too?" Heller asked, holding out the rest of his bread crust.

The child grabbed hold and before Heller could add a word it ran off, darting like lightning between people's legs, and soon disappeared from view.

Heller straightened up and gave the plate back to the kitchen lady. "Hey, my spoon!" he blurted.

"I told you! Didn't I tell you?"

February 9, 1947: Early Afternoon

Heller left the police station on Katharinenstrasse feeling unusually gratified. He had gotten coffee, ersatz of course, with sweetener instead of sugar, and the beverage was now warming his stomach. Even more pleasant, though, was that his phone call with Speidel had gone far differently than he had expected. He'd been preparing for a tough battle, for threats and recrimination and cynical reactions.

But the public prosecutor had turned extraordinarily obliging and friendly. They were getting off on the wrong foot, he told Heller. He intended to have Gutmann brought into police headquarters for questioning that very day—and intended to order a house search as well. Medvedev certainly had a hand in this, Heller supposed, or maybe he hadn't. He didn't waste any more time thinking about it, not wanting to spoil this small victory.

He pushed up his sleeve and checked his watch. It would take some time for all the forms to be signed and the operation organized. So Heller decided to stake out the Schwarzer Peter. He was certain that Gutmann was holed up there. If he left anytime soon, Heller could follow him. That might also reveal if there was an informant within the police. Or the judiciary.

Heller stepped behind the wooden fence along the grounds of the metal shop, searching for a good spot among all the objects people had left behind. He looked at the opposite building, his hands deep in his pockets.

After a few minutes, a window opened above him.

"Clear out of there, you old bastard!" shouted an angry man.

"I'm with the police," Heller shouted back.

"Ah, I see, I just meant, people are always doing their business there; it's an outrage!"

"Shut that window," Heller yelled. "You're interfering with a police operation!"

It took nearly an hour. Heller stepped in place, trying to keep warm. The effect of the ersatz coffee had long faded, as had the nourishment from that barley soup. Finally, Heller heard an engine approaching. Policemen ran up from the nearby station. Heller stepped into the street to intercept the cops, showing them where to keep watch in the inner courtyard and the various possible side exits to both streets.

Six more policemen rode on one of the trucks that rolled up; one carried a battering ram. Oldenbusch jumped out the passenger side and pulled two reports from his briefcase.

"It's blood on the tools, from two different people," he told Heller in a rush. "Kassner's trying to determine the blood groups so we can at least confirm Swoboda's. The ring's inscribed with 'Rosmarie, 08/16/1931.' I've already arranged for the city and church registrar's offices to check who was getting married on that date. Kassner examined the girl as well. Clear case of asphyxiation. The lungs full of flue gas. Also syphilitic, secondary stage."

"For God's sake!" Heller blurted. "The fire hoses! That's why her hair was frozen. She must have been in Gutmann's house. Did Speidel know? Does he have Kassner's report?"

Oldenbusch raised his eyebrows and shook his head.

Heller was disappointed. Did this mean Medvedev had interfered and Speidel's backing down really had nothing to do with Heller? Heller needed to pull himself together.

"You four, come with me," Heller ordered the policemen. "The others, spread out. We might encounter some resistance."

Curious onlookers were gathering yet again.

Heller crossed the street and hammered on the front door of the Schwarzer Peter.

"Police!" he shouted. "We're searching the building!" He pressed an ear to the door. "Open up, Herr Gutmann, or we'll break down your door!" Heller counted to ten, then stepped away from the door. "Bust it down," he ordered the cop with the battering ram.

The policeman was just about to swing the heavy iron when Gutmann said, "I'm coming already!"

They heard rumbling from inside, then the door opened. Gutmann looked at Heller with a disparaging gaze. "You're going to regret this," Gutmann barked at him. "Really regret it! I warned you. Which vehicle am I riding in?" He tried to push past Heller.

But Heller grabbed his arm. "Spare me the nonsense," Heller said. "And keep talking tough, see if I care."

Heller forced his way past Gutmann and into the bar.

"Smells like something burning," he said.

Oldenbusch sniffed. "He's trying to destroy something."

Heller hurried toward the smell until he reached Gutmann's room, where he spotted a small book on the floor, half-burned and still smoldering. He knelt down, slammed it shut, and smothered the rest of the embers with the cuffs of his overcoat.

He handed the book to Oldenbusch as he entered the room. "Keep this safe, Werner. There must be more rooms in here somewhere, and

I intend to find them. We'll tear open that walled-off stairwell if we have to."

Heller went back into the hallway, looked around, and pulled open a heavy curtain. It concealed a shelving unit fit into a recess, holding cleaning rags and linens. He rattled the shelving unit and noticed how easily it moved. He pulled it away from the recess with ease. This revealed a wall that was actually a door, which led to the walled-off part of the stairwell.

Heller blew air out his cheek in anger. He should've noticed this earlier. He stepped through the opening and looked around, using the weak daylight streaming down through gaps in the roof far above.

The way outside to Alaunstrasse had been blocked by a recently built wall, and the cellar appeared to be buried in rubble, but the stairs leading up were unobstructed and in use. Every third step held a candle, and the large amount of dripped wax indicated that many such candles had been burned here. Footsteps and dragging marks showed in the dust. Heller climbed the stairs to the second story. It was bitterly cold up here. The floor was covered with frozen puddles from the fire hoses, the walls dark from soot. Black icicles hung from the ceiling. It still reeked of smoke. Heller entered an open apartment. He stood at the first doorway, on the inner courtyard side of the apartment. He heard noises behind him, recognized Oldenbusch from the way he snorted when exerting himself, then listened to him squeeze by the shelving and narrow passage to the doorway before heading up the steps.

"This way." Heller waited for Oldenbusch, then pointed at the open door. Beyond it was a cramped, windowless room. He could make out a small stove, a bed, and a low shelf with a washing bowl. A thick layer of soot covered everything.

"Look at this, boss," Oldenbusch whispered and pulled the door all the way open with a finger. The soot-covered inside of the door revealed the tracks of fingers and hands, running from chest height down to the floor. Even lying on the floor, the girl must have tried in vain to open the door or make her presence known. From the ice made by the fire hoses, it was clear to see where she had lain. A shoe and sock were still stuck in the ice. Heller swung the door back and looked at the other side. It had been locked from the outside, the key still sticking out.

Heller wiped his face and forced himself to tame his rage. He really wanted to storm out and punch that filthy bastard in the face. Right after the fire, while he sat downstairs with Gutmann playing the injured victim, she had been up here, fighting for her life.

"Are there more rooms?" Heller asked, his voice raw. Oldenbusch went down the hall, propping himself against the wall so he wouldn't slip on the ice. "Two, but they're empty."

Heller nodded and took a deep breath. The girl might have lived if Gutmann had just come upstairs and unlocked the door.

Shaken now, both he and Oldenbusch stared at the ghostly imprint of the girl's body on the floor. They could clearly make out her calves, the folds of her dress, her arms, and even a few strands of hair that had frozen in the ice. It was eerie, as if she were still lying here.

"The firefighters should have checked," Oldenbusch muttered.

"They couldn't tell, not with the stairwell walled off," Heller said, though he'd had the same thought. The firefighters shouldn't have assumed anything and should've checked. Out of principle. It was always about principle. Yet he had to blame himself as well, for getting careless. The building should have been thoroughly searched the first day.

Heller tried to collect his thoughts. "We have some real hard work ahead of us, Werner. I need statements from everyone in the neighborhood. I need to know who saw the girl, how many girls were working here, how many Soviet officers were coming in."

Oldenbusch nodded. "No one's going to utter a peep; they're all too scared."

"Fritz Koch, that drunk living over in the metal shop? He'll tell us something. People just need a little tempting. They're practically bursting with curiosity and a need to talk to someone. It's up to us to draw the right conclusions from all their talk."

Heller took another glance into the room that had become a death trap for the girl. He chewed at his lower lip, deep in thought.

"Boss?" Oldenbusch asked.

Heller looked up. "When are you going to stop calling me that, Werner? If this girl had syphilis like Kassner says, the johns could've gotten it too. Maybe that helps us somehow."

"That means I'll have to question the Russians again."

"It does, Werner, and they're not going to like it. But we should be calling them Soviets. Because not all of them are Russians."

Heller sat at one of the tables in the bar and used the light from a kerosene lamp to look over the book Gutmann had tried to burn. More than two-thirds of the pages had been completely burned up, the rest charred and browned. Gutmann had written in pencil, and Heller could only make out a few figures. This was likely Gutmann's secret ledger that he used to record expenses or earnings he planned to hide from the taxman—many that Heller could read were in the single digits, possibly liquor or soup ordered. Other figures were higher. Gutmann had entered subtotals and totaled these up on a separate page. The date was still visible in places. One page drew Heller's attention.

Oldenbusch came in to show him something. "Look, I found these in Gutmann's desk." Oldenbusch put a small brown bottle on the table as well as a tobacco tin holding syringes and needles.

Heller took a good look but couldn't tell whether these were the same type of syringes he'd found in the doctor's bag. He pointed at the little bottle. "So what's this?"

Oldenbusch lifted it so Heller could see the liquid in the light of the lamp.

"My guess is Evipan or a similar preparation. The active ingredient should be the same. Hexo-something or other. Kassner will know. Hexobarbital, that's what it was. But take a look at the labels." He pointed at the Cyrillic script. "There's more drugs in his desk. Penicillin, if I'm not mistaken, worth a mint, I'm telling you. Labeled in Russian as well. I can't imagine this stuff getting diverted to Gutmann's inventory in any legal way. If only we knew who had access to—"

Heller raised a finger. "Hold that thought, Werner."

He ran his finger over the open page of Gutmann's charred notebook, going down the rows of legible letters.

. . . ov
. . . nko
. . . in
. . . mann
. . . da
. . . ier
. . . nov
. . . ili

These last three letters gave him pause.

As Heller stepped out onto the street, the cold caught him off guard yet again. It had been freezing enough in the bar. He looked at his watch, saw it was two thirty in the afternoon. He looked down the street, at the people everywhere. A child caught his attention. It was a young boy, as far as he could tell from his thick disguise of overcoat, scarf, and cap. The boy walked slowly, with his hands in his pockets, looking around. Heller put him at six years old, with a thin face and a black bruise on one eye. Only as the boy neared did Heller see he wore one of those standard Soviet fur caps with earflaps that could be tied up over the head. It looked new; only the red star had been removed. Heller stood in the boy's path.

"Hey, you, tell me: Where did you get that hat?" he asked and tried to grab the kid by the arm. But the boy eluded him and ran off. As he did, something fell out of his coat pocket and hit the street with a soft clank. The boy stopped and tried running back to pick it up. But when he saw that Heller was following him, he decided against it and bolted. Heller picked up the object. It was a small narrow blade, its handle driven into a piece of carved wood and secured with wire. Heller was surprised to find how sharp the blade was. In crowds, thieves used these sorts of knives to cut open bags and coats. He shook his head. The boy wasn't even school age yet. Heller pocketed the knife, intending to head toward the bar, when he suddenly caught sight of someone he thought he recognized. It was the girl with the overcoat from the slope. She must have gone right past him, and now she was walking up Louisenstrasse, taking oddly short steps. She looked exhausted. Heller was of two minds.

"Werner," he shouted across the street. "Werner!" But Oldenbusch was still inside the Schwarzer Peter and couldn't hear him.

"You there! Comrade!" Heller waved for a cop and kept glancing back at the girl, who had nearly reached the next intersection.

The uniformed cop reacted but, misinterpreting Heller's wave, headed into the bar. Heller snorted in annoyance and started running after the girl before he lost sight of her altogether.

The girl seemed to be walking aimlessly, first up Kamenzer Strasse, then back down Schönfelder Strasse, eventually turning onto Priessnitzstrasse and following that awhile, only to take a right onto Bischofsweg and soon a left onto Forststrasse. Heller followed her by zigzagging, keeping a good fifty yards' distance. Once he bent down and fixed his shoelace when she looked around.

The girl had now reached Nordstrasse. Heller caught up a little. He slipped between the trees lining the street, since there were fewer people around here to duck behind. The girl stopped within view of the Schlüters' villa, then took cover behind one of the trees so she could watch the house. She soon stepped back out, sprinted across the street, and slipped into the overgrown bushes in old Frau Dähne's yard. From there, she kept watch on the villa. Soviet Army men were still there, standing around looking bored, smoking, burning something outside in the yard. Several civilians were standing with them, likely getting food.

Heller waited a bit before attempting a quick look. The girl was now gone. Frustrated, he stood in front of the yard. He heard a noise and ducked down quickly. Then he poked his head through the leafless branches of the thick hedges edging the ruins of Frau Dähne's home. He soon spotted the girl, crawling out of an opening to the cellar of the collapsed house. She worked to pull herself out sideways, partially propping a hand against her puffed-out stomach or whatever stolen goods were under her overcoat. For a moment Heller wondered whether he should confront her, but then decided to keep watching.

The girl darted back onto the path, moving with purpose now. Heller took pursuit again at a measured distance with no idea where she was going. He figured she lived in one of the old ramshackle buildings on the edge of Neustadt. Yet the girl kept marching farther. She turned off suddenly for a path into the woods, to Heller's surprise, and followed that along Priessnitz Creek, continuing into the Dresden Heath.

Heller fell back a bit. They weren't the only people passing through here, but most who came out of the woods were loaded down with brushwood and branches. It was growing dim between the tree trunks, with little snow and plenty of shiny dead leaves. The droning of Russian trucks along Carola-Allee could be heard, yet the sound only reinforced

Heller's perception that he had found himself in the middle of the wilderness. The creek was quite wide in spots, and it rippled and gurgled, ice lining the banks, its wide, flat bends frozen over. The girl was making good progress now. It was clear she knew her way around. Heller felt unsure. He hadn't been in the heath for years. Up to the right of them had to be the barracks and the military cemetery. The vehicle noises were little more than a distant rush now. Instead, the twigs cracked under his feet and frozen leaves crunched. Heller fell back a little farther, and soon they were alone in the woods. He looked at his watch again. It was hardly 3:00 p.m., but it seemed as if hours had gone by since he'd taken up pursuit. The sun would soon go down, though. He'd lost sight of the girl and rushed to catch up, frantically trying to get back on her trail. Then he spotted her again. She was crossing the stream, leaping expertly from stone to stone as if she knew the way. Heller waited for her to disappear among the trees, then followed.

He paused at the dark bank of Priessnitz Creek, eyeing the frozen mud, the icy water, and the protruding rocks, scarcely bigger than cobblestones. At the spot the girl had nimbly leapt across, he'd have to weigh his every step and hope his bum foot didn't give out. He dared his first leap and immediately had to keep going as he realized he'd lose his balance otherwise. After five successful leaps, he was lucky to land in the high forest grass. He kept going up a slope, thinking he'd seen the girl disappear over it. But he had to watch out, since there was the possibility that she'd noticed him and was lying in wait.

Yet the girl, who hadn't looked back once, moved ever deeper into the heath. Somewhere, Heller knew, there was a moor here. Was that where she was going? Or to the old Heath Mill inn? Had they already passed Kannenhenkel Trail? Heller didn't know where he was anymore. It would soon be dark, and getting lost in these woods with these temperatures could have fatal consequences. Yet he had to keep going, and it was obvious that the girl knew where to go.

They crossed through two clearings before plunging into a dusky pine forest where Heller had to hold his arms in front of his face to protect against branches. Right as he passed through, he smelled fire. A sliver of smoke rose from a hollow. Heller took cover, hiding behind a fallen beech tree and pressing himself against the trunk. He watched the girl climb back down a slope. Something moved far below. He'd first taken it for a low mound or a boulder. Then he saw that it was a tent, camouflaged with twigs and leaves. A small child went up to the girl. Another child came, and the girl greeted it. Then she pulled something out of her overcoat and passed it around.

Heller crept closer, crouching. He slowly made his way down the slope, approaching the primitive shelter with caution. No one had noticed him yet. He was about ten yards away when he realized that the hollow held more of these dwellings. Dug into the slope, and not visible from above, was a shelter secured with lumber and covered with blankets. Heller stood in the open and made for the camp. The little kids had already spotted him. They stared at him until he'd gotten within ten yards. One of them held up a hand without taking its eyes off him, which alerted the older girl to him. She turned and stared.

It nearly scared him how filthy, unkempt, and feral she looked up close. The little kids were in the same wretched condition—undernourished, freezing, noses running.

"What do you have under your overcoat?" Heller asked gently. He then felt a shove from behind.

"Hands up!" shouted a young voice.

Heller raised his hands above his head. "I'm not the only one here," he said, without knowing whom he was talking to.

"What do you mean?" asked the young voice behind him.

"There're Russians in the woods. If you shoot, they'll come this way. You can be sure of it."

"I could stab you!" the voice replied defiantly. The opening to one of the tents shifted, and a boy of about ten came out carrying a machine gun that he pointed at Heller.

Heller spoke clearly and gently, avoiding any quick movements. "They'd search for me. Listen, I don't want anything from you." He turned, very cautiously, his hands still up.

Standing before him was a tall boy of probably sixteen. He had on a threadbare German military uniform stuffed with cotton in the arms and legs. He wore a German helmet as well and even had army boots. He, too, was armed with a German machine gun. He had eczema along his lip and was missing one of his lower front teeth. Heller noticed several decorations on his chest—an Iron Cross and two Russian medals. A big knife hung from his leather belt, and on his back, Heller was astonished to see, he wore a bow and quiver with arrows.

"May I see your bow?" Heller asked. "Did you make it yourself?"

"Keep them hands up!" warned the armed kid behind him.

Heller obediently put his hands above his head.

"Don't let him out of your sight, Johann," the taller boy said. "Who are you?"

"My name is Max Heller. I'm with the police. I was pursuing a thief and got lost here. And you, what's your name?"

"You were chasing Fanny!"

"Don't you say my name!" the girl said, outraged. Only now did Heller see that she had psoriasis spreading from her temples below her hair.

Heller looked around. More children crawled out of the other dwellings, slowly approaching. Heller guessed there was a dozen of them, maybe more. Most seemed barely four years old, very few of school age. They all looked haggard and hungry. They were covered in dirt and had blackened teeth and clogged noses. They wore ragtag clothing stitched together from old clothes, parts of uniforms, curtains, and bed coverings. Most had weapons on them—knives, pistols, spears, and lances. They looked at him with near apathy. Heller felt a heat rising through his jaw and behind his eyes. He didn't dare blink.

"What are you carrying under your overcoat?" he asked the girl again, his voice breaking.

"Don't show him!" the boy ordered.

"Don't make no difference, plus he needs feeding." Fanny unbuttoned her overcoat, revealing a little bundle. She pulled at a knot and unwound a long cloth. A tiny, skinny infant appeared, wrapped up in a blanket, its little head bright red and its mouth contorting into a faint, weak whimper.

Heller intuitively lowered his hands and reached out for the infant.

"You can't carry it like that," he told the girl. "It's barely getting any air that way. See?"

"Hands off!" warned the tall boy.

"I'm only trying to help," Heller said, undeterred. He held the baby. It was as light as a feather and smelled as if it had been wearing the same diaper for days. Its eyes were stuck shut, and so were its nostrils.

Heller sighed heavily. He would have to ask her. It wasn't rare for infants to be left near hospitals by starving mothers unable to feed themselves, let alone a child. Had she found one and taken it? "Where did you get it?" he asked.

"He's mine!" Fanny shouted. "Had him myself, in that tent. Came right out of me, all on his own. Four days ago. All them here saw it. That right?" She looked around, and all the kids nodded.

"You had it here? In the tent? Without any help?" The little thing trembled in his arms, or maybe his hands were shaking.

"Wasn't the first time. One girl here already had one. She screamed, but not me! I scream?" Fanny peered at the kids. They shook their heads.

"See. Didn't make a peep."

Heller nodded. His heart had tensed up. He could barely endure the sight of such neglected children. He carefully gave the baby back to Fanny. "So where's she now, the other one?"

"Back there." Fanny and the other children pointed behind them. Heller looked in that direction and thought they meant one of the covered dwellings, but then he spotted a little mound of earth topped with a small cross made of tied-together branches. "We had to bury her. Poor Margi."

"Poor Margi," the kids whispered.

Heller couldn't speak. He felt so helpless in the face of such indescribable hopelessness and poverty. Yet at the same time, he knew the pity overwhelming him wasn't going to do any good. On the contrary. He needed to stay alert. He was still in danger. These kids weren't living here in secret for no reason. In their eyes, he was an intruder and a threat. He turned to Fanny.

"You have to give him something to drink regularly and wash him really well, with warm water, you hear me? And always keep him wrapped nice and warm. You have to keep his bottom clean and dry. Every day. Do you have any powder?"

Fanny shook her head.

"And when you hold him, always keep a hand under his head. He's still too weak to hold his head up on his own. You see? Right like this." Heller showed Fanny how she should carry the baby.

They heard a noise, like the chirping of a small, weary bird. The tall boy with the machine gun listened up. "Someone else is coming," he whispered.

"Go look," Fanny said and pointed her chin at Heller. "Johann and me'll keep our eyes on him."

The boy hesitated, then darted off and climbed up the slope, barely making a sound.

Heller relaxed a little. That boy had seemed to pose the greatest danger.

"How old are you?" he asked Fanny, who had sat on a log, opened her blouse, and, without any embarrassment, bared her chest to breast-feed the baby. Her chest wasn't fully developed, and her nipples looked sore. Heller could hardly stand to watch how helplessly and greedily the baby started wiggling its head when Fanny put it to her breast, hardly mustering the strength to suck.

"Fourteen, I think. Not really sure. February now, right?"

Heller nodded. "The ninth."

"Fifteen then."

"And your parents?"

"My mother never come out of our cellar bunker, and Father went missing during the war. I was in a home at first, but when the Russians come, I took off."

Heller had already suspected as much, yet every one of her seemingly unemotional words hit him in the heart. "So you're all orphans?"

Fanny stared at him.

"I mean, none of you have any parents left?"

"Well, most of them're dead. And his parents, Alfons's ones, took off without him." Fanny pointed at a seven- or eight-year-old, his left hand clamped around a lance consisting of a bar with a bayonet fixed on the end. The boy's right arm was missing.

"I brought a few of 'em with me from the home; other ones we found and saved from the Russians. And now they got parents again. Me, I'm now the mom, and Jörg is their daddy."

"Why aren't you in the city? There are places where people will help you. There are some good people. I know so."

"Russians are in the city. Plus, no one wants to have us. They all just beat us or run us off. You ever in a home like that? They hit you right in your trap, and you get nothing to eat, and then you're taken off to Russia to be one of their slaves. Nah, we're happier here. We're doing good, aren't we?" Fanny took another look around, and all the children nodded.

Heller looked at the pathetic group of kids. "I don't think you are. There are good homes, where you'll be warm and get a real bed and fed three times a day. No one hits you. And the Russians aren't all that bad. They don't have any slaves. You have to believe me on that."

Fanny shook her head. "The Russians, they go eating children, someone even saw it! That right?" The kids nodded again.

"No, that's not true," Heller replied.

"You're only saying that 'cause the Russians give you food. That true? What, you supposed to try and lure us out of the woods?"

"Fanny," Heller said gently. "That's your name, right?"

She nodded.

"Fanny, you were there three days ago when they found that dead Russian on that slope above the Elbe. You wanted that backpack. Did you know what was inside?"

Fanny hesitated, then shook her head. "I just saw it, wanted to have it."

"And I also saw you twice at Gutmann's bar, at the Schwarzer Peter."

Fanny frowned and scratched at her scabs. "Nah, nah, got no idea who that is."

Heller raised his chin. "The tall guy, what's his name? Jörg?"

"He's our leader, ever since Walter got shot dead. Poor Walter."

"Poor Walter," the children whispered, and it sounded like an amen in church.

"So you hunt animals? And you beg and steal in the city?"

"We don't filch nothing; we only take what we need. And Jörg, he goes hunting with Heinrich. Heinrich's a good archer and stalks real good too. Heinrich's good, isn't he?"

"Heinrich's good," the children replied.

Heller looked into their dirty little faces and saw his son before his eyes. How Klaus had stood there in the kitchen with that despairing smile because his father hadn't recognized him at first. These children were barely getting by in the woods, not even an hour by foot from civilization, left on their own, parentless, unwanted. Again he buried the thought. "May I look around?" he asked Fanny. "I won't run away."

Fanny shrugged, took her infant from her breast, and started to lay it in a dirty old stroller with no wheels.

"No, wait," Heller tried. "Place it on your shoulder, like so, then pat its back real soft until it does a little burp. You understand? Until it belches." He helped her and showed her how to pat its back. Once the baby gave a gentle burp, she giggled like a child, and the other children giggled along with her.

"If he doesn't do a little burp, he'll get a tummy ache, that or he could vomit in his sleep and choke on it."

Fanny stared at him a moment, deep in thought. Her face lit up. "You mean when he pukes."

Heller nodded. Then he stood and went toward the dwellings.

A pack of kids followed him. The small ones looked up at him, eyeing him with nervous curiosity and wonder. When he crouched to look into the tent, they did the same. The smallest one pressed especially close and observed his every move. Their penetrating reek brought tears to his eyes. They probably hadn't washed since the last warm days of fall, not to mention ever changing out of their ragged clothes. Their heads were swarming with lice, and sometimes the bugs ran right across their faces. All the kids had some kind of skin rash, and they twitched and scratched themselves incessantly. A little girl stood off to the side, holding a twig in her arms. It had cloth wrapped around it and had become her doll.

It stank inside the tents as well. Filthy blankets and pillows covered the floor, tin cans were piled up, old dolls and broken toy cars lay next to all manner of stolen goods—wire, batteries, and cardboard. In old pots and other containers, Heller found chestnuts, acorns, beechnuts, and frozen or dried lizards in a wooden box. In another tent, two children lay motionless under their blankets, seriously ill. Heller felt their heads—they were red-hot. A girl was cooling them with a rag she had soaked in cold stream water. In the shelter dug out of the slope, practically a cave, he discovered ammunition boxes with German carbines, Russian rifles, and hand grenades of German and Russian make. Several small fires burned in front of various shelters. Primitive stands held black pots. Heller picked up a big spoon and stirred around in one. It was apparently a soup. Small shreds of white meat and a little bit of green floated around in it; he took a cautious sniff. Their dishes consisted of odd plates, a few sawed-off steel helmets, and old tin cans. The children relieved themselves at a narrow stream. Heller tried to spot the one he had given his barley soup to. He thought it might give him some small comfort knowing that the child at least lived here with this group and didn't have to roam the city like a lonely, lost creature. He didn't see the child.

Fanny was suddenly behind him. He hadn't heard her coming. "Jörg, he says the Germans are gonna fight again and chase the Russians out. He says our soldiers aren't defeated yet. They're just resting and got new weapons built. He says, under the ground, Adolf's building a secret weapon gonna make all the Russians dead with one blow. He says we always need to defend ourselves. He says, if the Russians do find us, that they gonna shoot us all dead."

"So does Jörg sometimes go off to battle?" Heller asked her.

"Go, get away!" Fanny ordered the children around her. They obeyed and vanished into their tents without a word. She then puckered her lips and leaned her head to one side in an almost flirtatious way. "You secretly trying to question me, aren't you?"

"No, I'm just interested." Heller tried to placate her. "So, is he a good father to your child?"

Fanny took a quick look around, then stepped closer.

"He's not the father; he just thinks so. But he's got no clue how that works," she whispered and giggled. "He thinks it comes from kissing." She pulled Heller closer to her. "It's a Russian baby," she whispered in his ear.

"You go see the Russians? They give you things for it? Or did they make you?"

"Nah, didn't make me. I wouldn't put up with that. I'd kill any man dead who tries!"

"But you do go sometimes?"

"Sometimes, yeah, but don't go telling Jörg. He says he'd slit anyone's throat who touches me."

Heller took a deep breath. He'd like to know more, but he couldn't risk asking too much. Fanny seemed to have a simple disposition, yet she was also a fighter who'd managed to survive nearly two years without outside help and even gave birth to a child. Did the boy truly not know how babies were made? It was hard to imagine.

"And this Jörg is sometimes gone at night?" he asked, making it sound casual.

"He's gone a lot." Fanny pressed her lips together, screwed up her eyes in mistrust. "You *are* trying to question me!"

"Fanny, please listen. Your boy is sick. You need to get him to a doctor."

"He's not sick. He's got no fever!"

Heller took her by the arm, looking her firmly in the eyes. "Tell me, is there something running out of you down below, between your legs?"

Fanny turned away from him with a disgusted look.

"It's flowing, you have discharge down there? White and slimy?" Heller asked.

"Sometimes maybe, a little. That bad?"

"Fanny, it's what they call gonorrhea. The clap. And your boy has it in his eyes."

"Nah, that can't be true, can it?" She added an incredulous laugh.

"Fanny, I'm a policeman. You can believe me. And tell me another thing: Do you know Franz? They call him the one-handed man."

Fanny recoiled. "Best you get going now, before Jörg comes back. You never know what that one's gonna do, especially if he gets mad. You shouldn't be here no more."

Using the last light of the day, Heller navigated his way back out of the woodland maze. Though he had always been able to rely on his good sense of direction, he was nevertheless relieved when he finally reached Priessnitz Creek. He followed its path and found himself back out on Bischofsweg.

It was around 7:00 p.m. and fully dark when he reached the police station on Katharinenstrasse. There he got on the phone to headquarters and was grateful to hear that Oldenbusch was still working. Twenty minutes later, he picked Heller up in the Ford.

"So where have you been?" Oldenbusch asked. "With Kasrashvili?"

"I followed the girl, Werner. The one who tried fighting us for that backpack with Franz Swoboda's head in it. Just imagine this: there's a group of children living in the heath, led by a boy named Jörg. Some of them are little kids, orphaned, sick—breaks your heart."

"I don't know if I've ever seen you this troubled, Max."

"Werner, don't you understand? Children. In the woods. In this freezing cold. No mother, no father. All alone, fending for themselves. They can't even speak properly."

"Then we'll need to get them out of there. Child Services office can take care of it."

Heller touched Oldenbusch's arm, but Oldenbusch kept his eyes fixed on the street.

"It's not that simple, Werner. They have weapons. Machine guns, hand grenades, pistols, knives. The boy, their leader, he's around sixteen. He still believes Nazi propaganda, gives himself medals, believes in secret weapons, and thinks a new war is coming. And then there's the girl, Fanny. I'm not certain I can trust her. She has a baby, from a Russian, she says. I think she's acting dumber than she really is."

Oldenbusch slowly turned onto Königsbrücker Strasse, since there were potholes everywhere and tires were in short supply. "So is there reason to suspect these children had anything to do with the attack?"

Heller stretched his legs as far as he could. His ankle ached from the long march over rough terrain.

"We can only speculate. Remember that spelling mistake on the leaflet? 'Bolshevissm'—with two s's. Those kids have been living in that forest hiding place ever since the war ended. They've had no schooling for a long time, if ever. The two adolescents spoke with poor grammar. Mind you, I don't know how they could have produced the leaflets. I didn't spot a mimeograph in their miserable camp. They still could have had something to do with those dead Soviet officers. Like I said, I'm just speculating. But I'm pretty sure Fanny knew Swoboda."

"So what you're saying is, you want to keep quiet about this for now?"

"Just for now. I need to find out more. I'll go back tomorrow and try to gain her trust. I'm bringing them food. I'm just not sure where I'm going to get it. And I want to go see Kasrashvili too. And Frau Schlüter has to be questioned. And Gutmann." Heller rubbed his chin. "I have no idea what to tackle first."

Oldenbusch carefully steered the car around the next pothole. He seemed unruffled. "I suggest taking one step at a time. Frau Schlüter's sitting in the prison at Münchner Platz. Gutmann's in custody at police

HQ. Kassner sent over a report, and I have it here for you." He leaned forward and tapped on a folder on the dashboard.

Heller opened it and scanned Dr. Kassner's findings. In the case of Berinov, there were no detectable sexual diseases, though Kassner stressed that syphilis was quite difficult to detect in its early stages. In the case of Cherin, there was a suspicion that he'd been infected with gonorrhea, but this couldn't be proven decisively given the condition of the corpse. They still needed to take swabs. Attached were the final report on Swoboda's head and the autopsy report on the dead girl. In her case, the sole cause of death was smoke inhalation.

Heller read in silence, holding pages up to the window and using the light of streetlamps rushing by. He wondered if there was anything to the gossip about another victim, by Swoboda's hand; if there truly was another girl lying buried somewhere. Gutmann knew something, that much was clear. No doubt he was a tough adversary and wouldn't give in anytime soon. Heller really needed to question him again today.

He put the folder in his lap. He was exhausted and missed Karin and Klaus. He needed to speak to his wife, to unload some of this burden. Karin would understand him. Werner didn't have any children, and he hadn't witnessed all the misery Heller had seen in the woods. It wasn't hard for Oldenbusch to forget the matter. But Heller couldn't get the images of those neglected children out of his head. It was like something was pressing down on his chest, making it hard to breathe.

"About those severed hands," Oldenbusch said, continuing where he left off. "The registrar's office promptly replied about the wedding ring. On August 16, 1931, Rosmarie, maiden name Schuster, married an Armin Weiler, who worked as the head of the accounting department in a state-run food processing facility. But I'll bet you can't guess the rest, boss."

"Werner!" Heller groaned, exasperated.

"Armin Weiler used to be the accountant at Schlüter Printing."

Gutmann had to wait in the interrogation room quite a long time, and he received Heller with a pitiful smile. The guards had removed his handcuffs, and he was leaning back in the chair, looking relaxed, his legs stretched out under the table. Heller took off his overcoat, draped it over the chair back, and sat across from Gutmann. Oldenbusch sat next to him. He was under Heller's strict orders not to say anything, even if Gutmann addressed him. Heller stared at Gutmann, giving him the first word. "You really are making a mistake here," Gutmann said. "I warned you before. Taking me into custody might seem sensible, but there are many who won't like it. This isn't about me, no matter what you're hoping to gain from this. I'm not worried about me. This is about you and your future. You're deciding at this very moment. You understand?"

Heller expected no less. He kept cool. "The girl found this morning in the building behind your establishment . . . Who was she, where did she come from?"

"I didn't kill her. She suffocated in the fire. And I nearly suffocated too. I just wanted her out of my building. Listen, I wanted to spare you all this trouble. Because I knew you'd pursue the matter and only end up falling on deaf ears, especially among the Russians. I intended to keep the girl up there temporarily and get rid of her later that night. I was doing it for you, Comrade Heller. But these kids, I'm telling you, they're a plague. Always sniffing around. Anyway, I didn't kill her."

Oldenbusch was taking down every word.

"If you'd be kind enough to answer my questions," Heller said, not attempting to hide his weariness.

"I don't know who she was. She had a Silesian accent and called herself Eva. She was the one who came to me. I gave her food and shelter, but she knew she had to do things for it. Nothing comes for free."

"How old was she, is what I'd like to know."

"I don't know. She said eighteen."

Gutmann gave Heller a brazen look. Heller showed no expression. "How long had she been there with you?"

"A few months."

"What about the other girls? Do you replace them?"

"There's a new one every now and then."

"When did this all start? Was it your idea or someone else's?"

"There have always been women working there. Just walking around the neighborhood like they do, got scooped up by the Russians. They also got raped or the vice squad locked them up. This was still back in '45. I started organizing the whole thing after that. I gave them rooms; they paid me rent. I had nothing to do with their business. And when one goes, another comes. In the beginning I always asked their age. They all said eighteen. Most didn't have any papers on them, so how was I supposed to know? I had to trust them. That's just the way this works. I couldn't care less what they do upstairs."

"How do the girls know to come to you?"

"Word gets around. The SMAD knows about it. This is exactly what I'm trying to tell you, Herr Heller. They don't want scandal. After the attack, people were telling me I should be worried about the public finding out. But it will never reach the public. Why do you think the Soviets got there before the police?"

Heller leaned back in his chair and crossed his arms, staring. Gutmann truly believed he was safe. "More has reached the public than you think, Herr Gutmann. People in the neighborhood are neither deaf nor blind. Major Vadim Berinov and Colonel Vasili Cherin—were they johns?"

"Don't know, maybe. Like I said, not for me to worry about."

"We know both of them were regulars at your place, thanks to your notebook." This was a lie, but Heller figured it was worth a try.

"Even if that's true, you trying to claim I bumped off Soviets? I was in my bar the whole time—I've got witnesses!"

"Would you rather name your johns as witnesses or maybe your underage prostitutes?" Heller kept looking at Gutmann, his face blank.

"There are other witnesses. I have a secure alibi."

"For which days?"

"For every day! Plus, I don't believe you. You don't know a thing. You're groping around in the dark. You don't even have an actual reason to keep me in custody, and I still haven't had a chance to talk to a lawyer." Gutmann was growing indignant. Did he truly believe that all he had to do was utter a few threats and they'd just leave him alone?

Heller kept at it. "We also know you obtained illegal medicine and pharmaceutical goods from a Captain Lado Kasrashvili."

Gutmann shrugged, maintaining his tight-lipped expression. "No idea who that is."

"Does the name Armin Weiler mean anything to you?"

"Yeah, I know him. I get potatoes and flour from his business. He sometimes has a drink at my bar." Gutmann added a sideways grin.

"We know you were quarreling with your caretaker, Franz Swoboda."

Gutmann flew into a rage. "Yeah, so what? That against the law? You can't argue anymore? Got no reason to keep me here!"

"Swoboda's dead, Herr Gutmann. We found his severed head. Quite brutal. Based on witness statements, you're under strong suspicion of murder."

"You'd just love that," Gutmann hissed, but his expression revealed he was growing more uneasy. "Just who are these so-called witnesses?"

"We can't divulge that. But we have witnesses from the immediate vicinity as well as Soviet circles."

Gutmann released a disparaging laugh, yet he nervously tapped on the table. Then he leaned back, shook his head, pursed his lips, and crossed his arms.

Heller wasn't finished. He'd still saved a little ammunition.

"In the report from the coroner who examined Swoboda's head, there's mention of a drug addiction. They found an elevated concentration of a sedative in Swoboda's blood, probably hexobarbital, an injectable narcotic. In your office, we found a considerable amount of

Evipan and various syringes. So it's possible you sedated Swoboda with an injection, killed him, and cut off his head."

Heller went silent, to let his words sink in. He kept his gaze fixed on Gutmann. He was about to learn just how convincing his lie was. He couldn't add any more just yet without risking his bluff getting called. Heller pressed his knee against Oldenbusch's leg, having sensed he was growing nervous.

"Serves him right," Gutmann muttered, staring at the tabletop. His expression betrayed what was playing out inside him, a full spectrum of hate, rage, equanimity, doubt. Suddenly, he seemed to reach a decision. He leaned forward and repeatedly tapped his index finger on the table.

"Very well. Serves him right. Franz was a tough bastard. He was with the SS in Serbia. I'm still not exactly sure how it happened, but he lost his hand in battle. Apparently got trapped after an explosion and had to saw it off with an entrenching tool. It's true he was a bit of a lunatic. He kept things clean at the bar, sweeping and keeping organized. It worked out."

"Did he know about the girls?"

"Sure. He'd gotten them heating for their place and brought them water."

"Did he abuse any of them?"

Gutmann hesitated. "Could be, but they never said anything."

"Word is, he killed one of them."

"When?"

Heller ignored that. "Is it true?"

"I don't know. Sometimes they just take off, here one day, gone the next."

"How are they supposed to take off when they're locked in? Like that girl who suffocated upstairs in your building. Can you explain that? Were you keeping them prisoner?"

"It was for their own protection! So not just anyone could burst in on them. Listen to me, Heller. I was unconscious, I was wounded and confused, and I was scared of the Soviets. That's why I didn't say anything about her up there. I had no idea she'd croak."

Heller raised a hand. "Can you give us a list with the names of your guests?"

"You still don't get it. I'm not making any list—I might as well sign my own death warrant."

"But you had a list. Which you tried to burn."

"No . . . yes . . ." Gutmann shifted in his seat, waving his hands. "Jesus. All right. Franz, he'd picked a fight with one of them. It was like he'd made him into his own personal enemy."

"Who was it—Cherin?"

"How should I know? Everyone called him Vasili. They used to drink together, before Franz became verbally abusive. Calling him a Russian pig, fucking Ivan, how he'd taken out the likes of him dozens of times, and all that crap. I think Cherin was doing some snooping on Franz. I also think Cherin had something going with one of them."

"Had something going? With one of the girls?"

"Yeah, sometimes the johns *do* fall in love."

"So Cherin was one of the ones who'd go see the girls? And he was in love with one. Could she have been the one who killed Swoboda?"

Gutmann raised his hands, distraught now. "I don't know what went down. I wasn't there, goddamn it!"

"Cherin was snooping on Swoboda, you said."

Gutmann nodded, and his shoulders raised.

"Swoboda killed him because of that?"

"Could be."

"So then Berinov set out to find his friend?"

"Vasili and Vadim were friends, yes. They mostly came in together. Maybe he sedated Swoboda and sawed off his head. That Georgian sold his stuff to everyone, so why not Berinov?"

"Then Berinov goes running around the neighborhood with a backpack carrying Swoboda's head in it? Why?"

"How should I know?"

Heller nodded. "The only question is—"

"Is what? What's the question?" Gutmann gave Heller an impatient stare.

"Then who killed Berinov?"

"How did you know that, boss, about the hexobarbital?" Oldenbusch asked. Thanks to an unexpected gas ration, he had offered to drive Heller home. They were now traveling up Bautzner Strasse, the Ford's headlamps the only source of light.

Heller sighed, too tired to contest the nickname. "They were already using Evipan in the First World War. I was sedated with it myself when I was wounded. When you receive it often, you get addicted, as you said. Withdrawal isn't pleasant. It manifests as irritability, tremors, loss of motor skills and the ability to speak properly, and, in extreme cases, delirium tremens. That fits what little I've heard about Swoboda. Kassner's report has nothing about it, though. I'm not sure if it would even be detectable in coagulated blood."

"You really grilled Gutmann good about it. So this Kasrashvili really does have a hand in things."

"He might just be selling. I want to see about visiting him tomorrow."

"Shouldn't you inform the Soviets too?"

"Werner, I can hardly think at this point. I need to go home and get some sleep. I'll speak to Frau Schlüter first thing tomorrow. There must be a reason we found that doctor's bag among her things. And what's the connection between the Schlüters and this Weiler? Just that he had worked for them? That's what I want to find out. We'll see after that."

Heller rubbed his weary face. They slowly climbed the final stretch of street, listening with concern to the pinging engine.

"Stop, Werner. I'll get out here. Tomorrow morning at seven—"

"I'll pick you up, boss. Let's say six?"

Heller nodded, reaching for the door handle.

"Wait a second." Oldenbusch fished around in his overcoat pocket and pulled out a brown paper bag. Heller looked inside and discovered a few white pills.

"You told me that your Frau Marquart was sick."

"Where did you get that? Not from Gutmann's office?"

"He was only going to profit off it."

"But, Werner, it's not right. You can't just—"

"It's also not right when someone dies because they can't get any medicine, especially when it's readily available."

February 9, 1947: Late Evening

Karin breathed a sigh of relief when Heller finally got home. She rushed up to him from the kitchen. Though she could see his weariness and exhaustion, she couldn't contain her frustration.

"It's so late again, Max. It can't go on like this! We desperately need coal. You have to go to the coal office tomorrow. We have coupons, but they're not doing us any good. Others stand in line for hours every day. But you're never there. Because of work." She added a disapproving stare.

Heller opened his overcoat. He said nothing.

Karin knew what that meant. "Max, we need to worry about our own lives too. No matter what else is happening."

Heller nodded, stroked Karin's arm, and went over to Klaus, who was sitting at the kitchen table, picking out the leftover chaff from a little sack of grains. Heller set a hand on his, a fatherly gesture, yet also the sort of contact that he realized must seem odd to a grown man. But Klaus let Heller keep it there.

"How are you two doing?" Heller asked.

Klaus moved a little to the side, so Heller could sit next to him. "I had to register today. I also got food ration coupons and an employment card for now. I'll get fed at the garrison. My training should start in a week. I'll help Mother out till then. I was able to get a little lard, flour, and barley with your card. And I was in the backyard. If we sawed down that old cherry tree, we'd have wood for a month."

"But we'd have no cherries in the summer," Heller countered. He didn't want to imagine what Frau Marquart would say about this. She loved that tree more than anything.

"We got an invitation," Karin said and handed Heller a letter.

Heller removed the letter from its already-opened envelope. The Soviet Military Administration was inviting them to a cultural evening. The invitation announced nonration dining, and there would be singing and piano music by Prokofiev and Debussy along with some speakers from the Cultural Association. The letter wasn't signed, but Heller was sure Medvedev was behind the invitation. He took a look at the date. "That's only the day after tomorrow."

"I don't have anything to wear," Karin muttered. She wasn't being vain but simply stating the truth—neither of them had formal wear. Perhaps Heller could help himself to some of the late Herr Marquart's clothes, even though most of his pants and shirts would be too small.

"Is everything all right?" Karin asked. Heller nodded. He didn't want to tell her anything in front of Klaus. Then he remembered the pills. He fished the paper bag out of his overcoat and gave it to her. She took it, along with his hand. "Max, what is this?"

Heller tried signaling her with his eyes, but Klaus had already noticed and stood up. "I'll go see how Frau Marquart's doing."

"No, Klaus, you stay, please," Karin told him. "You can put the barley in the water; it'll take a little while for it to swell. I'll go see her. Her fever wasn't quite as high today." She went upstairs.

Heller faced Klaus. "I'm not trying to hide anything from you, Klaus. It's just that I still haven't gotten used to any other way. Under the Nazis, we couldn't ever say the real truth in front of you boys, for fear you might accidentally betray us."

Klaus came over to him from the stove. "I could always hear you two. Even what you told Mother about the Gestapo. I knew who I was going to war for."

Heller lowered his head. What a burden that must have been for his sons, having heard all of that yet knowing they couldn't speak to anyone about it.

Klaus sat back down next to Heller. He looked upset but was trying to keep his composure. "I can't believe how everyone talks!" he blurted out. "Everywhere, in offices and agencies, standing in line, on the street. They still have so much Nazism stuck in their heads. They whisper about Jews, that they're all going to come back and buy everything up, but they also talk about the Russians and how Hitler was betrayed. They believe Göring's the one to blame for all their misery, and Goebbels. They still don't get it, none of them!" He pounded on the table.

Heller nodded, trying to find the right words. Yet everything he could think of sounded like excuses and justifications. Everyone was trying to take care of themselves while not attracting too much attention. There were only a few who dared to resist openly, compared to the many who overacted—denunciating, profiteering, murdering. "They're not all like that," he said eventually, to at least say something. But it wasn't much comfort after having stared reality in the face all day.

Klaus wouldn't calm down. "Is it really so hard to understand? They really don't get where all this misery comes from, who caused it? All they do is whine and moan."

Not all, Heller wanted to say, but Karin had come back. She'd heard what Klaus just said.

"But the Soviets are going about things so clumsily," she said. "They have enough to eat, sure, but they don't share any of it. They let us go hungry. And they take away everything we have—bicycles, cars, machines, whole factories. They shouldn't be surprised people are upset."

Klaus looked up at his mother. "You didn't see what happened in Russia!"

"And people are still being arrested daily."

"Yeah, that's because there are still so many Nazis around acting as if nothing happened."

Heller saw his son tensing up. Karin sat at the table with them.

"But what if they take away everything we have at some point? Or arrest everyone?"

Klaus bristled. "You weren't there, Mother. You should be happy they're even letting us live. They have every right to wipe out our whole country. I saw the beasts, and they were German beasts. I saw what they did—"

"Klaus!" Heller warned him.

"And they weren't just there, these beasts, they were here too, in our homeland, our own country. You didn't know about the camp at Hellerberg? Father never told you about the Gestapo's torture cells? Don't act so stupid, Mother!"

Klaus sprang up and stormed out of the kitchen, but he stopped out in the hallway. He released a stifled sound and seemed to be falling apart. Heller looked to Karin, who sat frozen in horror. He had never felt so helpless. Even though he could sense what Klaus had seen and gone through, he still needed to make it clear to him that they, as a family, had to stick together. He rose beside the kitchen table.

"Klaus," he said softly.

Klaus returned to the kitchen looking remorseful. He placed a hand on the back of his mother's neck. Then he bent down to her, to hug her tight, feeling embarrassed. "I'm so sorry," he said in a low voice.

Karin nodded and wiped the tears from her eyes. "It's all right. But promise me you'll never talk to me that way again."

"Max, what's going on with you?" Karin whispered once they'd finally gone to bed. Heller stared at the ceiling a long while. He turned toward her. It always took time for the down blanket to warm up, and he'd had to rub his cold feet together so much that he regretted not putting socks on. Despite how cold the bathroom was, he had still washed himself, from head to toe, his hair as well. It had taken all the energy he could muster, and yet he considered it a luxury.

The alarm clock was ticking next to him. He could hear Frau Marquart's rattled breathing through the wall, and Klaus was sleeping downstairs on the sofa. The wind blew outside, making the branches of the old cherry tree tap at the window. The last time he'd looked at the thermometer, it had read 1 degree outside.

"I was in the heath today and discovered a group of children," Heller finally said.

"Children?"

"War orphans. They're led by a young man and a girl. He's maybe sixteen; she's just fifteen. Most are sick and riddled with lice. They live in tents and shacks made of branches, leaves. But you won't believe this—they're all armed, even the small children, and are determined not to be taken to a home."

It was quiet for a time.

"Can you do anything for them?" Karin eventually asked.

"Not without the Soviets' help. I don't have access to any such resources."

"So you can't tell them?"

"I can't," Heller said, and the way he stated it told Karin not to keep asking.

"Is it a lot of kids?" Karin asked.

"Ten, maybe more. The youngest are around three."

"Only three? For God's sake."

"And the girl, Fanny, she delivered her own baby. From a Russian."

Karin sat up. "She has a kid? A baby?"

"Yes, a boy. She just had him a few days ago, all on her own, there in a tent. A tiny little thing."

"What age did you say? Fifteen?"

"At the most. She doesn't even know herself exactly."

"Bring her here, Max."

"What?" Heller turned to face Karin.

"You should bring her here. She has a newborn. A baby!" Karin sounded resolute.

"Karin, I don't know if I can trust her. She could rob us blind if we let her in the house."

"Don't you dare go thinking like that, Max," Karin whispered, upset now. "You go there tomorrow and bring her back. It will all work out."

Heller put up more timid resistance. "You said earlier that we needed to start worrying more about ourselves."

"But a baby, Max, just a few days old. You don't want to be responsible for it dying, do you?"

Heller couldn't help thinking about that mound of earth with the cross. "No," he said.

"You bring her here. Promise me."

"All right, Karin, I will. I'll go back tomorrow."

Where were they supposed to put a girl and a baby? he thought. What were they supposed to eat? Could he trust her? That was the big question, and he already knew the answer: he couldn't. But he couldn't just leave her there in the woods with a newborn either.

He had returned to lying on his back and staring at the ceiling. The alarm clock on the nightstand ticked away. Frau Marquart was breathing easier. His feet were still cold.

"Max," Karin said, and her warm hand traveled under the blanket to him. "Come, Max. Come here to me."

February 10, 1947: Early Morning

Oldenbusch was very punctual the next morning, waiting at Heller's front door. After a quick hello, the two men fell silent until they reached the former regional court at Münchner Platz. A Soviet military guard let them pass through the gate so they could park the car in the inner courtyard. After the nearly half-hour entrance procedure, they were finally sitting across from Frau Schlüter in a small interrogation cell.

She wore the same clothes as when she was arrested two days before. Her face was ashen, her hair pulled back tightly but visibly unkempt, her hands shaking. Heller gave Oldenbusch a nod to offer her a cigarette. She grabbed one, looking grateful, let him light it, and took a deep drag. Then she wiped the corners of her eyes with the thumb of the hand holding the cigarette.

"Look what you've done to me," she said in a faint and hopeless voice.

"You could have spared yourself," Heller said, "by telling us about your son in the first place."

"Sure, and for what? So the Russians would arrest him and take him away? I can only hope the boy's smart enough to take off. I've already lost everything anyway. None of it matters anymore—none of it!" Frau Schlüter took another deep drag.

"Let's try to be constructive, Frau Schlüter. Not all is lost. Not even Friedel. You have to cooperate with us. We need to know what crimes he's committed, if any. If we find Friedel, if he appears before a German court as part of our criminal prosecution, we could point to mitigating circumstances. Your son's still young. He'll get one or two years in prison, no more. But this is assuming you cooperate."

She gazed at the tiny windows of her cell. "A German court? Don't make me laugh. Germany doesn't exist anymore. We're a Russian colony, nothing more. An enslaved people."

"Frau Schlüter, your son's life is at stake. If we can't prove his innocence, the Soviets will pin it all on him—the attacks and the murders of Swoboda, the two Soviet officers, and possibly even Armin Weiler."

She stared at Heller in horror. "Murder?"

"Yes, murder. He'd receive fifteen years in prison from a German court. How old is he—fifteen, sixteen? Who can say what the Soviets would do with him? Maybe take him to Bautzen or Siberia. No one knows."

"But he didn't kill anyone!"

"Tell us what you know. Is he responsible for the attack on the Victims of Fascism meeting at the Münchner Krug? We found the same type of hand grenades, as well as leaflets, among the items he was trying to remove from your cellar. Do you think he'd improperly write the word 'Bolshevism' with two *s*'s before the *m*?"

Frau Schlüter took another drag of her cigarette. "He was so excited that someone had attacked that Russian bar. 'Someone's finally doing something,' he said."

"You didn't tell him not to do anything?"

Frau Schlüter lowered her eyes. "What good would that do? He would've done it anyway. He would have attempted something or other. But he didn't want to kill anyone; I know that. He threw the grenades so they'd miss on purpose."

Heller had his doubts about that, but he didn't voice them. "Where did he get them?"

"No idea. I didn't even know he had them."

"So he's not responsible for the attack on the Schwarzer Peter?"

"He was at home, asleep on the sofa. And he didn't kill any Russians. Friedel is no murderer."

"Do you know Armin Weiler?"

"He worked for us, in accounting."

"We found a bag in Friedel's hiding spot. Inside were bloody tools and sawed-off human hands that belonged to Weiler."

Frau Schlüter's eyes widened. She forcefully shook her head. "No, no! Stop this! I don't believe that—it's all a bunch of lies! No one's going to pin that on him."

"He's fully steeped in Nazi propaganda. You yourself were a committed National Socialist; still are. You used Jews as forced labor and denounced people in your neighborhood for not displaying the flag correctly."

"That's what that Frau Dähne wants you to believe!" Frau Schlüter shot back. "That old bag isn't exactly on the straight and narrow herself. She's crazy! Who knows what's going on inside her place? I saw young girls going inside there. Wouldn't be surprised if she was procuring hookers for those pigs."

Heller had resolved to ignore Frau Schlüter's moaning and complaining, but this made him take notice. "What makes you think that?"

"That one-handed man, who works for that Russian bar—Franz the Stub. Everyone in the neighborhood knows him. He used to go in and out of Frau Dähne's. And everyone knows what was going on there wasn't exactly legitimate. I wouldn't be surprised if Franz the Stub had torched that bar himself. That or the Russians, trying to cover something up. And so now they need someone to take the blame."

"You saw girls going in and out of Frau Dähne's? What kind of girls?"

"All kinds. Nobodies. Filthy little sluts. They live in the woods or who knows where and rob people blind. They'll do anything for a meal."

Heller looked over at Oldenbusch and glanced at his notes. Then he gave his junior partner a slight nudge, for him to offer Frau Schlüter another cigarette. She grabbed it without thanks and let him light her up again.

"Where's Friedel?" Heller tried once more.

"I don't know."

"Frau Schlüter, you have to trust me. Tell me where he is."

She leaned forward. "I do not know," she said, stressing each word.

Heller leaned forward now too and looked Frau Schlüter in the eye. "We're the only ones who can help your son. The only way he can be saved is if we find him. Think hard. Where could he be? Does he have a hiding place? Do you have relatives in the city? Or is he hiding in the woods?"

Oldenbusch thought of something. "Maybe he knows those kids?" he whispered in Heller's ear.

But Heller ignored the comment. "Frau Schlüter, your son's life is at stake. He needs to eat, sleep. He might need you for something and come back. He'd end up running right into the arms of one of those policemen posted around the house. He might come creeping up at night and get shot dead by a Soviet soldier. All sorts of things could happen, and sooner or later one of them will."

Frau Schlüter showed no reaction. She considered her half-smoked cigarette as if just now realizing she was smoking it, contorted her mouth into a bitter smile, and stubbed out the butt on the tabletop. "We'll see about that."

Heller chided Oldenbusch after the interrogation. "Can you just keep your thoughts to yourself until we're alone?"

"Sorry for that. It suddenly hit me and came out before I knew it."

The two walked down the long corridor, passing the cells where two years ago people had sat waiting for the sentencing that would condemn them, all because they'd supposedly hidden Jews, shown themselves "hostile to military power," spied, uttered defeatist comments, or behaved in other ways damaging to the Third Reich. Now people sat waiting here again under lock and key. There certainly were actual criminal Nazis among them, yet many had simply been denounced and had no real way of defending themselves against the seemingly arbitrary Soviet denazification process.

"That Frau Schlüter is really stubborn," Oldenbusch said to mitigate their gloomy mood. The car didn't want to start on the first try.

"She doesn't trust us. And maybe she really doesn't know," Heller said. He had calmed down and was glad Oldenbusch hadn't gotten his feelings hurt.

"What about what she said about Frau Dähne? Should we look into it?"

"I'll go see her." Heller thought about that and went over his list of tasks for the day. "I definitely need to go back into the woods, to that secret camp. We have to speak with Gutmann again, and I want to see Kasrashvili too. And I can't forget to go to the coal office." He vacillated a moment before reaching a decision. "Wait here a moment, Werner," he ordered and stepped out of the car.

Ovtcharov poured tea into his cup. "People have told me that you always find a way to get your voice heard."

"Well, since I was already here I thought it was worth a try." Heller caught himself staring at the warm tea and made himself look away.

Ovtcharov's office wasn't nearly as large and imposing as Medvedev's. It was a normal office, with filing cabinets and metal shelving full of folders and binders, dull yellow curtains over the window, and a portrait of Stalin on the wall, a fatherly smile dancing on his lips. It smelled like stale smoke. The red flag behind Ovtcharov was the only dash of color in an otherwise drab backdrop.

The Russian stirred his tea, then pulled out a cigarette and lit it.

"So what do you want? To make a report? A strong woman, this Frau Schlüter."

"She is, yes."

Ovtcharov smiled. "It's admirable, all the pride you have, and how tough you are on yourself. I like that, Comrade Oberkommissar."

"The term 'pride' isn't of much use to me. Pride only creates suffering."

Ovtcharov was about to disagree, then gave it another thought. He pointed at Heller. "What do you want? I haven't been able to learn any more from this Schliter woman."

"I'd like something else from you."

Ovtcharov sat down and looked at Heller with amusement.

"I have to get a better picture of what sort of dealings the two murdered officers had. Cherin and Berinov. I have to know who they were friends with. When and how often they visited the Schwarzer Peter, and who else was with them. On top of that, I have to request that you provide me with a report on Captain Kasrashvili's conduct, anyone he surrounded himself with, his habits. I'm also requesting that you proceed with caution and discretion."

"This is what you request? Do you suspect Kasrashvili of something? And why so cautious?"

"His name comes up repeatedly in connection with my investigation. There's solid suspicion that he's peddling medication from Soviet stocks."

Ovtcharov didn't look convinced. "Kasrashvili has gotten himself into trouble many a time. He's been demoted twice already for negligent behavior. There were suspicions that Russian officers lost their lives because of his misdiagnoses and improper treatment, but these could not be confirmed. The concerns of the Soviet Union certainly don't seem to interest him all that much."

Heller felt forced to come to the Georgian's defense a little. "He's more of a musician by passion, not a doctor, a soldier even less." He stopped talking, unsatisfied by his choice of words—he didn't need to make the situation even worse.

"Well, none of us is doing what we'd like. The war made soldiers of us all."

Heller started over. "Did you know that Kasrashvili's father is a famous concert pianist?"

"Was. He's dead. He was shot in '38, in a purge ordered by Marshal Stalin." Ovtcharov let his words sink in a little, blowing cigarette smoke out of the corner of this mouth and tapping ashes onto his saucer. "Now, Comrade Oberkommissar, do you have any other information? Since you just happen to be here."

Heller cleared his throat and tried to find the right words. "Have you ever considered that the attack on the Schwarzer Peter was done to cover something up? Possibly by a member of the Soviet Armed Forces? According to Gutmann's statement, there was a dispute between Berinov, Cherin, and a certain Franz Swoboda."

"Franz the Stub." Ovtcharov picked up a file from a stack on his desk. "Vasili Cherin once told one of my men that this Swoboda was a war criminal but never wanted to discuss it any further. This was about ten days ago. We did find out that Swoboda was depending on Gutmann for drugs and did dirty work for him. Swoboda was considered unpredictable and truly violent. According to witnesses, when Cherin was drunk he threatened to ship Swoboda to Siberia. We weren't able to pursue this, since Cherin was found dead."

This amazed Heller. "It sounds like you've been running an investigation for some time."

"Naturally, when a member of our Soviet Armed Forces is killed. Our initial suspicions fell on Gutmann. But he has a strong alibi for the night Berinov died. He has friends in certain circles, people who are impossible for me to act against."

"High military circles, you mean?"

Ovtcharov just stared at Heller.

"So you do know what was happening in that bar?"

Ovtcharov said nothing, but his reaction was answer enough.

"You want to avoid a scandal at all costs, is that it?"

Ovtcharov sucked on his cigarette, burning down the last of his butt. Heller felt the man wanted to tell him something but didn't trust his own department.

"I will give you the files from our investigation, Kasrashvili's file too," Ovtcharov said. "However, it is crucial, Comrade Heller, that you do not mix the one matter with the other while you follow all leads."

"But what would you have done," Heller said, "had Berinov not been found dead and I didn't happen to end up on this case?"

"You did not 'happen to end up on this case,' Heller, so do not fool yourself. Now goodbye."

Public Prosecutor Speidel carefully ran his fingers along his part as he paged through the Russian investigation files. Heller observed him. He wasn't sure what Speidel could really do with the material. After a few minutes Speidel looked up, chewing on his lower lip, deep in thought.

"You have access to amazing sources," Speidel said. "It's clear to you that we're stepping into a minefield, yes?"

Heller didn't answer.

"According to your theory, Cherin and Berinov were regulars at Gutmann's bar. Cherin got into a dispute with Swoboda. Swoboda followed Cherin and stabbed him to death. After that, Berinov killed Swoboda, cutting off his head for revenge. After that, Gutmann would've killed Berinov to take revenge for Swoboda, wouldn't he?"

"It's just one possible scenario. Gutmann could've easily killed them both. Maybe he was even contracted to do it. Even so, Armin Weiler doesn't fit in the scenario, or he played a role we don't yet know about. We haven't found his corpse—only his hands."

"Let's leave Weiler out of it for now. How was Gutmann supposed to have managed it all physically? Sure, he's big, but he's not that strong;

more the flabby type, right? Judging from all we know about Swoboda, he was much brawnier and very strong. And how was Gutmann supposed to have gotten close enough to Berinov while wielding a bayonet, then attack him, without Berinov putting up a fight?"

Heller considered Speidel's objections irrelevant. "For one: someone actually did it this way. Two: Berinov had a prick on his upper arm. The murderer could have surprised him with an injection of Evipan and waited until he was sedated before stabbing him in the neck. Of course, it could also have been someone else, but we did find the medicine and needles at Gutmann's."

"Out in the open? And why didn't he take the backpack with him?" Speidel's skepticism was clear.

"Well, perhaps he was surprised by workers heading home from the late shift and had to flee. Like I said, it's only a hypothesis. We have two dead Soviets, some body parts from two dead Germans, a dead girl, rumors of a second dead girl, yet no concrete evidence or witness statements. It seems like all I do is wander the city following up on incidents. Unless we can come up with something more plausible, we might as well stick to this scenario. I've seen murderers with less motive, Herr Public Prosecutor. I'm happy to hear all your suggestions. I plan to question Gutmann again this afternoon. He caved a little yesterday evening once I made it clear that he could easily be charged with certain crimes—homicide, failure to assist, fencing stolen goods, and immoral behavior." Heller didn't want to reveal anything about Fanny for now. He'd pursue the lead just as soon as he could leave the prosecutor's office.

"About the Gutmann issue," Speidel said, avoiding Heller's gaze and brushing imaginary dust from his lapel instead.

Heller sat up in his chair, resolved not to give this former Nazi even an inch of room.

"Gutmann's free," Speidel said.

Heller stared at Speidel in disbelief. "That can't be. A young woman, just a kid, died in his building. He admitted to attempting to cover up her death. We also had solid suspicion that he'd suppressed evidence related to Swoboda's death."

"I know all this, Comrade Oberkommissar. I wasn't the one who released him. Nor a judge. Someone from the SMAD secured his release. Someone way up high."

"How long has he been out?"

"Since around seven a.m."

"Has anyone been assigned to track his movements?"

"I only learned of his release after the fact. And, Heller, between you and me? We'd be risking our own necks if we had him followed now."

"Just assuming Gutmann believes he's the main suspect, wouldn't he try to get rid of any other witnesses?" Heller was thinking about Kasrashvili, among others.

"If he were smart, he'd relocate to the west," Speidel said.

"He wasn't released so he could take off. Someone instructed him to clean house!" Heller rose and leaned across the table to take back the files Ovtcharov had given him. He wondered who in the SMAD had the most to gain from keeping the German population's emotions in check. A couple of names came to mind.

With every step closer to the Dresden Heath, Heller felt more exposed. Apart from the slice of bread inside his overcoat that was supposed to be his lunch, he hadn't been able to rustle up anything he could take to the children. It would have been impossible to ask Karin to donate something, since they only lived on what little they obtained during the day. He knew only too well how Karin scrimped and saved just to provide him with that tiny bit of extra sometimes; he knew she was giving

Frau Marquart some of what little broth she had left, even though the sick woman still kept spitting it out. And there was always that fear they wouldn't be able to scavenge anything today, or the next day. There were no reserves left, not anywhere. What if Karin were to become sick? What if she couldn't continue because of hunger or exhaustion? She was barely more than a shadow of herself already. She had felt so small in the night, so fragile.

He walked down Bischofsweg and onto Priessnitz Path and continued under the tall Carola-Allee overpass. Seeing it reminded him yet again that at the end of the war people in despair had jumped to their deaths from there because they couldn't bear the downfall of the German Reich and so deeply feared Russian retaliation.

There was another reason Heller felt exposed. He had given Oldenbusch his pistol for safekeeping because he intended to show the children that he meant what he'd said. For the same reason, he had ordered Oldenbusch not to follow him or make any attempt to search for him. He'd told Oldenbusch to keep an eye on Gutmann instead.

Heller knew he was putting himself in great danger. The boy, Jörg, was ready for anything and had posted his own guards. It was clear he was committed to protecting his little community. All the younger children had known was a life of battling for survival, a struggle that might have turned them into murderers. And did Jörg love Fanny? She'd given birth to a Russian's baby, one that he believed was his. What if he'd found out and already taken his revenge?

Heller had walked for nearly half an hour and had followed the creek for a good while when he suddenly heard a crackling sound. He peered around for the spot where Fanny had crossed the stream. Was he already being followed? He made himself continue on as if everything was normal, fighting the urge to take cover or hide. But the children had to see that he wasn't up to anything. He kept hearing a soft crackling and crunching, the same sound his footsteps made on the dead leaves.

Could someone be hiding behind the trees with a gun aimed at him? Heller continued a little farther along the creek. It had grown dim. Clouds covered the sky, and a light snowfall was beginning. He didn't need that.

Two people approached, a man and a woman of indeterminate age. They carried bundles of deadwood on their backs. Heller squeezed into the bushes and waited for them to pass. Only then did he continue, eventually finding the spot along the creek where he could reach the other side by jumping stone to stone. He made his way across, slipped on the last stone, and nearly fell in before taking an awkward leap onto the other bank. A deep pain shot through his right ankle. Limping along, his hands now raised to show his peaceful intentions, he trudged up the slope. Heller stumbled when his foot got caught on some roots, yet he kept his hands above his head. He finally reached the crest of the little hill concealing the camp on the other side. He slowly lowered his arms. The camp was empty.

It was a possibility he'd considered, but he was still disappointed. He slowly made his way down the other side of the hill. The tents had been taken down and removed, with only a few dark spots showing where they had stood. The snow would soon cover that too. The camp-fires had long gone cold, the shelter pulled down, the supports knocked over, the soil collapsed. Heller took a stick and poked at a few holes in the ground, pushing aside a pile of leaves without knowing what he was looking for. He discovered a pit containing garbage and tin cans as well as cooked and smashed bones. He spotted skeletons of squirrels or rats, but also larger bones, and the longer he looked at them, the more he feared they were human. Radial and ulna bones from an arm, possibly. He would've liked to banish the thought, but he couldn't.

He followed a few vague tracks that led to the narrow stream before disappearing. The children must have waded through the water, but Heller couldn't tell if they had gone up or downstream.

What could they have done with the sick? Carried them on their backs? One thing was clear: they had gone away because of him.

Heller eventually accepted that it didn't make any sense to continue his search. He wouldn't find the children here, not now. The heath and its roughly twenty-three square miles weren't exactly a vast impenetrable forest, but the area was large and confusing enough to hide in. It would take hundreds of police to comb through it, but even that left a way out through open fields on three sides, toward Ullersdorf, Radeberg, and Langebrück. It was hopeless.

Disappointed and exhausted, Heller made his way back. Thick snowfall set in, which wouldn't make it easier for the little group to survive. Their camp was sure to be even farther removed from civilization now. They would have to erect shelters and get settled in all over again. Even if the temperature did start climbing and spring came a few weeks early, these children were facing a bitter struggle.

Heller started to head back the way he had come in but then decided against crossing Priessnitz Creek in the same place. The danger of slipping and falling was too great. He kept following the stream instead, taking shortcuts at the major bends. He reached another trail that crossed his and rose steeply, leading up to the military cemetery, he guessed. From there it wasn't far to the garrison where Kasrashvili was posted. Before he could decide, he noticed movement on the opposite bank. He took cover and watched a person dressed in black approach. It was clearly a man, seemingly unarmed, yet clearly not the usual wood gatherer from the way he was acting. He kept stopping to look around, then hurried on. Heller thought he had seen the man somewhere before, or at least recognized the way he was moving. He let him pass and then followed at a distance.

After a strenuous hike that demanded Heller's complete attention, they finally reached Bischofsweg, which the man, looking determined, took until Kamenzer Strasse. They continued on down before making a slight turn into what became Martin Luther Strasse.

And suddenly Heller knew whom he was following. The man in front of him had just crossed Martin Luther Platz and was heading for the church. There he pulled a key out of his pocket and entered the building through a side entrance. Heller waited a few moments, looked at his watch, then followed the pastor through the large main portal into Martin Luther Church.

February 10, 1947: Early Afternoon

The tall edifice gave Heller a somber and chilly reception. It had survived the bombings nearly unscathed. Dull colored light streamed in from the smaller stained-glass windows of the apse. The broken large round windows in the transept were patched with wood, only a few thin rays of light breaching the cracks. Candles burned at the altar.

Martin Luther Church was large, with plenty of seating. Heller walked along the pews. Ever since the First World War, he had entered a church on only a few occasions. There were the weddings of his two best friends, both of whom lost their lives in February '45 along with their families, and his own wedding—like Karin wanted, having promised this to her mother, who'd passed away far too young. It was in the trenches of Belgium that he had lost the final shreds of the faith his own mother had once given him.

It had been a small wedding. Karin became an orphan after her father's kidneys had failed and led to his agonizing death in the hospital. Heller's parents had been sick then as well, looking so thin and shrunken, like an elderly couple, even though they hadn't even reached sixty years old. His mother had tears in her eyes, already sensing that she would never live to see her grandchildren.

Heller cast aside these memories and looked around. This house of God held only a few visitors. An old woman with a headscarf sat in one of the front pews. Farther back, off to the side, sat an older man who stared ahead in silent devotion. Heller could make out a few others in the darkness.

Instead of walking up to the altar, he made his way left along one of the pews and waited under a gallery in the dark to see what would happen. After a few minutes, the door to the sacristy opened, and the pastor came out. He wore a black suit with the collar, and his hair was parted. Taking gentle steps, he approached the old woman near the front, greeted her, exchanged a few whispers, and nodded. Then he turned to the altar, switched out the burned-down candles, and lit the new ones. When he tried to return to the sacristy, Heller stood in his way.

The pastor looked startled. "Can I—I know you. You're the police detective."

"Oberkommissar Heller. I have to speak with you, now. It's urgent."

The pastor took a good look around the nave, then nodded. He invited Heller into the sacristy and locked the door behind him using a key.

Heller looked around the small room. It was fitted with built-in cabinets, their door handles holding various vestments on hangers, and had a large safe and a massive oak table with various candleholders, chalices, and altar candlesticks, as well as boxes and packages. More boxes were piled on the floor. All told, the room seemed more like a storeroom, chaotic and disorderly. And among all this was a made bed—the pastor evidently lived here. Through the high-up window, Heller could see that the snow was coming down even harder. And that the window had bars on it. He turned to the pastor.

"Your name, please."

"Beger, Christian."

"Birth date?"

"August 20, 1910."

Heller wrote this in his notebook, which he then laid on the table, his pencil next to it.

"Herr Beger, I followed you here from the woods," Heller began. He didn't have much time. "I know you were with the children. I discovered that group yesterday. Today the camp was gone. Tell me where the children are. You know."

The pastor stared at Heller. "I couldn't find them today either."

Heller gave him a stern look. "Your backpack was empty on the way back. That means you brought them something to eat in the pack, I assume." Heller grabbed one of the boxes and pulled out a can of ham. Canned foods were stacked up in other boxes too. "I found the exact same cans in the children's trash." He'd seen the same cans on Gutmann's shelves too. It was possible Fanny had obtained them from there.

The pastor was beginning to look less certain. "How can I trust you? How do I know you won't sic the Russians on those children?"

"Listen. I'm worried about the infant. I'd like to persuade Fanny to come to my home. A mother and child can't stay out there."

The pastor blinked erratically, his narrow shoulders drooping as if the burden of his heartache were dragging them down. "What concern is it of yours?"

Heller didn't like putting so much pressure on the man, but he had to. "Two kids there are severely ill. They're already getting delirious. They might have died already."

The pastor squinted. He was battling himself, searching for words. He wiped his eyes, embarrassed. "I'm trying to help. I take them all I can. I give them what I can spare."

"Shouldn't you be making sure the children end up in a safer place with proper care?"

"You don't think I've tried? It's impossible. Jörg, their leader, won't allow it. He watches after them like they're his own children. Though, believe me, they're not doing much worse out there than here in the city." Beger had to fight back his tears again, and Heller couldn't blame him. He could only imagine all the misery the young pastor saw each day.

"But they're sick and undernourished, full of bugs and lice. They're literally being eaten alive."

"What do you know?" Beger barked. "Talk is cheap. No one wants them. No one has any compassion, not even for the littlest ones. People hit them, even shoot at them. They're alone. Don't you understand? Alone and abandoned. It breaks my heart seeing them like this. The youngest ones have forgotten they even had a mother and father. Some don't even know their own names . . ." The pastor's voice broke. His face was ashen, his worry digging deep creases into his otherwise boyish face. He took a deep breath and tried to regain control.

"But there are homes," Heller tried in a calmer tone.

Beger snorted and hissed a cynical laugh. "You know what these homes are? They're little more than child prisons. There's no love there. None at all. As if they were criminals, as if they had any choice about their fate."

"But aren't there Christian . . ." Heller saw the pastor's look and stopped himself. He wasn't exactly providing much insight. "This Jörg, he seems very dangerous."

Beger leaned against the door to stretch his back, frowning from the pain. "He knows no rules. He's an orphan, and fending for himself is all he's ever known."

"Do you think he's capable of murder?"

Beger hesitated again, gazing up at the ceiling as if hoping to find help there. "He's dangerous because he's so naïve, because he'd like to be her protector. Because he was raised to be a Nazi through and through. But he doesn't know any better. None of them know any better."

"He loves Fanny, am I right? Do you know if Fanny knew Gutmann, or if she ever prostituted herself for him? Do you know who fathered the child?"

Beger pushed off from the door. His face hardened. "Fanny told me you were looking to question them. Whatever else Jörg might have done, he does protect the children, and he looks after her. I don't want to know what would happen to him if the Russians caught him. And even less what would happen to those children."

The pastor moved to leave, but he had locked the door and first had to fiddle awkwardly with the key, which didn't want to turn, so he used his other hand to help.

Heller placed a foot against the door. "I don't want to tell anyone about the children. I don't want to hand them over to the Russians. I don't even want to know where they are. I only want Fanny and the baby. We will care for them, my wife and I. The girl needs to see a doctor. She has the clap, and she gave it to her child."

Beger yanked on the door handle in anger, but Heller was stronger.

"No," Beger said. "You can't demand that of me. I don't trust you. And Jörg wouldn't allow it anyway. You should be glad he even let you live."

"I'm coming back tomorrow, at six in the morning. So we can go together. I'll bring something to eat. I do mean well. You need to trust me."

Beger yanked on the door again, and Heller let him pass.

"I'm not doing it. I won't!"

Heller passed back through the open door into the nave of the church. The front pews were empty. The old woman from earlier had just left, the large main entrance door now closing.

"Early tomorrow morning. I'll be here, and I'm coming alone," Heller told Beger again gently. The pastor withdrew into his room without a word and locked the door, and Heller strode quickly out of the church.

The snowfall had let up. Heller stood on Martin Luther Platz, looked around, and spotted the old woman, who was just about to turn onto the next cross street. He looked at his watch and sighed. An unbearable hunger nagged at him. In his pocket was the bread, spread with liverwurst, wrapped in wax paper. But he wanted to save it for as long as he could. Hands in his overcoat pockets, he walked down the steps at the front of the church, following the old woman. She walked while leaning slightly on a cane, her overcoat practically reaching the ground. He didn't hurry to catch up. Once he'd reached her, he glanced at her from the side, acting surprised.

"Frau Dähne?"

"Herr Oberkommissar," she said.

"May I escort you home, on account of the weather?"

"You'd take the trouble of going all that way? That's quite nice of you."

Heller offered an arm, and the old lady took it.

"You know Pastor Beger well?" Heller asked. "Didn't he join the parish after the war?"

"No, he was already here in '44, when Pastor Kühnel died."

"He's still young. He never got called up?"

"No, he wasn't fit for service, something to do with his back."

Frau Dähne seemed willing to talk.

"He hands out food every Sunday," Heller said. "I wonder where he gets it."

"Alms from good Christians and people who'd like to be."

"You mean people who wish to clear their conscience?"

"Yes. So many try to buy their way to salvation. At any rate, he's always up to something, our good pastor. A fine man. He only needs to learn to handle his emotions better. He doesn't deal with the suffering of others very well. And that's something one should be able to do if one hopes to comfort others, don't you think?"

Heller didn't reply. Genuine compassion always seemed better than false comfort.

They walked along in silence until Louisenstrasse. Then Heller got back to it.

"Are you getting along all right, all alone in the ruins?"

"I can't complain," Frau Dähne replied.

Heller took a long deep breath and tensed inside. "Does Fanny visit often?" he asked and felt her arm, still linked with his, put up a little resistance.

"I give her something to eat when I can," Frau Dähne said in a low voice.

"Does she visit regularly?"

"She comes and goes when she wants. Poor child. She's an orphan."

They had turned up Kamenzer Strasse.

"And Josef Gutmann, you know him?"

Again it seemed as if the old woman faltered, though she might have only slipped a little on the icy sidewalk.

"Everyone in the neighborhood knows him, at least since his bar was destroyed."

"Is it possible that Friedel Schlüter had contact with him?"

"Contact? You mean because Gutmann ratted on them?"

That startled Heller. "Ratted on them—you mean denounced them as Nazis?"

"Isn't that what they say? That Gutmann joined the Communist Party right after the Russians marched in, then promptly denounced the Schlüters as Nazis."

"But everyone had to know they were Nazis. After all, their printing company had become a big business, growing fat from the war economy, using lots of forced labor."

Frau Dähne stopped and looked up at Heller. "Knowing that is one thing. Betraying it to the Russians is another. It's possible that was his way of gaining entry into the Communist Party. Right after the Russians came he was running around wearing a red armband with Antifa on it."

Heller stared at the little old lady, thinking things over. What she was telling him threw a whole new light on the attack on Gutmann's bar. Could Friedel be more than simply a misguided young man, far more dangerous than assumed? Yet why that ridiculous spelling mistake on the leaflet? Could someone be manipulating events?

"Let's keep going," Heller said. "Is it true that the one-handed man, Franz Swoboda, used to come and go from your house?"

Frau Dähne sighed. "After he returned from the war, he was assigned a room at my home. He soon found a new place to stay, though. After the air raids, he visited me now and then and helped me repair the damage. But I haven't seen him for a long time."

Heller kept silent, waiting for the old woman to tell him more. They had reached the intersection of Kamenzer Strasse and Nordstrasse. It wasn't much farther now.

"Would you have anything against my taking a look inside your home?"

"Inside what's left of it," Frau Dähne corrected him. "What are you hoping to find?"

Heller didn't answer. Nordstrasse rose a little. It was slippery, and Frau Dähne held his arm tightly while sliding around.

"Tell me, what do you want from the pastor?" she asked.

Heller considered what he should reveal, despite suspecting that she already knew far more than she was letting on.

"My wife would like to take in Fanny and the baby. The pastor's refusing to make it happen. He's afraid of betraying the group."

"I can take care of it."

"What?" Heller stopped and stared at her in astonishment.

"I can persuade Fanny that it's best for her and the baby," Frau Dähne stated with utmost confidence. "I know where she's staying at this time of day."

"Then tell me!"

Frau Dähne shook her head. "No, I'll go alone. Now. You can take a look at my house in the meantime."

"And she trusts you?"

Frau Dähne grimaced, then nodded. "I think so."

"You can go first. I'll follow you at a safe distance."

"You sure are an awfully stubborn man! Do what you need to, but if Fanny notices that you're following me, she'll disappear."

"How about we take our chances?" Heller said.

"Very well, but we'll have to go back the same way."

They continued walking together, back down Kamenzer along Alaun Park. Then Heller gave Frau Dähne a head start. He waited until she had reached the intersection at Bischofsweg, then followed her at a proper distance. A blaring horn made him start. He looked up and saw Oldenbusch in the black Ford. The car was swerving along the snow-covered cobblestones, its nearly treadless tires offering no grip on the slippery surface. Heller jumped to the side to play it safe. Oldenbusch braked and slid the car sideways up against the sidewalk. He then leaned over and pushed the passenger door open.

"Max, finally!"

"What's wrong? You're driving like a madman. Can it wait?"

"It can't!" Oldenbusch shouted and shot off as soon as Heller climbed into the car.

"You been looking for me long?"

"A few minutes now. I was making a second round on the off chance I'd find you. Gutmann's dead in his bar, hanged. Suicide, looks like."

"Looks like?" Heller said.

Oldenbusch nodded.

"Stop next to that old woman real quick, Werner."

"Is that the Dähne woman?"

"Frau Dähne, yes."

Heller rolled down the window. "Frau Dähne, I need to go. It's urgent. When you find Fanny, tell her to wait for me at the edge of Dresden Heath, at Waldschlösschen. She knows where. At five o'clock!"

February 10, 1947: Early Afternoon

Oldenbusch parked the car a little way up Alaunstrasse, near the court-yard entrance where they had carried out the dead girl.

"Didn't you post any men?" Heller asked warily, seeing no policemen.

"Two of them. Made it inconspicuous so we don't have another crowd this time."

Heller nodded and climbed out. "So who found him?" he asked across the roof of the car.

"The back door to the bar was left open. And old man from the neighborhood noticed; we got his personal details. He repeatedly called inside to no answer. So he went and grabbed a patrol cop. That's who found Gutmann."

Heller and Oldenbusch used the street entrance to reach the back courtyard. They made their way along the rear of the buildings to the Schwarzer Peter. A policeman was waiting there at the door and saluted.

"Nothing further to report," he announced.

"You found him?" Heller asked. "Did you touch anything?"

"The light switch, Herr Oberkommissar, but with a glove on. I checked the body for vital signs, but he was already cold. All I touched was his wrist."

Heller nodded, entered the bar, and found himself inside that narrow hallway again, the one leading to Gutmann's storeroom, his office, and the disguised door to the stairway. Heller kept right and then left until he was standing in the main bar area, where a slight reek of urine hung in the air. Oldenbusch followed. Two bare bulbs burned dimly above the bar; Heller was surprised that Gutmann had been able to get those lights working again in the three days since the attack. They bathed Gutmann's massive corpse, dressed in dark pants and a white shirt, in a sickly yellow light. Heller, who could only see the dead man's back, had Oldenbusch hand him a flashlight so he could shine light on the floor around the body. He spotted a row of damp spots, likely from the snow that had melted off the policeman's boots. Below Gutmann's sock-clad feet, a tipped-over chair lay in a larger puddle. The insides of Gutmann's pant legs were dark with moisture. His arms dangled limply, his palms facing out and his fingers stretched in odd angles.

Heller directed the flashlight to the ceiling. The thin rope Gutmann hung from had been thrown around one of the partially scorched beams. The other length stretched down to the radiator below the window and was threaded through the ribs and crudely tied off. This was all doable for one person, Heller reckoned.

He made a wide arc around the hanged man, pulled a table over, and climbed atop it to get a closer look at the noose around Gutmann's neck. It was knotted amateurishly, not a hangman's knot. Only now did he take a moment to look Gutmann over.

The rope had dug deep into his neck. Dark red bruises and scratch marks showed how hard Gutmann must have tried to slip his fingers under the rope, struggling in vain not to die. The dead man's stiff face reflected all the torture that being suffocated must have inflicted on him. His eyes bulged, his mouth was contorted, and his swollen tongue stuck out. It must have been a slow death. Heller knew that many strangulation victims lost consciousness because their carotid artery had been squeezed flat. In Gutmann's case, though, the noose had obviously strangled only his throat. He must have fought for minutes on end before finally losing strength. One last spasm had then made his limbs jut out.

Heller climbed back down from the table and shined the light on the tips of Gutmann's fingers. They were chafed, with broken fingernails.

Oldenbusch couldn't stand the quiet any longer. "To save himself, he would've had to pull himself up to the beam, hang on to it, and undo the noose. That certainly doesn't look very likely considering this thin rope and his body size. Me, I can barely manage a pull-up."

"Doesn't the fact that he struggled not to choke to death point to evidence of murder? It's also possible that he first meant to kill himself, then changed his mind." Heller said this knowing that Oldenbusch, being his assistant, wouldn't choose the easy answer.

"No, I think—"

Heller raised a hand. He first needed to gain his own impression. He carefully observed the corpse using the flashlight's beam.

"Is there a suicide note?" he asked as he gave his full attention to the cuffs of Gutmann's sleeves.

"There is, written by typewriter. Should I read it to you?"

"By typewriter? He has a typewriter?"

Oldenbusch nodded. "In his office. I've already taken a look. There's a high likelihood the typing comes from that machine—the small *r* is damaged; it makes a hole in the paper when struck. There are fingerprints on the keys. I'm assuming Gutmann only typed with two fingers, so a comparison shouldn't take long. The paper came from his desk too."

Heller listened without taking his eyes off the sleeves. On the fabric of both he discovered fine fibers that could have come from the rough hemp rope. He knelt and searched the floor around the chair and the puddle of urine for more fibers—and found what he needed.

"Just like I thought, Werner: someone tied him up, hanged him, then severed his restraints."

Oldenbusch came closer. "But wouldn't he have resisted? Why didn't he scream?"

Heller looked around again. At a table across from the body, one chair wasn't in the same position as the others. Heller sat down there without moving the chair. Had the murderer sat here watching Gutmann struggle as he died? Heller sat a few more seconds, then climbed back onto the table to inspect Gutmann up close. He shined light on Gutmann's mouth, looking for fibers or any clue that the bar owner had been gagged. But he couldn't find anything. Acting on impulse, he started searching the dead man's upper arms and shoulders. He carefully touched the body, rotated it very gently, then held it in place. He finally found what he was looking for.

"You overlooked this," Heller said, waving Oldenbusch over, and shined the flashlight on a tiny red spot on Gutmann's upper sleeve.

"Let's take him down," he ordered.

Oldenbusch sighed.

Heller climbed off the table. He placed a chair close to the dead man and immediately climbed up on that.

"Hold him tight by the stomach; I'll grab him under the arms and cut through the rope. Then we'll lay him on top of the bar. Do we have a knife?"

Oldenbusch got a knife, handed it to Heller, and grabbed the corpse around the torso. He let out a slight groan from the weight. Sliding his right arm under Gutmann's armpit, Heller leaned his head to the side to avoid getting the dead man's hair in his face, then sliced through the rope. The body slumped down. Oldenbusch wheezed from the strain but held on tight. Together they maneuvered the corpse over to the bar. Oldenbusch snorted and blew air out his cheeks, then had to take a seat.

"No excuses, Werner. Help me open his shirt." Heller started working on the buttons. Together they pulled the shirt over the dead man's head.

"Clearly a needle prick," Oldenbusch stated after brief inspection. "So he was sedated. Why tie him up?"

"To me, it looks like he was being tortured. The murderer let him hang there awhile before cutting off his restraints, so he could watch him struggle as he died."

"But how did the perpetrator get him up there? I could barely hold him, and I was only trying to pull him down."

"He pulled him up by the rope around his neck. You can see where rope rubbed against the beam up there. You can see it on the radiator too. And the way leverage works, it wouldn't have been as heavy with the rope at that length. It's the same as using a pulley. Maybe the perpetrator wasn't alone either. The chair was probably tipped over to make it look like a suicide. I'm sure it's the same with the suicide note. Show it to me."

Oldenbusch reached for the page and handed it to Heller.

"I'm a bastard," Heller read. *"A murderer. A disgrace to my parents. What's the point of living such a nasty life? There isn't one! May the Lord have mercy on me."*

Heller pursed his lips and scanned the text once more. "No sign of a break-in?"

"Neither at the front nor the back door. Maybe Gutmann knew the person and trusted them."

"Or someone had a key. Maybe the same person who murdered Swoboda. Or someone surprised him as he was entering the bar. Or they gained entry using a weapon. Werner, we should be clear about what we're doing here." Heller handed the page back to Oldenbusch.

Oldenbusch sat down again. "You mean, how best to deal with this? Max, you think the Soviets have a hand in this?"

"Not all. One or a few of them. Gutmann himself warned me to steer clear. I'm not sure who among the Soviets would be authorized to have Gutmann released."

"But that note, it has no mistakes in it," Oldenbusch offered.

"That doesn't explain anything. All it shows is a good knowledge of German. And that rope? Where do people get something like that these days? It's not a clothesline."

"But why cover up a murder so amateurishly? Why even go to the trouble? Does the perpetrator not think we're capable?"

Heller shrugged. He had to think hard about how to proceed. Someone had committed this murder without caring if the crime was discovered. Someone who felt safe or, even worse, was mocking him.

"All right, Werner, let's do it this way. We'll treat this case the way the murderer wants it to look: Josef Gutmann took his own life. That's how we'll pass it off, how the prosecutor will know of it. Let the perpetrator consider himself in the clear."

Oldenbusch, not satisfied, grimaced. "Or another possibility is that he knows we're playing with marked cards and is just toying with us the way he played with Gutmann. We'll end up bumped off too. Max, the Russians don't mess around—you're in Siberia before you know it."

"Speculating won't get us anywhere, Werner. Officially ignoring Gutmann's death isn't an option. We must do something. So get things under way like we discussed. I have my other appointment—I have to make sure I'm at the meeting place in time. I don't want to miss the girl." Heller started to leave, then came back holding up his index finger.

"Come to think of it, Werner. Go ahead and delay it for a bit. Take fingerprints, secure evidence, but only report the case to the public prosecutor's office *after* Niesbach has left for the day. I want to see if anyone brings it up with me before it's official."

February 10, 1947: Late Afternoon

It was still well below freezing, as it had been for days. Heller was starting to worry about feeling so cold all the time. Something was off, as if he had an illness coming on. He tried not to think about Frau Marquart's nightly coughing attacks.

He'd just made it to Waldschlösschen on time. His legs ached from his rushed march to the streetcar stop and valiant leap onto the car's platform as it departed. He checked his watch again. It was past five. He would give Fanny a half hour more, though he immediately regretted his decision, as each minute dragged on. He'd already let two streetcars pass. How easily he could've stepped onto one and been at home by now, sitting before the stove. Sometimes his adherence to principle made him mad at himself.

He bounced on the balls of his feet, raised his shoulders high, and buried his face in his scarf. He wouldn't be able to wait another half hour. Fifteen minutes maybe.

"I been watching you a long time," said a voice off to the side. Heller swung around. Fanny had crept up from behind. She wore her long coat, the baby clearly bundled underneath. A strong smell came off her.

"I'm glad you came, Fanny," Heller said.

"Sigrid, she tells me you're wanting to take me home and give me food and that. That'd be better for him." She pointed at her bundle. "Me, I just don't know if I can trust you. Jörg, he'd like to kill you off, was what he said." She gave Heller a defiant stare.

"You can trust me," Heller said.

"He'd go bump you right off, he hears I'm with you."

"Then he doesn't need to find out. I'd like to take you and your baby to see a doctor. What's the boy's name?"

"He's got no name. Aren't the parents together the ones supposed to give him one?"

"You, Fanny, are his mother. You have to give him a name."

"I'll think on it. Where's this doc?"

"Right nearby."

"So you're really not trying to play with me?"

Fanny stopped in the middle of the street in front of the barracks. "No, I don't think I'm going in there."

Heller gently took her by the arm and pulled her over to the other side of the street.

"It's fine, believe me. Don't be scared."

"But they got so many Russians around here." Fanny looked around anxiously.

"What they have most of all is a doctor who can help you." Heller let go of Fanny and went up to the sentry at the gate. He asked for Kasrashvili in a firm voice and waited. He watched Fanny from the corner of his eye. She approached with caution.

It took a while, since the soldier had to make a phone call, then he let them pass. Inside, Heller opened his overcoat and enjoyed the warmth. Not that he could relax. He was nervous. He was aware that he was taking a big risk. At the end of the long corridor, a door opened.

The Georgian came out of his office. When he saw Fanny, walking his way at a slight distance behind Heller, he tilted his head to the side.

"Captain," Heller said. Kasrashvili didn't respond. He kept looking past Heller, at the girl. Fanny stared back.

"I have to ask for your help," Heller began and waved Fanny over. "Come on, show him."

She opened her overcoat without taking her eyes off Kasrashvili and unwrapped the dirty cloth.

"That's an infant!" the doctor blurted.

Heller had to suppress a disparaging laugh. "You don't say. It's sick. Probably the clap. It needs to be examined along with the girl. We'll need medicine for both."

Kasrashvili took a few seconds, then he gave a gruff, almost angry nod and went back into his office.

A half hour later, they were back on the street. Fanny and the Georgian hadn't exchanged a word during the examination. Heller's coat pockets held pills, sulfur cream for Fanny's skin rash, and a little bottle of silver nitrate for the boy's eyes. The remedy was actually meant for prevention, yet Heller was still satisfied. He had also gotten the sense that his visit had nearly been too much for the Georgian. This time there had been no sign of his usual blasé attitude. Heller was sure of one thing: Fanny and the doctor had met before.

"You know the doctor," Heller said as they walked to the streetcar stop.

"He was always sitting in the corner, at the piano," Fanny muttered, "in Josef's bar."

"Did he go see the girls too?"

"Not me, he didn't," Fanny said and kept looking around as they walked.

"What were those two fighting about in the bar?" Heller asked.

"One girl was gonna have a baby from a guy there. And he wanted to marry her at some point. But Franz, I guess he got too rough with her because the baby went kaput."

"So who was the baby from? The doctor?"

Fanny grew wary, having noticed that Heller was trying to sound her out. "Nah, no idea. From someone or other."

Heller let it be. He didn't want to wear out what little trust she had in him.

Heller stood in the kitchen, at the stove, and watched his wife and Fanny strip and wash the skinny baby right on the kitchen table for lack of other options. Karin had warmed up a large pot of water and poured some into a bowl. Fanny stared wide-eyed at how confidently Karin handled the baby. The infant barely resisted. His squawking little voice fell silent when Karin lowered him into the bowl of warm water. He dozed off almost immediately.

"Why's he not saying nothing?" Fanny sounded worried.

"He's fine. Lying in that warm water is like it was for him in your belly."

Fanny looked amazed, her mouth open, and Karin gave Heller a grateful glance.

For the first time in his life, Heller couldn't understand his wife's decision. She had voluntarily imposed an even greater burden on herself. She not only had to take care of the gravely ill Frau Marquart—she'd brought in another mouth to feed and an infant who had to be washed and changed daily.

And yet she seemed happy, viewing the baby boy as a gift.

"You'll have to wash yourself too, Fanny," Karin said. "Once I'm finished with the little one, you can have the water. I also have a little soap left. You can have some of my clothes. What you have on needs to be washed. Max, please leave the room."

Heller nodded and briefly placed a hand on Karin's shoulder. She leaned her head and brushed her cheek against the back of his hand for a moment.

Heller shut the kitchen door behind him and sat at the living room table. Klaus, who at his mother's behest had been up in the attic searching for a mattress and blankets, came back in and sat with Heller at the table.

"Does the SMAD even know about this?" he asked.

Heller gave Klaus a pensive look and shook his head.

Klaus leaned forward, speaking more quietly now. "That's not good, Father," he said. "You can't trust her. You saw that they're armed. What if that boy comes here, that leader? What if he follows you or she brings him here? You can't hide that from the Soviets."

Heller ran his fingers through his hair. "What am I supposed to do? She couldn't stay in the woods any longer, not with a baby. And if I reported it to the Soviets, they'd start combing the woods with a whole regiment. You can imagine what that would mean for the children."

"But what are you hoping to achieve with this? Are you simply going to leave those children to freeze and starve? And what if they really are responsible for murder? This Fanny, I don't trust her. She's only acting naïve."

The door opened, and Karin came into the living room. She looked tired.

"It's a miracle that tiny thing is still alive. Do we have any schnapps left?" she said.

Klaus stood to get the bottle and glasses from the cabinet.

"You never went to the coal office, did you?" Karin asked Heller, staring at him.

Heller shut his eyes. He'd forgotten.

But Karin didn't blame him. "Did you two hear? They want to detonate the Semper Opera House."

Heller didn't understand at first. "But it's already destroyed."

219

"No, they want it gone altogether, people are saying. To make room for new buildings."

"High time that old imperial show-off was gone anyway," growled Klaus.

"Now hold on," Karin countered, "that's a true landmark."

Klaus poured them glasses of schnapps. "Is that even relevant, when there's such a huge housing crisis?"

February 10, 1947: Night

Heller awoke with a start and listened in the darkness. All were asleep, even Karin next to him, her breathing steady and shallow. Blowing up the Semper Opera House—he couldn't get the thought out of his head. So much had been detonated already. Just look at the bridges. What senseless destruction, one day before the end of the war, as if there hadn't been enough destruction.

But that wasn't what had startled him awake. It had been another thought, and now it kept eluding him. He stood, tossed his overcoat around him, and crept out of the room.

No sounds came from Frau Marquart's room. She was sleeping calmly now. Her condition had stabilized, though it wasn't improving much. Farther down the hallway, right under the window, lay Fanny. Heller went over there in a crouch and observed the girl in the moonlight. She was sleeping soundly. Next to her, in a little nest of a bed that Karin had made, was the infant. Heller flinched as he noticed the boy looking at him. The boy lay there completely still. Heller stretched his hand out and gently stroked the baby's cheek with his index finger. Suddenly he recalled the thought that had woken him up—he'd figured out where Friedel Schlüter could have been hiding. He quietly went back into the bedroom, took his pistol from his nightstand, and hurried downstairs to call Oldenbusch. It took forever for him to pick up.

"Where you heading?" Klaus asked after Heller hung up. Heller hadn't noticed him come from the living room. He'd probably been lying awake again.

"Into the heath. To the Wolfshügel. You know that stone lookout tower on the hill there, the one they detonated in '45?"

"I'm coming with you."

"No, Klaus. This is my job. You stay here. Please keep an eye on everything."

It was after midnight when they parked the Ford along Bautzner Strasse near the entrance to the Dresden Heath. Oldenbusch was drowsy and in a bad mood, but Heller ignored it.

"I don't like leaving the car here," Oldenbusch muttered.

"There's no other way. No one's passing through at this hour. Do you have your weapon? And a flashlight?"

Oldenbusch grunted affirmatively.

"Then let's go."

"Why didn't we call for reinforcements?"

"Because I'm not certain I'm right, and because I hope to speak to the boy first."

"Ah, so what makes you think Friedel's even there?"

"He needs a hideout. He knows the area and wants to stay close. He must have been planning to take all that stuff from the cellar somewhere. It couldn't have been far."

Oldenbusch grunted again, apparently not satisfied with Heller's answer. The two were soon walking the trail toward the Wolfshügel tower ruins. They left the path before reaching the spot and advanced by ducking low, moving from tree to tree for cover.

"All this white snow as a backdrop," Oldenbusch whispered, "makes us easy targets."

"Hush!" Heller ordered and released the safety on his pistol. Oldenbusch did the same. On the hill before them was the destroyed lookout tower. Its silhouette reminded Heller of dramatic cliffs or the ruins of a chapel in some Romantic landscape painting from Caspar David Friedrich. The foundation still stood, surrounded by stones and boulders lying in the snow. The entrance was on the rear side, Heller knew.

"You go around the right, Werner, and I'll go left. But don't shoot at me! Best not to shoot at all."

Oldenbusch snorted and disappeared.

They met again on the back side of the foundation.

"I'm guessing no one's here," Oldenbusch whispered.

"There's the entrance, see? You smell that, Werner? There was smoke." Heller pulled out his flashlight but didn't turn it on. As quietly as possible, he approached the entryway, which was the size of a normal door. He positioned himself to the left of it, Oldenbusch to the right. Then Heller switched on his flashlight and shined it inside.

Apart from the leaves and snow that had blown in, it looked empty. Heller could make out the remains of a campfire, and next to it empty cans of food. Suddenly something rustled in the farthest corner of the room. A shock of blond hair rose from under a mound of blankets. "Mother?"

"Friedel Schlüter? I'm Oberkommissar Heller, Dresden Police. You're under arrest."

The boy's hands shook as he reached for the cup. Heller had made tea in his office even though it meant having to draw from his own meager stocks.

Oldenbusch, who had taken the boy's fingerprints, now sat in the corner of Heller's office, fighting fatigue.

Heller took a piece of paper and pencil from his desk and set both before the boy. Friedel Schlüter looked at him in surprise. He was a tall and handsome blond boy with gray eyes and a straight nose. The perfect Aryan, Heller thought.

"Write the following," Heller said. "First, the word 'fascism.'"

The boy frowned tearfully, clearly having no idea what they were doing with him.

"Do it. Write 'fascism,' then 'socialism,' then 'Bolshevism.'"

The boy leaned over the page and wrote.

Heller stretched his neck to see. Then he gave Oldenbusch a telling look: all the words had been written with two *s*'s at the end.

Heller didn't beat around the bush. "Your mother's sitting in Russian custody because of you. I'm giving you the opportunity to tell us the truth. If you don't, we'll hand you over to the Russians first thing tomorrow morning."

The boy's eyes widened with fear.

"Are you responsible for the attack on the Schwarzer Peter bar?"

Friedel shook his head violently, apparently unable to speak. His chin quivered.

"Are you responsible for the attack on the Münchner Krug?"

The boy nodded.

Heller took a deep breath. "Did you murder Soviet officers Vasili Cherin and Vadim Berinov?"

"What?" Friedel yelped. "No! I didn't kill anyone. Never!"

"You tried to get into the meeting. Why did you throw those hand grenades?"

"I wasn't . . . I wasn't trying to kill anyone. Believe me!"

"So what were you trying to do?" Heller asked.

"I wanted to set an example, to call upon people to resist, because the Russians are making us their slaves. But I didn't want to kill anyone.

Ever. You have to believe me. I swear!" The boy tugged at his padded coat in despair.

"Where did you get the hand grenades?"

"I found them! In the woods. I really did. In a crate. I'll tell you where."

"Have you ever seen this bag?" Heller pointed at the leather doctor's bag sitting on another table.

"No, I've never seen it. I swear!"

"Josef Gutmann. You know him?"

"Yeah. Mother says he betrayed us to the Russians. But I didn't do anything. I was happy when that bar was burned. Finally, someone was doing something, I thought. I wanted to do something too. I wanted to do something for the Fatherland. Please believe me. I never wanted to harm anyone."

Heller believed him. But just tell that to the Russians, he thought. To them, anti-Bolshevik agitation was worse than attempted murder.

February 11, 1947: Early Morning

Heller got a bad feeling as he followed the Soviet soldier down the hallway to Colonel Ovtcharov's office. The colonel had Niesbach summon Heller to his offices on Münchner Platz. It wasn't a good sign. The soldier knocked on the door and opened when ordered. Then he looked at Heller and nodded at him to enter. It couldn't have been less civil. Heller stepped into the room, and the door closed behind him. Ovtcharov pointed to the seat across from his desk. Heller removed his cap but stood where he was.

"How long were you going to keep this resistance group in the woods from me?" Ovtcharov asked, clearly angry.

"Resistance group?" Heller said, playing dumb. His stomach tightened.

The colonel slapped the table. "Do not take me for an idiot! You were there twice already without informing me."

"Ah, you mean the children?" Heller acted surprised. "How did you . . . ?" He fell silent, after the Russian gave him an evil smile.

"I assume Frau Schlüter told you," Heller concluded. "She doesn't know anything. She only overheard it from a colleague of mine. She told you in order to save her son. If that isn't clear to you already."

"It doesn't matter where she got her information," Ovtcharov said.

"So what did she get from you in return? The promise to leave her son alone?"

A corner of Ovtcharov's mouth raised. "I let her go."

"But you don't even know how involved she is in all this." Heller's outrage swelled. Once again, he felt duped and at their mercy.

"Well, sometimes a person does have to compromise a little," Ovtcharov said and gave him a wry smile.

"So what now? What are you going to do?"

"Pastor Beger was kind enough to inform us of the group's whereabouts."

Heller was stunned. "He didn't do that voluntarily."

"In one way he did. It only depends on how you look at it, Oberkommissar."

"What did you do with him? Can I see him?"

"I've instructed my people to do whatever is required to restore the safety of members of the Soviet Army. No, you cannot see him. First, I must verify your integrity. Maybe you have some reason why you so stubbornly refused to join the Socialist Unity Party?"

Heller knew he had his back against the wall. Yet he couldn't stand Ovtcharov's smug condescension. "Of course I have a reason! I want to see the pastor, now! How did you even know about him?"

Ovtcharov leaned back in his chair, looking casual. "Someone reported his name. I've ordered a military operation," he said with a certain pride.

"You can't. No!" Heller stood over Ovtcharov's desk now.

The Russian saw this as a threat. He rose and reached for his holster.

"Rescind the order," Heller told him in a commanding voice. "They're just children!"

"We will see who and what they are. They are armed and have possibly murdered two officers! That's more than enough for taking such measures. Sit down, Oberkommissar Heller."

"We both know," Heller said, still looming over the desk, "that the murders of those two officers have something to do with what happened at the Schwarzer Peter, with the prostitution of minors."

"This is only speculation!" Ovtcharov bellowed.

But Heller withstood Ovtcharov's scathing glare. "Apparently, you don't have a clue what goes on in that bar. Your army officers are committing sexual offenses with underage girls. With children! And all you want to do is cover it up. You're just looking for a scapegoat," he hissed in fury, "for someone you can deliver to your superiors."

This was clearly going too far for the Russian. Enraged now, Ovtcharov pulled his pistol from its holster and aimed it at Heller. "That's quite enough! You know nothing!" he shouted. "You only see the good in people. You still believe it's possible to make things better. Look out that window! The way they go running errands, always lamenting how bad they have it. You, Heller, you look out on that street and see a thousand people. A thousand people you believe are so harmless, innocent, unknowing. But I'm not as blind as you, no. I don't see a thousand people. You know what I see? I see a thousand devils! And you, Heller, are one of them!"

Heller recoiled but didn't respond. It had grown loud out on the street. The howling of engines from heavy trucks penetrated the closed window.

Ovtcharov slowly lowered his weapon and put it away. He sat back down and ran a hand over the desk as if that would calm the charged atmosphere.

"Just sit down," he ordered in a reasonable tone and waited for Heller to comply. "What sort of people do you think we are?" he said, regaining his more composed voice. "We Russians. You think we do not love our children? You think we consider it a good thing when members of our armed forces behave like that? Ever since I heard about this disgusting behavior, I've wanted to put an end to it. But I need to proceed just as cautiously as you. I don't know who's behind it. From my informants among our officers, I do know that Colonel Cherin was having a lengthy affair with a girl. Then he got into a dispute with Swoboda, and it was apparently about this girl. What happened next is still not clear. Some of the officers who were visiting the bar on a regular basis were ordered back to Russia long ago. That doesn't necessarily mean anything, yet it might also mean that someone higher up knows about the matter. I naturally want to avoid a scandal. But you and I, Heller, we both have the same goal."

Heller was listening intently. "So why did you keep so much information from me? If we truly do have the same goal, as you say?"

Ovtcharov leaned back. Heller immediately knew what that meant: the Russian colonel had been using him. Ovtcharov sent him in first, so Heller would be the one poking the wasp's nest.

"I found Friedel Schlüter last night and arrested him," Heller said. "He's sitting at police headquarters. He's admitted responsibility for the attack on the Münchner Krug. Says he had nothing to do with anything else. He threw the hand grenades into the wrong window on purpose."

Ovtcharov had put his venomous smile back on. "I know."

Heller sighed. He was quickly realizing that it was pointless trying to figure out exactly who was working for whom, or who was spying on whom and passing on information. "What's the Georgian's role in all this?" he asked. "Kasrashvili. Is there more I should know about him?"

"Kasrashvili is doing large-scale business in medicines. Such a thing would not be possible unless someone was lending him a protective hand. He was a regular at the bar, but my informant couldn't find out if he just drank there and played piano or did other things as well. He provided Gutmann with drugs. It's not clear what sort of compensation he received. There was nothing of worth found in Kasrashvili's quarters."

"You know Gutmann's dead?" Heller said.

Trucks had passed through the front gate. Down in the courtyard, orders were being shouted in Russian.

Ovtcharov nodded and stood up. "Despite all this, there are other issues we need to tend to. Every form of rebellion and resistance must be prevented at once! Our mission in the forest took place in the early-morning hours—with success. The trucks are just coming back."

Heller stood too. "Let the pastor go! He only meant well."

"Some priest he is," Ovtcharov said. "His church was full of foodstuffs."

"He was handing them out! Do you not understand that?" Heller's anger boiled over again; the Russian's cynicism sickened him. "People like him *do* exist among all your devils. Are you going to release him or not?"

"Did you know that his predecessor, one Ludwig Kuhnell, was arrested by the Gestapo and executed soon after?"

"The man's name was Kühnel," Heller blurted. "Did Pastor Beger have anything to do with his arrest? Did he betray his predecessor to the Gestapo?"

Ovtcharov shrugged. "We have no knowledge of this."

"Then he's completely irrelevant. Let him go."

"If you so desire," the Russian replied sarcastically. "And might there be anything further I should know?"

Heller thought about Fanny. "Not that I can think of," he said, then nodded down at the courtyard. "May I go down there? I want to see what your men found in the woods."

Ovtcharov grabbed his coat. "We will go together."

Heller stood in the courtyard of the former courthouse, along with Colonel Ovtcharov. It had become light out. The cold didn't relent, and the sky was gray. It could start snowing again at any moment. Two Soviet Army trucks were parked in the courtyard, their motors chugging. Soldiers opened the tailgates to the canvas-covered truck beds. From one they dragged off a stretcher with a body on it, body and face covered with a tarp. Heller pulled the tarp aside. The deceased was a boy of about sixteen. It wasn't Jörg.

"Down! *Davai!*" ordered a soldier at the rear of the second truck, waving the barrel of his machine gun. When Heller heard the crying, he couldn't stand it anymore. He rushed over to the truck.

The image would be forever burned in his memory. Like all the other images that haunted him, this one would take its place on that black wall inside his head, tearing him from his sleep, wrenching at his heart.

About twenty children cowered on the bare wood planks of the truck bed. The youngest ones, having no idea what was happening, clutched at each other, sobbing, their tears leaving bright streaks on their dirty cheeks. Sheer horror was etched on the faces of the older children. They stared into space, trembling, and started when the soldier yelled again. But they didn't understand what they were supposed to do. They shoved back into the deepest corner of the truck, helpless. Heller had already noticed that Jörg wasn't among them.

The impatient soldier jumped up onto the truck bed and grabbed at the first child he could reach. The child screamed in distress and clamped on to the wood sides. In their despair the others grabbed the child, even the littlest ones, only two or three years old, helping. Total bedlam ensued. Only now did Heller see that the oldest children, the eleven- and twelve-year-olds, had been handcuffed.

"Leave them alone!" Heller shouted and pulled himself up onto the truck bed to break up the tussle between the soldier and the children. "*Stoi!*" he ordered.

The soldier let go and, not sure how to proceed, looked to his superior. Heller squatted before the children, looking around at Ovtcharov. "Take a look here! Are these your devils? These your Werewolves?"

The colonel gave a command to the soldier, who then jumped down from the truck in obvious relief.

The smaller children had pressed themselves up to Heller, clawing at his overcoat. They stank horribly, and it was tough for Heller to ignore the odor.

"No need to be afraid," he tried to convince them in a calming voice while keeping an eye on Ovtcharov. The colonel was getting a full report from his men.

Among the children Heller recognized the boy who'd threatened him with a weapon two days ago. He was about eight. "You—you're Johann, aren't you?" Heller whispered to him. "Where's Jörg?"

"Jörg, he says you the one shoulda got killed," the boy whispered. "Says you're a bad man, a traitor!"

"I never betrayed any of you; you have to believe me. They were spying on me. That's how they found you."

Heller was doing his best, but the boy wouldn't give in.

"You're the reason Heinrich's dead. Jörg's gonna come and kill you dead for that."

"What are you talking about there?" Ovtcharov cut in.

Heller turned away from the boy. "Listen, you have to inform Child Services. And take off those cuffs, will you? These are children. And send your soldiers away! You can see how scared it's making them. Can't you at least get a woman here to help?"

Ovtcharov looked unimpressed by Heller's appeals. "They must be interrogated first."

"No!" Heller was getting louder. "These children must see a doctor. They need something to eat and to warm up! Don't you have any compassion?" He tried to climb off the truck, but the children clung even tighter to him, their eyes full of panic.

"It's going to be all right," Heller promised them. "It'll be all right."

"I will have the children sent to a doctor," the Russian snarled, "once I know where their leader is. Results are what I need, not compassion."

Heller sighed and eyed him warily. "Very well. Let me see what I can do."

February 11, 1945: Midday

When Heller came home, a smiling Karin rushed up to him with the baby in her arms. She really wanted to show it to him. "Just look how happy he is."

Heller smiled and stroked his wife's arm.

"Guess what? There's a package for me to pick up—from Sweden!" Karin sounded excited now. "You know anyone in Sweden?"

Heller shook his head. He was tired. He had let Oldenbusch go home after driving him as far as Bautzner Strasse. He'd walked the rest of the way. "Where's Fanny?"

"She wanted to go out for a bit. But she promised to come back soon."

"You shouldn't let her leave the house, Karin."

"It's not a prison," she countered. "Sit down, Max. I'll warm up some food for you. Klaus cooked it. The dish is called kasha. Klaus said he'd been given it nearly every day for the last two years. Yet he's making it for us." She smiled again and made Heller go into the kitchen and sit down.

Heller could now feel just how exhausted he was. He really needed to get a full night's sleep at some point, he thought, rubbing his eyes. Then he went over the morning's upsetting chain of events in his head.

He didn't know anyone at the Child Services office but had wanted to avoid the children getting torn from each other and sent away to different homes. Lacking any better option, he contacted the Victims of Fascism and asked Constanze Weisshaupt to help. These children were victims of fascism too, after all. As half-Jewish and an orphan herself, Constanze had promised to help. She was always grateful for what he had done for her in '45.

"So where's Klaus?" Heller asked.

Karin hesitated. "In the yard. He's sawing down the old cherry tree. I told him he could."

Heller looked up, unable to hide his disappointment. Frau Marquart wasn't the only one who'd be sad. He had liked that tree a lot too, its gnarled trunk, those crooked branches. In the past two years of living here, he had always imagined himself sitting under its shadow one day, so happy and carefree, without hunger, without need.

"Max, the baby needs more warmth. And we do too," Karin said with a hint of warning. "We can trade those branches for things to eat."

There was a clatter at the back door, and Klaus came inside. He set down two armfuls of sawed-off branches in the kitchen, then put some into the stove. The damp wood hissed and steamed.

Then he sat down at the table with Heller. "Over at the water pump they were saying there was shooting in the woods early this morning."

"That was the Soviets," Heller said. "They took the children from the woods."

Klaus stared at Heller in silence, and Heller stared back.

"I'm telling you, she's dangerous," Klaus eventually said in a low voice. "They're still searching for the leader of that gang, I hear."

"It's not a gang," Heller shot back.

Karin had laid the infant in its basket. She cut in. "She's not dangerous. You just have to win her trust. You can't do that while suspecting her."

"Mother, all that miserable Nazism, it's still inside their heads. It needs to be driven out of them. All of them. The children most of all."

Right then the front door opened, and Fanny came inside. She beamed at them.

"Look what I went found." She placed four eggs on the table with pride and produced a few lumps of coal from her coat pockets as well, though it was barely enough to fill a dustpan.

"What *I found*," Karin said gently to correct her grammar.

"No, I found it," Fanny insisted. "So where's my little guy? He been sweet?"

"He was very sweet." Karin smiled and pointed at the basket. "Wash up, please, Fanny. Then you can breastfeed him."

"That'll have to wait a moment," Heller said and stood. "Fanny, could you come into the living room, please?"

Heller led Fanny into the living room. "The Russians were in the woods today and found the children. Someone snitched on the pastor, and the Russians forced it out of him."

"Really? You're not just trying to sucker me? They get Jörg?"

"He wasn't there. Tell me, who could've betrayed the pastor?"

"If you weren't the one, then maybe that Frau Schlüter's boy?"

"No, that's not . . ." Heller fell silent. Ovtcharov had already known about Friedel. He'd had Friedel put into a cell after two hours of interrogation during the night. The Soviets could have reacted fast enough to track down the pastor and force the information out of him, then headed into the woods to find the children.

"You two know each other, you and Friedel?" Heller asked. "Because you were visiting Frau Dähne?"

"I know him 'cause he wanted to go putting his thing in me. But I never let him. 'Cause of Jörg and 'cause he wouldn't give me nothing to eat. He got real mean about it too."

Heller would've liked to write all this down, but he was afraid it would keep Fanny from talking. "I know you sold yourself at

Gutmann's bar. Did you know a customer named Vasili and another named Vadim?"

"Could be."

"What about Swoboda? Was he fighting with those two?"

Fanny rolled her eyes as if bored by all the questioning. "There was one girl had something going with this one Russian. He was always giving her chocolate and all that. And that One-Handed Franz? He was a pig, that one, got real rough with her, and that made that other one a real rough bastard too. Then she was sick. 'Cause of him, and then she was dead. That's what I know. And the Russians were screaming at him, they were gonna send him to Siberia! And then the one got stabbed dead. And then One-Handed Franz, he was gone."

Heller couldn't make much sense of what the girl was saying.

"His head was inside that backpack you wanted. Did you know that?"

"Whose head?"

"One-Handed Franz."

Fanny looked at him, and a tentative smile spread across her face, as if she didn't believe a word Heller was saying.

"And Gutmann—Josef—how was he?" Heller continued.

"Sometimes he was fine and sometimes a real bastard. When someone wasn't playing along, he'd go and give them a good smack. But he didn't go touching the girls, not with his thing, I mean. He wasn't so bad."

"Fanny, who's the baby from?"

"From a Russian, just like I told you! Not sure whose."

"So, Jörg, where might he be now?"

"Got no idea. He knows his way around the woods real good and all the hiding spots."

"Max, Fanny, time to eat," Karin shouted from the kitchen.

Heller yawned and rubbed his face. "We'll talk about this again later."

When Heller woke, the light had changed. Still groggy, he pushed off the wool blanket and rose from the sofa. He could tell that he had slept far too long. He looked at the clock; it was nearly four in the afternoon. He'd been lying here for three hours.

It was quiet in the house. Too tired to put his shoes back on, he went into the kitchen in his socks. Maybe there was a bite of something to get his blood flowing. He found a half loaf of bread, light gray and crumbly, with a slightly bitter aftertaste that stayed on his tongue a long time. People said acorns were being used for filler. When he went to open the silverware drawer, he saw it was already slightly open. That wasn't like Karin. He banished his next thought and pulled the drawer open, looking for the bread knife. He didn't find it, not in the drawer or anywhere else. Could Karin have the knife in her bag?

Heller wrapped the bread back in the paper and put it away. He went upstairs. Karin wasn't up there, and neither Klaus nor Fanny were anywhere to be found either. He checked on Frau Marquart. She lay in her bed and appeared to be sleeping. He approached cautiously and felt her forehead.

"Max," she said softly, opened her eyes, and looked at him.

"How are you feeling?"

"Better. Much better. Thank you so much, dear Max, for everything." She placed her hand on his, and Heller sat on the chair next to her bed.

"Karin is the one you should be thanking, not me."

Frau Marquart nodded and smiled. "Tell me, is there a baby in the house? I thought maybe I heard one."

"There is, yes. It's from a young woman we've taken in for a short while."

Frau Marquart smiled again and didn't want to let go of Heller's hand.

"And did you notice our Klaus is here?" Heller said, glad to see Frau Marquart back to taking interest in what was going on.

"Yes, I saw him. At first, I thought it was you, dear Max. He's quite serious, isn't he?"

Heller nodded, hoping it was only temporary. Then he remembered something. "Frau Marquart, we had to cut down the cherry tree. We needed the wood."

To his amazement, she took the news in stride. "It's just a tree. We'll plant a new one."

The phone rang downstairs in the hallway. Heller stood. "I'm sorry, I have to go."

"I know. Go ahead. I'm just fine."

February 11, 1947: Afternoon

"I thought I sent you home." Heller tried to smile but failed.

Oldenbusch gave him a wry grin. "I was at home, but I just couldn't get the case out of my head. So I took a look at the fingerprints."

"Good thing you did." Heller left it there, and together they waited for Friedel Schlüter to be brought into the interrogation room. Heller didn't need to keep asking Oldenbusch just how sure he was about this. If his partner wasn't certain, he wouldn't have called.

There finally came a knock on the door. "Come in," Heller shouted. Two policemen brought Friedel into the room.

The boy looked completely exhausted and had trouble remaining upright on his chair. His cuffed hands lay in his lap. He stared at the leather doctor's bag without expression when Oldenbusch set it on the table. Oldenbusch opened it and started pulling out each tool, one at a time. He placed them on the table in a neat row. The severed hands weren't among them. They'd left those with Dr. Kassner.

"Do you know why we're here?" Heller asked the boy.

Friedel looked up as if just now realizing who was sitting across from him. Then he began shaking his head in a way that seemed like he wouldn't ever stop. "Where's Mother?" he asked.

"She was released. Friedel, we've thoroughly examined this bag and the tools. Last night we took fingerprints from the bag and compared them to the ones on the tools. They're your fingerprints. It's very clear."

The news of his mother's release had enlivened Friedel for a moment, but now he lowered his head. He said nothing for a while. Eventually he muttered, "Someone stole that from me."

"Friedel, you've gotten yourself into terrible trouble. Two men were mutilated with those tools." Heller kept his eyes on the boy every second.

"Those tools were stolen from me, out of the cellar. They were mine. I never saw that bag before!"

"Friedel, it won't always be us asking. When it's the Soviets standing over you, they'll want to know if you knew those two deceased Soviet officers and if you were the one who hanged Gutmann."

"But I don't know anything," the boy said in a dull tone. Heller noticed that the news about Gutmann's death hadn't caused him to react any differently.

"You can stop protecting people. The best thing you can do is talk. Do you know Fanny?"

The boy finally showed a little emotion. "I might," he muttered.

"That's not an answer," Heller barked. "Do you know her?"

"Mother says she's a whore. She flirts with anyone who has food. Can't trust her."

"And Frau Dähne. You know her?"

"That old hag—she's the one who was dragging the girls in to Gutmann. They took them into her house, gave them food, then sold them to Gutmann. Go see for yourself—she's always got things to eat, and always some meat."

"Are you telling me the truth?" Heller sounded stern. "Can you prove this, or is it just something you believe?"

"The one-handed man used to live with her. Go ask around the neighborhood." The boy was growing angry.

"We'll do that. Now, back to the bag. Have you ever seen it before?"

"No! I've never seen it, I'm telling you. The tools were stolen from my cellar. Days before." Friedel moved to rub his face, but his hands were cuffed. He was grinding his teeth, and his cheeks had turned red. He started blinking nervously.

"I'll summarize for you, Friedel," Heller continued. "Someone stole the tools and used them to mutilate two corpses. Then that same person or persons brought the tools to your hiding place, where we found them. So how did we end up finding your fingerprints on the bag?"

The dam broke now, and the boy couldn't stop it. Tears rolled down his cheeks, and he sobbed. "Mother, she told me you'd been there, and, and that you'd be coming back for sure. So I tried stowing it all in my hiding place, and suddenly the bag was just there!"

"Did you look inside? Did you know what was in the bag apart from the tools?"

"Yes!"

"So why didn't you report it—to us, the police?"

"Because you'd just pin it on me anyway! You were the ones who put that bag there. Mother says you're all in the Russians' pocket," he blurted in despair.

"I'm not planning on pinning anything on you. It's just that I find it hard to believe that someone put that bag in your cellar. Who would have done it?"

"If I knew, don't you think I'd tell you?" Friedel screamed in agony.

"Take it easy, Friedel," Heller told him. Even though the evidence did speak against him, the boy's despair was nevertheless real—of that Heller had no doubt. "Tell me about Fanny. Have you spoken with her? Where did you first see her?"

Friedel wiped his eyes with the backs of his hands, sniffed, and sucked snot back up. "That Frau Dähne, she brought her home one day. Last winter. I never talked to her much. She acts dumb, but she's not." The splotches on Friedel's face were now dark red. Something was gnawing at him, and he kept crying.

"What about you? Did you know Gutmann betrayed your mother to the Russians?"

"Of course, but I didn't kill him. Why won't you believe me?"

"What about Armin Weiler—you know him too?"

"From the printing company." Friedel sobbed in spurts.

"Did he know something about you and your family? Was he blackmailing you?"

"Mother says he's a traitor. When the war was still on, he reported the old pastor for hiding a pack of lowlife Jews in his church. Now that pig's with the Russians, filling his belly."

"Those were his hands in that bag, Friedel."

The boy lurched forward, against the tabletop, pressing his face into the crook of his arm. "I didn't kill anyone," he whimpered. "I just want everything to be like it was. Without any Russians! I want our German Reich back, the way it was, and our house, and my daddy."

Heller checked his watch for the third time. Tonight was the cultural event that he and Karin were supposed to attend. He still had some time, but by no means did he want to arrive late. He stood with about thirty other people at the Unity Square stop, waiting for the streetcar that refused to arrive. He went over his questioning of Friedel Schlüter one more time. Should he believe the boy? Had Friedel really just found the bag in his cellar? If so, who had put it there? It had to be someone who knew that Friedel was under suspicion. If he couldn't find any other suspects, he would have no choice but to stick to the facts. Heller knew how important it was to leave his feelings out of it, but this kid was a victim too, in a way, a child missing a father who was never coming back.

He looked at his watch again. The sky was already dimming in the east. More passengers were gathering by the minute.

"Excuse me, have you heard if there's a power outage?" a woman asked him. She bore a heavy bulging backpack, probably holding coal or potatoes. Heller couldn't tell. Then the streetcar finally came.

It was already overloaded with passengers, and hardly anyone stepped out. Yet everyone tried to climb onto the running boards anyway.

"Come on!" a man yelled to encourage the woman with the big backpack, holding out a hand to her and giving her some of his grab handle. Heller squeezed in next to them. The bell rang, and the streetcar continued on, past Martin Luther Strasse and Deaconess Hospital. At every stop, more people tried to climb on. But no one complained. They simply helped each other.

"She must have a whole piggy in that pack," someone joked, and everyone laughed.

February 11, 1947: Evening

It was a long distance for Karin and Max to cover on foot later that night. The streetcars weren't running anymore, and it had been impossible for Heller to arrange other transportation on such short notice. Either there was no gasoline, or car tires were shot out, or the Soviets had claimed all the remaining cars for themselves. Not even the Cultural Association, the founder of the event, could spare a car for the Hellers. Even on snow-covered roads, a car would have made the trip in just ten minutes. Yet now they were forced to walk first up the Rissweg, then down Bautzner Landstrasse out of the city until they reached Ullersdorfer Strasse, where the Bühlau Spa Hotel stood. Ordinarily, the two miles would have posed no problem. But the icy wind whipped, and the snowy sidewalks were slippery. Hidden beneath the fresh snow were potholes that made pedestrians stumble. Karin and Heller walked arm in arm, and he wondered when they had last done that. He couldn't remember.

The darkness caught up with them now, and Heller regretted going. He knew he would see Medvedev, Ovtcharov, and probably Kasrashvili as well, since he was cultural advisor to the local military and head of the choir. It was a good thing to be seen at official events, and he would use the occasion to find out whether word of Gutmann's supposed suicide was getting around. Yet he was mostly going for Karin's sake. He knew she was longing for this evening. He needed to indulge her. After all the deprivation of the past few years, he wanted to take her out for once, where it would be warm, where there would be food and music, where for a few hours the worries of everyday life could be forgotten. Karin had been taking care of everyone for far too long—severely ill Frau Marquart, Klaus, and now Fanny and her baby too. Heller's conscience had been slowly gnawing away at him, because he knew he didn't help out enough and had devoted too much of himself to his job.

He had secretly given Klaus his pistol and told him about the missing bread knife. He hadn't told Karin, though, not wanting to worry her. He also hadn't admitted to her that he didn't trust Fanny. The girl seemed happy and was caring for her baby in her naïve, childlike way. But the knife hadn't turned up. Klaus had taken the pistol from him, and Heller spared him any fatherly caution. It wasn't necessary. Klaus was now a grown man. The war had robbed so many people of their souls and had changed so many others' forever. Heller sighed.

"Why are you sighing?" Karin asked, squinting at the snowflakes blowing into her eyes.

"I'm thinking about Klaus, wondering if he'll ever be happy again."

Karin squeezed his hand. "He will," she said. "I'm sure of it."

The Bühlau Spa Hotel was lit up, and lots of vehicles were parked out front. The drivers stood smoking in little groups. Heller spotted two police trucks and at least twenty armed policemen in uniform. Warmly bundled Soviet soldiers with machine guns stood guard as well, smoking and looking around. On the bed of a Russian truck, Heller thought he saw a mounted machine gun.

Karin didn't notice any of it. She strode up to the entrance all excited, her eyes reflecting the warm light coming from the banquet room windows. Here, in April of '46, the regional associations of the Socialist and Communist Parties had agreed to unite. Now the hotel was being used for a celebration.

They were first checked by a Soviet, then a German sentry, and each time they showed their invitation and papers. Heller saw armed soldiers in the foyer too. Were they really that concerned about an attack?

They gave up their coats at the cloakroom. Karin was a little sheepish, smoothing and tugging at the dress that she'd gotten from Frau Marquart; she'd altered it quite some time ago. It was a summer dress, red with white dots, fairly simple, ruffled at the waist with a collar that could be unbuttoned a little.

Heller hadn't seen her in it before and couldn't take his eyes off her.

"What are you looking at?" Karin whispered to him with concern.

"You're lovely," Heller whispered back, smiling at her.

"Please, in this old thing?" Karin said, flushing a little. Heller offered her his arm, and she took it, so they could enter the hall together.

The banquet hall seemed enormous. The high walls were decorated with garlands and red flags. Gold chandeliers hung from the white vaulted ceiling, making the polished parquet floor glisten. Round tables covered with white tablecloths stood around the room. At the rear, a stage had been erected, with a piano on it and risers for the choir.

Now Heller was the one feeling underdressed in his old tight-fitting suit and the same shoes he always wore because he had no others. His white shirt came from deceased Herr Marquart's wardrobe, and Karin had sewn his black bowtie herself.

Yet Heller lost his unease once he looked around, seeing that most of the guests had also shown up in threadbare dresses and suits. Only the Soviet officers wore shiny black boots and their best uniforms, with polished medals glittering.

Heller didn't know any of the guests who had already gathered. So he steered Karin toward the stage, where he found Kasrashvili, just as he'd hoped. Kasrashvili sat in the shadows offstage, glancing at a sheet of music, looking bored. The Georgian looked up.

"Oberkommissar Heller," he said, then shook Karin's hand and gave her a hint of a bow. He shook Heller's hand too.

Heller introduced the doctor. "This is Captain Kasrashvili. Captain, my wife."

Kasrashvili nodded, then returned his attention to the sheet of music. It was clear that he didn't want to engage in a conversation with Karin present. Karin let go of Heller's arm. "I want to go see if I know anyone," she said to excuse herself, leaving the two men alone.

Heller watched her until she disappeared among the guests.

"From your reserved behavior, I gather Ovtcharov paid you a visit today?" Heller began. He had no intention of apologizing for doing his job. And he had no intention of spoiling Karin's evening. "Listen, I didn't plan on causing you any inconvenience."

Kasrashvili lowered the sheet music. "Calling it an inconvenience is sheer mockery. You should have just asked me if you wanted to know about Berinov and Cherin."

"Their corpses were lying right there, yet you never once gave me the impression that you might've known them." Heller looked around again, checking to make sure no one was listening. "So you would have recognized Swoboda if I'd shown you his head?"

"But you didn't show it to me, and you didn't ask if I knew them! Instead, you send the MVD my way. Now if you'll excuse me, I need to see to the choir."

"So what was going on with Cherin and Berinov?" Heller asked in a muted voice.

"They were arguing with the German. That's all I know. No more."

"And you? How often were you in the bar? What were you doing there?"

"I sat there and drank, occasionally played piano, nothing more. I knew nothing about the girls upstairs."

"But you do now?" Heller asked.

Kasrashvili seemed about to reply, then turned around and walked away.

Once Heller found Karin, they went looking for their seats, which were at a table up front to the right of the stage, with six other guests they didn't know. Everyone introduced themselves, but Heller quickly forgot their names and positions. Niesbach and Police Chief Opitz sat at the large neighboring table with several important Soviet military figures. Medvedev was there too, but he showed little interest in revealing that he and Heller knew each other well.

Heller was glad of that, since he'd been worried about such an encounter, considering those who were watching. Ovtcharov had also arrived and only nodded at Heller.

All the guests were now present, and the hall doors closed. The first speakers stepped onstage. First was a writer from the Cultural Association. All the talk was of Soviet-German friendship, of thanks to the liberators, of the latest accomplishments and how important culture was even in times of great adversity. Then a Russian general took the stage and spoke in such poor German that it was agonizing to listen to him. Yet no one dared make fun of him or complain. *Druzhba* was the only Russian word Heller understood—friendship. The man repeated it over and over, as if saying so would make it happen. Then a German, an active member of the Victims of Fascism, was back onstage. He had been in a concentration camp, he said, and described all the acts of cruelty he'd experienced there. He seemed horrified by people who didn't want to believe it and just took it for propaganda—all the more crucial to inform people and educate them and, above all, to further the denazification process. Children and young adults in particular needed to have Nazism driven out of their heads, he said.

This made Heller think of the public prosecutor, Speidel, who claimed never to have been a true Nazi. But what was a true Nazi? Was a person only a Nazi when they denounced Jews? When they voted for Hitler? When they went out demonstrating while carrying a swastika flag? When they had worn an SA or SS uniform or been a party member? Or was a person a Nazi simply by tolerating it all? Everyone now claimed not to have been a true Nazi, but all of them had gone along with the system. They were all the foundation upon which the German Reich was built. Heller didn't exclude himself. He, too, had performed his duty.

He wondered what people actually thought of the Nuremberg trials, which had been broadcast over the radio in excruciating detail. No one appeared to be interested. People had so many other worries—struggling to survive, seeking shelter, clothes, food, coal. Everyone preferred to look forward, toward a better future, rather than back to a cruel past.

"Don't fall asleep!" Karin whispered, nudging him. Heller started and nodded. He tried to suppress his thoughts. The next speaker was up, expounding on the accomplishments of the emerging socialism all while uncomfortably inserting the old Nazi vocabulary, referring to fresh blood, hard struggle, and a new national identity.

A certain discomfort was slowly spreading through the hall. The unaccustomed warmth bothered Heller. He tried opening his collar a little and would have liked to shed his jacket, but the event was too formal for that. He was sweating so badly that it was running down his forehead. It was only a slight consolation that he wasn't alone. Karin was sneaking dabs at her neck and forehead as other guests made a point of wiping their faces with handkerchiefs.

Finally, after what felt like an eternity, the final speaker left the stage to relieved applause, the lights came back on, and the food was served. The starter was noodle soup, followed by a proper pork roast, with dumplings, sauce, and red cabbage. Afterward, they served a cold fruit soup, followed by coffee and cake.

It was like paradise, like a leap into a different, much better age. The dishes had such appetizing aromas, and for a good long time all that was heard was the clattering of silverware on tableware. Heller couldn't take his eyes off Karin. It delighted him, the way she ate, how she took part in the discussions around the table, and how she bloomed. Heller chewed carefully, trying not to wolf his food down. But he couldn't eat any of the cake—his stomach was too full. Even Karin had only eaten a bite of her poppy-seed cake, even though it was her favorite, and she hadn't had any for years.

Cognac was served. The waiters darted back and forth, and toasts could be heard everywhere. *"Druzhba! Na zdorovie!"* shouted the Russians, who drank their brandy in one gulp and encouraged those at neighboring tables to do the same. Cigarettes were handed around. Everyone took them, even the nonsmokers. At some point the first guests stood to stretch their legs. The men at Heller's table finally rose as well. Heller had been waiting for that. He really needed to stand and get some fresh air.

But a hand suddenly appeared on his shoulder. It was Kasrashvili. He sat down in the open seat next to Heller.

"They can sure talk," the Georgian muttered and snapped his fingers at a waiter. "So, what do you think? To whom do you have to thank for this sumptuous meal? Ovtcharov? Or are you Medvedev's chained dog? Whose hand are you eating out of? It's not as if you could choose."

Heller could see Karin tensing up. She wouldn't like seeing her husband treated like this. He placed a hand on her knee to pacify her.

"You've been drinking, Comrade Captain," he said.

Kasrashvili gestured at the waiter to pour him a cognac and squeezed on his arm so he could take the whole bottle. "Of course I have. *Na zdorovie!* Or, as we Georgians say, *gaumarjos*. May you be victorious!" He raised his glass.

Heller hesitated, having had too many glasses already.

"You know it's an insult to a Russian when you don't take them up on their invitation?"

"But you're a Georgian, as you just made clear yourself." Heller raised his glass and took a drink. The doctor drained his and poured two more. He raised his glass again and held it until Heller grabbed the other and drank with him.

"Russians, Georgians, Ukrainians—we're all now one Soviet empire. Ready to rule the world!" Kasrashvili stood and nodded and clicked his heels in a manner that better suited the Wehrmacht than the Soviet Army. "I wish you a pleasant evening." Then he reached for the bottle of cognac and walked off.

"I need to get some air," Karin blurted out.

"I'm sorry about that, Karin."

"You don't have to be sorry, Max. Such a rude man! No comparison to his father. You remember? What a polite and courteous human being he was. What's wrong with him? Are you investigating him?"

"I think I might be harassing him on Ovtcharov's behalf," he said in a low voice once they were on the way to the foyer.

"I'm going to pop into the restroom quickly," Karin whispered.

Ovtcharov, who was also standing in the foyer, his chest decorated with a row of sparkling medals, seemed to have been waiting for this very moment. "Comrade Oberkommissar!" he called out. Heller shook his hand and gave a slight bow. The colonel smiled, yet Heller could tell by his eyes that something was worrying him.

"I'm pleased to welcome you here, Heller. I hope the speeches weren't too long for you?"

"What needs to be said must be said," Heller replied. It certainly wasn't the first time he'd said this.

"Have you been able to make any progress searching for the leader of that gang?"

"No, none. But we do have some evidence that strongly implicates Friedel Schlüter in the case involving Swoboda's severed head."

The Russian gave an emphatic shrug. "Heller, that doesn't interest me. The other boy is the important one. Was he acting alone? If not, how many are there still? What weapons do they have? What are they planning? These are the questions that most need resolving. And don't go trying to keep anything from me ever again!"

Heller said, "I'm doing everything within the powers I've—"

"Come on, are you really?" The colonel grabbed him by the arm. "Do you know about Captain Sergey Yakovlev?"

"Should I?"

"He's gone. Vanished yesterday without a trace. He, too, was a regular at Gutmann's place. Oberkommissar, I cannot afford to lose another officer. And if I find out that you are keeping things from me, then not even Medvedev can protect you."

Ovtcharov's face suddenly brightened. Karin was coming back.

"Frau Oberkommissar, I take it. It's an honor to make your acquaintance. Colonel Ovtcharov. I take it your husband has already spoken of me, and I do hope in a good way." He smiled broadly, took Karin's hand, and gave it a slight kiss.

Karin gave the Russian a slight nod. She took Heller's arm again. "Certainly, Herr Colonel. Thanks so much for the food packages."

"Do not mention it. I hope you enjoy the evening. It's been dragging on a little so far, but the best part should be starting soon. Let's go back in."

Heller was feeling uneasy. As Karin watched the stage in anticipation, having slid her chair next to his, he kept stealing glances around. Ovtcharov's displeasure was getting to him. If the colonel found out about Fanny, and that he was helping her, he would be in serious trouble. Ovtcharov wasn't known for showing consideration. A person would be held for a long time after getting caught in the fangs of the MVD, then shipped off to Bautzen. Heller knew of people who disappeared overnight and still hadn't turned up two years later. Others only gained their freedom after much effort and misery and paid for it with their health and vitality. So he had to watch out for himself, and above all he couldn't let Karin know about the risk he was taking.

The choir finally took the stage. More than twenty men stood up there, all broad-shouldered Soviet soldiers. Kasrashvili stepped onstage and stood at the piano. He seemed to teeter just noticeably and long enough to make whispers travel among the Germans. The Georgian held on to the piano with one hand, then gave a hint of a contemptuous bow. Heller sat up straight from the suspense and expected Kasrashvili to say something rash. A few awkward seconds passed before Kasrashvili bowed again, as if forgetting he'd just done so.

"Dear ladies and gentlemen," he began, his speech rather slow. "Despite the announced schedule, we shall first delight you with a piece that seems wholly fitting for times such as these."

Kasrashvili's words caused something of a sensation among the Soviet military men. Heller dared a look over. Officers were exchanging dubious glances. Ovtcharov waved one of his men over, whispered into his ear, and dismissed him. Only Medvedev remained cool, his face blank.

Kasrashvili sat on the piano bench. "Since my earliest childhood, when my father taught me how to play the piano at home, accompanying him at his side, I've harbored a certain passion for one of the greatest German composers. Johannes Brahms. His *German Requiem* is what we shall play for you this evening. Considering my somewhat limited facility, I'm restricting the piece to the second chorus."

Karin didn't seem to have noticed the anxiety in the hall. She sat next to Heller, small and fragile like a young girl, her hands clasped in her lap. As the first tones of the piano rang out, Heller could see the hairs of her neck stand up. He couldn't fathom why Kasrashvili had chosen a composition for a funeral mass, of all things. Right then the Georgian turned to Heller and looked him squarely in the eye.

"For all flesh is like grass," the choir sang, and Karin shuddered.

> And all the glory of man
> like the flower of grass.
> The grass is withered
> and the flower has fallen.

Certain chords affected a person's soul more than others. Heller wasn't sure which ones were doing it. Yet he could sense that the hearts in the hall were beating differently, that people practically forgot to breathe from such intense emotion, that they were succumbing to the Russian choir's fervent singing. He placed his arm around Karin and could feel her trembling. Karin had pressed a hand to her mouth and couldn't take her eyes off the young man at the piano.

Kasrashvili kept seeking eye contact with Heller as his fingers moved effortlessly across the keys. Heller returned the stare. And with every note, an ever-deeper grief appeared to grip Karin.

"So be patient now, dear brothers," sang the choir, "for the coming of the Lord."

Heller wondered if Kasrashvili's piano might have come from Frau Schlüter's house. It was an Emil Ascherberg model, and how many of those could there be in the city? Who had the Georgian gotten the piano from? Medvedev perhaps?

Behold, the plowman waits
for the delicious fruit of the earth
and is patient about it,
until he receives the morning and evening rain.
So be patient.

The key had changed, and Kasrashvili's playing grew louder and more impassioned. Karin couldn't hold back anymore. She had kept everything in for so long. She hadn't shed a single tear over the loss of her former life, her home, all her worldly goods, her memories. Not even for all the people she'd lost, having dealt with it all inside. She had only ever shared her worries over her sons.

Kasrashvili now worked the keys with a growing fury while staring relentlessly at Heller as if he were the cause of all evils. Heller looked to Medvedev and, sure enough, their eyes met as if the Soviet commander were expecting it. Was Kasrashvili Medvedev's little dog? Did he get to do whatever he wanted? If so, why? Nothing came for free. "LK" were the initials in that backpack, Heller recalled, and wanted to reach for his notebook. Then he remembered that he'd left it at home.

For all flesh is like grass,
and all the glory of man . . .

Karin took his hand and clutched it tight. She was lightly sobbing and couldn't calm herself now. Heller grew angrier at Kasrashvili, certain he'd chosen the piece on purpose. And he was angry at himself for having no good way of dealing with Karin's outburst.

Like the flower of grass.
The grass is withered
and the flower has fallen.

Where was Ovtcharov sitting? Wasn't it his job to prevent others from acting on their own like this? Heller looked around seeking help but only found more spellbound faces; even the Russians' eyes were glassy. Medvedev kept his eyes fixed on his boots. When Heller looked to the front again, Kasrashvili was waiting for him with a twisted smile.

> Those redeemed by the Lord shall return,
> and come to Zion rejoicing;
> and joy, everlasting joy,
> shall be upon their heads;
> they shall seize the joy and bliss,
> and the sorrow and sighing shall flee.

As the last chords faded, all remained still in the hall. Then Medvedev began clapping and rose from his chair. As if freed from a spell, the other guests rose too and clapped in frenetic applause.

Karin wiped the tears from her eyes and beamed at Max. "Oh, Max, how lovely! That was truly lovely! He truly is a great talent."

Her reaction took him by surprise. "But, Karin, I thought you couldn't stand that kind of thing."

"Doesn't matter, Max. That was just what I needed. For the past two years, everything inside me has seemed dark and hollow, as if there was no reason to live anymore. And I just couldn't get the awful memories of the night of the air raid out of my mind and my heart. It's as if the music liberated me just now. You know? Didn't you feel it too?"

"It made me furious."

Karin stared in amazement. "Furious? But why?"

"He played that because of me. And he was staring at me the whole time. 'For all flesh is as grass.' Rubbing salt in the wounds."

Karin placed a calming hand on his upper arm. "Max, please. A performance like that takes months of practice. And they're performing for all of us. Don't you understand? It's a song of solace, not of mourning. Brahms believed in the kingdom of heaven. Solace is what that song is supposed to bring, and hope of redemption."

Heller nodded. Karin was right, of course. Yet he didn't trust Kasrashvili, not a bit.

The evening grew late. After several more announcements, plenty of alcohol, and the cake platters repeatedly replenished, the atmosphere turned looser and more informal.

Heller felt like he'd been dipped in thick honey. Every motion became a battle against stiff resistance. He could only get out words with effort, and they sounded distorted to him. He didn't dare to stand because he thought he might topple over. He had tried to decline every Soviet officer who stepped up to the table wanting to drink with him, yet he stood no chance against Russian tenacity. As their level of alcohol increased, the Russians turned more and more sentimental, opening their uniforms, hanging their belts on the backs of chairs, and embracing anyone who crossed their paths.

"We're going home," Heller said at some point, his tongue heavy, and he stood. Karin, who'd grown quieter over the course of the evening, agreed.

"Could you possibly pack a little of this up for us?" she asked a waiter.

"Help yourself. I'll bring you some newspaper to wrap it in. At the cloakroom," he told her jovially, "there are packages waiting for everyone too."

Suddenly Kasrashvili was standing before them. "You're leaving?" he said. His uniform still looked immaculate, and he seemed amazingly sober for the vast amount of cognac and liquor he'd consumed. Had he really been drinking, or was he only acting like it?

"Drink one more vodka with me." The Georgian gestured at the waiter.

Karin pushed by Heller. "My dear Comrade Captain," she said, offering her hand, "you are so amazingly talented and play with an astounding ease that I have never seen in any other pianist. I do hope you'll be able to devote yourself to your artistic endeavors again soon."

Kasrashvili raised his eyebrows. "From your wishes to God's ears, madam. But Communism does not demand that which the individual may accomplish but rather that which itself requires. Isn't that right?" He then gave her hand another kiss, grabbed two well-filled vodka glasses from a passing tray, and handed one to Heller.

"Here's to not selling our souls. To your health!"

February 11, 1947: Shortly Before Midnight

The nighttime cold was a shock. It was as if all their limbs had frozen, their faces, noses, and mouths solidified too. Karin snuggled close to Heller, and together they battled the biting wind. The packages were a heavy weight to carry. And the trip home seemed to drag on. A car raced by, a second one soon after. Both disappeared into the night, leaving only darkness. Heller could feel the cold sucking the strength from his body. He wanted to say something to reassure Karin, but he didn't know what. Suddenly Karin stopped.

"Someone's there!" she said. Heller let go of her, shoved their package under his other arm, and tried to reach for his pistol. Then he remembered that he'd left it with Klaus.

"Come on," he said into the wind. They walked slowly on until Heller noticed the shadow rising against the snow. He reckoned they were skirting the Dresden Heath. They could have turned left onto one of the side streets, but that meant taking the long way. And those streets were all dark, offering plenty of hiding spots for an ambush.

"We'll keep walking," Heller told her. The snowfall picked up. Heller didn't let the shadow out of his sight. The closer they got, the more certain he was that someone was standing there waiting for them.

"Could you shoot at it?" Karin asked. Heller could see that she was scared. But he couldn't tell her that he wasn't carrying his pistol.

"I don't just fire at anything. Stay here. I'll check it out."

"I'm not staying here alone," she said and didn't move an inch from him.

They continued on their way, and the shadow parted from the darkness and darted across the street. The figure was holding something. Heller thought he saw a gun. About twenty yards separated them now.

"Jörg, is that you?" he asked, taking a chance. "Jörg?"

The figure stayed still. Suddenly Heller knew how the doctor's bag could have gotten into Friedel's cellar. "Frau Schlüter? Put down the weapon. I'm doing all I can for Friedel."

Suddenly an engine roared, and two headlights bathed the snowy street in glaring light. The figure quickly disappeared into the heath. A Soviet Army jeep came down the hill, braked, slid, and stopped right next to them. Someone shouted in Russian, which brought cackles of laughter. The doors opened, and two Soviet soldiers staggered toward them. Heller shielded Karin. He frantically wracked his brain for Russian words. *Druzhba, menya tovarish Medvedev, menya politsiya.* Would they understand? He cursed himself and his inability to learn that damn language. The two soldiers weren't armed, and one was waving.

"Alone here not good, *tovarish*. Danger big. You two coming with we!" he shouted. "You now come!"

"What should we do?" Heller asked, staring at Karin.

"Go with them, of course," she replied without hesitating.

"Stoi! Ochen spasibo!" Heller patted the driver on the shoulder and climbed out of the jeep. "Klaus!" he shouted as he helped Karin out. The light was still on in the kitchen window. Klaus had already spotted them and came running out of the house. Fanny peeked out from

around the front door even though Heller had drilled it into her to remain hidden from everyone.

"Klaus, please tell them to wait a moment, then drive me a little farther."

"Where do you think you're going?" Karin looked concerned.

"I just need to check on something. Go on to bed. And get Fanny upstairs."

"I don't like this, Max. Does this have anything to do with Kasrashvili? Or that colonel who was so nasty to you?"

"No, nothing of the sort. Don't worry. Please go inside." Heller held Karin close a second. "Klaus!"

Klaus had spoken with the Russian and now came and gave Heller the pistol.

"I need a flashlight too. Can you get it for me? And try reaching Oldenbusch. Tell him I'll be over on Nordstrasse. Better yet, call police headquarters or the detectives' division and have them call him."

"You're not going to wait until reinforcements arrive?"

"Yes, yes, I'll be waiting. But I just want to get there." All at once, an immense clarity filled Heller's head.

The ruins of Frau Dähne's home were still and dark. Heller stepped onto the property, quietly walked up to the small door, and shined his flashlight. He tried the door, but it was bolted from inside.

"Frau Dähne?" he said but got no answer. He walked on and discovered a narrow stairway that led up to a balcony area between the first and second floors that had once provided a rear exit to the yard. Up there he saw a door and window repaired with boards and cardboard. He slowly climbed the five steps, entering the balcony's unlocked solarium. He knocked on the door leading inside.

"Frau Dähne? Heller here. I need to speak to you." No one stirred inside, so he opened the door.

The room wasn't very large, and it was crammed with everything the woman had been able to save from her house: several cabinets, a table, pictures, lamps, and a great deal of cracked porcelain. There was hardly any room to move, but she seemed to have adjusted. Heller could see the corner she slept in. "Frau Dähne?"

It was really cold. Her little steel stove had long cooled even though there were enough piles of wood to heat the whole place for a week. Heller stepped closer, to touch her possibly sleeping form. He was already fearing the worst when he realized it was only a blanket gathered in a bundle. The bed was empty.

Heller felt uneasy. Shouldn't she be at home? He stood, shining his flashlight around the room. Something on a shelf caught his attention. It was a leather spiked helmet from the First World War, worn by soldiers before the steel helmet was introduced. He himself had worn one. It was just good enough for deflecting saber blows but completely useless against bullets and shrapnel. Heller touched the helmet and spotted an old framed photo beside it. It showed a middle-aged man in uniform and a woman in a nurse's outfit. It was clearly a young Frau Dähne. Heller took a closer look around. He pulled out boxes and opened cabinets. He found a broken saber, only the handle and about four inches of blade remaining. In a cardboard box he discovered various mementos: a yellowed nurse's cap, a booklet of codes of conduct, a dinged-up bullet, shrapnel, and more photos, many showing vast field hospital collection points for the wounded and the amputated, images of captured Cossacks and dead horses. And even though this was from the Russian Front, a different war zone than Heller had experienced, it still shot him back thirty years. He hadn't expected that.

Heller had already seen images from collection points like this, where hundreds of moaning, fading men lay bleeding to death, having to wait and wait because the field doctors couldn't keep up with even the barest of necessities. And when a field surgeon finally did arrive, he would decide in just a few words whether a soldier lived or died, whether he received surgery or an amputation. If Heller hadn't been conscious at the time and hadn't protested and begged, they would have given him the anesthetic and taken his foot off. Caught off guard, he now felt the memories overpower him, dragging him back into the hell of those muddy trenches full of a foul stench, a bloodred clay soup of legs, arms, and torsos. Those artillery shells hammering. For days. Every hour, every minute, every second. You could lose your mind. Yet he had endured it, and he owed his ticket out of hell to a single sharp piece of wood. Big as a bread knife, driven right through his ankle after an explosion. On the first day in the field hospital, the constant drumming barrage from the French had begun haunting his dreams. What he would have given to be rid of them.

He had never gotten rid of them, not even after that terrible night in February of '45. When he had staggered through that thundering hell of flames. When he had crawled through a cellar for minutes so interminably long that it seemed he was damned to wander in that darkness for all eternity. That was his price for surviving, Heller was forced to realize. Nothing came for free. In a place where so many people had lost their lives, it was a simple fact that you would pay somehow for still being alive. He paid with his dreams and with that strange fear that always overcame him whenever he so much as thought of stepping into a dark cellar.

Heller forced himself to banish the images from his mind, then placed the items back where they belonged. He eventually followed his instincts and climbed onto a chair to reach the high shelves. It didn't surprise him when he got hold of a rifle—Russian booty from the First World War, a Mosin-Nagant. It was covered in dust but otherwise in good condition apart from some newer scratches. Its normally attached bayonet was missing.

Heller thought he heard a faint sound. He turned around and directed the flashlight beam down into the room. But nothing was there. He climbed down from the chair and put the rifle back. He took another careful look around. That made him realize that one of the large wardrobes was standing a little way out from the wall. When he shined his light behind it, he discovered a passage. He pushed the wardrobe out a little more, so he could squeeze through. The room behind it must have once been a hallway, and half of it was now caved in. Stairs led down into the cellar. A wide board leaning against the wall caught his eye. As he pulled it away, he discovered a nook with food stacked inside—cans of food, dehydrated rations, rice, a bucket of potatoes, a crate of apples, fruit preserves, conserved leeks, even chocolate and fresh meat in ceramic bowls. Where had the woman gotten it all? Heller glanced at his watch. At least thirty minutes must have passed since he'd instructed Klaus to call for backup. How long would Oldenbusch and his men need? Twice that long maybe?

He heard the sound again, like a moan. He shined the light down the stairs again but could only see a few yards, where the stairs turned left. Heller saw something lying on the fifth or sixth stair. It was a single candle, half burned down. Could the old woman have fallen down the stairs?

Heller hesitated, unable to muster the resolve to go down the stairs, not even with his flashlight. He had no fear of ghosts, didn't believe in demons, yet he knew that if he climbed down into that darkness, something would happen to him. He would start hearing things that had happened long ago. Start smelling fire, burned flesh, charred hair. Feel those hands reaching for him, trying to take hold.

The darkness was already grabbing for him, creeping upward, enveloping him, dragging him down when he moved the flashlight beam to another spot. He felt like a small boy, scared of the bogeyman. But he wasn't a boy—he was a grown man. You can handle this, he told himself, you can. You've gone through far worse hells. Yet he couldn't. He needed to get out of there and wait outside for Oldenbusch.

He heard the moaning again.

"Frau Dähne, is that you? Are you all right?" What a stupid question, yet he did feel a little encouraged hearing his own voice. But what if she really was lying down there? What if she needed help?

Heller drew his pistol and felt his way down the first step, then the second. He aimed both flashlight and gun together at the dark cellar entrance. Keeping his back to the wall, he forced himself down, step by step. He knew that he'd be fully at the mercy of his fears should the flashlight go out. Once the stairs turned, he shined light into a cellar corridor. It was far longer than he would've guessed and branched off into several rooms.

He didn't see Frau Dähne, but he did make out dark stains on the floor. He crouched and touched one of them. It was clearly blood, even if it had dried a long time ago. He now spotted footprints and shined the light along the floor. The prints led to a door at the far end.

Heller straightened himself. He shouldn't stay here on his own. It might be a trap. Oldenbusch would be here any minute; it had been long enough. So Heller needed to go upstairs, secure the scene, and wait. He used the flashlight to light his way to the stairs and was on the second stair when he heard the sound again, loud and clear, as if someone were trying to scream with a gag in their mouth.

Heller cursed. He was torn between reason and wanting to help, and he hated not being able to remain reasonable. Yet he turned back around and went to the far door, which was open just a crack. Heller pushed it open with his foot, keeping his pistol aimed. When he finally dared to enter the room, a chilling stench hit him. The smell was overpowering. He shined his flashlight beam to the left, along a wall, and stopped at shelving and collapsed masonry. Heavy beams supported the ceiling there. Someone had put in a lot of effort even though the house above was beyond saving.

Heller was running the flashlight over the unstable brickwork when the moaning sounded next to him. He whipped around and shined the light.

He saw him now. It was a Russian officer, gagged, with his hands tied behind his back and hanging from a rope around his neck. Just as with Gutmann, the line had been tossed over a ceiling beam and tied to an iron rod sticking out of the wall. The man screeched and moaned and reeled back and forth. Heller directed his beam down and saw that the man could just stand on his very tiptoes. His naked toes painted streaks on the smudged cellar floor. Heller scanned the surface and saw it was covered with blood as far as he could see. He was standing in the middle of it himself. He stepped to the side in disgust, incapable of thinking clearly, then bumped into something heavy that first yielded before swinging back at him.

It was a second hanged man. He'd lost his battle long ago. It had to be Weiler. He wore civilian clothes. His arms ended in dark stumps, his hands cut off. Heller stepped to the side again so as not to get hit by the swinging corpse. His flashlight beam landed on a workbench that was dark from blood. Something lay on it, a human torso missing its head, arms, legs.

Heller had to stifle the urge to gag. He thought of the meat upstairs in the hiding place and in the pots with the children in the woods, and he thought of Frau Dähne, of her chopping wood.

The Russian officer moaned, reminding Heller what he needed to do.

"Wait, I'll find a knife," Heller said, then felt a sharp pain in his left shoulder. He dropped the flashlight, and it clattered to the floor and went out. He grabbed his gun with his left hand, reached for the painful spot with his right, and felt a syringe sticking out of his shoulder. He was about to yank it out when something struck the back of his head. He ducked, and a second blow flew over him. Numbness began spreading through his arm, and he started to panic. He held the pistol with his right hand, aiming into the darkness. But he heard and saw nothing of his attacker. Now his arm was numb, and everything was spinning. He needed to keep a clear head. He needed to get out of here. He went by touch, one arm stretched out. He bumped into a wall and felt his way along it. Suddenly he sensed movement, then metal on stone. He threw punches around him, made contact. Something fell to the floor. Then, finally, he could feel the doorway. He staggered into the corridor. His numb arm dangled wildly, and his knees grew weak, the floor seeming to dissolve under his feet. He fell, then crawled onward to the stairs. It smelled like mold and blood. He was nauseous.

"Don't you recognize me?" he heard. *It was Klaus, peering at him gravely, as if he'd given up believing in any and all goodness of man.*

Heller opened his eyes wide, staring into the darkness. Had he been hallucinating? Or had he lost consciousness for a few moments? Faint footsteps neared. Heller rolled onto his back and tried to raise his gun, but he was far too weak.

"Werner!" Heller shouted. "Werner!"

Then a foot stepped onto his throat and pressed him to the floor. Heller reached for the leg, his fingers numb and weak. His consciousness waned, yet he still felt his attacker's breath on his face as he bent down to pull a noose over his head. With a firm jerk, the noose tightened around Heller's neck.

February 12, 1947: After Midnight

"Max! Boss!" Someone was lightly slapping his face. Then something ice-cold touched his forehead.

"What's that?" Heller asked, dazed.

"Snow, Max. Get up. What happened?" Oldenbusch grabbed him and hauled him to his feet.

"When did you get here?" Heller's tongue felt foreign inside his mouth.

"Just now."

"What time's it?" he slurred and only now noticed all the light. Several flashlights were brightening the cellar corridor. Heller tried to check his watch with his numb fingers; he could have been unconscious only a few minutes. "Did you see anyone running away?" He felt at his neck but found no rope there. Had he imagined that?

"Not on the street," Oldenbusch said.

"Werner, have the whole area searched now! Frau Dähne, she . . ." If only he could've prevented it. A sudden wave of nausea swept over him and he vomited.

Oldenbusch patted his back. "An aftereffect of the anesthesia. I've already launched a manhunt for Frau Dähne."

Heller retched and gasped for air. "You've been in the cellar—you helped the man?"

"Yes. We got him down. It's Yakovlev, the missing Soviet. He's still alive, but it's unclear if he'll make it. His throat is probably crushed."

"Werner," Heller whispered, grabbing his colleague's arm. "You think it's possible that the meat, that she . . ." His voice gave out, and he started vomiting again.

Oldenbusch shrugged and nodded, as if he'd considered it already.

"Thus the injection of anesthetic, because she's much too weak to fight against a man," Heller panted, pushing damp hair off his forehead.

"So it's not just coincidence that all these men were regulars in Gutmann's bar?" Oldenbusch asked.

"No. She knew Gutmann, Swoboda, and all the girls. Frau Schlüter even alleged that she was procuring the girls for Gutmann. She owns a rifle that fits the bayonet. She was a nurse and knows anesthesia. She could even have betrayed the pastor to the Soviets to divert suspicion to those children in the woods."

"Come on now, Max. Let's get upstairs. We'll drive to the office. We need to get you back in shape."

"No, we're staying," Heller ordered. "Get some more light in here, and start securing the evidence. Call Ovtcharov over here. I'm going to go sit upstairs until I feel better."

Forty-five minutes later, Heller was sitting on a chair upstairs, still unable to stand. Coffee was doing him good. A kerosene lamp provided feeble light. Cables from a generator outside ran through the room and down to the cellar. The door was open, and Heller was freezing despite the blanket draped over his legs. When Ovtcharov came up from the cellar with Oldenbusch, he grabbed a chair and sat across from Heller. Outside in the yard, twenty of his soldiers stood around smoking, waiting for orders.

"It was an old woman?" Ovtcharov said. "She lured my men down into the cellar here, and the one-handed man and that Weiler as well?" Disbelief was written all over his face. "She numbed them, strung them up, then butchered them? Did I understand that correctly? And to divert attention, she stuck those two severed hands in the neighbor boy's cellar?"

Oldenbusch held up a hand. "In her oven we found the remains of bones—she apparently incinerated anything left over from her victims," he explained.

Ovtcharov eyed the small metal stove with skepticism. He then shouted something to his soldiers outside, who moved out.

Heller rubbed his aching shoulder. His chest too. "I realized something this evening. You know what it was?"

"I'm so eager to hear," the colonel said, though it sounded sarcastic.

"I was wondering if it was possible that Medvedev ordered Kasrashvili to take care of the issue in the Schwarzer Peter bar. I mean, he would have been in a position to get them out of the way, one after the other. Avoiding a scandal. You yourself led me to the idea by telling me that the commander didn't dare officially interfere."

Ovtcharov's body began shaking oddly. Only after a few seconds did Heller comprehend that the Russian was laughing. Heller had to give him credit for at least attempting to hide it.

"Comrade Heller, you truly must reexamine the image you have of us Russians. Sure, you may appear to represent the moral authority of your police force, but you really do harbor a most grim resentment. I've asked you before what you think of us. Now I'm asking you, do you really think we'd order one of our own officers to kill a fellow officer? Kasrashvili is a prisoner, as we all are. He, too, cannot live the life he'd wanted. He drinks too much, he plays funeral music, and he's destroying himself. Didn't it ever occur to you that Medvedev might feel sorry for him? And that's why he's giving the man some slack? But it is true that he was the one who told us what was really going on in Gutmann's bar. And now I wish to hear from you just what happened to Cherin and Berinov."

"I can only speculate as to how Berinov died. He must have been here in the ruins and found Swoboda's head, which he took with him. Frau Dähne followed him, gave him the injection, and then, once he was numbed, rammed the bayonet into his neck."

"So how did the head get into the backpack? Did Berinov himself put it in there?"

"Potentially. As evidence."

"Why didn't the woman take the backpack with her?"

"Because it was early morning, and people were already on their way out," Heller offered, unsure. The more he talked, the more it became clear that something wasn't right. Did Berinov have the backpack with him, or had he found it here in the house?

"How did she lure the men inside? Why would they go see her?"

"You'll have to ask her once we've caught her. The day before yesterday, I started to walk her home. She went along with it at first, but then she cleverly diverted me away. I'm only realizing that now."

Ovtcharov gave Heller a quizzical look. "How did she divert you?"

Heller pursed his lips, wondering how to respond. Ovtcharov knew every trick in the book. He didn't want to give too much away.

He asked a question back instead. "First tell me: Was Frau Dähne the one who told you about the pastor?"

"We have eyes and ears everywhere, Oberkommissar. Most people are not as straight-ahead as you."

"It's 'straightforward,'" Heller said, correcting the Russian yet again.

"Right. And for that I admire you, how you pursue a cause the way you feel is right, no matter the consequences. On the other hand, I'm also surprised by how unbelievably naïve you can be. But I prefer to think of you as more stubborn than foolish. We've known for some time who you've been putting up in your home. So I think it would be a good idea to wait and see what happens." Ovtcharov kept his gaze fixed on Heller.

Heller stared back. He didn't respond to what Ovtcharov had said. He had just gotten another nagging thought. He rubbed at his throat, where that foot had stepped down on him so hard. It still hurt. However strong of will old Frau Dähne might be, stringing up a man by a rope required plenty of strength, and she didn't possess it. He only had to recall how hard it was for her to set back up that fallen chopping block.

He stood and looked at Oldenbusch. "Werner, did you find the weapon I was assaulted with? I think I might have knocked it out of the attacker's hand."

Oldenbusch nodded. "One second," he said and went to the cellar stairs in the next room. "It's not an actual weapon," he shouted on his way back. "More like a bread knife."

Heller took the knife from Oldenbusch and caught his breath. "This is mine. This afternoon I noticed it was missing. Fanny must have stolen it. But I also saw she was still at home right before I came here. It's not possible for her to have gotten here faster than me."

Ovtcharov stood up with a pleased look on his face. "So it must be this Jörg," he said. "I will sound the alarm. He can't be far. Do you have an idea of where we need to be looking?"

Heller nodded. "I need a telephone, right away. Is Frau Schlüter's still working?"

Ovtcharov took him by the arm. "Come."

Together they rushed across the yard to the Schlüters' villa. Ovtcharov hammered on the door. "Open up!" he shouted, but no one responded. The Russian cursed, took two steps back, and gave the door a mighty kick, busting the lock open. Heller took the stairs two at a time, a sharp pain running through his right ankle every other step. He gritted his teeth, yanked the handset off the wall phone in the hallway, and dialed home. He only got a solid tone. Heller hung up and tried again. But the connection was dead.

Ovtcharov's driver zoomed up Bautzner Strasse despite the slippery surface. Heller tried not to imagine what might have happened back home. If it was Jörg who'd assaulted him in the cellar, a half hour would have been enough time for him to reach Frau Marquart's house on foot.

Heller blamed himself. He shouldn't have let Karin persuade him to take the girl in. In doing so, he at least should have informed Ovtcharov. Now he'd put his wife and Klaus in danger, as well as gone behind the Russian's back, which would only make the man mistrust him more.

On the bridge over Mordgrund Creek the car almost started to slide. Heller clamped onto the back of the front seat. They couldn't lose momentum or they'd never make it up the grade.

They finally reached his neighborhood, Weisser Hirsch. The driver decelerated hard so as not to slide on the steep incline down the Rissweg. Ovtcharov instructed him to park away from the house, then climbed out with his pistol drawn. The driver grabbed his machine gun, and Heller pulled out his pistol.

"Tell him he shouldn't shoot to kill," Heller pleaded to Ovtcharov.

"This I know," grumbled the driver. They hurried across the street and crouched to approach. The house was dark and still. Ovtcharov ordered the soldier to go around to the back door while he and Heller crept to the front. Ovtcharov kept a lookout while Heller tried to open the door without making any noise.

He pushed it open quietly and listened. He couldn't hear a sound.

"Klaus?" Heller whispered. "Klaus . . ."

No response. Heller crept down the hall and looked into the living room. His son lay on his back on the sofa. His left arm hung off, his hand touching the floor.

"Klaus!" gasped Heller.

Klaus shot up and peered around. "What? What is it?"

"It's fine, Klaus. All fine. It's me. I need to see Fanny."

"She's sleeping upstairs." Klaus stood, now wide awake.

Heller went upstairs and peeked in the bedroom, where Karin sleepily raised her head.

"It's all fine, keep sleeping, Karin," he whispered and shut the door. He was feeling relieved and could breathe easier. "Comrade Ovtcharov, tell your driver that all looks to be in order," he called down the stairs in a low voice.

Then he stood over Fanny's sleeping spot. It was empty. Fanny was gone, along with the baby and all her meager possessions. He squatted down and felt the bedding. It was cold. He stayed in a crouch, thinking things over. He only rose again, slowly, when he heard a sound.

It was Ovtcharov, who had followed him up the stairs. Karin came out of her room, her robe wrapped tightly around her.

"Is she gone?" the Russian asked.

Heller nodded. Where could she be going in the middle of the night? To meet Jörg? Was she planning to waylay him, or was she running away? When he looked up, he noticed a certain schadenfreude spreading across the Russian's face.

"She is shifty and cunning. That's how you Germans say it, yes? She had settled right in with you, just like she first did with old Frau Dähne. She aroused your sympathy. And now? What does he say now, our straightforward man? How does he sleep at night now?"

"Are you mocking my husband?" Karin asked, glaring at the colonel.

"Mother, he's right," Klaus cautioned from halfway up the stairs.

Karin didn't like being silenced. "I was the one who insisted he bring the girl here. She has a baby! Don't you understand? And don't think I didn't notice how unfair you were to my husband back at the Bühlau. Why do bad people always have to make fun of the good and decent ones?"

"You're saying I'm a bad person?" Ovtcharov asked, his tone harsh.

"I don't know you well enough to say," Karin replied, staring him in the eye. "But you were sure acting that way."

Her determined stance seemed to unsettle the colonel. He stared at Heller, looking almost helpless. It was awkwardly still. Suddenly the driver shouted up to them in Russian. Ovtcharov asked something in return. Then he grinned, turned to Heller, and spread out his arms like a gratified circus ringmaster. "My men have found the boy. He's been holed up in the river tunnel under Deaconess Hospital. He had a gun on him."

"Is he dead?"

"What do you think? He gave himself up."

"Come on, I need to speak to him." Heller was eager to get going, but the Russian held him back.

"Oh no, Comrade Oberkommissar. This one's mine. I'm talking to him. He will tell me where that girl with the baby is. You go to bed. I will let you know what happens." Ovtcharov saluted, then turned on his heels and went whistling down the stairs.

February 12, 1947: Early Morning

Heller left the house before sunrise, his head full of unanswered questions. Since the phone line wasn't working, he hadn't been able to confirm whether Oldenbusch was coming to pick him up. So he decided to take the streetcar. He made the difficult trek up to the stop at Bautzner Strasse. The numbness had almost disappeared from his body, but the injection spot on his arm ached, and there were a few sore spots on his neck that his overcoat collar kept rubbing. It wasn't even six yet, but many people were out and about. Some of them were already waiting at the streetcar stop, though it was never certain whether a train would arrive. Everyone stared listlessly into space. After a few minutes, some of the men set off on foot. After ten more minutes, the streetcar arrived. Heller got a ticket from the conductor, found a seat, and wearily leaned against the window, where his carousel of thoughts started revolving again.

He wondered where old Frau Dähne was now. Had she fallen victim to Jörg and Fanny? Had Fanny blackmailed her, taken advantage of her? Heller didn't want to believe that. Or had it been compassion that compelled Frau Dähne to help Fanny, to let her live with her and allow Fanny to kill? Could compassion be so great that someone would allow such a thing? Perhaps the whole matter had gained such momentum that it had spun out of the old woman's control.

The streetcar traveled alongside the Dresden Heath now, over Mordgrund Creek, by Lingner Park and Albrechtsberg Palace, and eventually passed the Hotel Heidehof, which now housed the MVD offices. Heller wondered whether Jörg was in custody here or if they'd taken him to Münchner Platz.

When the streetcar halted at Waldschlösschen, not far from where that first body had been found on the icy slope, Heller was still lost in thought. It was slowly becoming light out. To his left, the view over the Elbe River opened wide to include the snow-covered ruins of the central city, appearing like a wild, rocky wasteland. Heller's eye suddenly caught something—a little figure standing at the slope along the river, staring up the road. The streetcar continued on.

"Halt!" Heller shouted as he jumped from his seat and forced his way through the crammed-together passengers. "Hold up! It's an emergency," he shouted, and the streetcar slowed again.

"What's wrong?" the conductor said.

"Someone must've fallen asleep," a passenger said, and people laughed.

Heller fought his way up to the door and jumped out. He waited until the streetcar was gone, then crossed the tracks and the street.

"Were you waiting here for me?" he asked the girl.

Fanny stared at Heller with a blank expression, showing no surprise. She didn't have her baby with her. "You give me my Jörg back."

"I can't do that, Fanny," Heller told her. "The Soviets have him. There's nothing I can do."

"Sure you can! They're your friends, the Russians! Just go see them and tell them he didn't do nothing."

Heller shook his head and tried taking Fanny by the arm. She pulled back.

"Fanny, you need to come with me to the station. I have to ask you about Frau Dähne's house."

"Don't you go touching me. Go see the Russians and get Jörg outta there. We're gonna take off. To the west." She drew her hand from her overcoat pocket and scratched at her temple. Heller noticed that the angular bulge in her pocket resembled a pistol.

"Was it you who happened to be at this very spot six days ago? You were looking for the backpack."

Fanny's right eyelid started twitching.

Heller stepped closer. "You killed the one-handed man, Franz Swoboda!"

Fanny turned irate. "He took me against my will. Called me a stupid brat, 'you're gonna do whatever I tell you.' And then he hits me. So I bit him and ran away, 'cause I knew what he already done to Margi. He came after me, and when I went and tried to hide at the old lady's, he saw me, and he came inside. So I surprised him and killed him dead!"

Heller looked around. They were alone on this side of the street. "How?"

"With one of them spiky rods from the rifle. Stabbed him in the back. Frau Dähne, she got mad at me and said that meant big trouble. Then we tried cutting him up so we could get rid of him."

"So Jörg—he didn't know about it?"

"No, not a chance! It coulda just been self-defense, was what Frau Dähne said."

Heller raised his chin. "And killing Vasili Cherin, was that self-defense too?"

Fanny lowered her gaze and pouted.

"Cherin wasn't with just any girl, right? He had something going with you. What did he promise you?"

"The baby's his. He wanted to take me with him at first, back to Russia. And then he says I should go disappear and that it's not his. And if I didn't leave him alone, he'd lock me up. That got me so mad, I went after him. Then I stabbed him with the same spiky thing."

"But Berinov was his friend, and he was looking for him. He followed you into the ruined house, and you numbed him with the syringe. But it didn't work right."

"Snuck right in was what he done, tried taking off again. Had the backpack with the one-handed man's head inside. I stuck him in the arm with the syringe. But he didn't fall over right away, he was so drunk, and he didn't even fall over after I stabbed him. Then he went running out of the house, with that thing sticking out of his neck. But there were already people out, so I couldn't go after him."

"People didn't notice he was injured? No one tried to help him?"

"How would I know?"

"And Yakovlev and Weiler? How did you lure them into the ruins? And Gutmann—how were you able to string him up? You weren't acting alone, and you definitely didn't write that letter."

Fanny shrugged.

Heller seized her by the arm, turned her, reached into her coat pocket, and pulled out the pistol. It was a TT-33, a Russian officer's gun.

"You have to come with me. We need to clear this up."

Fanny resisted, ramming the back of her head against his chest. "You're not gonna lock me up," she gasped. "No way you are. I hid my baby and I'm not telling where. So if you arrest me, he's gonna starve and freeze and it's all your fault!"

"Where's the baby? Tell me!"

"You let me loose!" Fanny hissed.

Heller let her go. "Where's the baby?"

"I'm not telling!"

"Be reasonable, Fanny. It's your child."

She shook her head. Rage brought tears to her eyes. "Russian baby is what it is."

"Don't act like it doesn't matter to you. Otherwise you wouldn't have cared for it, nursed it. You're a good mother. Karin told me. Fanny, where's your baby boy? You can tell me."

"My Jörg wants him, don't you understand? He cares, he does. He's always so good."

"Karin and I can take the child, Fanny. We care too. You understand that, right? And I can talk to the public prosecutor and put in a good word for you both. You two have had it really rough, and you were only acting in self-defense. But you need to come with me now, and you have to tell me where your baby boy is . . ."

Heller paused. He'd just figured out where the baby was. It was actually quite simple.

Fanny was eyeing him with mistrust, trying to read his face. Then she whipped around and ran off.

Heller wanted to run after her, but it was clear he wasn't nearly as fast. He wondered how to proceed.

He spotted a policeman in the distance.

Exhausted and sweaty, Heller arrived at Martin Luther Church ten minutes later, right as the streetlamps turned off for the day. He'd lost sight of Fanny, but she couldn't have gained much of a head start. He stood before the church, panting, unable to keep an eye on all three entrances at the same time. He had to go inside. The side door, which was closest to him, was locked. He rushed on to the main entrance. It was open.

Once the large door closed behind him, darkness reigned inside the church. The altar at the far end appeared in silhouette, the pews barely visible. Heller listened in the dark and caught himself reaching for his gun. He forced himself to leave it in his overcoat.

"Fanny?" he said into the darkness.

"You're not supposed to come here." Fanny's voice was quite close. He turned her way.

"I had to. I'm a police officer. It's my duty. This isn't only about you, Fanny—it's about the baby. Your baby. You carry a responsibility."

"She didn't choose to have it—she's still just a child herself." Frau Dähne's voice.

Heller tried to spot the old woman in the darkness. "That excuses some of it, but not all. Everyone should exhibit a certain amount of reason."

"You don't know a thing! You don't know her suffering!"

"How do you know? What do you know of me?" Heller kept moving toward their voices.

"Stay where you are; I see what you're doing," Frau Dähne hissed. "Leave the girl alone. She's only trying to survive. If you don't, I'll be forced to shoot."

Heller's eyes finally adjusted to the darkness, and he saw the old woman. She was holding an MP 40 machine gun.

"No, don't—he's gonna free my Jörg," Fanny whispered, sounding tearful. "He's gonna go to the Russians."

"Fanny. I'll tell you one more time: I cannot do anything for your Jörg!" Heller gradually neared the old woman. "The Russians wouldn't believe me, that he's done nothing." Only two yards separated him from Frau Dähne and the barrel of the machine gun.

"The meat that you gave the children," he said gently. "What animal was it?"

"Why do you want to know? It was pig. I know a butcher, a relative of mine. He gives it to me."

The old woman stepped back.

Heller stepped forward at the same pace, step for step. He could only guess where Fanny was.

"Give me the weapon, Frau Dähne. You're only making things worse for yourself."

"You listen to me, Herr Oberkommissar. You know how old I am? I have nothing to lose, not a thing. What's it all good for, anyway, living like this, in struggle? One freezing night after the other, and you wake the next morning resigned to your fate, having to make it through yet another day. I could shoot you dead." The old woman's eyes flashed.

"I know what you would lose if you did," Heller replied. "Your salvation."

Frau Dähne didn't respond.

Heller broke the silence. "Where's the pastor?"

The old woman stepped back to the left, moving into the darkest corner of the church, where, as Heller recalled, there was more than one door.

"Don't you have any sympathy for those children?" she said. "Don't you wonder how it came to be that they had to live in the forest, that they had to sell themselves?"

If he were fast enough, Heller thought, he could snatch the gun from her. He only needed to slap the barrel to the side and rip the butt from her hands.

"Frau Dähne, that's enough!" It was Pastor Christian Beger. His silhouette had separated from the corner shadows. He stood next to the old woman and gently took the weapon from her hands. In his black clothing the young man remained a dark blur to Heller, only his collar glowing.

"Fanny, go!" the pastor said. "You hear me, Fanny? Go now. Take your boy and go."

"But my Jörg . . ."

"I'll see what I can do, but you must go. And you, Frau Dähne, go with her." The pastor's voice was firm, assertive.

"But—"

"Go, now!" insisted Pastor Beger.

"Fanny," Heller said. "Remember what Karin showed you. Your baby needs to be fed, and warm, and clean. And you, too, need to keep clean, you hear? And you have to talk to him."

It was silent for a moment. Then Heller heard soft footsteps moving away from them. The main door opened a crack, and for a few seconds the early light of day sliced through the darkness like a sharp razor. The two women darted outside, and the heavy door shut forcefully.

In the darkness, Heller and Pastor Beger remained motionless, waiting for the shadows to reveal shapes again. Yet in those few seconds, Heller had seen a face smashed by the Soviets, the image still etched in his mind like a photo negative. One eye nearly swollen shut, the bridge of his nose with a gaping gash, and an eyebrow split open.

"You're a good man, Christian," Heller said. "You're like me. Always searching for the right way, constantly despairing on account of those who never become wiser, who never learn from their mistakes. Despairing about all the injustice out there."

Pastor Beger said nothing, but Heller could hear his labored breathing.

"And you keep finding, over and over, just how hard it is to do the right thing. But not only is it tough, it's actually impossible. Am I right? Who are you supposed to help? Who deserves sympathy, and who is truly guilty? It's enough to drive you insane, don't you think? You're put to the test again and again, trying to make the right decision, yet you repeatedly end up disillusioned."

Heller could still hear his words, hoping they would stir the pastor. Yet Pastor Beger said nothing.

"Frau Dähne, she only wanted to help. She wanted to help the children. But what did she do in return? Is she guilty? Is she a good soul?"

The pastor now released something like a laugh.

But Heller had heard another sound. He raised a hand.

"You know," the pastor began, then gasped in shock.

Heller knew what it meant. He bounded forward and ripped the gun out of the pastor's hands.

"Go easy on him," he told Oldenbusch.

Oldenbusch had crept up with barely a sound. "Got here as fast as I could, boss. The church is surrounded." He held the pastor in a tight armlock.

"Let me go, please, my back! I can't stand it." The pastor groaned and writhed in pain.

Heller had slung the MP 40 on a shoulder. He shifted it onto his back and patted down the pastor for hidden weapons. Once he nodded the all-clear, Oldenbusch released the pastor. "Werner, have the men fan out at once. Fanny just took off with her baby along with Frau Dähne—they should still be in the vicinity."

"Yes, sir!" Oldenbusch rushed off.

"No use of firearms!" Heller shouted after him. The door opened again. Light streamed in once more, fading when the door shut. Now it was just Heller and the pastor.

"When did it happen?" Heller asked gently.

"What?" the pastor said, looking around.

"When did you lose your faith?"

Pastor Beger smiled, trying to dismiss the question as a joke. Yet Heller's face was like stone. The pastor's mouth contorted as if in pain.

"You know why I got this position here?" he began. "The Gestapo took away my predecessor. He was hiding two Jews here in the church.

Someone from the parish reported him—someone who came to the service every Sunday, who prayed to Jesus, begging for salvation. They took the pastor away in the night and killed him. And what did the national church do? The bishop? They didn't send a single note of protest. They acted as if nothing happened." His voice sounded constricted, as if he were forcing himself not to yell.

"Was it an accident? Acting on impulse? Rage alone isn't enough to make a murderer. Who died first—Vasili Cherin or Franz Swoboda?"

Pastor Beger gritted his teeth.

"When Fanny showed up here the first time, I had no idea where she'd come from. Frau Dähne brought her in, and I gave her food. Later she told me about the children in the woods and I, I . . ." Pastor Beger stopped himself, then bit at his lip. "These children, these poor little creatures. It's not our concern, people told me. No one wanted to care for them; everyone only worries about themselves. These children didn't seem to matter to anyone. I did what I could, for months on end." The pastor breathed harder. "There was such hunger everywhere and no one accountable, and there in the thick of it people like this Weiler, like those officers, like Gutmann. He donated food, bread, and sausage to me. And I was so stupid, so naïve, I didn't understand what they were doing. At first, I thought they were really going to help those girls. And then here came Fanny, already carrying a child. And she believed it was normal. She believed she had to sell herself to get food. That is so . . ."

He searched for the right words. And suddenly they erupted out of him. "All those people out there, such stupid, pigheaded narcissists, with no decency. They all think of themselves as victims. No one, not one, admits to being an offender. All the while they betray each other, stealing and killing. The worst criminals are already back in office, assuming the highest posts. And it's precisely the people who voted for a murderer to be their leader who are now sitting on their stocks of food and getting fat while those children in the woods perish. I ask you: Where is God in all this? Where is my God, whom I'm supposed to believe in? There is no God, I can tell you that."

The pastor's voice cracked. "He's not here. He never has been. He's a lie. You understand me, Oberkommissar? I've beseeched him, pleaded to him, begged. He must show himself. He must show me some kind of sign. Yet nothing happened. Instead this fiend, this war criminal, he beats on this young girl, nearly a child herself. Margi was far along in her pregnancy, you see, like Fanny, and she fled from him, into the woods, and she died from a miscarriage. That's when I knew someone had to do something. Someone had to act, had to punish them, if He wasn't going to. And if there's no heaven and no hell, no divine punishment, then people like Swoboda need to be punished right here on earth."

"You're right about that, but not when it comes to vigilante justice," Heller replied. "Every person has a right to a fair trial."

"You of all people say that?" screeched Pastor Beger, his voice breaking. "You are the one who betrayed me to the Russians. They took me and beat me the very same day. And I've been forced to realize that I'm weak. I wasn't strong enough. I couldn't take it and was so afraid of the pain. No faith could make me strong, since even Jesus on the cross was just a lie. I betrayed those children because I couldn't take the beating." The pastor sobbed. "They shot poor Heinrich because he wouldn't put down his weapon. He was trying to protect the group. And now they're all gone, and I don't know what's happened to them. The outside world doesn't care, not the Germans or the Russians."

"That's not true. I care about the children," Heller said. "I never betrayed you. And I took Fanny into my home. Without telling the Russians."

"A hypocrite's what you are. You serve the Russians, just like you served the Nazis," Pastor Beger hissed, making a fist.

Oldenbusch was back. He quickly stepped in to protect Heller from the raving pastor. But Heller shook his head.

"Do you want to tell me what happened? Did it start with Swoboda?"

"Fanny took me into the woods to help Margi, but by the time I got there she was already dead—her child too. The only thing left to do was bury them. I said a prayer for the children, to give them some hope. But me? No one was giving me any hope. Hell had opened up right before me. And while I was still praying I was seized by this unbridled rage at a murderer like Swoboda lying there all fat and smug in his warm bed even though he deserved to have been hanged long ago. I took that bayonet, ambushed him, and rammed it into him. But he fought back. I had to stab again and again. Then during the night I dragged him over to Frau Dähne with my handcart, since I didn't know what to do with him. She had to help me get rid of him."

A favorable judge might decide this was an unpremeditated emotional act, Heller thought. "And Weiler had to die because he'd betrayed the previous pastor?"

"Frau Dähne knew. Weiler had found out about the pastor accidently. He must have told Frau Schlüter at the printing company, then she reported it to the Gestapo. But Weiler, he kept on going to church every Sunday; he survived that inferno of an air raid without a scratch. Even got a good position after the war. Provided Gutmann with food, got invited to the bar, sexually assaulted those girls, yet still came every Sunday, saying the Lord's Prayer like a good boy, donating candles and canned food. Nearly drove me insane with his hypocrisy. I lured him into the ruined house, numbed him, and strung him up. A person like that should suffer, you see. Shouldn't ever be allowed to experience a merciful death. I watched him, the way he struggled for his pathetic life, the way he pleaded and whined. And the way he pleaded, it was . . ." Pastor Beger cut himself off, needing to compose himself.

Heller wanted to keep the pastor talking. "And then it was Cherin's turn?"

"Cherin wasn't any better. He didn't care what happened to Fanny. First he promised her a new life, then he disowned her. He didn't want a child, especially not from Fanny. After she told me about it, I followed him and stabbed him."

"Whereupon Berinov started searching for whoever killed his friend. Did he suspect you?"

"I wanted to take the head to Gutmann and nail it to his front door. I wanted to teach him real fear, that hypocrite with a crucifix in that frightful building of his, him and everyone who visited that place. Berinov surprised me there. He wanted to know what was in the backpack. I ran back to the ruined house, and he followed me. He attacked me down in the cellar, took the backpack, and tried to run off with it. I chased after him, injected him with the anesthetic, but it didn't work right. He staggered up the cellar stairs, and I tried to stop him. He kept pushing me away. I got desperate and rammed the bayonet into his neck. But he kept going, right out of the house, and I couldn't stop him, didn't dare follow him. There were already people out on the streets. I didn't know what to do. A little later I heard that they'd found a dead Russian."

"And you sent Fanny to go fetch the backpack?"

"She found out about it and went there on her own. She was only trying to help."

"Found out about it from whom? Frau Dähne? She knew everything?"

"I put her in a difficult situation. Please don't punish her for it." Pastor Beger sounded exhausted.

"That's not for me to decide," Heller said. "Were you the one who hid Weiler's severed hands in the Schlüters' cellar, along with those bloody tools?"

The pastor's face darkened again. "They deserved what they got. Always complaining about their own fate, all without ever questioning who actually bore the guilt. I can't stand it!"

"What about you, Pastor Beger? Do you not bear any guilt? What did you feel seeing those men die? You watched Gutmann suffer. Did it give you pleasure?"

The pastor laughed. "It was agony, an awful torment. Seeing him twitching and soiling himself. But I had to endure it. I had to sit still and watch. I had to bear witness to these fiends paying for their crimes."

"What about me? Were you planning on stringing me up too? And watching me die?"

Pastor Beger lowered his gaze. It was completely still in the church.

"That would be murder, Herr Beger," Heller said. "You do understand that?"

Pastor Beger looked up and shook his head. "I didn't murder. I only did what needed to be done."

Heller, stunned, shook his head. "But it's not up to you to play judge, to rule over life and death. Every person, no matter the crime, must have the chance at a fair trial."

"Fair!" blurted out the pastor. "You really believe it's fair what the Russians are doing here? Did I get a fair chance not to betray those children? And would I ever receive a truly fair trial?"

The pastor pushed Oldenbusch aside and ran off into the darkness.

Heller was expecting that. He gave chase. The pastor disappeared through the door to the church steeple and threw it shut. Heller stormed into the stairwell, but Beger was already climbing the first steps of the tower staircase. Heller stayed close on his heels, taking two steps at a time in hopes of sparing his right ankle. But he wasn't able to catch up.

After climbing countless stairs, Pastor Beger reached the bell tower, which was open to the outside. He charged around the bell and climbed onto the surrounding stone parapet. He looked down, gasping, teetering between mortal fear and fearlessness. Heller had just reached the bell tower and was out of breath. He stopped in his tracks. Wheezing, he slowly approached the parapet, keeping his eyes fixed on the pastor, making sure not to get too close. Five yards separated them. Heller took a quick look around. From up here he could see far above the roofs of the surrounding buildings and the voids ripped open by random bombings. He had a view of the entire Neustadt area and could see the fire-gutted spire of Trinity Church, the vast ruins on the other side of the Elbe.

Pastor Beger balanced on the parapet, pressing his back to one of the four sturdy columns at each corner, clawing at the sculptured stone relief. The snow-covered pavement was about 150 feet below them. No chance of surviving a fall.

"Beger, listen to me. There are good people too!" Heller said, still panting. "People who *do* help others."

The pastor didn't respond. Heller took another step closer.

"I, too, lost my faith. When I lay there in the trenches, in 1915, while all around me countless young men were dying, randomly, senselessly. But I haven't given up."

The pastor turned his head to the side, toward the abyss, so as not to look at Heller.

But Heller knew what would move the man more than anything else. "You couldn't do anything about that girl dying. It's not your fault, Christian."

Pastor Beger shuddered, clearly affected. "But I set that fire, don't you see? She suffocated because of me! Because of me. Did you see her face? Her horror?" Tears rolled down his cheeks.

"She suffocated because Gutmann was thinking only of himself. Because he lied to the police and the fire department. Herr Beger, look at me!"

The pastor shook his head. He stared in the direction of Gutmann's bar, about three hundred yards away. He suddenly looked composed. Straightening up a little, he released his left hand from the stone and wiped his face. "I'm guilty one way or another. But I'm not going to let myself be taken prisoner, no—I don't want to die in some hole. I don't want to be hanged! I'd rather jump from here. What do I have to lose now? Absolutely nothing."

"Don't do it, Christian. I need you!"

"Me?" Pastor Beger turned his head and gave Heller a quizzical look.

"The MVD have taken Jörg prisoner. The same people who beat you. They think Jörg is the one responsible. They're going to sentence him just like Friedel Schlüter. But he doesn't deserve the punishment. The two of them could be executed. Christian, you're the only one who can help those boys. Let's get down from here. You make a statement and confess. After all you've done, you do want truth and justice to prevail, don't you? Now's your opportunity. Absolve the boys with your confession. Don't just leave those two to die."

The pastor's face contorted into a despairing grimace. Heller could see him battling with himself and knew he wouldn't be able to hold out much longer.

"Where would you take me?" Pastor Beger whispered.

"I'd put you before a German judge. But I should also tell you that the Soviets would do everything in their power to charge you in one of their courts. That could mean Siberia or even the end of a rope."

The pastor gave him a sad smile. "You could be lying."

"I'd never do that," Heller replied, his eyes fixed on the pastor's.

Pastor Beger gazed back out into the distance. In the east, the sun had fully risen over the horizon. When he turned to face Heller, more tears ran down his cheeks. "Will you take care of the children? Will you promise?"

Heller nodded.

"Will you tell them how brave I was?"

"I will."

"Give them my best and tell them I will never forget them? And that they should never forget me?"

Heller nodded again and stretched out a hand.

"I'm coming," Pastor Beger said and climbed down off the parapet with Heller's help. "Let's go."

February 12, 1947: Late Afternoon

"I suppose you have the head with you this time, Oberkommissar?" said Lieutenant General Medvedev with a hint of a smile. He had Heller take a seat at his desk, then waved his secretary out of the room.

Heller wasn't quite sure how to handle the commandant. He felt just as used and deceived by him as ever.

"You know, I'm actually quite pleased they didn't put you in administration," Medvedev said, taking the initiative. "It would've been quite a waste."

"I assume Ovtcharov was keeping you informed about the investigation?" Heller said, ignoring the general's satirical undertone.

"Yes, as far as Ovtcharov himself was informed. It has always been important to me that my and Ovtcharov's organizations work hand in hand. Together one is stronger. Or, as you Germans say, four eyes see more than two. The colonel indicated to me that you were insinuating I had Kasrashvili kill all those men on my behalf."

Heller shifted uneasily in his chair. Medvedev seemed to be taking this rather seriously. "I never said it like that."

Medvedev snorted. "Well, however you express it, the gist remains the same. Explain to me what prompted you to suspect the pastor."

"Berinov was clearly killed by a left-handed person. Pastor Beger appeared to be left-handed. I'm sure he was taught to write and do his work with his right hand, but if he wants to make certain of something, he uses his left hand. I noticed that when his key got stuck in the lock to the door of his quarters. In addition, that fake farewell letter from Gutmann didn't seem to fit any of the suspects."

"Gutmann didn't hang himself?" the commandant asked.

Heller hesitated, then nodded. "I thought it wise not to make that public right away."

Medvedev shook his head indignantly. "Do I look like the public?"

"In addition, Gutmann knew Pastor Beger because he donated food to him. So Gutmann had let him into his bar without becoming suspicious. That was how Pastor Beger was able to stick that anesthetic into his arm from behind. The deciding factor came in a conversation I had with Ovtcharov. He was explaining to me that the pastor's predecessor had been arrested by the Gestapo, and he said his name: Ludwig Kühnel. LK for short, just like the initials stitched into that backpack holding Swoboda's head. Pastor Beger had taken over Kühnel's church and parish and all his things along with it. Either he had obtained the syringes from Gutmann or Fanny got them for him. She was wholly capable of gaining access to Gutmann's rooms."

Medvedev let Heller's words sink in before nodding. "So shouldn't we be searching for her? For her and the old woman?"

"We already have a manhunt on for Frau Dähne," Heller responded, looking the commandant in the eye.

Medvedev frowned. "Well, I suppose I will be reading all this in your report someday."

Heller nodded again. "I do have one request."

The commandant let out a little grown. "Do not try my good nature too very much, Oberkommissar. If it's about this boy, this Jorg? I'm taking care of it."

"It's *Jörg*, with an *ö*. What's that mean? Has he been released?"

"He will be released, once it's been proven without a doubt that he did not take part in any attack."

"Herr Commandant, I had to promise the pastor that the boy would be taken care of. I promised that he would be released."

"Then don't make promises that you can't keep," Medvedev snapped. "He must be checked out first."

Nevertheless, Heller sensed he could press things a little further.

"But he's practically a child. He needs affection, a firm hand, and above all a little luck in life. Somewhere Fanny's hiding with her infant, waiting for him. Shouldn't we give them a chance at a future?"

"You're one formidable individual, Oberkommissar. The way you never let up." Medvedev rubbed his chin. "I will call Ovtcharov. That's a promise from me. All right?"

"And Friedel Schlüter—he should get a proper trial, and I think he should be shown some mercy."

Medvedev stood. "He conducted anti-Soviet agitation, calling for armed resistance!"

"But he's never known otherwise. He's still a child."

"I will see what I can do. But now I think it's time for you to go!"

Heller stood yet didn't budge from his spot. "There's one other request I have, Herr Lieutenant General."

"*Yob tvoyu mat! Yebis vse konem!*" thundered the commandant, and Heller figured that this time it was probably just as well he didn't know much Russian.

February 12, 1947: Late Afternoon

"It's from Erwin!" Karin shouted from the front door before Heller had even stepped into the yard.

"What is?"

"The package! A package from Sweden!" Karin ran out and hugged him, then eyed him dubiously. "Are you all right?"

"I am, yes. You never called. Fanny wasn't here?"

Karin shook her head. "The telephone's still busted. What about her?"

"She's gone away with the baby. I'm guessing she's waiting somewhere for the boy, Jörg. I pressed Medvedev to let him go. We arrested the pastor this morning. Beger. Fanny fled with Frau Dähne."

Karin raised her hand to her mouth. "The pastor? The one who was helping the children? So Fanny knew—she knew from the beginning? She's the one who stole that big knife from us, wasn't she? I, uh, might not have told you . . ."

"Don't worry about it, Karin. Pastor Beger took all the blame. We'll talk about it later. I'd like you to go on a walk with me. I just hope Fanny's managing all right with the baby."

"She learned quickly. She'll be able to care for him."

Heller nodded, lost in thought. Something just wasn't right. Fanny and Frau Dähne shouldn't have been able to escape so easily. Both were accessories, if not more. He wondered if they were still in the area. Even though they had fled no more than a couple of minutes before Oldenbusch arrived, they seemed to have vanished. Heller put an arm around Karin's shoulder. "First let me see what our boy sent. Did he write too?"

Karin perked up a little. "Yes, he's doing well. You won't believe it, Max—the only way he can send packages is through Sweden because domestic mail is being held up at the zonal border. He sent coffee and canned food, soap, baking powder, and zwieback." Excited, she pulled Heller into the kitchen.

Klaus sat at the table in front of the opened package, staring at a can with a label in English. He put it aside when Heller came into the kitchen. "Erwin always was good at arranging things," Klaus said and smiled, thinking about the brother he'd not seen for more than three years.

Heller looked in fascination at the items his youngest son had sent from the west, then reached for one of the white paper bags and looked inside.

"Klaus, can you look after Frau Marquart for a while?" he asked and carefully closed the bag again. "I need to go see about something with your mother."

Heller gave the heavy front door a cautious knock, then took two steps back. It was already quite late in the afternoon and growing dark. Since her husband had knocked so timidly and nothing came of it, Karin stepped up to the door and knocked again, this time harder and louder.

They finally heard footsteps, and a stern-looking woman in a nun's habit opened the door. "Visiting hours are over. You'll have to come back tomorrow—"

"Good evening." Before the door slammed in his face, Heller quickly added, "Oberkommissar Heller, I'm a detective."

The nun's expression turned friendlier. "Ah, you're the one we owe all this to? Come on inside. And this is your wife?"

Heller nodded and entered the building with Karin. They stood there hesitantly and waited for the nun to close and lock the door again.

"I'm Sister Martha. That was quite the surprise this afternoon, I can tell you. We were horrified at first, seeing a Russian truck, but then . . . May the good Lord thank you!"

Heller waved a hand in embarrassment, unsure of what he was supposed to say. But Sister Martha didn't tolerate modesty. She took Heller by the wrist. "We received coal, potatoes, and milk. Rice too, and raisins. I want to show you."

Heller gently freed himself. "All I did was ask the commandant to give you a little support."

Sister Martha gazed at him with wide eyes. "Perhaps, but the point is that you did so."

"Could we see the children?" Karin asked.

"Of course! Come along. We have to go upstairs." Sister Martha went first, in a hurry, her broad skirt gathered in one hand, the points of her cap bobbing with every step. She quickly made her way along the hallway upstairs. "Our home isn't very big, but we have plenty of children here. We have to put up the new arrivals in the large dormitory. That way they can stay together at first," she explained before opening a door. "Attention, children!" she shouted.

Heller let Karin enter first.

"Heavens!" Karin whispered and nearly froze. Heller wasn't sure where to look first. The large room held at least twenty sleeping arrangements— small beds, cots, and, for the older children, simply straw mattresses on the floor. Twenty pairs of eyes stared up at them.

"Children, say 'good evening,'" Sister Martha said.

"Good eve-n-ing!" the children said in chorus. They were all washed and had their hair cut. They looked a little wary, as if they weren't comfortable in walled rooms, as if they still couldn't believe that something good had happened to them.

"This is the good man who brought us such joy today."

One of the youngest children ran up to Heller and wrapped her arms around his leg.

"Heavens," Karin whispered again and bent down to the little blonde girl wearing nothing but rags. She stroked her hair and had to fight back tears.

"We don't know what her name is or where she came from," Sister Martha explained. "The Red Cross tracing service has thousands of such cases."

"May I?" Heller asked and showed the nun the white paper bag he'd brought along.

The nun took a look inside and hesitated at first, then nodded. "Only one each," she told him. Heller crouched down, reached inside the bag, and took out a cube of sugar. He handed it to the girl, who had probably never seen such a thing in all her life. She took it, though she wasn't sure what she was supposed to do with it. Heller took another cube out and licked at it. The girl copied him, and her eyes widened.

"Tell Herr Oberkommissar thank you," the nun whispered, but the girl didn't hear a word as she was dreamily licking her sugar cube. Now the other children jostled for space around Heller, stretching out their hands.

"Just one each," Sister Martha told them. "Tell Herr Oberkommissar thank you."

Heller distributed the sugar cubes into all the little hands while Karin could barely take her eyes off the little girl, who savored the cube with the tip of her tongue, over and over.

Once all the children had received one, Heller gave the bag to the nun. Now one of the older boys was standing next to him, and it took a moment for Heller to recognize him.

"Johann, hello," Heller said. The boy lowered his head with a hint of a bow, pursing his lips. He stretched out his hand. Sister Martha rustled inside the bag for another sugar cube, but Johann paid no attention to her. He was looking Heller in the eye. Heller finally understood and shook the boy's hand.

"Thank you, Herr Oberkommissar." The boy bowed again. Then he stuck his hands in his pockets and went back to his bed.

ABOUT THE AUTHOR

Photo © 2017 Jens Oellermann

Frank Goldammer was born in Dresden and is an experienced professional painter as well as a novelist. *The Air Raid Killer* was the first book in his Max Heller series, and *A Thousand Devils* is the second. Goldammer is a single father of twins and lives with his family in his hometown. Visit him at www.frank-goldammer.de.

ABOUT THE TRANSLATOR

Photo © René Chambers

Steve Anderson is a translator, an editor, and a novelist. His latest novel is *Lost Kin* (2016). Anderson was a Fulbright Fellow in Munich, Germany. He lives in Portland, Oregon.

www.stephenfanderson.com